DRACULA UNMASKED

A Journey through Time

DRACULA UNMASKED

PAMELA J. RAUCH

LifeRich Publishing is a registered trademark of The Reader's Digest Association, Inc.

LifeRich Publishing books may be ordered through booksellers or by contacting:

LifeRich Publishing
1663 Liberty Drive
Bloomington, IN 47403
www.liferichpublishing.com
1 (888) 238-8637

Because of the dynamic nature of the Internet, any web addresses or links contained in this book may have changed since publication and may no longer be valid. The views expressed in this work are solely those of the author and do not necessarily reflect the views of the publisher, and the publisher hereby disclaims any responsibility for them.

Any people depicted in stock imagery provided by Getty Images are models, and such images are being used for illustrative purposes only. Certain stock imagery © Getty Images.

Dracula Unmasked: A Journey Through Time is a work of fiction. All incidents, dialogue, and all its characters with the exception of some well-known historical and public figures, are products of the author's imagination and are not to be construed as real. Where real-life historical or public figures appear, situations, incidents and dialogues concerning those persons are entirely fictional and are not intended to depict actual events or to change the entirely fictional nature of the work. In all other respects, any resemblance to persons living or dead is entirely coincidental.

ISBN: 978-1-4897-2354-3 (sc)
ISBN: 978-1-4897-2355-0 (hc)
ISBN: 978-1-4897-2356-7 (e)

Library of Congress Control Number: 2019909958

Print information available on the last page.

LifeRich Publishing rev. date: 7/19/2019

I dedicate this novel to my sister-in-law, Irene. Without your continued support and encouragement, I never would have made it to the finish line. You believed in me when I needed it most, and I thank you from the bottom of my heart.

I would also like to thank my husband, Joseph for always being my rock. I know it can be a challenge sometimes, to live with a woman who has one foot in another century; your love helps me stay grounded in this one.

A special thanks to Robin Norgaard, my Consulting Editor and dear friend.

Vlad Dracula - New York City - (September 11, 2001)

A flood of painful memories assaulted the ancient vampire as he took a deep breath and beheld the ruined dream of America. His city was in flames, but worse yet; a faithful friend had betrayed him. The sun was no threat to him, veiled as it was by a thick cloud of smoke that wove a fabric of despair into the very atmosphere. He beheld his wounded city as the piercing shrill of fire engines and first responders drowned out the anguished cries of people suffering the kind of loss, from which there was no recovery. Riddled with guilt as he surveyed the epitome of human cruelty, Vlad Dracula abandoned his regret and finally embraced his love of humanity. This, after spending more than five hundred years taking human lives on a regular basis, to satisfy his burning hunger.

In all fairness, some deserved to die, and others were victims simply because they crossed his path at the wrong time. He'd used up a lot of animals too, snapping up their lives without a thought, when his hunger became unbearable. He'd lost count of how many humans he had killed, too many to count; some still haunted his dreams. Most vampires were incapable of compassion and for Dracula this was true, but that didn't mean he lived without guilt. Could he have done anything to stop this? There were no answers today. His city was burning and Dracula blamed himself for misplacing his trust; he had failed his city and himself. In his pivotal moment, the ancient vampire wondered why he had been chosen to live as a creature of the night, no longer believing it was a blessing to live forever.

THE OLDE WORLD

PART I

Chapter 1 - The Omen - Carpathian Mountains - (April 1431)

The majestic white wolf stood on a snow-covered peak of the Carpathian Mountains, with keen eyes that could spot its prey from a distance of more than five miles. Slowly the great beast descended down the mountain, moving purposefully as if responding to a mating call. Above him a full moon shone with an eerie glow, which only enhanced a sense of impending doom. The surrounding forest was a refuge for his kind but tonight, he was summoned by a higher power. As its presence grew closer, the vegetation visibly wilted. The wolf raised a wet nose to the air and caught the scent of something so foul; it forced a host of wildlife into hiding. A steady wind combed through the lush forest as he scanned the treetops and waited for a sign from the Dark One.

"He has been born," a solemn voice whispered, as the night became suddenly still.

"Tell me...," the white wolf responded with building excitement, at the thought of grooming another like himself.

"A most evil one named, Vlad Dracula...in Wallachia. He is born a prince, but we will make him a *Prince of Darkness.*"

"Is he the one, master?"

"Yes...he is the one we have been waiting for," the Dark One replied impatiently.

"And how will I serve him?" the wolf asked unsure what was expected.

"Fool...you serve me and no other!"

"Forgive me, master...how may I serve *you*?"

"We need the assistance of something more innocuous, something that will be unnoticed by those who serve and protect him."

The white wolf ran his tongue over yellow teeth with relish as a plan began to formulate, "I will seek out the ancient oak, master...surely the answers will be there."

"It is not the tree that will serve you...seek out the vine and make it your own," the Dark One replied, but the wolf was still confused.

3

"Master…I don't understand."

"You must feed it! Your blood will fuel its waning fire and only then, will we have the means to groom this child into the dark lord he is mean to be."

"But master…where will I find him?" the wolf asked, but the Dark One had already vanished leaving a gentle wind behind.

The forest floor started moving beneath him, and the white wolf realized the Dark One was taking him to the Western Woods, where the sacred oak lived and breathed. It had been planted by the Druid's shortly after the birth of Christ. As the wolf cautiously approached the ancient tree, he felt a darkness spreading over him that had nothing to do with nightfall. The tree was taller than any the wolf had ever seen and its branches reached out hungrily with the bony fingers of a crone. The tree's massive trunk was covered with corroded gray bark and exuded a noxious odor clearly not of the living world. A tangled mass of spoiled greenery wound itself tightly around the ancient oak and seemed almost part of the tree itself. The white wolf stood only a foot from the tree now, certain he was as close to hell as he could get. The tainted vine was withered and appeared almost frail but the great beast knew better, and so had the Druids.

Determined in his mission, the white wolf stepped closer, nuzzling the brittle bark and the sleeping vine came instantly awake, feeling a hunger that could not be satisfied by water and sunshine. The wolf let his body go limp and the vine began to wrap itself around the animal's neck; leafy tentacles caressed the only thing that could nourish its burning hunger. When the vine appeared ready to consume the subdued beast, a human hand emerged from the tangled mass and then another, as the wolf took on his human form. The vine hummed as sharp tentacles began to pierce the man's breast, desperate for a taste of glorious human blood. As the vine drank, it writhed about erotically and the human responded in kind, making their dance look like a mating ritual. The wind suddenly picked up and the human pulled away, grasping his naked chest as he resumed his canine form. The rejuvenated vine loosened its grip and patiently listened, as the white wolf explained the Dark One's plan. The sinister vine had already begun to detach itself from the ancient oak, unable to resist the intoxicating call of the human world.

Chapter 2 - Prince Vlad Dracula III - Wallachia - (1431-1442)

Most babies are born innocent; Prince Vlad Dracula III most certainly was not. The Dark One understood this royal child had been born for great purpose and would use the faithful vine to help guide the new prince in his quest for human carnage. Gifted with a keen sense of direction, the vine had already tunneled its way to the church where the new prince was being baptized; with little effort, the vine found its way inside through an open window. The church was packed with royalty and peasants alike, as they gathered to catch their first glimpse of the new heir to the throne. The royal prince was brought out by his wet nurse wrapped from head to toe in purple velvet; his eyes were open wide as though inspecting the crowd. As the infant was disrobed he started to kick and scream with such a vengeance, the crowd became deadly silent. When the priest dunked the child into the basin of holy water, the baby released such an explosion of farts and feces, his vestment was completely soiled. Gasps of horror could be heard from the peasants and many crossed themselves for protection. The baby continued to fuss and cry, until every last drop of holy water was wiped from his body. The vine was encouraged by this turn of events and thought, "This is going to be one nasty son of a bitch."

By the time the royal family returned home from church, the vine had found its way to the castle, working its way up the stone wall, just outside the nursery window. When the windows were left open at night, the vine would crawl inside and wrap itself around a leg of the infant's cradle. As the prince grew into a toddler, the vine was present to observe Prince Vlad take his first steps; baby steps soon became the sure-footed gait of a crowned prince and the two spent as much time together as possible. When the prince turned three, he was joined by a baby brother, Prince Radu. By the time the prince had his fourth birthday, he understood his parents had found a new favorite in his younger sibling; this merely helped cement the bond he had with his precious vine. By the age of five, Prince Vlad considered the vine's constant presence as much a part of being Prince of Wallachia as the uncomfortable and restrictive garments he had to wear. On his eighth birthday, the vine began showing Vlad how to torture and mutilate small animals and with each kill, the young boy's heart began to darken into the cold, calculating killer he would someday become.

The years passed quickly and eventually the prince reached an age where he refused to be treated like a child. Prince Vlad loved his pony, Ludwig, but had been begging his father for a horse since his eleventh birthday. At twelve years old, he was an accomplished rider and rode on his own many afternoons when his lessons were finished. His current course of study was anatomy, and the subject bored him to tears. As always, he carried a sword for protection but never had the opportunity to use it. Prince Vlad finished his ride and paused with Ludwig under a massive evergreen, a favorite resting place they both knew well. The chestnut pony scratched the ground to signal it was time for dinner. Vlad watched his pony's head move from side to side in confusion when his master did not dismount; the boy was studying the animal's muscular neck, wondering what it felt like to cut through muscle.

"If I must learn about anatomy, I will see it for myself!" Vlad finally screamed, then wielded his sword; in one swift movement he decapitated poor Ludwig, who collapsed just as Vlad dismounted. The blood was magnificent. The sunlight made it sparkle like rubies, and the boy was overcome with a desire to become part of his favorite pet in a most special way. Vlad fell upon the carcass and like a demon possessed, went into a feeding frenzy. Still unsatisfied, the boy dragged himself to where the severed-head lay, and drank from the horse's neck until his thirst was finally quenched.

Upon returning from his ride, clothes saturated with blood, Prince Vlad approached his father and demanded a horse. The king snapped his fingers, calling for a stable boy to grant his son's request. Eventually, members of the royal family and servants too, learned the details of the unfortunate pony's demise. From that day on, rarely did anyone say no to Prince Vlad Dracula.

The Dark One was thoroughly pleased at the sequence of events and a silent communication ensued between the vine and its master; that night, the twelve-year-old prince dreamed of tearing human flesh and drinking blood from a ruby studded chalice.

Chapter 3 - Reign of a Tyrant - (1456-1463)

Vlad Dracula grew into a fierce warrior, most satisfied when planning war strategies or engaged in battle. His country was his first love; all others came including his wife, Princess Ana.

In the fall of 1462, when the ongoing battle with the Turks began to accelerate, the royal prince was called to battle. At dawn he rose and dressed, but his wife begged him to stay because she was with child. He kissed her on the forehead as he buttoned his shirt. "My love, I am forever your husband, but our sons will need their father to set an example. I must lead my men and I promise you and my God, I will be victorious."

A week passed with no word from Vlad; Princess Ana began to fear the worst. The following morning at dawn, she heard the castle guards sound the alarm, but the warning was too late. Princess Ana gasped in horror when she realized a band of Ottoman Turks had already surrounded the castle. Despondent and convinced capture was imminent; the princess threw herself into the Arges River, killing herself and her unborn child. Upon his return, Vlad was greeted by his wife's lifeless body; in anguish he cursed God, Jesus Christ and all that was holy. He stormed up to the church's marble altar, swiping across it with his arm; horrified priests watched candles, statues and the royal chalice crash to the floor. The holy men crossed themselves, and moved away as the royal prince continued his tirade with wild staring eyes.

After Princess Ana was buried, Prince Vlad locked himself in his room for days, eating very little and refusing to talk to anyone. On the eighth day as Vlad brooded in his bedchamber, the Dark One finally made its presence known; the evil entity revealed its plan to help make Prince Vlad an invincible warrior. The Dark One was clever in its methods; it promised to teach the Prince about the intoxicating allure of human carnage. Vlad listened and actually felt himself growing thirsty for the taste of human blood. The Dark One stayed a while, taking time to explain military strategy, even recommending several new forms of torture. The grieving prince grew optimistic, as he absorbed everything the Dark One explained; however, it was the promise of immortality that finally motivated the leader out of mourning and into action.

On a crisp autumn morning while the castle was still asleep, the prince arose fully dressed and came out of his chamber. Everyone scurried about, frantically trying to tidy up and prepare breakfast for their lord. Those who saw Prince Vlad that day noticed a dramatic change in his appearance. Servants and family members were known to comment that all traces of compassion had evaporated. His face had thinned, leaving behind a more well-defined jaw and thinner lips nearly absent of color. His hair usually given to unruliness was now pulled back severely in a pigtail tied with a strip of leather. Most startling, were his eyes; they had turned to an icy green.

As changed as the Prince of Wallachia was to his family and servants, on the battlefield Vlad Dracula was much worse. To say his tactics were less than honorable would be an understatement; Vlad Dracula killed without conscience and with extreme brutality. As time passed, the prince fought endless battles with a drive and ferocity unparalleled by any other ruler of his time. Enemies and allies alike would openly agree, there was no ruler fiercer the Prince of Wallachia. He was eventually nicknamed "Vlad the Impaler" because of his unique form of execution. Turkish soldiers unlucky enough to be wounded, instead of killed would be subjected to impalement, a slow and agonizing death. In 1463, the year after Princess Ana's death, the Wallachian army realized their greatest victory by killing nearly thirty thousand Turkish soldiers. Those who were killed on the battlefield were the lucky ones; those taken captive were impaled, left to die alone and rot in the sun.

As the sun set on a battlefield wet with human carnage, Prince Vlad admired the endless rows of impaled soldiers and held his arms up to the sky screaming, "Without the help of God, I am victorious!"

CHAPTER 4 - COUNTESS ELIZABETH BATHORY - SARVAR CASTLE - (1581)

Her bedchamber was adorned with more than thirty mirrors of every shape and size. Dozens more were located throughout her castle, so she could admire her reflection anywhere she happened to be. The countess had commissioned the design and construction of many; some were truly one of a kind. A woman of such exotic beauty should expect nothing less; she didn't really care if people thought her vain. Countess Elizabeth Bathory was eccentric and self-absorbed, often subject to fits of uncontrollable rage, which made her an incredible tyrant. The countess was born into the Hungarian royal family in 1560; during most of her childhood, she was spoiled, but largely ignored by her parents. The countess was adored and indulged by her wet nurse, Darvulia, who openly practiced witchcraft and taught Elizabeth her many methods of torture. The young countess took to the practice of inflicting pain, like a fish to water. Countess Bathory began abusing her servants by the time she was twelve, under the tutelage of Darvulia; servants at Sarvar Castle were treated no better than common livestock. Countess Bathory's methods of punishment were extremely harsh; she always made a point of beating servants until they bled. The coppery smell and taste of human blood was intoxicating to the countess; with each passing year she craved more. Over time, Countess Bathory became convinced drinking blood would keep her young and beautiful.

Count Ferencz Nadasdy was Elizabeth's husband, but he was rarely in residence at Sarvar Castle. There were battles to fight, he claimed, but according to castle gossip; he spent most of his time whoring around. While the count lived a life of thrill and adventure, his wife was stuck inside a dreary castle; because of this, the countess created her own private chamber of horrors in the dungeon. Utilizing what she had learned from Darvulia, the countess became a master at inflicting pain and perfected new methods of torture. At the age of twenty, Countess Bathory had already been married for five years, but her life was anything but glamorous. Before they married, she dreamed of seeing foreign lands, but her husband never took her anywhere; in fact, the countess rarely left the castle. She toyed with the idea of taking a lover, but the risk seemed too great, until one summer night when a fire began to burn inside her. Elizabeth decided she was unwilling to tolerate a life of continued celibacy. It happened one night in late July, just after sunset. The countess felt restless and found herself walking with determination toward the stables; she decided it was time to quell her growing hunger. Tonight, Countess Bathory allowed desire to be her guide, and sought out her Captain of the Horse Guard, DesioVas.

Desio heard her approach and turned to smile at her, as the sun dipped behind Sarvar Castle. Without saying a word, Desio moved to the countess and took her hands in his. Tonight, the countess felt a passion that neither station nor status could dispel; once the electricity between them ignited, there was no turning back. Desio took the countess in his arms, burying his face between her breasts as he praised her astonishing beauty. Their clothes almost fell off and Elizabeth allowed herself to be lowered onto a pile of fresh hay, where she let this beautiful gypsy of a man take what many men would die for. The urgency between them was overpowering; when he entered her, Elizabeth rose up and gave herself to him completely, but only for a moment. When Desio finally collapsed on top of her, he was pushed aside as a plaything; the countess was already up and gathering her discarded clothes. Before she left, Elizabeth made a point to remind him that her horse still needed grooming. She would be a tough one to break, he thought, as he got up to dress. Desio didn't really care how Countess Bathory spoke to him, as long as she continued to warm his bed; he was fairly certain she would come back for more.

The countess viewed Desio as a delightful distraction and nothing more. Besides, she had other interests to pursue in the dungeon of Sarvar Castle. After all, servants who misbehaved simply had to be punished. With the assistance of Darvulia, they practiced sadistic methods of torture on countless young girls, who suffered in silence because they had nowhere else to go. It was the sight of their blood that thrilled her. She ordered Darvulia to collect it in bottles; the countess couldn't get enough of it. As her obsession grew, it drove her to acts of extreme cruelty that became more maniacal with each passing year. On her nineteenth birthday, Countess Bathory hired an ironsmith to build a customized torture chamber called an iron maiden. Kept hidden in the castle's dungeon, this unique device was responsible for the demise of several young girls in her employ for more serious infractions. If it was ever suggested the countess might be mentally unbalanced, she would throw her head back and simply say, "Madness is a privilege of royalty."

The summertime meant open windows and cool night air; alone in her bedchamber, Elizabeth absentmindedly brushed her long dark hair. Summer nights were fleeting and made the countess feel pensive; she could hear the soothing sound of crickets chirping outside. This was a peaceful time of night; servants were dismissed and Elizabeth had time for her own private thoughts. Desio was likely waiting anxiously for her in the barn, but she wasn't coming tonight; the thrill of copulating on damp hay had already lost its allure. Her canopied bed was already turned down, but she was not even remotely tired. Outside her bedchamber, musicians played an endless stream of melodies that all sounded the same. In her white lace dressing gown, Elizabeth Bathory looked anything but evil, so overpowering was her astounding beauty.

Through the open window, Elizabeth could see a flock of bats flying in frantic circles above the treetops below; as she watched, the largest one left the circle and flew up to perch on her window sill. The bat tipped its head from side to side, as if waiting for an invitation. Elizabeth held out her finger and on cue, the bat flew into the room only to disappear behind the wall tapestry. She shrugged and continued brushing her hair, deciding the creature was harmless and would eventually fly away.

As she resumed counting brush strokes, Elizabeth felt a sudden chill permeate the room; she heard someone behind her. She turned around slowly, her dressing gown flowing in sync with her graceful movement, as the stranger studied her from across the room. Elizabeth could have screamed, but realized she didn't want her nocturnal visitor to leave. He was nothing short of beautiful; at first, she didn't believe he was even real. The countess took a step toward him with her hand extended, but he didn't move. Her strange visitor made no attempt to disguise that he was sizing her up; he had piercing green eyes that captivated her instantly. His skin was alabaster white and he had thin lips she longed to kiss; to her he was the image of sheer perfection.

Before he spoke, Elizabeth had already dreamed his voice.

"My name is Count Dracula," he spoke in a deep, rich voice. "I thank you for inviting me inside. I have come to offer you something you crave more than anything in life."

"I'm listening..."

"I will make sure that your stunning beauty is preserved for all time...in return you will help me amass an army of undead servants, who will literally take a bite out of this quaint little village."

Without missing a beat, the countess responded, "Just one village?"

Dracula smiled with sharp teeth, as he moved toward her. The countess pushed him away with her hand. "You may taste me...but do not kill me."

"My dear Countess Bathory, why would I want to destroy your beautiful wickedness, when it is the very thing that makes you so exciting?"

"Come and taste me then," the countess said, as he scooped her up into his arms. She gasped when Dracula sank his teeth into her fleshy softness.

The countess pressed herself against him as he drank, and whispered, "My dear count... I am a woman with many needs."

CHAPTER 5 - THE DARK ONE CALLS -
THE WESTERN WOODS - (1581)

The hiss of a rattlesnake permeated the air as the malignant vine floated in a dream-like sleep. The thorny growth was wrapped tightly around the ancient oak, the only comfort it had ever known. The hissing sound grew louder and the vine was finally ripped from its peaceful slumber.

"He needs your presence now," the Dark One whispered.

"Master, I have rested well and am ready to do your bidding." The vine had no voice, but that didn't prohibit a silent communication between them.

"He stays with a countess, Bathory by name. She resides in Hungary at Sarvar Castle. I have chosen her to be his partner in evil. You must stay near him, a reminder of the vow he made when he drank human blood and gave up his humanity. You will find him much changed, now that he has been turned."

"Turned where…I don't understand. Is my lord still alive?"

"He is a vampire now; he left his mortal life behind in Bucharest. He died in 1476, over a hundred years ago," the Dark One answered.

"What year is it, master?"

"The year is 1581. Vlad is no longer Prince of Wallachia. He is Count Dracula and Wallachia is no more. As I have already explained, the count can be found at Sarvar Castle with his countess. Let him tell you his sorry tale…now get thee gone and go to your lord!"

The vine activated its keen sense of direction and newly replenished, burrowed into the ground beneath the Western Woods for its journey to Sarvar Castle. As the moon rose higher in the sky, the malignant growth weaved its way beneath the forest floor until finally; there it was in the distance. The vine paused to take in the breathtaking view; Sarvar Castle stood proudly in the moonlight, like the magnificent structure it was. It welcomed the vine with windows that beckoned it to claim the castle for its own. With little effort, the agile vine climbed up the castle wall where it located Countess Bathory's suite of rooms.

The excitement began to build as the vine reached the window sill of her bedchamber. The tainted vine entered the window from all sides and rapidly began to climb up the inside wall, spreading itself like the thin legs of a spider.

Upon entering the room, the vine observed his lord and the countess locked in a sexual embrace. The vine had never encountered human beings engaged in sexual behavior and was surprised by the violence of their passion; it looked more like a wrestling match than lovemaking. The Dark One chose this moment to make its presence known.

"This is something humans do; they are driven to it in a futile effort to escape the absolute loneliness of human existence. There is procreation, of course, but that is only a small part of it. Dracula cannot impregnate the countess, but he still continues to pantomime the act of human love."

"Do humans enjoy doing these things to one another?"

"Yes, but for reasons that don't matter here. Your lord is unfortunately, falling in love with our Countess Bathory…and we can't allow it."

"But why, master…I thought we wanted them to be together?"

"Yes, but love was not in my plans…"

"What should we do, master?"

"Nothing right now…these things have a way of working themselves out."

The countess fell back against the comfortable pillows as an evening breeze kissed the dewy softness of her supple skin. Elizabeth gaped in disbelief, when she saw the thorny vine climbing up her bedroom wall. She poked her lover in the side to show him. "What the hell is that?"

Dracula got up and moved to the window. "My vine…my strength," he whispered as he dug his fingers into the soft down of his faithful vine. The vine responded by detaching from the window sill and curling its way up the vampire's arm. When it beheld Vlad Dracula up close, it was astonished that despite the passing of more than a hundred years, its lord had not aged at all.

The count turned away from the window and the vine gently released him. "My dear Countess Bathory, I am ready now to tell you my story…how I came to be a vampire and the truth about how I died… in my human life that is."

The countess rose from the bed to pull a silk nightdress over her head, as she coaxed Dracula to a seat by the fireplace. "Dearest Dracula, I would love to hear your story while the night still lingers and you've already fed. Perhaps you can start by telling me about this enchanting vine that has decided to impose itself on the walls of my castle."

Chapter 6 - Vlad Dracula's Tale – (In the Year 1476)

Dracula never expected to narrate the story of his death but that was exactly what he was now prepared to do. The lovely countess sat next to the fire as he spoke and her eyes sparkled like polished diamonds. The castle was eerily quiet this time of night. Most of the candles had already burned out; the dwindling fire provided the only light by which the count could begin his epic tale. Elizabeth's ivory skin glowed softly in the firelight, as she waited anxiously for his story to begin. Her pet falcon, Akos was unusually quiet as he perched beside his mistress, craning his neck as though poised to listen to the amazing tale. The clock over the fireplace rang in the two o'clock hour, when Dracula reluctantly began his painful story.

"The great plague was upon us that year and Wallachia was caught in the disease's evil clutches. You have to live through something like that to fully understand it. Castle Arges was hit hard when the plague arrived with a vengeance during the winter of 1476. I had a new wife by then, Princess Isabella. Although there were many pregnancies, we only had one son; Mikolai had just turned thirteen. My queen and I lost several housemaids and three of our stable boys to the illness; eventually, cook came down with it too. By late March, the fighting started to escalate in Bucharest; as Prince of Wallachia, it was my duty to lead my army into battle so I had to leave my family behind.

April 2, 1476 was the day I died, and gave up my human life. I had a feeling of apprehension the moment I opened my eyes that morning; I knew the odds were stacked against us. I fought for what seemed like a long time, and then a lethargic feeling overcame me...it felt like I was moving in slow motion. My confidence waned as I watched my men fall one by one...we were outnumbered and I knew Turkish reinforcements were on the way. In the end, it was a boy fighting a man's battle who took my human life. The Turkish soldier who killed me looked younger than my own son; his extreme youth made me underestimate him. Before I could strike, I felt the sting of his blade, as it cut deep into my abdomen. I knew it was a killing blow, when blood poured through my fingers soaking my clothes; at some point I lost consciousness and was left for dead. I managed to find my way to a shallow cave bordering the battlefield; I didn't expect to live through the night, but I wanted to die alone with dignity. Eventually sleep came, that is…until I woke and faced the blackest wolf I had ever seen. He towered over me and I assumed the beast planned to make a meal of me. I didn't have the strength to fight him, so I lay perfectly still and suddenly the wolf spoke to me."

Dracula paused for a moment as he watched Elizabeth take in every word, her face glowing with excitement. Dracula continued his tale as the night waned on.

"I understood right away, the wolf was not of the living world…he actually called me by name…"

Elizabeth interrupted, "What did the wolf say?"

"He promised me the gift of immortality."

"What happened next?" Elizabeth asked, leaning closer to him.

"Before I could respond, the wolf lunged at me and all I could manage was to slash my attacker's flank. The wolf seized my exposed neck with his massive jaws; we wrestled on the ground with my neck flayed open as I fought for my life. Suddenly, we were eye to eye and I saw myself reflected in the wolf's eyes…only then did I understand this is what I had been promised. I stopped struggling…and let the wolf drink his fill. Although I felt lightheaded, I was no longer afraid and now certain the beast would not kill me. When the wolf finally released my neck, he lowered his body to the ground exposing his wounded flank so I could drink his blood. Driven by an insatiable hunger, I put my lips to the wound and began to drink like a newborn nursing for the first time. I drank until there was nothing more and when I was finished, my own wound had nearly healed itself. I fell into a dreamless sleep. While I slept…the black wolf slipped away leaving me with incredible new powers, yet no instruction on how to use them.

When I woke hours later, I was surprised to discover my wound had completely healed; there was not even a scar. Refreshed and filled with a renewed sense of purpose, I ran back to the battlefield to see if I could save any of my men. At first, there were only corpses, but then I heard a moan coming from a wounded soldier a few feet away. His name was Nikos Fabri, and he was a friend and a faithful soldier. The man was clearly dying…and I wanted to help him…at first, but as I watched the wound from his neck weeping warm blood…I felt a hunger beyond anything I had ever known. I seized my comrade and drank from him until his body went limp. In that moment, I knew what I had become. Still hungry I combed through the sea of bodies, until I found another dying soldier, an enemy this time. I drained him in minutes. When I was finally sated…I was horrified by the savagery of my actions. I had killed and tortured thousands of Turkish soldiers, but in my mind, nothing could equal the atrocity of killing a friend and comrade."

"Is it a crime to feed on what is necessary to survive?" Countess Bathory asked. She was not the least bit horrified at how a vampire lived.

"But Nikos was one of my own men…and a friend."

"Never mind…can we please go back to the story?" Elizabeth replied with a wicked grin.

"Very well…let's see…the battlefield…I faced a dilemma and began to formulate a plan to ensure I was declared dead. You see…if I planned to start my new life as a vampire, Prince Vlad Dracula needed to be eliminated…I saw an opportunity right in front of me. I chose one of my soldier's corpses with a similar build and changed clothes with him. I even placed my family's heirloom ring on his finger…a sure way to confirm the identity of the former prince. Before leaving, I took his head….planning to dispose of it later. The sky grew lighter so I needed shelter from the sun. I claimed an abandoned horse and we made our way back to the cave I'd used earlier."

Dracula paused and glanced at the mantle clock. "Three o'clock… the witching hour," he whispered, signaling that he would need to stop soon. A captive audience waited breathlessly to hear what happened next.

"When the sun set the following evening, I rode the mare I'd befriended back to Castle Arges. When I arrived, the hour was late so most were asleep. I ditched the horse because I had to get past the guards without being seen. I used a secret entrance unknown to most, where royal family members could come and go in times of trouble. My eyes adjusted to the darkness instantly; I could see without need of a torch, despite the pitch blackness. I moved quietly through a maze I knew from memory toward the royal suites. As I reached my son's bedchamber, I felt something I hadn't planned on; I was thirsty and there was only one thing that would quench my thirst.

I crept in quietly and approached Mikolai's bed. I moved to draw his bed curtain and was startled to find his wet nurse, Ursula attending him. Believing me dead, she crossed herself and fled the room. My boy opened his eyes a bit, attempting a smile through weeping sores that covered his face. I understood my son was dying; when I moved closer, I could feel the rush of blood racing through his veins and his life force called to me. I remember crying...and then, Mikolai sat up and embraced me; his neck pressed against my lips..." Dracula had to stop for a moment, the memory too painful to recall.

"...I was overcome by the sweet smell of my dying child...I did the unthinkable... I sank my teeth into his neck and...I drank from my own son..."

"You were going to make him a vampire?" the countess asked.

"It was the only way to save him...but it didn't work out."

"What happened?"

"As luck would have it, Princess Isabella burst into the room, and let out a blood-curdling scream. I knew my guards would be coming soon and my secret would be uncovered, unless I moved fast. When the first guard entered my son's bedchamber, I leapt at him....but halfway through the maneuver; I became airborne and no longer in my human form. Instead, I had become a ferocious black wolf, just like the one who made me. My guard was so startled by my transformation...he fell backwards which allowed me to escape." Dracula stopped speaking; signs of impending daylight were fast approaching and it was time for all to rest.

"When will you finish the story?" Elizabeth asked with sleepy eyes, when she realized his gripping tale had stopped.

"My Lady Bathory, I will come to you again tomorrow night." Dracula turned away, and in one swoop, became airborne on a mission to beat the sunrise.

As Darvulia changed the bed linens the next day, she worried about her mistress. Of late, the countess had taken up the habit of staying up all night with a mysterious count; he had apparently imposed himself as a permanent house guest. This strange count had shown up one night a few months earlier; Darvulia already learned that several gypsies had disappeared from caves at the foot of the Bakony Mountains. A few locals claimed several bodies had recently been discovered completely drained of blood. Darvulia understood the curse of the vampire better than anyone; she also took note the killings started not long after Count Dracula began frequenting Sarvar Castle. Darvulia had nursed Elizabeth from birth and always tried to ensure that should her mistress take a lover, it would be someone common like Desio Vas. A mere stable hand was completely expendable if he became a problem, but a count from another prominent royal family was another matter altogether. Either way, Darvulia didn't trust Count Dracula one bit, and was certain her mistress would end up with a broken heart.

Chapter 7 - Dracula's Tale Continues - (In the Year 1476)

Today, as she rode her horse across a field of lush green grass, Countess Bathory reflected on the tale her nightly visitor had told, and realized how complex Count Dracula really was. Man or vampire, whatever he was, she found him most compelling; he was also the only person who didn't fear her authority. Elizabeth's faithful falcon, Akos, flew above her as she rode through the rolling hills with her dress billowing in the wind. The countess realized she was still learning about this mysterious man who called himself a vampire. Every night she would ask the count to turn her; Elizabeth was desperate to remain eternally young and beautiful. She would be twenty-one in only three months' time, and already she could see a change in the softness of a beautifully sculpted face. Countess Bathory's greatest fear was aging; she spent much of her free time wondering where the next wrinkle would show up on her nearly flawless face.

Since the night Count Dracula first arrived, Elizabeth had started dismissing her ladies early, insisting on getting herself ready for bed without assistance. Each evening the countess would secure herself within her bedchamber shortly after sunset, and wait with much excitement for her vampire to arrive. Darvulia was the only one who knew about her strange visitor, but she had never seen him. Elizabeth was intrigued by the count's story and wondered how he had lived for the past hundred years. The countess breathed deeply as she thought about her lover, and the mysterious circumstances surrounding his death. She knew one thing for sure, he was still a handsome man despite the fact that he had been born nearly a hundred and fifty years ago. According to his story, Dracula was forty-five when he died; to her, the count looked no more than thirty-five. The handsome vampire had the glorious power to help her stay young and beautiful, too; for this, she would make herself a slave to Count Dracula.

Engaged in a series of violent battles west of Moldavia, Count Ferenc Nadasdy was not expected back from his travels until at least

November; this gave Elizabeth the freedom to spend all her nights in a most uninhibited way with the Romanian count. Of course, there were restrictions to observe, such as the count's aversion to daylight. On that first night, she had asked him where he could rest during the day; Count Dracula confirmed her husband's family crypt would work just fine. Gifted as the count was with the ability to shape shift into a bat at will, he was able to enter and depart from her bedchamber without ever being noticed. The countess waited impatiently for the long hours of daylight to fade; she watched as the sky turned orange and ash gray, a sure sign her count to arrive soon to continue his story.

The night was unusually cool for early September. As Elizabeth waited for Count Dracula to arrive, she shivered and wondered if tonight would be the night, her vampire granted her eternal life. Gazing into a gilded mirror, Elizabeth didn't even notice the count enter her bedchamber. Akos flapped his wings, as he observed Count Dracula's amazing transformation to his human form.

"You look quite bewitching tonight, Countess Bathory," Dracula said softly, as he came up behind her. The count began kissing the back of her neck; Elizabeth turned to face him with the light of love in her eyes.

Anxious for Dracula's story to continue, the countess poured a glass of Tokay wine and sat before the fire. "So...tell me something, count... how is it that you cast a reflection in these lovely mirrors of mine? I thought creatures of the night avoided mirrors for that reason...please enlighten me." The countess was clearly challenging him.

"Just another myth about our kind," Dracula replied, pointing to his reflection for emphasis. "By the way...I love the smell of garlic, so don't believe everything that crone, Darvulia tells you."

The countess shrugged and took a sip of her wine; Dracula moved to take her glass, putting it down gently. Elizabeth moaned softly as the count took her in his arms and laid her gently on the bed. She was a vision to behold, perhaps one of the most desirable women the count had ever known. The vampire desperately wanted to taste her, and he knew she would let him, but first he had to please her in a most human way; that he knew how to do very well. There was no moon tonight; and night breeze had its way with the bed curtains, as the two lovers spent themselves again and again. The hour was quite late when Dracula's story began again; the night's candles still burned brightly as the vampire continued his tale.

"That first night I remained a wolf...I didn't want to leave myself vulnerable in the wild. Once the moon rose, I headed deep into the woods to hunt for sustenance. I soon discovered I could satisfy my hunger by killing small game; it seemed a better option than killing humans every night."

Elizabeth interrupted impatiently, "Why would you kill animals when you could drink the delicious blood of humans?"

"After the end of my human life, much of my burning anger left me; I still lust for blood, of course, every vampire does. It is our curse...but what you can have every night becomes as mundane as any other habit."

Elizabeth folded her arms across her chest and replied, "You sound like a rather reluctant vampire to me. Please go on..."

Dracula moved to the window and continued. "My plan...was to assume the identity of my brother, Radu. You see, he was there during that final battle...but he now fought with the Turkish army. I watched as Radu clashed swords with a Wallachian soldier. My younger brother was a traitor! Without hesitation, my henchman decapitated my brother and threw his severed-head into the Arges River. My heart ached for the brother I once loved...but a battlefield was no place for sentimental thoughts. Eventually, I realized his death was a way for me to retain my title as a count...I could claim my lands, including Castle Arges. My brother and I shared such a striking resemblance growing up...people often confused us when were together. I was confident I could make myself a believable changeling for my brother. I don't want to bore you with all the details...I enlisted the help of an old family friend and sent him back to Castle Arges with signed letters stating that I, Radu Tepes had survived my battle wounds...and that per my birthright, I would be coming within three weeks time to take up residence in Castle Arges."

The clock struck the one o'clock hour as Dracula continued his tale. "I spent the next few weeks at my country estate outside Moldavia, while I waited for the castle to be vacated. The first few nights, I was so busy with my travel preparations; I paid little attention to the distinct aura I felt as I walked through my childhood home. Usually this was a place I found warm and welcoming…as a vampire, I could detect a veil of sadness in the air. The manifestation itself came from an oversized mirror in our front hallway, a family heirloom that had been hanging in the same spot for years. It happened the night before I planned to make my journey to Castle Arges. I was looking in the mirror, and my reflection suddenly faltered…as the face of an old friend appeared….my first kill as a vampire, Nikos Fabri."

"What did he say?" the countess asked her eyes hungry for more details.

"His first words were: 'Touch me you unholy thing!' He begged me to let me out…he promised to be my servant for all time. I wasn't sure what to do…and then Nikos flashed me a hopeful smile…only then did I realize how much I needed a companion."

Elizabeth jumped up to pour herself another glass of wine, never taking her eyes off the count as she completed her task. "My dear count, are you telling me that you have a friend who is a ghost?"

"I assure you countess, ghosts are very real."

"Prove it then."

"My lady…I can do much better than that." Dracula took her hand in his, as they approached an oval mirror in the back corner of her bedchamber.

At first they only saw themselves, but then everything turned to mist. Dracula took her hand and put it to the glass; the countess flinched because it was cold to the touch. The mist began to dissipate and the face of Nikos appeared. For a brief moment, Elizabeth became lost in the spirit's penetrating stare. When she felt his palm against her skin, she tried to pull away; Dracula held her there until the specter grabbed her wrist and pulled himself through the mirror in a blinding light. The countess stood frozen, as the ghost of Nikos Fabri stepped fully into her bedchamber.

As the countess stood speechless, the sound of children whispering echoed from the mirror; it began to glow once more. Like before, the mist came and when it started to clear, the countess could see two boys in long white nightshirts; they stood together at the bottom of a wooden staircase. Both boys had blonde curls and their eyes were the color of ocean water on a summer day. With trembling lips, the oldest boy spoke, "We are searching for our mother, the queen…can you help us please?"

The younger boy spoke now, "My name is Richard, and I was once Duke of York. My brother is Edward…we thought he would be crowned king of England…but he died before it happened."

Countess Bathory was mesmerized by the young spirits and didn't want them to vanish. "When did you die?"

"We were murdered," the younger brother confirmed.

Young Richard continued establishing himself as their official spokesperson. "We died in the year 1483, but my brother doesn't like to talk about it. Edward thinks we just have to find a way out…then everything will be as it was before." Dracula pulled Elizabeth away from the mirror; the last thing he needed were more ghosts in his life.

Nikos spoke up now, "They cannot hurt you, countess…these are the two young princes who were imprisoned in the Tower of London during the summer of 1483. They were twelve and nine years old when they vanished. Edward, the oldest was heir to the English throne…but they disappeared that summer after being imprisoned and were never seen again. What adds to the mystery is that their bodies have never been found. Some say their uncle; King Richard III was responsible for their deaths. Who knows…Henry VII had good reason to want them dead as well. They have been with me in the Otherworld for a long time now… they cannot rest because their remains were never interred." The mirror returned to normal, but Elizabeth unexpectedly found herself wanting to know more about the young princes.

CHAPTER 8 - DESIO VAS - SARVAR CASTLE - (1581)

His mood was foul this evening as he groomed Gaspar with growing resentment; he had nothing against the poor horse, just his mistress. He and the countess had not been together for two weeks, and he was certain she had taken another lover. Despite the fact Desio had no claim on her because she was a married woman; he felt a sense of possessiveness that was just part of his nature. Eventually he would tire of her but she surprised him by taking another lover, which made him insane with jealousy. When the countess missed the first few nights, Desio took it in stride however; after a week he knew something was going on and began to seethe with anger. For the past few nights, Desio had been watching the window of Elizabeth's bedchamber. She had been staying up all night entertaining a male visitor who wore a black cape. The strangely dressed man arrived every evening, just after sunset; Desio couldn't figure out how he was getting past the guards unchallenged and apparently, into her bed. Tonight, as he watched shadows moving back and forth, Desio could swear he saw two men; how were they getting into her private chamber without being seen? Another thing he found puzzling was the sudden appearance of ivy, now covering the exterior of Sarvar Castle. Desio had never seen climbing ivy grow that fast and there was something sinister about it; especially the way it grew thicker in the area surrounding Countess Bathory's bedchamber. Desio was convinced there was a connection between the mysterious nightly visitor and this unnatural growth.

Desio finished grooming Gaspar, giving him a gentle pat before leaving the stall. He grabbed his glass blown pipe and sat underneath a darkening sky planning to smoke a bowl and stay alert. Tonight, he planned to follow Countess Bathory's lover to see where he spent his daylight hours. Blowing small puffs of smoke into the air, Desio closed his eyes and basked in the memory of Countess Bathory's scented skin against his own. The hour grew late and Desio Vas, weary from his day, drifted off to sleep propped against the stable door. As the moon dipped lower in the sky, Dracula flew over Desio's sleeping form, oblivious to who he was or that his intentions were at the very least, to turn Countess Bathory against him.

Chapter 9 - Countess Bathory's Vanity - Sarvar Castle - (1581)

She was horrified when she looked in her favorite mirror this morning; the one she felt was the most flattering. Her reflection was ghastly. Elizabeth let out a gasp and covered her mouth as she observed dark circles under her eyes; the countess knew it was from lack of sleep. Staying up night after night had become her constant habit and when morning came, the countess found herself still stuck in the human world. The countess was losing patience with her vampire; he had been promising to turn her since the first night they met. Each day her face got a little older and she wanted to be turned now, while she was still young and beautiful. Elizabeth applied lip color with precision as she felt another one of her fierce headaches coming on. The countess fumed at not being turned yet; more than anything, Elizabeth Bathory longed to bite into sweet human flesh.

Taking one last look in the mirror the countess called to her maid, Theresa who had just started recently. The timid girl rushed to her mistress with an awkward curtsy.

"Close the door and come closer, dear," the countess said in a silvery voice.

Theresa moved closer, but with obvious reluctance. When she was within arm's length, Elizabeth snatched her arm and took hold of her face with both hands, kissing her passionately on the lips. Theresa wiggled to get free, but her mistress held her arm tightly, as she pulled the girl's dress down to expose her breasts. "You have such smooth breasts, dear," Countess Bathory whispered as she pulled the girl closer.

Theresa nodded as tears filled her eyes, but the countess refused to let her to. It happened so fast, the girl was taken by surprise. Countess Bathory clamped her teeth onto Theresa's upper arm, biting all the way down until she had a piece of the girl's flesh in her mouth. The poor girl shrieked, holding her arm as blood sprayed over both of them. Before the countess could stop her, Theresa fled the room. When Darvulia heard the screaming, she came running into the bedchamber; Elizabeth sat on her chaise lounge happily chewing on Theresa's flesh with a bloodied mouth, as though she were eating a breakfast roll.

Chapter 10 - An Undeniable Bond - Sarvar Castle - (1581)

It was early evening when Count Dracula made his usual appearance in Elizabeth's bedchamber. Upon seeing the room empty, he moved to the window to stroke the vine's downy softness. The night was still warm despite the season, so he unbuttoned his shirt and tossed it on the dressing chair. Wearing only his pants, the count moved back to the window and leaned against the sill; before long the vine covered its lord's neck and torso. The hungry vine found a soft spot on Dracula's chest and began to burrow inside, where a warm flow of blood traveled through the vampire's body. The wicked vine began to ingest the intoxicating substance, which tasted like liquid gold. The countess entered the room and discovered them, automatically reacting like a spurned lover.

"So that's how it is then, that filthy vine can drain your blood and know eternal life…but this you will not do for me!" the countess screamed, as she slammed the door.

"I had to do it, the ancient oak was dying…my vine needed sustenance or it would wither and die."

"I don't believe that! Why *should* I believe that! You promised me eternal life, but here I am nearly twenty-one years old. Is that awful vine more important than I am?" The countess was clearly angry, but Dracula had learned how to calm her.

"Please Elizabeth, sit down…get yourself some wine and let me finish my story…all will be explained," Dracula pleaded until the countess agreed to sit down to listen.

"Tell me the rest of this never-ending tale of woe then," Elizabeth demanded, "I want you to finish your story tonight…then give to me what you promised!"

Dracula placed his hands tenderly on her shoulders and once again continued telling his tale. Tonight, Nikos was also in attendance, content inside his mirror; it was a story he already knew, because he had been Count Dracula's companion for a very long time.

Chapter 11 - The End of Dracula's Tale - (In the Year 1476)

"**I** returned to Castle Arges in the summer of 1476, with a new horse named Midnight. Nikos Fabri rode beside me, and would be presented to the staff as my newly appointed Captain of the Guard. Nikos was able to pass for human but more importantly, he could withstand the one thing I could not…the light of day.

As we approached my castle, we could see night torches burning bright however, within the castle walls most were asleep. When we reached the drawbridge, the nighttime sounds were suddenly silenced and it grew quiet as the grave. It was after eleven when we passed through to the inner walls of my fortress. At last I was back in my family home, where I could maintain a home court advantage and defend myself against those who persecuted my kind…"

"I need more wine," Elizabeth interrupted, getting herself another glass.

"…I was officially welcomed back to Castle Arges the next evening. When I introduced myself as Radu, my kinsmen and staff welcomed me home without question. As my first order of business, I officially changed my name to Dracula Tepes in honor of my father's house, the house of Dracul…insisting my actions were simply to honor my father's legacy.

"Have you ever been bested by a human being?" Elizabeth asked with an evil grin. The countess was beautiful, but deadly; Dracula knew he would never be able to trust this woman as a vampire. He knew her well enough by now to know she could turn on him at any time. Dracula had fallen for the countess, but he was not blind to the blackness of her heart; truthfully, he had no desire to take her human life anyway. Deep down, the vampire knew this was the reason he hadn't turned her yet; it was time to leave, before the countess bullied him into changing his mind.

"Well…have you?" the countess persisted.

Dracula signed deeply and continued his narrative, "The first time

I died it was from pure carelessness. My son's wet nurse, of all people...
was the one who took my vampire life."

The countess looked up, surprised to hear this part of his story. "Are
you saying a silly servant was clever enough to take down a vampire?"

"Sadly, yes. But then I was still new to the world of vampire and
left myself vulnerable."

"Please, go on."

"I was advised all who worked at Castle Arges had never been in
service to our family. I believed my instructions had been followed,
until the night I came face to face with my son's former wet nurse,
Ursula. Somehow she had managed to get herself a position here in
my most intimate quarters; when she saw me, she crossed herself and
backed away in fear. I laughed it off, insisting I was my brother Radu.
Eventually she seemed to relax and I thought she believed me, but I
soon found out I was mistaken.

A day or two later...as I lay sleeping through a cool autumn day,
Ursula and two of the kitchen staff entered my bedchamber armed
with wooden stakes. In my twilight state, I could vaguely see and feel
their presence, including their purpose, but I was powerless to stop
them. Ursula plunged a stake into the hollow cave of my chest...I
don't remember if there was any pain...I just stopped feeling anything.
Next, I heard the sound of smashing glass as window shudders were
torn down...my assassins finished the job by flooding the room with
sunlight. Vlad Dracula was bested by a simple housemaid...but, it was
a long time ago." Dracula paused for a moment, no longer wanting to
recant a painful past he longed to forget.

Elizabeth was so moved by this part of the story; she did not realize
Dracula had stopped speaking. Overcome by the painful memory,
Dracula's shoulders sagged as he moved to kiss her soft neck. For a
brief moment, the countess believed her time had come, but when she
looked look into his eyes, Countess Bathory saw only pain and regret.

"I must go now, my lovely countess. My tale has ended and there is
nothing more for me to tell. I died and believed it was a way to atone
for my sins...so I accepted my fate with grace and dignity."

"But you lived again...you came here to find me." The countess felt
him pulling away, but didn't understand why.

"Yes, love. It was a wonderful ride…but the season of love is brief."

"What do you mean? You made a promise to me!" Her voice began to tremble at the thought of losing him.

Dracula cupped Elizabeth's cheek, putting a finger to her lips, as he spoke the words she didn't want to hear. "I will not make you a vampire. I cannot sentence you to a life of regret…I just can't. I'm sorry." Before the countess could object, Dracula flashed his cape and became airborne, riding an autumn wind into the mysterious night.

Countess Elizabeth Bathory cursed Dracula as he flew into the darkness; she felt a sense of betrayal she had never experienced before. Frustrated and hungry for the taste of pain, suffering and glorious blood, the countess woke two of her servants and brought them to her dungeon, where she and Darvulia tortured them until their bodies gave up.

Chapter 12 - Desio Vas –
Sarvar Castle - (1581)

He could hardly believe his luck when he caught sight of the large bat as it flew out of Countess Bathory's bedchamber, gliding with the wind before making a sharp turn toward the Nadasdy Crypt. At last, Desio Vas was able to confirm his suspicions. He advanced on foot keeping a safe distance, and then watched in disbelief as the bat turned into a well-dressed man. The man wore a cape and his skin was impossibly white; he ducked inside the crypt, unaware he was being watched. Desio was stunned at his discovery and now understood his adversary was the most despicable kind of predator, a nosferato or, as some called them, vampyre.

Desio believed Countess Bathory was under the vampire's spell; it was well-known that creatures of the night practiced the dark arts. Desio knew exactly what had to be done, something that could only be done just before sunrise; he would need a priest and had to plan things carefully. He would bide his time until he could make the necessary arrangements, because it was all about timing. No one knew better than Desio Vas that in most matters, timing was everything.

Desio took one last swig of his warm ale and started humming as he skipped down the narrow pathway to the barn, where his loft bed was waiting for him. It would take him a week or so to set things up and make sure this unnatural abomination was destroyed. The last thought Desio had before he drifted off to sleep, was how lovely it would be when the countess came crawling back to him.

Chapter 13 - The Water Goddess – Sarvar Castle – (1581)

Elizabeth sat by her open window watching the sunset; the night had lost its special magic. It had been nearly two weeks since she last saw him; the countess wondered if he had left Hungary altogether. Dracula's absence had taken away her zest for living; the excitement of being with the count had been a whirlwind of endless nights full of passion and discovery. Countess Bathory admitted to herself she might be lovesick; this was not a feeling she was accustomed to having for any man. He had left her to grow old and ugly in a in a world where beauty was revered above all else. How could Count Dracula treat her this way? How dare he make empty promises to a member of the Hungarian royal family! Tonight, there was a fire burning inside her and try as she might to let her anger go, Elizabeth was unwilling to allow Dracula to have a victory over her. It wasn't in her nature to be bested by anyone, and she wasn't about to allow a vampire to make a fool of her.

Theresa entered her bedchamber, preparing to braid Elizabeth's hair. She approached her mistress who of late, had been sullen and quiet. Theresa preferred her mistress this way; she had seen the angry side of the countess and had the scars to prove it. As Theresa began to braid her hair, Elizabeth hummed a sad song and watched the last colors of the sunset fade, as the day surrendered itself to a sky full of stars. The air had become frigid and there were rumors of an early snowfall; just the thought of winter made Countess Bathory shiver. Her hair finished, the countess looked out the window, hopelessly searching for her count; deep down, she knew he wasn't coming. Elizabeth turned to Theresa to say good night, and saw the girl rubbing her neck.

"What's wrong with your neck...is it your lace collar, dear?" Countess Bathory asked with genuine concern.

"It's nothing, my lady...just a rash," Theresa replied, looking a little too nervous.

"Let me see." Elizabeth moved to her and before it could be stopped, Theresa's neck wound was exposed; there was no denying Dracula had found himself a new companion. Before Theresa could even speak, Elizabeth grabbed her arm and threw her down on the bed. "How dare *you* give yourself to him! I am ten times more beautiful than you are!" screamed the countess as she grabbed a scarf, and began tying Theresa's hands together.

Darvulia entered the bedchamber in response to the sound of her mistress screaming. Upon seeing her wet nurse, Elizabeth began smashing mirrors all around her, as shattered glass flew everywhere. "I'm a crone, Darvulia! I'm hideous and my count would rather have a peasant girl...when he can have a countess!"

Elizabeth hung her head and burst into wracked sobs; Darvulia moved to comfort her mistress, knowing from past experience she had very little control when the countess decided to throw a tantrum. As the bizarre display of Countess Bathory's uncontrollable rage continued, Theresa cried hysterically, certain a horrific punishment awaited. All Theresa had done was accept a little kindness from a handsome stranger. She had no idea the charming gentleman she'd just met, was Countess Bathory's secret lover.

"If Dracula wants a perfect and beautiful companion for all time, I will give him that. My dear Theresa, I will give you eternal beauty starting tonight. Won't that be nice?" Elizabeth asked. She pulled Theresa to her feet, tearing her dress as she pulled on her arm with uncontrolled rage.

Darvulia seemed unsure what her mistress was up, to but followed Countess Bathory as she hurried Theresa unwillingly down the marble staircase. Theresa struggled to get free, crying for mercy as she was dragged down the steps so fast; she kept tripping on the hem of her gown. When they reached the main foyer, two guards approached and unlocked the front door for the countess and her entourage without comment. Cold air assaulted them, as the countess dragged Theresa out onto the marble columned patio; a three quarter moon shone brightly in the night sky. Without the sun's warmth, the temperature had quickly dropped below freezing and Darvulia shivered, wondering what her mistress had in mind. Theresa finally stopped weeping, as Countess Bathory commanded several of the kitchen staff be woken from their slumber, to gather buckets of cold water. Already shivering from the cold, Theresa wrapped her arms around herself in a futile effort to keep warm. Elizabeth stripped what remained of Theresa's clothing off, exposing her lithe young body to the bitter night air. Paralyzed by fear, the girl couldn't even feel ashamed of her nakedness. The countess ordered Theresa be tied to a stone column to receive her punishment, and then laughed with maniacal delight as servants poured continuous buckets of cold water over her naked body; when Theresa's body finally slumped in surrender, her skin was slick with a thin coat of ice.

Elizabeth smiled at her wet nurse, completely satisfied with the punishment she had decreed for Theresa. Darvulia returned a forced smile and went back inside the castle; her only thought was to find forgetfulness in sleep. Pleased that her rival was finally dead, Elizabeth moved closer to inspect white flakes of ice forming on the girl's eyelashes. Theresa's dead eyes held an expression of surprise, as though she were trying to comprehend her own death. Determined to taunt Dracula and guarantee he would come to see what had become of his new mistress, Elizabeth had two of the stable boys woken and instructed to build a bonfire in the front courtyard. As flames grew higher, the icy sheen on Theresa's body vanished as excess water trickled down her arms and legs; the dead girl had been transformed from an ice sculpture into a water goddess.

In her death, Theresa was even more beautiful, which only fueled her jealous rage. Countess Bathory stood alone in front of Sarvar Castle with her arms raised to the sky and screamed, "Dracula...come and rescue your water goddess...she is waiting for you...and so am I!"

Chapter 14 - Dracula –
Sarvar Castle - (1581)

The night was fading fast as he flew toward Sarvar Castle, searching for Theresa. She had been late to meet him, so Dracula assumed she was kept late by the countess. She was a pretty thing, but he felt no passion for her at all; this made her the perfect choice. Properly dressed, she would make an ideal female consort. Unlike the headstrong countess, she would prove a demure and pliable companion. Theresa was docile, a woman he could easily groom; over time, he was certain she would make a faithful servant and occasional mistress. Dracula thought about the time he spent with Countess Bathory. At first, she provided him with everything he craved; excitement, desire, tireless passion and a regular taste of her succulent blood. As time passed, Dracula began to fully comprehend Elizabeth's capacity for evil and actually feared turning her; he believed it possible she would start a colony of her own vampires, to be turned against *him*. She was beautiful, but ruthless; that kind of complication he didn't need. Dracula had enough demons chasing him, he didn't need any more. He would be better off with someone like Theresa. The girl was young and naïve, much easier to control than a willful countess. Dracula planned to turn her tonight, before Elizabeth discovered their secret; it was time to get out of Hungary.

The castle was just up ahead, but something didn't look right, and then Dracula caught the unmistakable smell of smoke. Quickly descending toward the ground, the vampire put his feet forward and glided back into his human form, as though putting on a pair of pants. He landed on the open drawbridge as though he was expected, which indeed he was. Now in his human form once more, the vampire saw a huge bonfire burning in front of Sarvar Castle and surmised it had been set deliberately. He didn't see her at first. Dracula was trying to find something to extinguish the fire with, when he finally saw what the countess had done. Theresa had been sacrificed to make him suffer, by further fueling his precious guilt. In the cruel orange glow of a burning fire, Dracula beheld Theresa's body as it glimmered with colored light, electrifying the surface of her skin. He had to leave this country now, and find a new place where he was completely unknown. He had broken a golden rule in the world of vampire; he had allowed himself to fall in love. Dracula doubted Countess Bathory was even capable of love and now, he was certain she had no heart at all.

"I curse you, Countess Bathory...and I hope you live to be eighty!" Dracula screamed up at Elizabeth's bedroom window, but the room was dark.

Rolling up his sleeves, Dracula untied Theresa and gently lifted her body from the column, where she had been left to the elements. There wasn't much time before daylight, but he planned to spend all of it giving Theresa a proper burial; in his mind, she deserved that much.

Chapter 15 - Desio's Revenge - Sarvar Castle - (1581)

Tonight was the night, Desio thought smugly as he finished up his chores, anxious to carry out his plan to best his adversary, Count Dracula. Most of the time, he was carefree and happy to be alive; even as a child, Desio had been this way. Some called him "happy go lucky" while others called him a "simpleton," but in reality, he was much smarter than he looked. Desio had been in residence at Sarvar Castle for a long time now, and had eyes and ears everywhere. He had slept with royal daughters, and was prone to taking the virginity of young housemaids. Desio Vas was a man who could charm just about anyone and it served him well.

Tonight, he had more important things than women on his mind. Desio Vas was deep in thought about his *secret mission*, one that would rid Hungary of an abomination. When the sun rose tomorrow morning, Count Vlad Dracula would be sent back to hell, where he belonged. The following morning Desio met Father Tamas at 4:30AM outside the Nadasdy Crypt. Desio understood well the importance of attacking just before dawn, when a vampire is weakest. The priest brought along a large hulking man named, Otto to do the deed. Desio led them inside and instantly felt a bone-chilling cold.

The air was musty and damp making it difficult to breathe, but not for a vampire. Dracula sensed they were coming and assumed his bat-like form. The morning sun was still obscured by the mountains, but would not be for long. As he hung from the ceiling waiting for the trio to enter, Dracula prepared to fight for survival. When the vault door opened, Dracula descended from above, transforming instantly into a wolf. The unfortunate priest tried to flee, but was much too slow; within seconds, the ferocious wolf tore his throat out. Otto pulled out his long knife and charged the wolf; he had been expecting something human and struggled against the size of his canine adversary. Despite the size of his foe, Otto was determined to collect his bounty, so he continued slashing the air, but never once hit his target. Dracula pounced on him, clawing at his face and chest, as blood cascaded down the front of his tattered shirt. Otto's knees buckled and the black wolf knocked him to the ground, clamping its powerful jaws onto the man's exposed neck; Otto was no match for a vampire defending his lair.

Desio stood in the corner as the black wolf hurled Otto's mutilated body against the wall. He was now left to face a ferocious beast unarmed. The two locked eyes, now only a few feet away from one another. Dracula advanced, changing back into his vulnerable human form, and Desio saw his opportunity. He raced to the vault door and threw it open; a brilliant burst of morning sunlight flooded the crypt. Dracula's face contorted, his arms stretching up to the ceiling as he began to ignite. The vampire's body twisted in a most unnatural way, as the sun cut through the core of his being like a red hot blade. He screamed in agony as his pale skin began to melt and burn. Desio watched dumbstruck and unable to move. The vampire continued to sizzle and burn until Count Vad Dracula was reduced to a pile of gray ash.

The vine awakened during the confrontation and made its way to the corner, where Desio was attempting to hide. It wrapped itself around his ankle and with amazing speed, climbed up to his chest. As its grip tightened, Desio felt something sharp pierce his chest; it took only minutes for the vine to drain most of the life-sustaining blood from his body.

Nikos entered the crypt after hearing the noise, and quickly realized he was too late. Nikos knew he had failed to read the warning signs that Dracula was in danger of being exposed. He had started to feel safe here at Sarvar Castle, but he now understood the signals he had missed. Nikos beheld the pile of ashes that had once been his friend, Dracula. Grief-stricken, he watched numbly as the vine moved to the pile and slowly regurgitated the blood it had drained from Desio Vas; Nikos watched in amazement as the blood spread, mixing with the ashes of Count Dracula.

At first, nothing happened. Then suddenly, there was movement, followed by a most amazing transformation. Gradually the pile of ash began to form into a cowering infant; the grotesque thing emitted a screeching sound that echoed throughout the crypt. The form continued to age, as toddler became an adolescent; finally the adult form of Count

Dracula, appeared once more. His body was covered in thick gray slime, as through he had been born again. Naked and still locked in a fetal position, the vampire finally opened his red eyes, just in time to see Desio Vas close his own eyes for the last time.

CHAPTER 16 - DECLINE OF ELIZABETH BATHORY - HUNGARY – (1581-1614)

The moment Dracula was turned to ashes; Elizabeth Bathory collapsed onto the floor of her bedchamber, and became violently ill for days. She took almost nothing to eat and drank much more than her normal quota of Tokay wine, as she mourned the painful loss of her love. Desio's demise brought the entire sequence of events out into the open; naturally, no one knew a vampire had been slain, because there was no body. The only bodies found were Desio's and a brute named Otto. Elizabeth eventually learned her former lover had been responsible for turning her count to dust; her only consolation was in knowing Desio perished too. Elizabeth could hardly bear the thought of his suffering, and wondered if vampires felt pain. Despite being a cold-hearted woman, the thought of Dracula in pain was agonizing. The countess was unaware the vine had revived Dracula, and that he and Nikos were in hiding. For the countess, the future seemed a vast wasteland of emptiness that would pale in comparison to the memory of soft velvet nights in the arms of her handsome vampire.

Countess Bathory would always love her vampire, but she had no choice but to settle back into domestic life. Count Nadasdy began spending more time at home; he decided it was time to start a family. They had several children together, but the countess never found love again as long as she lived. Her bloodlust continued and many believed she suffered from severe mental illness, as evidenced by chronic migraines that plagued her since childhood. As the years passed, the royal family relocated to Cachtice Castle, where the torture sessions continued on a regular basis. Inevitably, as her methods became more extreme, young girls began to perish; bodies had to be disposed of on a regular basis. After the daughter of a Moldavian noble went missing, authorities were finally brought in to investigate; they discovered dozens of bodies strewn about the castle. Darvulia and five other accomplices were tried and convicted for the murders of over six hundred young girls. Despite her heinous crimes, Elizabeth Bathory a.k.a. the "Blood Countess," never spent a day in jail due to her royal status. After the trials, authorities declared the countess insane, demanding that Elizabeth be locked away in her private chambers, for the rest of her life. Before her confinement, the countess requested that every mirror she owned be removed from the premises; there she lived all alone until her death at the age of fifty-four.

Chapter 17 – Dracula Unmasked – Castle Arges

Over the last hundred years, Castle Arges had begun to crumble; Dracula realized this would likely be the last visit to his family home. The count occasionally returned for personal items and other valuables when he was feeling nostalgic. His clothing was no longer usable, having become too tattered to wear. Most of his other possessions were no longer needed; however he retrieved his favorite walking stick, along with a silk top hat he pilfered from one of his unlucky victims. Dracula gathered what remained of his family's heirloom jewelry to barter with humans at a later date, if necessary. His primary reason for returning tonight was to retrieve the balance of the vast fortune; it was discreetly hidden within the bowels of the castle.

The voices of his past echoed through the walls of the castle, as he packed up his belongings. Dracula could still hear his father's wise words spoken when he was a boy. "Vlad, always remember it is far more important to be feared, than to be loved." Dracula had taken these words to heart and tried to live as his father had; who knew he would become one of the undead, traveling with the most unlikely companions? Dracula took a deep breath as he moved past a hallway mirror, but something made him stop what he was doing. The vampire moved closer to study his reflection in the mirror. His face was still handsome though pale; his skin still fairly smooth and free of the deep lines associated with human aging. As a vampire, Dracula knew wrinkles would never come, but this realization gave him no satisfaction. He closed his eyes and tried to imagine himself as an old man. As if reading his mind, the mirror showed him the face of an ancient man who was so weathered; his eyes almost disappeared inside the loose flesh of his sagging skin. His hair was white and so sparse it barely covered his balding head. Dracula's high cheekbones jutted out like misplaced elbows, and his lips were merely a joyless slash of crimson. The old man's face was ugly and frightening to behold; the vampire could not make himself look away, so fascinating was the transformation. Dracula finally shook the vision off, and once again beheld a handsome man of forty-five. His green eyes were completely void of emotion, as a fuzzy apparition of his son, Mikolai floated in the air behind him. Suddenly the vision changed into a bloody battlefield, filled with impaled Turkish soldiers; against a vivid red sunset, their bodies writhed in agony. Dracula cupped his hands to his ears, and cried, "Show me no more!"

The mirror responded by providing another vision of twelve-year-old Vlad, beheading his pony, Ludwig. As the blood of his slaughtered pet filled the mirror, Dracula finally forced himself to look away. Unnerved and certain he had taken everything he could possibly need from Castle Arges, Dracula prepared to return to the Otherworld which from now on, would be his refuge and home.

Chapter 18 - Nikos – The Otherworld

The Otherworld had always been a place where Nikos felt truly safe. After his death on a battlefield that ended with a vampire's kiss, he was summoned by the sound of ocean water and an explosion of light. When the light dimmed, he beheld a beautiful arched doorway, and then he saw the strange mirror; without hesitation, Nikos entered the Otherworld, and remained there until Vlad Dracula pulled him into the living world again. Nikos spent the first year with Dracula, both loving and hating him, for ending his human life in a most unnatural way. Over time Dracula proved himself to be an honorable lord, but there was another reason Nikos remained loyal; he craved life in the human world. He no longer ate or had other physical human needs, but he could pass for human anywhere he went. Nikos had regrets about losing his humanity; sometimes he even missed the sweet warm feel of a woman's skin, but his sexual appetite had long ago been extinguished. In this way, Nikos and Dracula differed; Dracula could still enjoy the pleasures of a woman. Nikos was grateful his lord had decided not to turn Countess Bathory; like his lord, he feared someone so wicked might turn against them. Nikos had to admit she was a beautiful woman, but cringed to think about how difficult her temper would be to manage. Fortunately, that was over now, and Nikos was ready to leave this chapter of his life behind. It was Nikos who helped get Dracula out of the Nadasdy Crypt, on the night of the attempted assassination. Fortunately, no one heard the battle until Nikos had already brought Dracula into the safety of the woods. Neither of them knew Darvulia had spread rumors throughout the castle, claiming Desio Vas and his accomplice had slain a vampire; her aim was to protect her mistress and to quell any hope she might have that Count Dracula would return.

Now residing in a place without time, Dracula and Nikos made future plans. In the Otherworld, there was no need to feed, and here daylight could not find him. No one at the castle realized they had escaped from Hungary through Darvulia's heirloom mirror; the only one the countess didn't smash to pieces. The faithful vine had followed, spreading its leafy tentacles around the opening so it could closely guard its lord. Dracula and Nikos were engrossed in a discussion of where they should travel next. Neither yet understood their powers of mobility; they believed themselves dependent upon others to bring them through the threshold to another time. They had been considering London, as their new home; Dracula was intrigued by the country's rich history and admitted an attraction to the infamous moors. Nikos suggested they jump ahead in time, stating the sixteenth century was a bit archaic. They chose their travel destinations carefully, to minimize the risk of a violent confrontation with inhabitants of a future time. To Dracula, the future was a vast unknown; being quite superstitious, Dracula feared going too far ahead in time, lest they be unable to return.

The royal princes giggled behind them, catching them by surprise. The boys were always sneaking up on Nikos, and he'd gotten used to it. Dracula was still trying to adapt to the idea of their company. In the human world, Edward had been a sturdy twelve-year-old and heir to the English throne. Richard, Duke of York, was nine when he was murdered and their remains never found; hence, the reason they were both trapped with Nikos in the Otherworld. The two princes had been with Nikos since the day of their deaths in 1483, and were his constant companions. Edward admired Nikos who showed him respect, but still didn't fully trust Dracula. Richard was very fond of Nikos and considered him a second father. The princes were boys, but because of their experiences and the education they received through Nikos, they were well beyond their chronological age in every possible way. The boys told an incredible story about what had happened during the summer of 1483; through research, Nikos discovered several theories surrounding their deaths, but found nothing about anyone discovering their bones. Based on an English history book on the subject published in 1604, historians claimed the children were smothered by their Uncle Richard (King Richard III) *or* by his order; their bones likely hidden within the Tower of London. Since the first day the princes arrived in the Otherworld, they have been asking Nikos to help them find their bones. As Dracula and Nikos were making plans, Richard came up with an idea he believed might help them solve the mystery of their bones once and for all.

"What about going *back* in time?" Richard asked unexpectedly. Dracula scowled but Nikos held up his hand, and nodded for the boy to continue.

"My Lady Mother…Elizabeth Woodville can help you. She was Queen Consort of England in 1483. If you visit her in early summer, she will be in sanctuary at Westminster Abbey. I know she will help us." Richard longed to see his mother's face again.

"We can't let children make such an important decision," Dracula replied impatiently.

"Please let the boy speak. I think he has an idea we should consider… their mother might be able to help us." Nikos replied.

"I thought we wanted to skip *ahead* in time?" Dracula complained.

"For once in your life…do something to help someone else, you selfish shit!" Nikos barked, and Dracula was duly silenced.

Edward surprised everyone by chiming in. "My brother, Richard is correct, Count Dracula. In the year 1483, my Lady Mother was one of the most powerful women in all of England. She will help us; she would do anything for her sons. I am sure of it." Edward pleaded his case like the royal prince he was.

Dracula nodded, finally willing to commit himself to helping the boys with their quest. They could always visit the future after they found out where the princes were buried. A free admission to the year 1483 and an introduction to the Queen of England might just prove interesting, if nothing else. Nikos had become very fond of the boys, and was torn between wanting them to stay in the Otherworld and helping them find peace. It didn't matter how he felt; he had made a commitment to help them. In order to accommodate Dracula's aversion to daylight, they would wait until early evening to make their entry into the year 1483.

CHAPTER 19 - QUEEN CONSORT OF ENGLAND - WESTMINSTER ABBEY - (AUTUMN OF 1483)

The gilded mirror could not do justice to the finely carved image of the queen's lovely face. Admired for her beauty as well as her intellect, Elizabeth Woodville was uniquely gifted with insight beyond the boundaries of normal human consciousness; because of her special talents, she had even been accused of witchcraft. According to popular opinion, Elizabeth Woodville used sorcery to bewitch King Edward IV and many believed her mother, Jacquetta taught her daughter the craft. Elizabeth scoffed at these rumors because she had married for love, been loyal to her country and given the king two male heirs to the throne. Tonight, a light burned in her blue eyes as she gazed at her image in the glass. The queen's head was adorned with unruly blonde curls that hung to her waist; although lovely, hers was difficult hair to manage. Alone in her bedchamber without her husband, the queen wore only a sheer nightdress trimmed with the finest lace money could buy. She studied her reflection, satisfied that for a woman of nearly forty, she was still holding her own.

The queen missed her husband, but it was necessary for her to seek sanctuary at Westminster Abbey with her children, until the political unrest settled down. The queen applied face cream imported from France to her delicate skin, as she admired her flawless complexion. Her naked breasts were clearly visible through the translucent garment she wore; her nipples were the color of fresh strawberries. She had narrow hips and her thighs were clearly outlined by the glowing candlelight; a slight shadow where her thighs met at the center of her womanhood was enough to tempt any man. If there was a rival to the astounding beauty of Countess Elizabeth Bathory, Elizabeth Woodville would be at the top of the list. When Dracula saw her for the first time, he was temporarily love-struck.

The queen put down her brush as the mirror became cloudy; an apparition appeared before her, it was a stern-looking man with hard eyes, but she was not afraid. "Who are you?" the queen asked, grabbing a robe to cover herself. Supernatural beings did not frighten her; under her mother's tutelage she had learned ghosts were harmless and nothing to fear.

"My name is Nikos Fabri...," he began. The princes moved next to Nikos, revealing their presence. The queen gasped and put a hand to her mouth, tears filling her eyes. "So it's true then...he did kill my babies, after all." The queen sobbed and covered her face.

Prince Edward finally spoke, "Lady Mother, please do not cry we are safe here...and will be with you again someday." The queen looked more closely at her boys still wearing the nightgowns they were buried in. Although they were dead, she had a difficult time seeing them that way; their reflections in the mirror were so vivid and alive.

Prince Edward put his hand to the mirror; he pleaded with his mother to touch the glass. The queen approached and when her palm touched Edward's, there was an icy cold, followed by a blinding light. The boy grabbed onto his mother's arm; when the queen pulled away, Prince Edward entered her bedchamber. The queen dropped to her knees and hugged him, as tears flowed down her cheeks. She planted kisses on his face and neck, as if needing to confirm he was really there. Her son was cold to the touch and the queen understood he was no longer alive, but she didn't care. Prince Richard moved to the mirror and his mother pulled him into the room to join his brother. The queen engulfed both boys hungrily in her arms, as though afraid they would vanish.

"Lady Mother," Prince Edward said, "these men, Nikos and Dracula, have most unusual powers. We have lived with them for a long time... they have graciously agreed to help find our missing bones...so we can leave this lonely place."

The queen smiled at the men in the mirror, but remained cautious. Count Dracula approached and put his palm to the mirror. The bewildered queen had no choice but to pull him into the room; Nikos entered last, feeling like an afterthought. He bowed humbly to the queen and then stepped back, unsure of the protocol when greeting such royalty. Dracula turned on his charm, bowing in gentlemanly fashion, as he kissed the queen's hand in a most seductive way.

The queen beheld the shadows of her sons, because that is exactly what they were. Although Edward and Richard were merely ghosts of her lost children, that didn't stop her from wanting to protect them. Were these men trustworthy and how did they come in contact with two princes who also happened to be heirs to the English throne? Someone was always trying to take advantage of royalty in any way they could; Elizabeth Woodville always remained wary of strangers.

"It is impossible for you to remain here. My sons, even if they are ghosts, must not be seen by any of my kinsmen...these are very dangerous times."

"I assure you, my lady, we will not stay for long. We need to ask what you know about current custom for royal burials," Nikos replied.

"Royal burials?" the queen asked confused.

"Yes, my lady," Dracula interrupted, "our plan is to travel into the future so we can discover when and where your sons' remains were found and laid to rest. If we are to seek peace for the young princes, we could use direction on where their remains might be buried if they were discovered say...one hundred years from now."

The queen tried to comprehend a time so far into the future. "It could be here in fact, or possibly Windsor Castle." As they spoke, the queen started to believe in the integrity of her visitors' strange mission.

"So in theory, the royal princes would be buried wherever you and the king will be laid to rest, is that correct, my lady?" Nikos asked.

"Well, yes... I suppose that is true...then, my answer would be here, at Westminster Abbey...but how can you possibly determine when this will happen?"

"We can't, my lady...but we are willing to try," Dracula responded wishing they had a better plan.

The queen directed her focus back to her sons as they stood in their bedclothes; they looked back at her with the wide blue eyes of innocence. "Royal princes, even if they are ghosts, should not be dressed in their nightgowns," the queen stated, as she moved to a large wooden chest to retrieve more suitable garments.

"My doublet!" Prince Richard exclaimed, as his mother held the garment up to him. He had to admit, he was rather tired of wearing a nightgown all the time. The two boys dressed quickly and the transformation was amazing.

"It is not safe for any of you to be seen here. The walls have eyes and ears. I do not fully trust some of those who have come with me to Westminster…as proclaimed protectors," the queen explained. She handed each boy a small sword, which made her feel a little better about their safety. It was difficult for the queen to understand they were now in a place where swords were unnecessary. Naturally, the princes were quite happy to have weapons they could call their own.

"Go with God, my sons. I will assist your friends and rest assured…I will make certain they fulfill their promise." With tears in her eyes, the queen hugged her sons once more, then stepped back to look at them for the last time. The royal ghosts regretfully bid their mother goodbye on a late fall evening in 1483, and returned to the Otherworld to wait for their bones to be discovered. The two boys enjoyed being the center of attention and often referred to their endless search as "bone hunting." For them, the quest was more of a game, than something they actually expected to find.

Chapter 20 - Dracula at Westminster Abbey – (Autumn of 1483)

Dracula found himself captivated by the beauty of England's queen. The vampire immediately took note the queen was nothing like Countess Bathory. Elizabeth Woodville appeared to be a very kind, intelligent woman who seemed genuinely interested in what he and Nikos could do to help her sons. Because it was necessary for Dracula's presence to be kept from prying eyes, the queen was forced to entertain visitors in her private rooms. It was growing late and Dracula's need to feed began to gnaw at him like a dull knife.

"My lady," the count began, "my true nature has not yet been revealed to you. I am a vampire and therefore, a necessary creature of the night."

"I did not think such creatures were real, Count Dracula, so please tell me more," the queen replied, surprised to find she was not afraid. Certainly, if he meant her harm he would have done so by now.

"I must leave you now and attend to my needs, but will return later this evening to tell you anything you want to know." The count flashed his trademark cape and assumed his bat-like form, flying out the open window into the night. The queen moved to the window but lost him in the darkness; suddenly the room felt so empty. As she lay between the sheets waiting for sleep to come, Elizabeth Woodville stroked her neck and wondered whether a vampire's victims felt any pain.

It was close to midnight when Dracula returned to the queen's bedchamber, where she had fallen asleep. She was a vision of loveliness, as she lay on her bed with her eyes closed; her full lips were the color of rosebuds and the vampire was overcome by an unexpected wave of desire. Hearing him approach the bed, Elizabeth sat up with a start, flipping her heavy braid to one side as she reached for a robe. The queen moved to her settee, anxious to hear how Dracula and his friend planned to travel to the future.

"Come now...and tell me where you came from, let's start there." The queen used a tone that both intrigued and challenged the count.

54

"My queen, if this is where you want me to begin…then, I fear I will confuse you even more."

"And how is that?"

"We most recently came from the year 1581, after spending time in Hungary, with the Countess of Bathory."

"Bathory, never heard of her."

"Of course you haven't…she hasn't been born yet, my lady."

"I don't understand…"

Dracula continued, "My lady…we have the unusual ability to visit other times in history. We mostly target dates in the future, but tonight, we chose to return to the past…to find you. Your sons insisted you could help them to the other side."

"I thank you for your willingness to assist my sons…but how could anyone be expected to believe it?"

"You watched me turn into a bat, my lady…what additional proof do you need?"

The queen smiled at this. "Let's say I give you the benefit of the doubt…and believe your story. If what you say is true and you really can time travel, why haven't you found my sons' murderer yet?"

"My lady, I'm afraid the crime remains unsolved."

"Ah-h-h, but I have only your word that this is so. How can I confirm what you are telling me is the truth?"

"You can't, my lady. But…I can tell you much about what will happen to you and your remaining children…if you want to know," Dracula replied.

"Should a mother know these things before they happen?" the queen asked, yet her eyes were hungry for information.

"Your firstborn daughter, also named Elizabeth, will marry King Henry the VII. Their son, Henry VIII, will marry six times. The king's only son, your great-grandson, Edward…will inherit the throne at age nine."

"Interesting to be sure," the queen replied, now worried about the future of England after she was gone.

The queen certainly couldn't deny what she had seen; a man turned into a bat and flew out her bedroom window. The astute queen was still guarded; otherworldly creatures often had the power to bewitch human beings and make them see things that weren't real. Having spent her childhood being tutored in white magic by her mother, Elizabeth did not always have faith in what she saw.

After a pause, the queen responded, "You give me food for thought... but you must admit your story is quite fantastic."

"My lady, your own son confirmed my story."

"He is a child," she replied with a shrug.

"True, but why would he lie to his own mother...who we traveled back in time to find?"

The queen suddenly switched tactics. "So, what's stopping you from biting me right now and making me a vampire, too?"

"I would, if I thought it was something you wanted...but I can see that you are too in love with your human life."

"I am in love with my husband, the king. As queen; I have a duty to produce heirs. Even if your lifestyle interested me at all (and it doesn't), I would never allow myself to live as you do...killing without conscience."

"What makes you think I kill without conscience?"

"How can one have a conscience and kill at all?"

"My guilt is the shield I wear against the pitiful crying of humanity. I scrape the lowest kind of man off the street, and with very little pain... put an end to his suffering. I hunt in neighborhoods you've never heard of, drinking the life blood of derelicts that have one foot in the grave already. To kill a man like that is a favor to him...and to society itself. A man like that is completely dead inside...so how can it be cruel to end his life?"

"Dear count, that was well spoken...but I believe you are just avoiding my question. Don't you *ever* felt guilty about killing humans?" The queen found his story fascinating, and really didn't want him to leave.

Upon hearing this statement, Dracula sat down next to the queen and proceeded to explain how he came to be. He told her the story of his family and admitted killing his own son. He told her about Nikos, his vine and the fierce battle for his life when Desio Vas and his accomplices tried to kill him. Dracula ended his story with the horrific torture and death of Theresa. The queen was silent throughout his tale, which lasted until well after midnight. At times his eyes brimmed with tears, and the queen slowly began to feel compassion for this "so-called" creature of the night.

When Dracula became silent, drained from the telling of his tale, Elizabeth Woodville finally spoke softly, "I am sorry you have suffered so."

The queen raised her hand to wipe a stray tear from his cheek; Dracula leaned against her for a moment, and that became his undoing. His vampire eyes turned red as he became solely focused on the pulsing vein in the queen's neck; Dracula was dying to taste her. The queen sensed his bloodlust, and reached to cover her exposed neck, but was too late. Everything turned to red as the vampire took the queen in his arms, and claimed her smooth white neck for his own. When Dracula's teeth pierced her flesh, the queen moaned with a distinct pleasure he had not expected.

When he was finished, Dracula gently pulled away. "I am sorry my lady. As I explained already…I don't always control my impulses. Your wound will heal in a few days. By then I will be centuries away, and no further threat to you…you have my promise."

The queen searched his eyes, they had returned to their normal color. She loosened her braid and whispered, "Take me as a man now… my nights are very lonely while my king lies with his mistress…and I am left to sleep alone."

"A woman like you should never sleep alone," Dracula replied in a husky voice, as he carried her to the bed. He slowly undressed his prize, taking in her loveliness as she raised her arms to bring him closer. Tonight, she didn't care about anything except her own human need for physical love. Dracula, of course, was more than happy to accommodate. The queen could feel the coolness of his skin, which only made him more exciting. Dracula made love to her in a most human way; when he entered her, she felt an instant surge of energy that went well beyond mere sexual gratification. Dracula left the queen's bed well before dawn, but the queen didn't hear him leave; she was fast asleep and already dreaming about him.

Morning came and the queen found herself alone. No doubt, the count was hiding inside her mirror, now that her bedchamber was filled with yellow light. She was surprised when Nikos came to the mirror seeking release, so she pulled him into the room.

"My lady…we have decided on a plan that should hopefully lead us to the discovery of the princes' remains."

"What is your plan?"

"We need to travel ahead in time…to the seventeenth century, in fact. Our plan is to take the boys and search The Tower of London itself, specifically where your sons were imprisoned. Only they can lead us to the right location."

Nikos stopped speaking when he noticed her telltale neck wound; he knew only too well who was responsible. He seethed with anger at the realization that once again, Dracula had put his primal needs above everything else. Seeing his face redden, the queen quickly put a hand to her neck. Nikos simply sneered and turned his back on her.

"Wait, please…you don't understand…"

"I understand very well, my lady," he replied, turning to look at her once more. "I hope you understand that, to him, you are just one of many."

CHAPTER 21 - A BATTLE FOR HONOR

Though safe from daylight within the Otherworld, Dracula still continued his habit of sleeping through the daytime hours. As he lay resting peacefully, Nikos approached with an anger the count could immediately recognize.

"You son of a bitch!" Nikos shouted, giving the count a hefty kick in the ribs to rouse him. Dracula rose to his full height, ready for battle as he confronted his angry friend.

"She's the damn Queen of England, for God's sake, Vlad. How could you even think of turning her into the abomination that you are!"

"Hold on now...who said I was going to turn her? I have no such plans at all. I just wanted to taste her and guess what...I think she actually liked it."

Nikos threw a punch at his undead friend, but Dracula was too quick. The two danced together with fists clenched as their anger piqued, with Nikos trying desperately to cause his lord some much-deserved pain. Prompted by the noise, the princes came running toward them; they were surprised to see the two men fighting with fists instead of swords. The boys always carried their swords with them, safely tucked into their belts.

"Nikos!" Dracula shouted, pointing to the princes. He hoped their presence would make him come to his senses, but his friend was hot and still wanted to fight.

"Count Dracula, I despise you. You corrupt everything you touch!" Nikos exclaimed, as he moved to take a sword from Prince Richard's belt. He was so quick, the boy couldn't stop him.

Prince Edward decided a fair fight was called for; he tossed his sword to Dracula, who caught the weapon in midair. The two men resumed fighting with swords, as the princes watched in awe; during their short lives, they had never seen men in battle.

"What is it now, Nikos? Do you have a crush on our lovely queen?" Dracula taunted.

"She is too good for the likes of you, unholy being!" Nikos countered, skillfully dodging his lord's blade.

"That's not what she said to me last night…when I was in her bed," Dracula replied, and with one well-aimed strike, he knocked the sword from Nikos' hand.

Nikos fell backward from the force and found his lost sword, charging at Dracula who had not expected such a quick recovery. Nikos erroneously slashed Dracula's abdomen, instead of just grazing his shoulder.

"Nikos, my friend…you have fought well…let's call a truce," Dracula pleaded, holding onto his gut, as blood seeped through his shirt. Nikos dropped his sword and moved to help his lord; the vampire had managed to remain standing, despite his injury.

"Truce, my friend?" Dracula asked again, offering his hand.

"A truce it is…but Vlad, if we're going to travel together through time, can you at least try not to climb into bed with every beautiful woman we meet?"

Dracula nodded, tipping his head toward the two princes; they had suddenly come to understand more than they should about the reason for their argument.

Chapter 22 - Countess Elizabeth Bathory - Cachtice Castle - (1614)

Now considered an old woman, Elizabeth Bathory, at age fifty-four, was nearing the end of her days. The countess had been locked in her suite of rooms for the past four years; her punishment for the countless lives she had taken. Lately, she felt more tired than usual and had a persistent cough she hoped would take her life, a blessing she really didn't deserve. During the final hours of her time on earth, the countess began to hallucinate; what she often saw were the faces of her victims. The one, who haunted her most, was Theresa; during the darkest of winter nights, the dead girl's presence filled the room. The former countess still dreamed of her precious time with Count Dracula, remembering his skin glowing under soft candlelight and promises of a life without end. She had his heart once, and then something changed; in the end, he left her broken and doomed to the curse of aging. Imprisoned and alone, Elizabeth Bathory prayed he would suffer for leaving her to grow old and ugly, alone in a castle where no one spoke to her. She had lost her beauty, her power and her will to live, even as each new day dawned with endless hours to fill. She cursed the count once more as she shivered in a room that was always too cold. Countess Bathory was a beaten woman now, waiting only for the day her miserable life came to an end.

The Dark One whispered to Elizabeth in the darkness, she was certain Satan had come to take her to hell.

"Elizabeth!" the Dark One hissed again, "I have come to make you an offer…a chance to escape the fate of eternity in the underworld."

"I will do anything you ask," she responded, ready to negotiate anything that might save her wretched soul.

"I can send you to be with Dracula once more. He resides within the Otherworld and travels with Nikos to places I'm sure you would like to see."

"I want to be young and beautiful again. Tell me what I must do…"

"I will agree to make you young and beautiful again…but then you must do what you failed to do before...turn the count's heart black, so he kills without guilt and fully understands how insignificant human life really is."

Elizabeth wasn't entirely convinced that all humankind was expendable, but she would do anything to be released from eternal damnation. Confident she and Count Dracula could take the human world by storm, she gratefully agreed to the Dark One's conditions.

"Rest now and speak to no one. Before the night is over you will be reunited with Count Dracula...and our work can begin again."

Elizabeth lay on her bed, too weak to move; the cold now unbearable as the growing darkness made the furnishings around her disappear. Eventually, Countess Bathory slipped into a sleep from which she never awakened.

Chapter 23 - The Dark One

The Dark One was truly the purest definition of Machiavellian. It had no heart, no soul and absolutely no ability to feel guilt or remorse. It served the master of evil and no one else. A disciple of Satan, the Dark One was simply a force of nature, no different than wind or water; except that it never relented. The evil entity slithered its way into the Otherworld, where it waited patiently for the right moment to reveal itself once more.

The year was 1614, when Dracula and Nikos tried to gain entry into the Tower of London. They left the princes behind as they continued their search more than a hundred and thirty years after Edward and Richard vanished. The princes had no sense of time when inside the Otherworld; Dracula and Nikos could be gone a few days or a few years and the boys would never know the difference. A place without time was like living inside a dream, there was no beginning and no end.

The Dark One hoped to have another opportunity to create a partnership of evil with Dracula leading the way. This time it would be infinitely shrewder in its methods. Accepting its former defeat, the Dark One had come to understand the vampire it created would never dominate mankind without assistance. Countess Bathory would need to reclaim the vampire's heart and win his trust once more. It was she who would help Dracula realize his power and take command of his tremendous capacity for evil. Upon her death, the Dark One had granted the former countess eternal life; the evil entity expected much in return.

The princes had inhabited the Otherworld for a very long time and made it a special place of refuge. Life within the Otherworld was comfortable, since food and warmth were no longer required. Sometimes the boys talked with much longing about their favorite dishes, and how nice it would be to taste food again. Although the Otherworld was a place without time, there was always a sense of being; the companionship the royal princes shared kept them from utter loneliness. By using their vivid imaginations, the boys created a world of their own making just by thinking of it; in this manner, they duplicated their royal nursery inside the Otherworld. Candles were their only source of illumination; as specters they could light them with a touch of their finger. When they first learned of their ability to ignite things, it was exciting; now it was just another mundane function of daily life within the Otherworld.

The Dark One had waited patiently for hundreds of years to set its master plan into action, but first and foremost, it needed to establish trust between the princes and Countess Bathory. An introduction to the newest ghost was best done while Dracula and Nikos were absent. Since there was no way to confirm when they would return, there was no more time to waste. The princes were engaged in a mock duel with their swords, when the Dark One decided it was time for introductions to be made. Careful not to scare the young boys, it decided the best course of action would be to let Elizabeth present herself at the mirror and request entry. If the Dark One had hands, it would be rubbing them together with relish as it carefully mapped out its nefarious plan.

Chapter 24 - Eva - The Otherworld

The first thing she noticed when she came back to consciousness was how close to the ground she was; it almost felt like she had suddenly grown shorter. The air around her was a mass of blue smoke and bone-chilling air. She followed the glowing light ahead, noting her feet moved in slow motion. For the first time ever, she was afraid and wondered if the Dark One had double crossed her; perhaps she would find the entrance to hell up ahead, and not the eternal life she had been promised. The glowing light loomed as she continued walking toward it; she was fearful but determined to follow the source of illumination.

"The Otherworld awaits your presence, as I promised. Come now… you will see a whole new world," the Dark One whispered.

"I am scared," she replied.

"Here, young one…I have sent you someone for company," the Dark One replied. From the pitch blackness came a squawking sound as her pet falcon, Akos, flew to his mistress.

"Akos!" she exclaimed with pleasure, and instantly became braver in her quest.

Further encouraged to proceed, she walked a few more steps and beheld the glowing mirror, instantly recognizing the gateway to the Otherworld. She stood before the mirror and put her palm to the glass and tried to peer inside; she had no idea how to gain entry. The vine abandoned its daylight slumber and came into instant awareness; it recognized the visitor despite her changed appearance. The princes continued their play fighting, but abruptly stopped when they saw a stranger approach the glass. On their guard in the absence of Nikos and Dracula, they grasped their faithful swords and cautiously stepped toward the mirror. Facing them was a beautiful young girl of about eleven or twelve, who looked vaguely familiar.

"Who is it, Edward?" Richard whispered.

Before Edward could respond the young girl answered, "Don't you remember me?"

"No, we do not," Edward replied pushing, Richard behind him.

"I am Countess Bathory, of course." This statement caused Richard to giggle out loud, which seemed to make their visitor angry.

"The countess was a woman...you are just a girl with a speckled bird," Edward challenged.

Elizabeth swiped the mirror with her hand, finally able to see her reflection; she had become a young girl again! The countess had been tricked by the Dark One after all! Anxious to enter the Otherworld, she smiled and decided to try another angle. It was best to present herself as a lost soul looking for refuge, and hope the princes would grant her entry. She quickly came up with the name Eva, deciding she was quite tired of being called Elizabeth.

"My name is Eva. Please let me in...I mean you no harm. Please don't make me stay out here alone...I'm frightened."

Richard posed stubbornly with hands on hips, still uncertain of their visitor's intentions. "How did you come to find this place?" he demanded.

Eva whipped up some tears, making Richard suddenly ashamed of his harshness. Edward immediately softened and with only a slight hesitation, put his palm to the mirror. With a flash of blinding light, Eva and Akos were pulled into the Otherworld to join the former princes of England. Once she was safely inside the Otherworld, Eva was anxious to befriend the two boys and hoped that Dracula would help her understand what she had become.

"Lovely bird," Richard said, as Eva extended her arm to let him inspect Akos more closely.

"He was my pet in life...we died together," she lied, pleased the boys found him interesting.

Edward and Richard had been alone with each other for a long time, so they were quite happy to have a new playmate. Neither boy had ever seen a live animal within the Otherworld, so there was much excitement as Akos flew about exploring his new surroundings.

"Are you both here alone?" Eva asked looking around in wide-eyed wonder.

"They've gone bone hunting," Richard offered as though that explained anything.

"Bone hunting?"

"For our remains, of course…that's why we're in this place. Why are you here, Eva?" Richard asked.

Eva quickly improvised. "I think I died of the plague but am not sure. My body was burned and never buried…I guess that's why I'm here."

"But why did you say you were Countess Bathory?" Edward challenged.

"I was just playing a joke on you…that's all."

Richard was convinced and took her hand so he could show her around. Eva followed with Edward behind, still unwilling to completely let his guard down with this strange new visitor.

CHAPTER 25 – BONE HUNTING – THE TOWER OF LONDON – (1614)

The Tower of London was surely a haunted place, Dracula thought, as they zeroed in on the iconic place of murder, intrigue and a most colorful history. Nikos and Dracula had no trouble reaching their chosen destination; they patiently waited for someone to pass the mirror in which they hid. Dracula had a plan, but it all depended on who encountered them first. Dracula had brought with him a pair of emerald earrings he hoped could be used to barter for their passage. None of them yet realized the extent of their ability to move through time, so they continued to remain dependent on someone to release them. After several hours, a silver-haired guard entered the room; he stumbled awkwardly toward the mirror when he saw what he considered, a hallucination. Dangling a pair of emerald earrings in his hand, Dracula tempted the guard who instantly took the bait by putting his hand to the mirror. Grabbing hold of the guard's arm, Dracula pulled himself into the room. The guard drew his sword but Dracula advanced on him, and sliced open his neck; the man's body slumped to the ground, as he pulled Nikos into the room.

Unsure exactly where they were in the Tower, they moved swiftly down a narrow hallway that led them into an older section of the building. The air got colder as they began to climb a set of crumbling steps; at the top, they discovered the wooden staircase. They recognized it at once, because the princes had created a replica within the Otherworld they sometimes used for playing hide and seek.

"Let's check each step to see if one is loose...that's our best bet," Nikos suggested, rolling up his sleeves.

Dracula prepared to assist, when the ghost of Elizabeth Woodville appeared to them, a beautiful vision in white. At once they both understood she had been condemned to haunt the place of her sons' murder. "Please do not befoul the place where my babies were killed..."

"My lady, don't you remember us? We have come to find your sons' remains so they may receive a proper burial," Nikos reassured her.

"You'll not find their remains buried there…no one has…"

"How do you know for certain we won't discover them, if we search under each step?" Dracula argued, unwilling to abandon their mission so quickly.

"A mother always knows…," she whispered, turning away as the sound of guards thundered in the hallway.

Dracula had to act fast. He motioned for Nikos to return to the mirror. When the doors burst open, the vampire morphed into a ferocious wolf ready to fight off his attackers. Several guards retreated upon seeing the amazing transformation, while others drew swords and tried to wound the beast. He leaped up to an open window; but it was too small for him! With a distance of only a foot between himself and his pursuers, Dracula took on his bat-like form and flew into the night.

Chapter 26 – The Otherworld

Nikos re-entered the Otherworld alone, and unsure what had become of his longtime friend. He hoped his lord had escaped from the guards who chased him, but had no way of knowing for sure. Expecting to see the princes upon his arrival, Nikos was surprised to find a young girl of about twelve; she stared at him with wide eyes and an insolent expression on her face.

"Who might you be, miss?" Nikos asked.

Eva did not answer and instead raised her right arm; her per falcon descended from above and landed with a graceful flapping of his wings. Akos offered a loud squawk as he beheld the first adult ghost he had ever seen. "And where is Count Dracula?" Eva asked, ignoring his request for her name.

The princes appeared from the darkness and ran to greet Nikos, happy for his safe return. Eva stepped forward, putting on a lost little girl face as she introduced herself to Nikos. The boys fired questions at Nikos about their search, and were anxious about Dracula's whereabouts. Nikos reassured them Dracula would find his way back home in due time, and abruptly changed the subject.

When Dracula returned, it was just after midnight in human time. The vampire appeared as a ferocious wolf with sharp teeth and mean red eyes. Quite out of breath after being chased, the beast panted heavily as blood pooled around his massive paws. The wolf looked up at Nikos in recognition and let out a howl that brought the princes and their guest out to see who had arrived. As they watched in awe, a human hand sprung out from the mass of matted fur and then another, as Dracula assumed his human form. Fascinated by the amazing transformation, Eva couldn't take her eyes off the count. Edward watched in stunned silence as Dracula became recognizable once more.

"You! What are *you* doing here?" Dracula pointed at Eva with instant recognition.

Nikos stepped forward in her defense. "Her name is Eva. She has come to stay with us...she has nowhere else to go."

"Bathory…I can't believe it's you…what pact with the devil did you make to get here?"

Eva feigned innocence as she moved forward and attempted to shake his hand, but Dracula swatted her away. Playing her role to perfection, Eva burst into tears and ran away into the darkness. Edward chased after her. Richard hesitated for a moment, and then followed them; he was fearful of Dracula for the first time.

"Vlad…what is wrong with you!" Nikos shouted.

"Eva is no child, Nikos. I could smell her the minute I entered this place. She is Countess Bathory…and the devil's incarnate to be sure!"

"She claims to be an orphaned child…who died from the plague, Vlad…and I believe her."

"You are too trusting, friend…but I am tired and need to rest now," Dracula responded as he walked away to find his place of solace.

Nikos stood alone at the entrance to the Otherworld feeling lost and very confused. How could a twelve-year-old girl be the ghost of an evil countess? Was it possible his lord could actually recognize the scent of a woman he knew a lifetime ago?

Chapter 27 – An Unexpected Journey

Edward and Richard brought Eva back to their room, and soon they were talking together as though they had known each other for years. The boys offered to show their guest how to use her imagination to create a beautiful room of her own within the Otherworld. The three finished a game of cards and began to talk more about the search for their remains. Eva let Edward speak, because she was fascinated by their quest; the hour was late, but none of them felt like feigning sleep after hearing Edward's gripping story.

"So, basically...you need to find your bones, right?" Eva asked just to confirm her understanding.

"Yes, that's right...but we don't know when our remains were found or...if they ever were," Edward responded, and Richard nodded in agreement.

"Do you mind if I ask *how* you were murdered?" Eva asked brazenly.

"Smothercated," Richard said softly.

"Please excuse him...he had a horrible tutor. What my brother means is...we were suffocated. Two cowards used pillows to take our lives as we slept. I saw one of their faces...he was no one I knew...and definitely not my uncle," Edward responded, as Richard's eyes filled with tears.

"Please don't talk about it anymore, Edward," Richard pleaded holding his throat.

"I guess we'll never know who did it...my brother and I just want to find our bones."

"I think I can help you...let's go to the entrance. The others are resting, so now is a good time to go." Eva jumped up to take the boys' hands in hers. While Dracula and Nikos were otherwise occupied, they tiptoed toward the portal that led to the human world.

Eva explained that she had seen the future and confirmed their bones had finally been discovered in the Tower of London, during the spring of 1674. The boys felt excited and fearful at the same time, trying to grasp they might finally uncover their remains. As they wiped the glass with their sleeves, they were able to peer into a future date at the Tower of London. The boys were notably disappointed to find the same location Dracula and Nikos already searched in the year 1614.

"We were already here before!" Richard exclaimed.

"Yes…but you were looking in the wrong place. Come, I'll show you."

Edward put out his hand to stop her. "Eva, you need to understand… we cannot enter a future time without assistance from someone on the other side…"

"Just watch me," Eva replied putting a hand right through the glass. With a quick flash of light, she entered the year 1674, as the princes watched from the confines of the Otherworld.

CHAPTER 28 - A NEW DIRECTION – THE OTHERWORLD

Nikos grew tired of being alone with his thoughts; he approached Dracula's chamber, knocking softly on the door. Dracula waved him in and Nikos entered a suite of rooms designed to replicate Prince Vlad's royal suite in Castle Arges. The ornate bed was stamped with the royal crest of Dracul and above it hung an upside-down cross. Other than this one oddity, it was an authentic reproduction from another time. These furnishings were all a fabrication of the mind; Dracula even added a fire burning hearth that was merely an aesthetic recreation for the eyes only.

Fresh-faced and clean of blood; Dracula stood tall in knee breeches and a brocade dressing robe. His chest was exposed revealing ivory skin as thin as parchment, and his dark hair was pulled back in a pigtail. The seasoned vampire's stance was authoritative, yet his face appeared quite serene. At times, he could easily pass for a stately gentleman, and not the cold-hearted killer he was.

"What is it, Nikos? I am very tired."

"We need to talk about things. I think I deserve an explanation on where you've been for three days…I was worried about you."

"You sound like a nagging wife, my friend."

"No wife would put up with you, Vlad," Nikos fired back, but smiled when he said it. Dracula let out a deep sigh and offered his friend a chair.

"What are we doing here, Nikos?" Dracula began.

"Paying for our sins?"

"Is that the best you can come up with?"

"What do you want from me, Vlad?" Nikos replied impatiently.

"I am tired of this solitary life…and having no other vampires for company."

"It must be difficult at times…"

"I don't need empathy! What I need is to find another male companion, someone I can turn into a creature of the night. Don't you understand? I need a protector with powers like mine!"

Nikos paused for a moment. "A decision like this must be made carefully…if you put your trust in the wrong person…it could backfire."

"Let me worry about that…I have no one in mind just yet."

"That's reassuring," Nikos replied with undisguised sarcasm. His lord was known for being impulsive.

"When this endless bone hunt is over, I want to move to a time where people are more civilized. I see no reason to loiter about in such barbaric times…when a modern world is waiting to be explored."

"I thought the modern world made you uneasy."

"It's just a matter of picking the right time. We need to settle somewhere and establish ourselves…so we can discreetly penetrate the human world…it's time for vampires to rule the night!"

"Creating more of your kind comes with some degree of risk, Vlad."

"I've been doing a lot of thinking about that over the last few nights. I believe it's possible to cultivate civilized vampires…creatures of the night that are strictly under our rule. I will be responsible for their tutelage to ensure their loyalty; in return, we will offer opportunity and protection. In our order, we will establish a code of behavior and command only authorized killings be permitted."

"And what of this place? Surely you don't plan on staying here."

"Of course not…we cannot build a life in a place without time."

"I agree…where do we begin, then?"

"We need another vampire to join us, Nikos. Someone who is dynamic, with natural style and sophistication…but with a killer's instinct. The man we seek will have a natural love of carnage…and distain for the banality of human existence. I feel certain my chosen candidate is waiting for us in the modern world. Together, he and I will establish our own vampire community."

"And what about me? I may not be a vampire…but you can't deny I've served you well," Nikos responded, clearly offended.

"You have, my old friend…but now it's time to secure my legacy…"

"…by making more like you." Nikos finished for him.

"You're a quick study."

"The more vampires we make, the greater the demand for human blood. I suppose you've got that figured out too?" Nikos asked.

"As a matter of fact…I have! Our vampires will need to feed, so why not have them assist the fair city of London, by reducing the population of shall we say, *undesirables*."

"Vlad…it could be dangerous to allow fledglings to multiply without supervision. A notable increase in the number of vampires could also draw unwanted attention."

"Let that be my problem. My plan is quite simple, really. During my brief stay in the year 1614, I discovered there are various neighborhoods throughout London, that house the poorest and most wretched of humankind. Many live on the streets…making fresh blood easy to come by. Let's face it…what loss is it to the world if a few homeless people go missing?"

Nikos listened and found it hard to argue with Dracula's logic. "So your plan is to satisfy your bloodlust, while simultaneously cleaning up the streets of London?"

"Well, there's more to it than that, but…essentially, that's the plan."

"Of course, you're right! We would be providing a service, at the very least." Nikos was inclined to be agreeable; he was tired of living inside a world of mirrors.

Dracula continued, "Our plan should also include the necessary acquisition of allies, specifically those in positions of power…it would make life easier if we had associations with officials who were willing to turn a blind eye now and then…"

"I knew the plan had to be more complicated…go on," Nikos said.

"It would be a mistake to limit ourselves to the lower classes, when droves of wealthy and powerful men can be turned into willing puppets. The offer of eternal life is hard to refuse…I suspect we'll find less resistance than you think."

"It's a good plan…who knows, we may discover unexpected opportunities only powerful men can provide."

"Indeed, but not in such barbaric times…we must seek a more civilized time in history."

"I wouldn't mind exploring London…a hundred years from now…," Nikos replied.

"Perhaps even beyond that…but nothing needs to be decided yet."

"Who knows, Vlad… in a hundred years maybe man will have learned to fly," Nikos said with a snicker.

"Perish the thought!"

CHAPTER 29 - PRINCELY REMAINS
UNCOVERED – TOWER OF LONDON - (1674)

Eva found herself outside the entrance to the Otherworld, and helped the two boys enter the Tower of London in the year 1674. As they took in their surroundings, they heard the sound of workmen shouting with excitement; something important was apparently being discovered. The three moved toward the source of the commotion and saw two men carefully extracting a box from underneath the floor, not far from where Dracula and Nikos had conducted their search sixty years earlier. They ducked behind a stone wall before the workers could look up and spot them.

Richard spoke first, "What do you think is in the box...is it our bones, Edward?"

"Sh-h-h!" Eva hissed.

They hid in silence, watching in awe as a makeshift wooden coffin was lifted from its resting place by the excavating crew. Everyone seemed to hold their breath, until at last; a hand was raised above the crowd holding the skull of a young child. The room started to grow very bright, and Richard became lightheaded; he leaned on Eva for support. Several workers began to back up as the light grew brighter; all but one of them ran from the room, abandoning the bones of the princes without a second thought. The last remaining worker took one look at the princely ghosts, and ran screaming from the room.

From the shadows, Eva watched as the portal between life and death opened up. A mist gathered around the princes' remains and a shape began to form. Elizabeth Woodville looked as she did when they saw her last; she beckoned her sons to a place of eternal beauty and white light.

"Edward," Richard gasped, "I can't breathe..."

"Richard...it's not real...none of this is real," Edward replied without conviction.

Richard felt his knees weaken as he reached for his mother's hand. She extended her delicate finger, illuminated by the whitest of lights.

The former queen beheld a vision of her toddling baby boy running toward her, with eyes the color of a summer sea.

"Mummy!" Richard cried out, when he reached the soft folds of her dressing gown. Edward stepped closer to them, unsure what to do, and then he heard another voice call to him.

"Edward...please don't go. Please don't leave me," Eva pleaded with tearful eyes.

Edward's heart leaped as he turned back to look at Eva, once more. He couldn't leave her. He wouldn't leave her. It was as simple as that. His bones were found, but that didn't mean he had to go. What if he chose to stay in the Otherworld with his adopted family? Who would stop him? His brother was where he wanted to be, but Edward had found someone else to love. She was the one standing in the shadows. She was beautiful. She was exciting and her name was Eva. It took Edward only seconds to realize all these things, and to understand what he had to do. Stepping back from the light, he moved to join Eva taking her hand in his. As the light began to fade, the former queen blew her son a kiss and took his brother with her to the other side.

Chapter 30 - A Boy Named Prince - The Otherworld

By the time Dracula and Nikos realized Eva had taken the princes into the year 1674, Richard, Duke of York, had crossed over to his final resting place. As Dracula and Nikos searched the Otherworld hoping to find them hiding or playing a game, a bright light flashed, and Eva crossed back over the threshold into the Otherworld with Edward tagging along behind her.

"Where have you been and where is Richard?" Nikos demanded.

"He's with our mother," Edward answered defensively.

"Edward, you know better than to travel anywhere without us being with you," Dracula said harshly.

Nikos stepped forward and asked once more, "Where is Richard?"

Eva would not be intimidated so she shot back, "We already told you…Richard crossed over to the other side."

"Edward, why would you do this without us?" Dracula asked angrily, glaring at Eva.

"Stop right there. I don't want to be called Edward anymore. I think from now on I should like to be called, Prince," Edward declared, holding up his hand as if making a royal decree.

Eva let out a snort of laughter, before she realized he was serious. "Just Prince...not, Prince Edward?" Eva asked tauntingly.

"Edward is dead. I just want to be called Prince from now on...the same way everyone calls you, Dracula," he said, pointing at the count.

"So, Richard is really gone?" Nikos asked again, hoping for a different answer.

"We thought you'd both be happy," Eva said impatiently, "they finally found the missing bones."

"Then why is Edward still here?" asked Dracula, still not fully convinced of their story.

"My name is Prince, if you please…and to answer your question, I decided not to go with them."

"Has the mystery been solved then? Did they discover who actually murdered the princes?" Nikos asked.

Eva responded based on what she knew, "I don't think so, at least not at the time the bones were discovered. They buried you and your brother in Westminster Abbey, alongside the king and queen." Prince was glad to know they had been reunited with their parents.

"Eva, how did you do all this without help?" Nikos asked a little more gently.

"What do you mean? I can travel anywhere I want."

"She's telling the truth. Eva brought us to the Tower of London in 1674…and we walked right through the glass without anyone's help… we even saw them digging up our bones."

Nikos and Dracula let out a collective sigh when they realized their quest was finally over; the search for the princes' remains had consumed them for such a long time. Nikos also felt a wave of sadness at the unexpected loss of young Richard, but Dracula seemed indifferent. Alone together in a place without time, the two found no need for further conversation and retired to their rooms.

Chapter 31 – Eva – The Otherworld

Eva sat at her dressing table brushing her long dark hair. Although a bit young for makeup, Eva decided she was going to do whatever she could to look like a woman, despite being trapped inside a child's body. With a little color on her lips and some shading above her eyes, Eva could easily pass for at least fifteen. She had also chosen a dress meant for an older girl, and managed to pad the inside of her bodice to create a hint of cleavage. A knock on the door interrupted Eva's thoughts; Dracula entered and moved to the mirror, standing behind her.

"You've not changed much at all, count," Eva said with a sly smile. Dracula's suspicions were instantly validated.

"Bathory…" Dracula whispered.

"So, now you know my secret," Eva replied, as she turned from the mirror to look at him.

"Well, you brought that damn bird with you…"

"Tell me…you still love me, despite all that has happened," Eva said, her dark eyes hungry for his touch.

"You were ruthless."

"This, from a man who killed tens of thousands in battle…without an ounce of remorse!"

"Soldiers, at least have the ability to defend themselves."

Eva put a finger to his lips. "I don't want to argue. Can't we just pick up where we left off?"

"Eva, you are a child…I have no idea how this happened, but you need to understand…we can't be lovers anymore."

"I have lost you in a most unexpected way," Eva replied, pulling away from him.

"You will never lose me, countess."

Eva rose from her chair and moved to Dracula, sitting beside him on the bed. She took his hand in hers; he felt a tinge of desire as he took in her unique scent. "Will you love me as a daughter, at least? I cannot be happy if I don't have your love at all."

"You must let me love you in my own way," Dracula replied with

81

a dry smile. Eva leaned in to kiss his cheek, as Dracula rose to leave a room that looked much like her bedchamber in Sarvar Castle.

A chilling presence entered her room, the moment she closed the door. "It is time for us to get to work, young one," whispered the Dark One.

Eva sat up instantly upon hearing the Dark One speak. "Yes... please, I'll do anything to get out of this place for a while. Where will you send me?"

"I have found someone worthy of our cause. This man has many admirable talents; he is a sexual deviate and enjoys inflicting pain. He has been accused of pedophilia as well..."

"And...his name?"

"He will be known as the Marquis de Sade..."

"He sounds interesting...,"

"One other thing...he hasn't been born yet."

Eva paused for a moment, intrigued she was being asked to skip ahead in time. "So, how far ahead are you sending me?"

"The eighteenth century...I think you will enjoy the fashions very much," the Dark One added, to make her assignment more appealing.

"Is he living in London?" Eva was already thinking about the need for new clothes.

"No, you will find the marquis living in France...Paris, to be exact." Eva smiled at the thought of spending time in France, but hated the idea of making her debut in a child's body.

"May I ask a question first?"

"Of course, young one."

"Why did you bring me to the Otherworld as a child? I have a right to know the reason...before I agree to help you."

The Dark One decided the truth was best. "As a woman, you were too much of a distraction."

"Really, that's the only reason?"

"Quite so...Dracula was much enamored of you...and that interfered with his drive to start building legions of his own."

"Will I have to stay a child forever?" Eva asked, hoping her condition was not permanent.

"I am afraid so…but remember, only your body will remain as a child. Your mind will have no limits."

"You will target Paris in the year 1768. I will show you where the marquis can be found. Beware! He has quite a fondness for pretty young girls…and I do mean *young*."

"Well, then…I should be perfect!"

"So, *Eva*…I assume you are fluent in French?" the Dark One asked.

"Not only French…I am also fluent in Italian, Latin and Portuguese."

"Excellent."

CHAPTER 32 - THE MARQUIS DE SADE - PARIS, FRANCE – (SEPTEMBER 1768)

First of all, he was much less handsome than Eva expected, which was a complete disappointment. As the Marquis de Sade shaved his pasty white face in a gilded mirror, Eva chose to present herself; she startled him so much, he almost sliced his cheek.

"Mother of God...who are you?" the marquis asked, when Eva's face came into view. The marquis put his razor down and backed away from the mirror.

Eva put her hand to the glass. "My dear marquis, I come to you with an offer I am sure you will not refuse."

The marquis responded by summoning his personal bodyguards. He pointed at the mirror and screamed, "Smash the glass to pieces... do it now!"

The first guard hesitated, but the second guard struck the mirror with a hatchet; until the glass was shattered, leaving broken shards on the floor. The marquis waved the men away and bolted the door from the inside. Hands on his hips, the marquis studied the mess with satisfaction.

He turned to retrieve his shirt, when he heard her voice call to him again. The marquis saw a jagged piece of glass lying at his feet; the young girl's face sneered at him. "You'll have to do better than that... to be rid of me!"

CHAPTER 33 – THE DARK ONE

Dracula primped in front of a mirror, trying on clothes he had acquired through centuries of time. Most were too tattered to wear, but he was quite attached to his cape and top hat. He had kept some of his royal armor and a few swords he'd taken from Castle Arges on his last visit. Left in the Otherworld, clothing and personal belongings tended to have a longer shelf life than in the living world. As he admired his reflection in the mirror, the ancient vampire wondered what it would be like to have another of his kind as a companion; someone who understood bloodlust in a way Nikos never could. His thoughts were interrupted by a voice Dracula recognized and dreaded at the same time.

"The one you seek will begin his earthly life in the nineteenth century…"

"Dark One…you have stayed away too long," Dracula replied to the mirror, his eyes scanned the room for an actual glimpse of the nefarious presence.

"That is where you're mistaken. I am always with you…although I might not make my presence known."

"And what of the man you mention?" Dracula asked, unsure how he felt about being watched all the time.

"Ah-h-h…he'll be a most brutal killer…with a taste for carving his girls up a bit. I think this one will give Scotland Yard a run for their money."

"Where do I find him? I will go at once." Dracula replied, swinging his sword back and forth in a mock duel with himself.

"It's further ahead than you've ever traveled before…a much more modern time. In this place you will finally have the perfect opportunity to start building a colony of undead servants!"

"In what year will I find him? I am anxious to shake off the dust of this dreary place."

"1888. The first killing will happen on the last day of August. This man is a killer of women…unfortunates who sell their bodies to survive. You will find him in London…look for a neighborhood called Whitechapel."

"Whitechapel?"

"One of my favorite places…a neighborhood in what I like to call, London's underbelly. The stench of opium dens will lead the way…to where most of his killing will take place. You'll find him among the worst sort of characters…those who troll the night once the public houses close up. The one you seek is different; he dresses well and has a taste for killing prostitutes…at least we know he's not squeamish…"

"How does killing whores make him the ideal candidate?"

"Believe me when I tell you…this man has everything we need! A burning hatred, a stomach for blood and a lust for carnage…sound like anyone else we know?"

"What name does he go by?" Dracula asked, ignoring the Dark One's last remark.

"Few know his real identity…you are looking for a cold-blooded killer the newspapers call, *Jack the Ripper.*"

"And you are certain he will embrace what we offer?" Dracula asked doubtfully.

"It doesn't matter how he feels about it. In the end you will make him a nocturnal creature and fulfill your destiny!"

Dracula knew there was no point in further conversation, so he agreed to an alliance with someone who hadn't even been born yet. The Dark One was a mysterious presence and one Dracula was ill-prepared to defy.

"I will seek out this man as you command. It is time I had one of my own kind beside me, to help build our legions." Dracula tried to say what he knew would please the Dark One.

"It is where your destiny lies. Jack will be there…waiting for you. Together…you will be unstoppable!"

Dracula felt a bit rattled at the thought of going so far ahead in time; he took comfort in knowing the Dark One had at least visited the nineteenth century. Dracula's thoughts were interrupted by the sound of Prince frantically calling Eva's name.

CHAPTER 34 – THE MARQUIS DE SADE –
PARIS, FRANCE – (SEPTEMBER 1768)

As Eva was quick to observe, the Marquis de Sade was not a handsome man. He had dark beady eyes set into deep sockets, and a classic Parisian nose that was just too big for his face. The marquis rarely smiled; when he did, his eyes remained cold rendering his overall demeanor aloof and insincere. He had a pronounced double chin and was prone to portliness, due to his fondness for rich foods. How he looked didn't matter much to the marquis. He had wealth and status, which allowed him the freedom to indulge without consequence, in just about anything that gave him pleasure.

Although wealth and status were very important to the Marquis de Sade, what mattered most to him was the continuous conquest of almost every attractive woman he met. The marquis was a master of seduction; women happily shared his bed to engage in both pleasing him and allowing themselves to enjoy his many skills in the boudoir. His sexual prowess was well known; on several occasions, the marquis had to compensate an outraged father who discovered his daughter had been quite willingly deflowered. With a man like the Marquis de Sade, sexual gratification was always the ultimate prize.

The leaves were just starting to turn as the marquis stepped outside into the bustling streets of Paris. Adjusting his powdered wig, the marquis began the brief walk to the Grande Taverne de Londres restaurant. Thoughts of the mysterious girl occupied his mind as he tried to focus on what he would have for dinner. The starry night was filled with sounds of lighthearted conversation and the clip-clop of horse hooves pulling grand carriages in the street. As he reached the corner, the restaurant came into view; his stomach growled in anticipation of a delicious meal. The musky smell of leather and horse manure assaulted his nostrils as he approached the sidewalk, and that is when he saw her.

She was a tiny slip of a girl, barely at the peak of her womanhood. The dark-haired girl could not have been more than fourteen years old. She wore a lovely red frock; it was a bit out of date, but she made it work.

Her breasts were almost non-existent, but her gown brought them out to their best advantage. Her hair was piled high on her head, with spiral curls that draped around her face and neck. She wore a red plumed hat and her face was exquisite, yet one he immediately recognized. It was definitely her. She was the ghost from his mirror; the girl stood at the entrance to the Grande Taverne as though she was expecting him. Cold fear gripped him as he got closer, but the marquis would not give her the satisfaction of letting it show.

Leaning on her parasol with a look of extreme arrogance, Eva finally spoke in perfect French, "Good evening monsieur…I hope you aren't going to break anything this time."

The marquis offered a winning smile, showing teeth that were less than perfect. He decided to call her bluff. "So glad you could make it, mademoiselle," he said politely, then took her arm and led her into the restaurant.

Upon entry, they were immediately fussed over by the maître de, who led them to one of his best tables. The waiter quickly brought them menus and presented the marquis with a bottle of his favorite wine for inspection. The marquis waved him away impatiently, after nodding his approval.

"So, my beautiful apparition, what is your name?" the marquis finally asked.

"Eva," was all she said. She wasn't going to make this easy for him.

"Such a lovely night, isn't it, Eva?" The marquis struggled to fill the silence.

"Evenings this time of year usually are."

"Of course, you're right…," he trailed off, suddenly feeling awkward.

Eva leaned forward and spoke softly, "How much time are we going to waste in this place making small talk?"

The marquis leaned back and released a howl of laughter. "Now that's what I like…a woman who gets straight to the point."

"It is the only way to be," Eva replied with a seductive smile.

"Just how old are you anyway?"

"I'm much older than I look." The marquis chuckled softly as he leaned toward her. Eva studied him more closely, determining he was quite ill at ease, despite his efforts to disguise it.

88

"I come from another time in search of someone special…someone who can lead, but still be ruled by someone greater than himself."

The waiter arrived with their wine and poured them each a glass as the marquis considered Eva's words carefully. He held his wine glass by the stem, and swirled the liquid around a few times before taking a sip.

"I've had many propositions in my lifetime, Eva…but none as interesting as this one. Please, tell me more. But first, have some wine… it is the house special and highly recommended."

"Thank you, no. I do not drink wine anymore."

"Anymore?" the marquis asked, raising an eyebrow.

"I come from another place and time. It's hard to explain without showing you but…if you join us; you will have eternal life *and* never grow old."

"Ah-h-h…the devil's promise," the marquis replied taking a sip of his wine.

"Yes, I suppose it is but, then again…I have seen your death and I know what I offer is an improvement on what awaits."

The marquis stopped smiling and took another sip of wine. "You claim to know all about me…yet I know nothing of you. How is that fair?"

"What do you need to know?"

"Everything."

Their food arrived and although it looked very good, Eva did not eat. The marquis devoured his food, along with several slices bread. He finally looked up and noticed his guest had not even touched her food. "Will you not take anything to eat?" he asked.

"I no longer eat."

The marquis shrugged and kept eating until his plate was clean. All the while, Eva just watched him, knowing he was just buying time. The marquis dabbed his mouth with a linen napkin. "So, you don't eat or drink, you frighten people by appearing in their mirrors…and you come from another time. Is that correct so far?"

"Correct."

"Are you a ghost?"

"Of a certain kind, but not exactly. When you join us…you must become one of the undead too."

"What…a vampire? What makes you think I would be interested in drinking human blood?"

"You will learn to crave the taste, I assure you."

"Wine is one thing, but drinking blood…I think not." The marquis wrinkled his nose in disgust.

"Dracula will change your mind about that."

"And who is this, *Dracula*…your leader?" he asked with a smirk, now just playing along.

"He is a most powerful lord…worshipped by many."

The marquis laughed out loud. "I follow my own rules and worship no one but myself."

"Yes, I know…that is what will send you to prison."

"It's too late to stop that from happening…"

"They will come for you again, marquis…that I promise you," she said evenly.

The marquis refused to take such a young girl seriously, but was unnerved she knew so much about him. "Will you let me walk you home, Eva?"

"I have no earthly home, marquis," Eva replied, as she stood up to leave.

"Where are you going, then?" He was clearly disappointed she was leaving him.

"You can call for me anytime you want… and I will answer." Eva replied, then turned her back on the marquis and left the restaurant.

The Marquis de Sade watched her go, following the swing of her hips with his eyes. His only thought was that he had to have her; however, he would only be satisfied when she begged him for it. The mere thought made the marquis cross his legs uncomfortably, in an effort to conceal the conspicuous swell in his breeches.

Chapter 35 – Search for Eva

"Damn it…I knew she would be trouble!" Dracula exclaimed. He and Nikos had searched every square inch of the Otherworld looking for Eva.

Prince felt certain Eva had left to find her own adventure. "I have combed through every possible hiding place and I'm telling you, she's gone."

"The journal, Nikos…did she write anything in the journal by any chance?" Dracula asked. Nikos retrieved the sacred journal and began thumbing through it.

"How are we going to find her, when she could be a hundred years into the future?" Prince asked.

"Let's calm down and view this situation logically. Did she talk to you about any plans at all? Do you think she would have gone *back* in time?" Dracula asked, putting his hand on the boy's shoulder.

"Not really…all she ever talks about is living in a more modern time," Prince replied, pulling away from Dracula's touch.

"Did she talk about a specific time in the future, then? Something or someone she wanted to see perhaps?" Nikos asked.

"She *did* mention wanting to see Paris. I think she speaks French, too…I heard her practicing in front of a mirror." Prince ruffled through papers on the desk.

"We must go and find her, Nikos!"

"Go where, Vlad? We have no idea where she is."

Despite a thorough search, they found nothing to indicate where Eva might have gone. Prince called to Akos and they retreated to his bedchamber. Angry and frustrated, Prince released Akos to his perch and laid on his bed, closing his eyes as visions of Eva filled his young heart with a longing he could not understand. Unable to turn his mind off, Prince decided to search Eva's room for clues as to where she might have gone. Her room was an absolute mess; Prince shuddered when he nearly tripped over a pile of discarded clothing. Eva had many books in her room but nothing stood out as he sorted through them. He picked up a book on anatomy and thought it was an odd topic to interest her. Akos began circling the room trying to get Prince's attention, and then dove under the bed. As Prince bent down to chase him away, he discovered the hidden book. It was a well-worn library book and was written in French. He read the title out loud, "Biography of the Marquis de Sade." Prince wondered who he was, and why Eva would be interested in him. As he flipped the pages, a small piece of paper skittered to the floor. Akos swooped down to retrieve it, and delivered it to Prince's open palm.

Everything they needed to locate Eva was here! The note written in her neat script contained a date in the future and an address in Paris. Filled with a renewed sense of purpose, Prince ran to find Dracula and Nikos. "I know where she went!" Prince exclaimed waving the note. Dracula snatched it from his hand then passed it to Nikos.

"1768…she's traveled ahead in time…apparently to meet a man named…Marquis de Sade," Nikos confirmed.

"I can read…who is he?" Prince asked.

"I have no idea…but I assume that book can help us," Dracula replied reaching for the book, but Prince held it to his chest.

"It's written in French and besides…I can read faster than both of you," Prince replied, already flipping through the pages. "Book was written in 1825…Eva actually visited the nineteenth century! It's the only way she could have gotten this book!"

"Why does she take such crazy chances?" Dracula hissed.

"Apparently, our young Eva has no fear of interfering with the future," Nikos replied. Prince continued to scan the book for any information that might be helpful.

"It says here the Marquis de Sade was quite wealthy and powerful in his own right. He published a lot of controversial writings and was always in trouble with the law. It also says here he was a *philanderer…* whatever that means. I don't understand why Eva would want to get involved with someone like him." Prince began to feel uneasy about the man Eva traveled in time to visit.

Prince fanned the pages to a portrait of the villain himself. "It says here…that the Marquis de Sade spent thirty years of his life in prison.

The book calls him a *sexual deviate...*" Prince trailed off, feeling himself blush.

"Do you speak any French at all, Nikos?" Dracula asked changing the subject.

"No."

"I am fluent in French...let me go," Prince insisted, tired of being treated like a child.

"It's too dangerous for you to go alone...but I can take you with me," Dracula replied, and Prince puffed out his chest a little.

"What has that girl gotten herself mixed up in now? The man is a pedophile!" Nikos just knew Eva would be a handful.

"What's a *pedophile?*" Prince asked, but neither answered.

Dracula took the open book from Prince, his face dark with anger. "Should this Marquis de Sade dishonor her in any way...he will curse the day he was born."

Chapter 36 – Marquis de Sade – Chateau Lacoste – (September 1768)

Eva came into his room through a mirror in his bedchamber while he slept. Creeping past his sleeping form, she navigated her way down a narrow hallway. The marble staircase was magnificent; even in dim light Eva could appreciate the marvelous craftsmanship. When she reached the landing, a gray Persian cat skittered across the floor in front of her. She nearly let out a scream, but was able to stop herself in time. The front entrance was a grand affair, adorned with golden statues of angels in every corner. In the center of the great hallway was a majestic gilded fountain adorned with more angels; their faces illuminated by a reflection of aquamarine-colored water. Accustomed as she was to lavish furnishings, Eva began to feel right at home.

A grandfather clock in the parlor chimed the twelve o'clock hour, as she tiptoed past a huge marble fireplace where a dying fire still glowed with red embers. Moving to a chair by the fire, Eva made herself comfortable while she waited for the marquis to wake up from his slumber. As she sat in an overstuffed chair thinking about the future, her body grew warm in the comfortable heat and she drifted off to sleep.

When Eva awoke, she found herself standing upright; her hands were secured with metal cuffs that were attached to a stone wall. She tugged at the cuffs to test their strength and gave up with a sigh; what was the marquis planning to do with her? The place was damp and cool, which led her to believe she was somewhere underground. Yanking at the cuffs in exasperation, Eva became angry that she had allowed herself to be so vulnerable. As she surveyed her surroundings, Eva quickly observed this was no ordinary place. There were two large metal tables in the center of the room and these were equipped with straps. On one wall hung a collection of swords and weapons of every size and variety. There were also other items, including a long black whip with carefully placed knots; Eva knew exactly what it was. In another corner was an ornate bed, richly adorned with silk sheets and copious pillows; this was also fitted with leather straps. Eva immediately understood this place was made for more than just seduction. Above the bed was a huge mirror, where the perverted marquis could view his acts of conquest. The room had only one door, and it looked sturdy enough to withstand attack by even the strongest battering ram. The only ray of hope Eva could see, was a full-length mirror standing in the corner; it could provide an escape to the Otherworld, but only if she could get free. Hearing the jangle of keys, she prepared herself for a visit from the master of the house. The marquis came into the room wearing only a dressing gown and slippers. His powdered wig was gone and she noted he was already going bald. The marquis was determined to grill his prisoner until she told him the real reason for her visit.

"Now that you are my prisoner...you will tell me who you really are...and why you broke into my residence." Eva said nothing, but fear was etched into her face.

The marquis moved closer to caress her cheek and softened his tone. "Such a pretty young thing. Tell me, how old are you really?"

Eva flushed and answered truthfully, "Twelve...last birthday."

"Oh my...that is much younger than I expected," he replied fingering her curls.

"It would still be a mistake to underestimate me...I assure you," Eva said bravely.

"And what will you do, my child...chained as you are to my wall?"

"If I don't return soon, I shall be missed," Eva replied weakly.

"Well, then...I should like to meet your rescuer...that is if he is able to find you. But first, he must get past my rather large bodyguards."

"My lord is very resourceful."

"I don't have time for fantasies! Tell me now, how you know so much about me?" the marquis placed both hands on her shoulders; his touch made Eva cringe.

"I already told you, I can see the future..." She was silenced when the marquis backhanded her across the mouth.

"I'll hear no more of this nonsense...I have many enemies. So, tell me...*who* sent you?" The marquis had lost all composure now, his ugly face colored with rage. Eva's eyes filled with tears as she hung her head in defeat.

"Only the truth will set you free," he said more softly, lifting her chin to look into her eyes.

"I am telling the truth."

Chapter 37 – Prince in Charge – The Otherworld

From the portal of the Otherworld, Prince and his companions set their sights on Paris, France during the autumn of 1768, three days after Eva was imprisoned by the marquis. The portal started to glow and from the mirror, Prince could see an ornate bedchamber that could only belong to a man of extreme wealth. The room appeared to be empty; they would need to remain behind the glass until the marquis retired for the evening. While they waited, Prince occupied himself playing cards; Dracula joined in just to have an activity to keep him busy.

After winning the first round, Prince asked a question that had been lingering in his mind, "Are you going to bite the marquis…as soon as he enters his bedchamber?"

Dracula slapped down a queen of hearts, and let out a bellow of laughter, then replied, "Nothing quite that dramatic!"

"Are we inviting the marquis to join us or not?" Prince persisted; he had a right to know what Dracula planned.

"Why would you think that?"

"Isn't that why she came to this place…I mean, wasn't it to ask the marquis to join us?"

Dracula didn't answer and eventually, Prince moved away to play his own game of solitaire. As they waited for the marquis to return home, Dracula realized it hadn't occurred to him that Eva might have been trying to recruit someone without telling him.

CHAPTER 38 - MARQUIS DE SADE – CHATEAU LACOSTE – (SEPTEMBER 1768)

The Marquis de Sade was quite intoxicated, as he mounted the stairs to his bedchamber. He had consumed nearly two bottles of red wine and his head was pounding. Taking a moment to steady himself, the marquis continued up the remaining steps as he tugged at the scarf around his neck. Unlocking the door to his room, he let himself inside. Kicking his shoes off, the marquis debated undressing, then decided it was too much effort; he flopped down on the bed with a thud. His bloodshot eyes looked up at the ceiling, but he could not focus because the room was spinning. He put a hand to his head, wishing he had consumed a whole lot less wine.

Dracula took this moment to step through the mirror, and present himself to the marquis. The inebriated man tried to bolt, but wasn't fast enough to get away. Before the Frenchman could scream for help, Dracula subdued him on the floor, where he lay helpless and unable to move. Prince stood over the marquis, holding his sword inches from the man's face.

"What do you people want from me?" the marquis asked fearfully.

Dracula put his boot on the man's chest. "What have you done with her...you snake?"

"Who are you talking about? I don't understand." Dracula had no time for games; his eyes grew red with anger. The marquis was certain his nocturnal visitors meant to kill him.

"I will ask you again...where is Eva?"

"D-d-downstairs...she's in a private place...but I assure you, she is well. I have not harmed her in any way," the marquis croaked in a womanish voice.

Dracula grabbed the marquis, and pulled him to his feet. "Put your shoes back on and straighten yourself up, man. We are going to take a walk to where you are holding our friend hostage."

"No...it's not like that at all, I assure you. Eva is free to go at any time."

"Prince, you need to stay here and make sure no one comes in or out, while the marquis escorts me to his den of iniquity," Dracula commanded. Prince was clearly disappointed to be left alone; he planned on playing a larger part in Eva's rescue. Once again, Dracula was taking center stage.

"Can't I come with you?" Prince pleaded.

"I need your eyes and ears here…just look over there," Dracula said, pointing to a bookcase full of books. "You can have yourself a field day while I am gone."

CHAPTER 39 – EVA'S RESCUE – CHATEAU LACOSTE – (SEPTEMBER 1768)

Eva had been a prisoner for three days now, yet the marquis had not abused her as she expected. She had been made comfortable in his "chamber of horrors," however; her wrists were bound with leather straps fastened to the headboard. The marquis gave her a lovely dressing gown and thus far, seemed disinterested in a sexual encounter despite the opportunity. He appeared to have a fetish for prostitutes however; each morning he came to visit and applied garish-looking makeup to her face. Eva let him do it; she considered herself lucky she wasn't strapped naked to one of his metal tables. She was overcome by a feeling of hopelessness; how would Dracula ever know where to find her?

The sound of jangling keys abruptly stopped her tears, as Eva braced herself for a visit from the man who held her captive. The marquis had indeed come to visit, but he was not alone. Dracula had bound his hands and thrust him into a chair; the Marquis de Sade begged for mercy, but no one was listening. Eva beheld her savior and smiled through her tears, as Dracula ran to her side. He unbuckled her straps and released her. Eva threw her arms around her rescuer; Dracula forgot himself for a moment, and kissed her deeply. The door was burst open by two bodyguards, who heard the commotion. Dracula morphed into a black wolf, pushing Eva behind him. The first bodyguard approached as Dracula lunged at him; within seconds, the guard's neck was opened, and his body dropped to the floor. Cowering and whimpering like a child, the marquis decided he would never drink Bordeaux again. The second guard pulled out a pistol, and emptied it into the raging beast; Dracula kept coming with claws drawn, his teeth still red with the blood. Out of ammunition, the guard threw down his weapon and the wolf pounced; snapping his neck to silence him. Dracula resumed his human form, as Prince and Nikos rushed into the room.

Nikos observed the untouched corpse at Dracula's feet. "What, no dessert tonight, Vlad?"

"Actually, I'm full."

Nikos pointed to the mirror, hastening Eva and Prince through first, with Dracula close behind. Nikos went last, taking one last look at the marquis, who sat in a pool of his bodyguard's blood.

CHAPTER 40 - THE PROMISE

After the daring rescue, Dracula carried Eva back to the Otherworld, despite the fact she had not been injured. After having almost lost her, he accepted his love for Elizabeth Bathory would never die; she was a wicked soul, but he blamed her family tendency toward madness. In his mind, the former countess was a fragile thing to be protected. The seasoned vampire brought Eva directly to her suite of rooms; Prince followed, but Dracula turned and gave him an adult look that said, "We want to be alone." Prince turned away, feeling foolish and out of place; suddenly he missed his younger brother very much.

Laying her gently on the bed, Dracula stroked her forehead. "You scared the death out of us, you know," he said finally.

"I just wanted to show you I could do something meaningful to help. This man seemed a perfect fit for us. I thought I would get to know him, first but...well, it kind of backfired." Eva was careful not to mention who commanded her actions.

"Did the marquis hurt you in any way?"

"No...but the marquis had a fetish for young prostitutes. He claimed prostitutes used makeup as a barrier between themselves and their paying clients. As you can see, the marquis tried to make me look like one, too."

"You look beautiful to me."

"Yes...but only as a lovely child," Eva replied sadly.

"You know that I would love you again, as a man...if I could, don't you?" Eva remained silent.

"All I can offer you now is a father's love, and it will have to be enough. It would break my heart if we couldn't work this out between us."

"I thought vampires had no heart."

"A vampire can't afford to show compassion...but that doesn't mean we have no heart."

"Touché."

Eva touched his cheek and leaned on his shoulder. "Tell me more about the first time you died...as a vampire, I mean. How did you come back after the women incinerated you?"

"My faithful friend, Nikos was responsible for that one. He rescued my ashes after the women scattered."

"What did he do with them?"

"He took them to the Otherworld, where I could be preserved in a dormant state without the need to feed."

"So, you didn't really die exactly...more like your life force was suspended in time, right?"

"I guess that's true. Nikos saved my life and gave me another chance...I owe him greatly, but he has a difficult time accepting what I must do to survive. Unfortunately, Nikos has more of a conscience than I do...at times, he seems tormented by the life we lead."

"It is the human way," Eva replied with resignation.

"Eva, I will always love and protect you as a daughter, but I also need a promise from you..."

"Go on," she prompted.

"If something happens to me..."

"Happens...like what could happen?"

"Don't make me say it...you know what I'm talking about. Silver bullet, wooden stake...a big fireball called the sun..."

"All right...I get the point. So, what do you need me to promise?"

"If something happens, you must rescue my remains in any form at all...you must find a dark place to hide them...until the time is right to bring me back to life again."

"How would I revive you, without a fresh human to kill?" Eva didn't fully comprehend her role.

"Remember what I told you all those years ago in Hungary. Human blood *or* human tears can bring a vampire back to life. That is what saved me the second time I was killed; my vine was the one who brought me back to life again."

"I always wondered how you came back...I was told by my nurse that your ashes were scattered to the wind."

"Perhaps it was better that you believed her. Strangely, I am alive today...thanks to the blood of your former lover." Eva was surprised Dracula had been revived by the blood of Desio Vas.

Eva held up a hand to make her promise. "I solemnly pledge that I will rescue your remains and do everything within my power to restore them by whatever means necessary."

"Thank you, my love...and my daughter," Dracula replied, kissing her forehead chastely.

"I guess I'll have to call you uncle...or it could be confusing."

"Then I shall be your Uncle Vlad...now and forever."

Eva jumped up suddenly full of energy; she grabbed his arm to pull him toward the door of her bedchamber. "Let's go flying and visit a time you've never seen before."

Dracula thought about the Dark One's words, and its promise he would find a companion in the late nineteenth century; why not take a peek into the year 1888 tonight? "How about...the summer of 1888?"

"That's pretty specific," Eva said.

"Well...let's just say I'm researching a more modern time."

"So *mysterious*, uncle," Eva replied with a charming giggle.

"My survival often depends on it."

"1888...I have never been that far ahead, but I've come close."

"I know...your miscellaneous adventures will be the death of me."

"What part of London should we visit?" Eva asked, changing the subject.

After a slight pause, Dracula finally said, "Whitechapel."

"Whitechapel? Never heard of it."

"It was in a book Prince found...sounds like a good place to remain anonymous," Dracula lied. With a burst of energy they headed toward the portal, holding hands like children running toward a new adventure.

CHAPTER 41 – RIDING THE WIND – LONDON, ENGLAND – (JULY 1888)

After convincing Eva to target the year 1888, Dracula thought hard about a man he had never met, and wondered what would happen if they didn't get along. The vampire was old-fashioned and set in his ways. He hoped his chosen candidate was, at the very least, well-educated. Either way, Dracula knew it was time to start making more of his own kind. A visit to Whitechapel would give Dracula an opportunity to become familiar with the neighborhood, in which the Dark One predicted a brutal killer would soon emerge.

Once through the Otherworld portal, Dracula felt a sense of apprehension as he followed Eva down a narrow hallway. "I see a window up ahead. Where exactly are we?" Dracula asked, noting it was an extremely small window.

"Inside the brand new clock tower…they call it *Big Ben*," Eva explained, as they beheld an aerial view of nineteenth-century London.

Dracula put his hand to the glass, and then passed right through it. Eva followed and soon they were standing outside the clock face of Big Ben.

"And now, I will be your travel guide as we fly over the city together," Dracula said, flapping his glorious cape behind him.

Dracula coaxed Eva onto his back, as a gust of wind obliged and carried them into the soft summer night. The big dipper was clearly visible and to Eva, it felt like they were flying right through its opening. Dracula dipped his cape occasionally, making her stomach lurch as the night breeze whistled in her ears. Just like children, they began to search for other constellations as they marveled at the wonders of a star-dappled sky.

Looking down at the streets below, Dracula became alarmed when he saw burning white light everywhere. "The city of London appears to be on fire!"

"No, not fire. It is called electricity… artificial light created by humans," Eva explained.

"This is most amazing!" Dracula turned and made a half circle back to where they came from; they really had flown out of a gigantic clock!

"Big Ben?"

"Isn't it beautiful?"

"Westminster Castle looks completely different...from what I remember," Dracula said with surprise.

"The original castle was burned to the ground in 1834...it was rebuilt, but looks much more contemporary than the old castle. The clock tower is part of the new structure...it's not quite finished yet." As she spoke, the ten o'clock hour struck; the comforting sound echoed in the night.

As they cruised through the night air, the need for conversation left them; each became lost in their own thoughts as they crossed over London Bridge. The illumination of London was breathtaking; Eva held onto her count, feeling optimistic about their uncertain future. Anxious to test the streets of London, Dracula began his descent into a neighborhood called Whitechapel; the Dark One was right, this was surely the underbelly of London. The pair landed on a side street, and ducked into an alley while they observed their surroundings. Neither one considered they were dressed in clothing sorely out of date.

Dracula took one look at Eva and blurted out, "We need some new clothes!"

Eva laughed and pulled him further into the darkness; lest they be discovered. "So, what will it be? Are you going to satisfy your hunger by killing only the well-dressed...or can we do something more civilized... like buying new clothes?" Eva asked.

"We have no money," Dracula said, turning out his pockets.

"That's never stopped us before," Eva said. She took his arm, as they strolled down the street looking for a clothier. The fog was thick, but they had no trouble navigating their way around London's infamous East End. They managed to break into an establishment called Hennigan's on Baker Street, and came out dressed in the height of London fashion. In addition to clothing, they also took a few pieces of costume jewelry; Dracula emptied the cash register, because it had been left open. Over the years, Dracula had made a habit of collecting currency from everywhere they traveled; on more than one occasion this had proved a valuable practice.

The public houses were now closed, and most residents had returned home for the evening. As Dracula walked with Eva on his arm, he was astounded by the number of homeless people who, as far as he could tell, were literally living outside. A small child came up to them with a hopeful look on her dirty face. Dracula thrust a coin into her open palm and she snapped it shut before he could change his mind.

"We could start a vampire community, right here in London. Just look at all these people in the street! It would be like taking candy from a baby," Dracula said, as he watched the girl disappear into the fog.

"Yes, a place like this would be ideal...for hunting. I certainly hope you plan to procure a respectable residence somewhere outside the city." Eva wasn't about to live in a neighborhood like this.

"Naturally...Nikos will handle the details, once we make a firm decision on where we want to settle."

"And you are certain about London, then?" Eva asked unexpectedly.

"What other place did you have in mind?"

"Across the ocean...there is a relatively new country where they also speak English."

"Ah, yes...America."

"I am still partial to Europe though...perhaps America is too modern for the likes of us," Eva said with a snicker.

"London has a feel for me. I don't know why...but I'm convinced we could be happy here," Dracula replied. Once he found a killer named Jack, it might be necessary to remain in nineteenth century London for awhile.

"I can be happy wherever you are," Eva said in agreement.

"Now...I must take you back to Big Ben, so I can seek out a proper dinner, before I die of thirst." Dracula pulled Eva behind a crumbling stone wall, and they became airborne on a perfect summer evening they would always remember.

CHAPTER 42 - JACK THE RIPPER - WHITECHAPEL DISTRICT - LONDON - (SEPTEMBER 8, 1888)

For Dracula, flying was one of the best perks of being a vampire. When flying near populated areas, it was prudent to adapt his rodent form; as a bat, Dracula was able to remain inconspicuous. With tiny wings spread wide against a midnight sky, Dracula's red eyes scanned the darkness for prey; tonight, it would most certainly be human. After the vampire fed, he began to search this wretched neighborhood for his new companion. The week before, a prostitute was killed, but Dracula missed it because he had been hunting on the moors. He cursed his rotten timing, when he read about the murder in the newspaper the next day. Tonight, he planned to troll the streets of this foul neighborhood until dawn, if necessary, to ensure he didn't miss his opportunity to catch a killer in action. By this time of night, anyone still walking about was likely up to no good. Dracula was amazed at the devastating effect of abject poverty, and what it did to a neighborhood. Those who were employed might be lucky enough to secure a roof over their heads however; houses in this area were not much more than hovels. Prostitutes seemed to have it hardest, Dracula thought, as he watched one across the street trying to negotiate her fee. For them, lodging houses provided the only shelter; it was not uncommon for several women to live together in order to make ends meet.

Within moments of landing, Dracula took in his surroundings and readied himself for a confrontation. As Dracula brushed off his cape, he picked up the sound of police officers, no doubt making their evening rounds. Gas lamps provided illumination on the streets of Whitechapel; alleyways were rarely lit, and often a breeding ground for criminal activity.

The vampire spotted a police wagon, and instinctively ducked out of sight. He backed further into the darkness and heard a faint gasp, certain it came from a woman. Curious, he moved toward the noise, and nearly stumbled over M. J. Druitt; he was busy carving up the corpse of Annie Chapman. The killer spun around, wielding a surgeon's knife as he slashed at the air.

"Don't let me interrupt your work," Dracula said with a gentlemanly bow. At last, he had found Jack the Ripper."

"Who are you?" the killer responded with snarl.

"It doesn't matter, does it? Let's just say I'm intrigued by men who are killers of women."

"Mine is a solitary crime...go find your own victim!" Jack said, anxious to immerse himself in carnage.

"You misunderstand...I am here for another reason..." Dracula replied, as a barrage of police whistles pierced the night.

The killer studied Dracula with hard blue eyes, and then pointed behind him. "Best get off the street, mate...look about!" In response to pounding footsteps, the killer sprinted away leaving him alone with the ruined corpse.

The smell of fresh blood was intoxicating, but every vampire knew it was lethal to drink blood from the dead. As he turned away, Dracula noticed a bunch of half-eaten grapes in the dead woman's hand, and for some reason this oddity stayed with him. Dracula quickly came to his senses and dashed into the Nag's Head Pub, on the corner of Farrant Street. He sat at the bar nursing warm ale, as he listened to locals talk about a vicious killer who had carved up a prostitute the week before. Dracula studied the pulsing necks of several patrons, feeling his burning hunger grow. A buxom young woman smiled at him, believing he was admiring her cleavage when truthfully; it was her glorious blood he lusted for. Looking away, the vampire paid his tab and exited the pub.

As Dracula walked down the nearly vacant street, he thought about the man he had met so briefly, trying to remember details about his face. Dracula wasn't sure he'd be able to even describe him very well. If the man he had met tonight was indeed Jack the Ripper, it was high time they were better acquainted.

Chapter 43 - Mary Jane Kelly - Whitechapel District – London - (September 10, 1888)

As Dracula walked through the desolate streets of Whitechapel, his penetrating stare and stern expression kept even the bravest street thug at bay. Now armed with a bit more information about a killer named Jack, Dracula concluded this particular killer enjoyed playing a game of cat and mouse with detectives. The vampire was impressed by Jack's ability to confound Scotland Yard's attempts to discover his identity. By all accounts, the killer of unfortunates seemed to have everything Dracula was looking for in a companion. He hadn't spotted him yet, but wasn't about to give up that easily; maybe it was still too early for the Ripper to make an appearance. The vampire stood out in a crowd, with his walking stick and genteel clothes. He always dressed a bit more formal than those around him; though unaware of it, Dracula wore his loneliness like a veil over his chiseled face.

The streets were bustling with activity, and as Dracula observed the crowd, he couldn't help but notice people seemed less amiable, now that a killer was on the loose. There were now two unsolved murders, according to the Glasgow Herald and The Standard. So far, Scotland Yard had not a single clue as to the identity of the alleged perpetrator. A throng of protestors assembled on the steps with signs that read, "SAVE WHITECHAPEL" and "SCOTLAND YARD OUT TO LUNCH." Local residents cried for better nightly patrols and guarantees for personal safety. The vampire's mind wandered, as he surveyed the crowd; he searched for anyone who remotely resembled the nocturnal killer he had met only once. Dracula was just about to move on, when a flash of glorious red hair caught his attention; in that moment, time literally stood still.

The young woman turned to look in his direction with a knowing smile, and it stopped him in his tracks. She was anything but a classic beauty. Yet, to a lonely vampire, she was exactly what his dead heart had been searching for. He realized immediately, she was a refreshing change from the women he usually courted. She had flaming red hair that fell in lush curls, framing a lovely heart-shaped face. Her eyes were a golden brown and she sported a mass of freckles across the bridge of her pointed nose. The ancient vampire took in the very essence of the red-haired woman, committing every detail to memory. Despite her worn clothing, Mary Jane Kelly carried herself with extreme grace. As she exited Scotland Yard, Dracula studied her gazelle-like movements and actually found it hard to breathe. The woman held her head high as she walked toward him, not paying much attention to her surroundings. Dracula was captivated; this woman was the most enchanting creature he had ever seen. There was no one else for him; her very presence made his knees weak, and electrified his sexual appetite. Desperate not to let her get away, Dracula stepped into the street to make his presence known.

"Good evening, miss...," Dracula said, with a slight bow of his head.

Mary offered a bright smile to the handsome, well-dressed stranger. "Good sir, good evening to you." Dracula held out his hand; she was a prostitute yet, he felt certain this was the least important thing to know about her.

"Where do you want to go?" Mary asked when he remained silent.

"I just want to understand everything you are."

"Suit yourself...I charge by the hour."

Dracula put a finger to her lips; when he leaned into her, she smelled like ginger. "What is your name?"

"Mary Jane...you can call me Mary."

"Beautiful Mary...," he murmured, as they approached an unlit alley. He looked around and realized no one was watching; before he could stop himself, the vampire pushed her into the darkness and pressed her against a brick wall. She gasped with surprise, at first, but then found herself responding to this strange gentleman who began tearing at her dress. He buried his head between her breasts as though trying to devour them. The vampire's teeth pierced her flesh so gently, Mary didn't feel the sting of his bite. Stopping himself to seek a more private place, Dracula lifted Mary up and carried her to a vacant hansom cab; it was conveniently parked on a secluded street corner. Mary went limp in his arms, willing to let the night take her where it would. Tonight, Mary

Kelly knew she would give her body willingly, and for free. Mary tore at Dracula's clothes with undisguised lust; for the first time in her life, her desire was authentic. Mary opened her legs to him and when he felt her wetness, he could wait no longer; Dracula plunged deeply into the intoxicating woman he had just met, but felt he had known a lifetime. Mary's violent thrusts brought Dracula to a height of passion he had never experienced as a vampire, and he wanted more. As their bodies continued to move together, Dracula's mouth returned to Mary's breast and he drank once more; her blood was so sweet, with its velvety texture.

"Mary," Dracula began, as they dressed hastily before the owner of the carriage returned, "Where will you go tonight?"

"Where I always go...to my flat in Miller's Court. I share it with a few others like me...lately we have been frightened to death...over these bloody murders. Surely, you've heard about Jack the Ripper."

"Actually, yes...when I was over at the pub."

"He killed my friend," Mary said with a sniffle, as she buttoned up her boot.

"Is that why you were at Scotland Yard? I saw you leaving and you looked rather shaken." Dracula inquired, as he stroked her hair.

"I was there to identify her body. My friend's name was Annie Chapman...that monster dumped her mutilated body in the street, like so much garbage." Mary lost her composure for a moment at the thought of her dead friend.

"I'm so sorry."

Mary straightened her skirt, and then realized the bodice of her dress was stained with blood. "Why did you bite me? Is it some new kind of fetish or something?"

"I am not just an ordinary man, Mary."

Upon hearing this, Mary threw her head back and cackled loudly, as she jumped from the coach. "So, tell me something I don't know!"

Before Dracula could stop her, Mary Kelly disappeared into the dense fog. When she was gone, Dracula felt the night air suddenly change; her absence already cut like a knife.

CHAPTER 44 – A MYSTERIOUS KILLER – WHITECHAPEL DISTRICT – LONDON - (SEPTEMBER 29, 1888)

Elizabeth Stride, nicknamed "Long Liz," had once been a reasonably attractive woman full of promise. Unfortunately, her looks soon faded as the mean streets of Whitechapel took their toll on an unmarried woman with no prospects. Dressed in her Sunday best, Liz strutted proudly making sure she smiled brightly at any man who crossed her path. Within minutes, she had found her first client, who was more than happy with a quick tryst in a dark corner. Once she had the cash in hand, Liz quickly hiked up her dress, and gave the nameless stranger what he wanted against a rickety wooden fence. It was not uncommon for her to service two or three men a night, which provided Liz with just enough money to keep a roof over her head and her belly full of gin. After reapplying her lipstick, Liz proceeded toward Berner Street where she felt sure another opportunity waited. Liz shook off her bonnet and let her blonde hair fall loose about her shoulders, trying her best to exude sexuality. The air was starting to turn cooler; Liz embraced autumn, happy to see the oppressive heat of summer depart. A dense fog hovered in the air, creating an eerie landscape that sent a chill down her spine.

As Liz walked down a narrow cobblestone street, she heard the sound of a hansom cab as it pulled up beside her. The horse gave his head a shake and the door opened; Liz kept walking in an effort to play hard to get. Before long, the clip-clop sound of horse hooves confirmed the carriage was in motion again; once more, it pulled alongside her. The door was now closed, but a hand was extended from the carriage window, holding a bunch of plump red grapes. Her mouth watered at the sight of a delicacy she had only tasted once in her life. She decided to approach the carriage, certain only a man of wealth would be able to afford such exotic fruit. Liz got into the carriage and grabbed hungrily for the grapes, as she leaned in closer to get a look at her killer's face. He smiled and tipped his hat, and Liz thought to herself, this night was getting better all around. Her handsome gentleman poured her a glass of absinthe, as she gobbled down grapes in rapid succession. She leaned back in the grand carriage and decided this was her lucky night. Elizabeth Stride couldn't have been more wrong.

Chapter 45 - A Kindred Spirit - Linden Hall Library - (September 1888)

It took Prince a few minutes to realize he was the only one who could see her, as she sat reading a huge volume on American history. Occasionally she glanced at him with pensive eyes that appeared to see right through him. He just had to talk to her! Dressed in clothing sorely out of date, the girl managed to fit in; likely because she was seated at a table surrounded by volumes of American history. People passed by her table without comment and eventually, Prince realized she was invisible to everyone else but him.

Attempting to appear nonchalant, Prince approached a bookshelf randomly choosing a volume on the American Revolution. He sat down at the table facing the young girl. "You have chosen a book about my father." The girl had the voice of an angel.

"Who was your father...is he mentioned in this book?" Prince asked with genuine interest.

"Paul Revere. My father and his friends practically started the American Revolution."

Prince was delighted by her strange accent. "What is your name?"

"Sarah...my name is Sarah...but father always called me Rory."

"Rory," Prince repeated her name. "I like it!"

"I believe we are one and the same."

"Ghosts?"

"Exactly."

"Why am I the only one that can see you?" Prince asked.

"Because, I don't want them to...but I wanted you to see me," she responded, with a bashful smile.

"Where are you from?" Prince pressed for more details.

"Don't you mean, *when am I from?*"

"Sorry...I'm not used to talking to others like me," Prince replied, with a sheepish grin.

"I come from the state of Massachusetts...in America."

"What year did you die?"

"1776…I was just thirteen at the time." This made Prince feel sad; on impulse he took one of her hands in his.

"Why do you haunt this library?"

"I come here to learn more about the country my father fought against. I don't know why…but I have always been drawn to England. There is so much to study in this vast library…I could spend eternity here."

Prince smiled and replied, "Sounds like an awful boring way to spend eternity." Rory pulled her hand away.

"I'm sorry…I didn't mean…" Prince began, but she cut him off.

"It's all right…I've been trapped here for a long time."

"Do you mean to tell me you are stuck in London?"

"Actually, I am stuck here in this place…whenever I try to leave; I always end up back inside the library somehow." Prince wondered why a girl born in America would end up here.

"I come here a lot myself…but I'm here by choice. I'm rather fond of libraries, too."

"I could not live without books," Rory replied, hugging a volume to her chest.

Eva approached the table, certain she heard another voice. "Who are you talking to?" she asked Prince. Rory promptly vanished in a rush of cold air.

Chapter 46 – The Otherworld

Although he could not age, Nikos felt every year of his endless life, as they made plans for living in the human world. He had his doubts about partnering with a psychotic killer named, Jack. His nickname seemed to indicate he would be trouble. Nikos worried Dracula might be making the wrong choice; he voiced his opinion, but there was no point in arguing with a vampire. Adjusting his spectacles on the bridge of his nose, Nikos plucked up a volume of seventeenth-century poetry and got lost in the sanctuary of another time.

Dracula took up the habit of hunting on the moors, as he waited for Jack the Ripper to commit his next murder. Some nights he hunted game, but tonight he craved the taste of human prey. There was always some fool, careless enough to walk the moors after dark; tonight was no exception. Dracula had been following a middle-aged man for half a mile, without being noticed. The unique terrain of the North York Moors, made it easy for him; as a wolf or a man, no human was safe from harm when the seasoned vampire was thirsty. The man turned his head at the sound of a snapping twig, and was instantly thrown to the ground; Dracula opened his throat beneath a heartless moon.

On a rock high above the place where a vampire savagely fed, a white wolf took in the sights and sounds of a crystal clear autumn night. The wolf was heartened to know the count still had a taste for killing and had not gone soft, as the Dark One feared. Tonight, the wolf had no call to answer other than its own primal needs; the beast had already picked up the scent of a red-tailed deer.

CHAPTER 47 – AN INDECENT PROPOSAL – WHITECHAPEL DISTRICT – (SEPTEMBER 30, 1888)

Dracula finally decided to trust Eva, and told her of his plans for a man named Jack. Her response was one of pleasant surprise; she was always itching for a new adventure. Dracula explained his plan to catch Jack making his next kill, on the thirtieth of September. Yes, he had skipped ahead in time, but it was necessary; the bonus was in discovering the Ripper would strike twice in one night. Dracula's plan was to present his offer to Jack, while his hands were wet with carnage; what better time to make a pact with the devil? Oddly, it never occurred to the ancient vampire for even a minute that Jack would refuse.

Deliberately dressed to blend in tonight, Dracula could barely contain his excitement at the thought of finally making a vampire of his own. He did not plan to take no for an answer; a promise of eternal life had always proved a great motivator. Right on schedule, the black carriage pulled up to the curb on Dorset Street; Jack lumbered out holding the arm of his first victim of the night, Elizabeth Stride. The whore was quite drunk, as evidenced by the way she stumbled from the hansom. For a moment Dracula almost felt sorry for her, but refused to let anything interfere with tonight's sequence of events. Following the two as they moved into a dark alley, Dracula watched Jack kill his victim with artful precision. It was over in seconds. The killer took a furtive glance around, before opening his black case with everything he needed to dissect a corpse in record time. It was now or never. Dracula made his presence known, moving slowly out of the shadows. Jack looked up and immediately recognized the stranger he had seen before. Wielding his weapon, the man challenged Dracula to speak first.

"I am sorry to interrupt you...but I have a proposition for you." Dracula's eyes glowed red, at the sight of blood bubbling from the woman's neck.

"Why do you keep following me around?" Jack asked gruffly.

"I had to be sure you were the one...before I presented my offer."

"What's wrong with your eyes, mate?" Jack asked, taking a step back.

"I am no ordinary man," Dracula replied. Jack's eyes grew wide, but he did not seem afraid.

"I've heard rumors about your kind...do you *really* drink blood?"

"Yes...but not from a corpse," Dracula replied, eyeing the growing puddle of blood.

"I knew there was more than one killer on the prowl! Scotland Yard has been dealing with several killings on the moors...bodies drained of blood. I read about it in the paper. Those killings weren't mine."

"You're probably right." Dracula held his attention with a hypnotic red-eyed stare.

"I didn't believe vampires were real..." Jack trailed off and lowered his weapon; his knees felt wobbly as Dracula continued with his proposal.

"Vampires are very real...we are a rare breed with very special powers..."

"What kind of powers are we talking about?"

"We are graced with eternal youth...for one."

"What else?"

"How about the ability to travel to any time or place you wish... just by thinking about it?"

"What's the catch here...why do you seek me to join *you* in eternal life?"

"As I said before, I am intrigued by men who are killers of women."

"Who exactly are you, anyway?"

"Forgive me...my name is Count Dracula, and I have been a vampire for more than four hundred years."

"You look damn good for your age, mate." Dracula nodded but said nothing.

Jack laid his scalpel down, as he considered what was being presented. "Thing is...I don't understand what I have to offer you in return."

"As I just explained...I have been a vampire for a very long time. I have seen and done many wonderful things, but have also known the pain of losing everyone I ever loved."

"Your offer just became less appealing," Jack responded with a nervous laugh.

"Let me speak plainly. I've lived without the companionship of my own kind for too long. I've had plenty of company in ghosts, but never one of my kind...someone who understands bloodlust and the thrill of killing. I want you to join me...I promise you will see the world in a whole new way. The limitations of your physical body will no longer hold you back. A vampire is the most invincible being on earth!" Dracula made his very convincing argument.

Jack could feel his excitement growing as he listened. He was not a young man any longer, but it would be nice to never grow truly old. A chance to start a new life was also quite appealing. "So, we will be making more like ourselves...you and I turning others until we have enough of your... or should I say, *our* kind?"

"You understand my proposition well. All I ask is for your loyalty; in return, you will have access to all the carnage you desire."

"I can be loyal to a fault!" Jack boasted, unsure if this was really true.

"Your greatest responsibility will be in helping me sire a community of well-groomed vampires. On occasion, we may also need you to mete out punishment when one of our own goes rogue...it happens sometimes."

"I can handle that...killing and mutilation are my specialties."

"We will expect a certain amount of restraint; we can't make vampires if you kill every human you feed on."

"Sounds like I'll be busy," Jack replied with a maniacal grin.

"How long have you been in the mutilation business?" Dracula asked.

"I was eight years old when I killed my mother. She was my first kill...the one you never forget. No one even looked my way because I was so young. I just thought you should know the worst thing about me," Jack said.

"Why did you kill her?"

"She was a bloody whore!" Jack said vehemently.

"Is that why you kill unfortunates?"

"One reason...among many."

"Your past is what makes you an ideal candidate; I believe destiny brought us together so we can begin what I should have started years ago," Dracula said.

"Forgive me, but I just want to confirm this is for real. You are Count Dracula…and a vampire. You followed me here tonight…because you are trying to build an army of vampires and I'm to be your first victim?"

"That pretty much sums it up. You have been chosen for a very important mission…you must fulfill your destiny, Jack.

"I get to kill whenever I want?"

"Within reason…we don't want to draw unnecessary attention to ourselves." Jack still looked puzzled.

"Don't worry…you'll still be able to kill for sport on occasion. But, Jack…no sending letters to the newspapers, okay?"

"So, basically you just want me to be myself." Jack dropped his knife into his black bag and snapped it shut.

"Please don't let me stop you in what you were doing…I actually like to watch," Dracula said with a sly smile.

"Lost my interest, I guess. Where can we go to talk about this further?" Jack asked, handing a bunch of red grapes to Dracula, who declined them with a wave of his hand.

"So, grapes are your secret weapon then?" Dracula questioned, raising an eyebrow.

"Absolutely…whores just love them!"

Dracula smiled because he knew Jack would accept his offer. He wasn't concerned that he requested a few weeks to tie up loose ends. It would give Dracula a chance to get to know the man's character a little better, before he made a firm decision to turn him. The vampire knew Jack would kill again this same night. He planned to follow him, and savor every glorious moment of Jack the Ripper's savage butchery. Observing a woman's murder was a rare thing for Dracula to witness, despite his unnaturally long life. Jack was smooth as silk in his craft; the whore was dead before she could even scream. Her eyes remained wide open, as if trying to delay the blackness that surely followed. Because Dracula never killed women, he found himself captivated as he watched Catherine Eddowes die. A woman expired so much more gracefully than a man; her invisible life force lingering for a moment before fading into nothingness.

CHAPTER 48 – THE OTHERWORLD

Dracula entered his mirror world once more, anxious to talk to Nikos about his night with Jack and his new love, Mary Jane Kelly. As usual, Nikos was in his library surrounded by stacks of weathered books. He didn't need reading glasses, but had recently started wearing a pair Dracula found during one of his adventures. Nikos looked up as Dracula entered, pulling off his glasses. His lord merely grunted at him in response.

"Good to see you, too, Vlad."

"You've got me thinking…maybe I should start wearing glasses. It would make me look distinguished…don't you think?"

"You can find them anywhere," Nikos answered, returning to his book.

"Not the kind I'm looking for. I need you to find me a place where they make custom glasses…more like spectacles. I almost forgot…the lenses have to be red."

"Red?"

"Yes, red. I want something stylish but classic. We will all need them as our legions grow, and we move about the human world on a regular basis."

"Why the sudden desire for setting a fashion trend?"

"The answer is quite simple. Red lenses will protect us when our eyes change before we strike. I have no wish to give my victims advance warning."

"Anything for your comfort, *master*," Nikos responded sarcastically.

"You're in some mood tonight. Just find me someone to make the glasses, damn it!"

"Did you feed?"

"Yes…I'm sorry…let's start over. I have something to tell you anyway, good news. I met a beautiful woman tonight. Her name is Mary and I want her to join us. Jack will be my right hand and I will take Mary to be my life mate!"

"You go too fast, Vlad. Please, tell me what happened with Jack. Did he accept your proposal?"

"Yes...of course, why wouldn't he? He says he needs a little more time to sort things out in his personal life. Since I know where he lives, we can wait."

Nikos noticed drops of blood on the floor and became alarmed. "Vlad, are you hurt? There's blood on the floor...let me see your hand."

Dracula laughed, then pulled a bloody handkerchief from his pocket and plopped it on the table. "My God...what is it, Vlad?"

"It's the severed ear of Jack's latest victim. He let me watch the kill and gave me a souvenir!"

CHAPTER 49 - A VAMPIRE IN LOVE – LONDON – (OCTOBER 1888)

$\mathbf{M}$ary met him behind the abandoned barn; she had been with him every night, since they first met. To say Mary was in love was an understatement. Having been a prostitute most of her adult life, she usually felt no emotion when engaged in sexual acts for pay. Some of her clients were reasonably adept, but no one made her feel like he did. Making love was heaven each and every time she surrendered herself to Count Dracula. Mary was a simple girl, and found it hard to understand why the count was so smitten. One reason appeared to be, that she was reasonably well-read. She had her mother to thank for her education, a fringe benefit of her employment as governess to Lord and Lady Whitford.

As the strong odor of damp hay filled her nostrils, her vampire drank wantonly from a neck wound he inflicted several nights before. Dracula wanted to give Mary everything she never had, fancy clothes, jewelry and a life of ease. He would make her a countess and everywhere they went, people would admire the reclusive couple with titles and land in Romania. As they lay together, Mary felt a sense of contentment she had never known.

Dracula ran his hand along her naked hip, as an idea came to mind. "Mary, let me take you with me tonight. I want you to experience the night as I do...from a sky full of stars," Dracula pleaded, as he jumped up to view the glorious night.

"I'm afraid of heights...I already told you." She reached for him to come back to her, but Dracula pulled her up and gathered their clothes.

"Let's go to the roof, then...let me take you that far, Mary." They quickly dressed and ran outside into the autumn night.

Mary ran barefoot like a child through the soft grass, sprinkled with evening dew. She raised her hands to the night, knowing she would fly anywhere with him.

"Is this so bad then...to say goodbye to the sun? Look at me...I can run barefoot in the grass and have the stars above for company!" Dracula exclaimed.

Mary moved behind Dracula and placed her head on his shoulder. "Take me flying then...gentle man," she whispered with a smile. Without saying a word, Dracula lifted them to the roof of the barn. Mary held tight as they became airborne, and flew into the glorious night.

From the ground below, Eva watched them flying together as one. She felt physical pain when she finally realized, Dracula had found love in another woman's arms. In a fit of jealous rage, Eva stormed into the barn and discovered the love nest her count and his whore had used just moments before. She grabbed a pitchfork, and thrust it into the stable door of Vlad's new horse. Eva was sorely tempted to kill the animal, but it would do nothing to stop the budding romance between the ancient vampire and his whore.

CHAPTER 50 – THE DARK ONE

As an entity of evil, the Dark One thrived on the pain and suffering of others. The nefarious being grew weary of existing in a dormant state, as it waited with infinite patience for its protégé, Vlad Dracula to fulfill his destiny. Lately, the vampire seemed far too interested in chasing the illusion of human love. Worst of all, he had chosen a base woman as his bride, someone who was well beneath him. It was time to intervene and put an end to this foolishness. Eva had become the Dark One's only source of hope, as it watched her gradually assume her role, as a right hand to evil. Jealousy was a powerful human emotion; no one knew it better than the former countess. The Dark One would make a puppet of this woman-child, so they could be rid of the red-haired whore once and for all.

Eva sat perusing a book in her room with much longing; the book contained pictures of beautiful women wearing richly designed dresses. Of all the things Eva missed, it was her earthly body with its soft curves and supple breasts. Eva still carried resentment because she no longer seemed to have a place in the adult world; no matter where they went, she would always be viewed as a child. As she flipped through the pages, Eva ruminated about Mary Kelly and how she could come between her count and his new found love.

A hissing sound alerted Eva the Dark One was near. As always, she awaited his voice and command. "Young one," the serpent-like voice spoke. Eva instantly snapped to attention.

"I am here."

"You are unhappy…are you not?"

"Very…I am bored and tired of being treated like a child. I am sent all over God's creation, searching for books…and now my lord is off every night consorting with his new whore."

"You must have patience," the Dark One replied in a soothing voice.

"But I'm tired of waiting for things to happen."

"What things would you like to happen, young one?"

"That woman cannot join us…I will not share my lord with her."

"Who says you have to do so?"

"You said I had to be patient."

"The woman is not necessary to our cause. We both know that when Dracula is in love…he becomes distracted. So, why not take care of it yourself?"

Eva leaned toward the sound of the Dark One's voice. "Do you mean…kill her?"

"Don't act like the thought hasn't crossed your mind, young one. Remember, I see everything."

"If I kill his new plaything…I risk making an enemy of my father and pushing him further away."

"Perhaps…but, not if Dracula can be convinced someone else was responsible."

"Who else?"

"One who is already a killer," the Dark One replied. Suddenly, Eva understood everything.

Chapter 51 – Prince and Rory – Linden Hall Library - London – (November 1888)

Prince found his greatest happiness in discovering the world through the safety of books. He was not a soldier like Nikos or Count Dracula. He was just a boy who never grew up. Even if he'd had the chance to become a man, the former prince recognized he was not brave at all. His mother had taught him to trust no one, including their own relatives. He and his brother were raised to be fearful, and it left them defenseless. As Prince told Rory the story of his short life on earth, she studied him with growing adoration. She knew how the tale ended; their mysterious disappearance a matter of historical fact. Prince's life had been a sad one but certainly, there had been some adventure.

"Where do you live now?" Rory asked. The library was the only home she knew.

"In a place without time...I come here occasionally to be around people. It is so dark and quiet where I come from."

"Does time matter to a ghost...I mean, why would you need any home at all?"

"It might be easier if I just show you," Prince replied. He looked into her eyes and felt compelled to bring Rory to the Otherworld.

Behind the reference section on American history, Prince discovered a hidden alcove where he often spent time reading in private. He remembered a mirror hanging there which could be used as a portal. Prince took Rory's hand and led her through a flash of colored light into the Otherworld. The vine stirred when it caught the scent of another ghost but sensed no threat, so it went back to its dreamless slumber. Nikos was nowhere to be seen, as they passed by the growing library they had amassed. Since candles burned forever in the Otherworld, there was always an amber glow to welcome them.

Rory immediately felt comfortable in this quiet, yet mysterious place. "So, this is where you all live then...like a house, but really just a private world behind mirrors."

"I guess you could describe it that way. We've made a home here of sorts. I am much more interested in hearing about your adventures."

Although she died at a tender age, Rory had been an important part of American history. Unknown to most historians, she had been on the horse ridden by one of America's greatest heroes, Paul Revere. Desperate to be part of history, twelve-year-old Rory had hidden in the boat her father used on that fateful night; he had to cross the Charles River to retrieve the horse he rode on that historic night. When Rory finally revealed herself, her father had no choice but to take her with him. Her presence was never noted in history books; her father made sure her identity was protected. Sometimes when Rory closed her eyes, she could see her father's smile and hear him calling out those famous words.

"Tell me about it. What was it like to be right there when history was being made? We have nowhere to go. I would love to hear the story of your father, Paul Revere."

Rory smiled as she began to speak from pure memory, telling him the events that spawned a revolution, while Prince leaned forward like a child listening to a bedtime story. When she was finished with her amazing tale, Prince wished there was more to tell, because he liked listening to her unique accent.

"I wish I had done at least one brave thing before my brother and I were murdered," Prince said, then proceeded to tell her the story of how he came to be a ghost.

"I can't believe I'm talking to one of the princes in the tower. I found a book about it. I had to know and understand who you really are. Where is your brother?" Rory asked.

"He ascended...my mother came for him." Prince felt a lump in his throat; he missed his brother more than he ever expected.

"Hard to believe I'm having a conversation with *the* Prince Edward!"

Prince bowed to her, and then gently kissed her hand. "The very same...Prince Edward and uncrowned king of England. In this realm, they call me Prince."

"It sure is a fantastic story...Prince."

"Maybe you should stay with us...we're just getting ready to travel to a more modern time...," Prince said hopefully.

"I hate the modern world…and the way people dress," Rory said, cutting him off. She was self-conscious in her out-of-date clothes.

"I wouldn't change a thing about you," he said with a smile. Rory leaned into him and kissed his cheek; Prince knew she was going to stay.

CHAPTER 52 - LOVE FOUND, LOVE LOST – LONDON – (NOVEMBER 9, 1888)

It was rare for Dracula to spend time with Mary at her flat in Miller's Court. The place was dingy and sparsely furnished, but no matter, the count was in love and could see nothing beyond his passion. She was a woman of the streets, but somehow it didn't matter. As the two lay together in a tangle of limbs and Mary's glorious hair, Dracula felt a sense of contentment he'd rarely known in his human life. He was in love with a beautiful woman: in just a few days, she would be his loving partner for all eternity. Until he met Mary Kelly, Dracula had not realized the depth of his isolation and loneliness.

As she lay sleeping, Dracula studied the lines of her body, marveling at her milky white softness. A gentle breeze came in through the open window and Dracula caught her intoxicating scent, honey sweet with a hint of ginger. She was gentle and kind-hearted despite her occupation and now, he was going to make her a vampire. Dracula had reservations about turning Mary, but there was no other way. In order for them to be together through time, she would have to give up her human life.

Mary moved to nuzzle his neck. "When will I become like you?"

Dracula suddenly became serious. "It will be very painful, you know."

"What my love, when you leave me tonight?" Mary teased.

"No, I mean when I turn you. It will hurt...a lot." Dracula saw confusion in her eyes. "There will be no pain when I bite your neck, Mary. What will hurt...is the transformation."

"Did it hurt when it happened to you?"

"Yes, but it passed quickly. When I awoke, I saw the world in a whole new way. The stars were brighter...and things seemed to explode with color. I could even hear voices coming from houses miles away." Dracula lowered his voice and continued, "I also never again saw a sunrise or felt its warmth against my skin. This life has its consequences, but you will discover a world that never looked more beautiful."

Mary's eyes sparkled with excitement. "I can picture it in my mind, love…a black sky filled with stars…and a man on horseback seeing the night for the first time, through vampire eyes."

"Actually, I spent the first few days as a wolf."

Mary's jaw dropped. "I hope you don't plan to turn me into a wolf! I wasn't counting on that."

Dracula laughed and caressed her cheek. "All vampires have shape-shifting abilities, Mary. I can also change into a bat which…believe it or not, comes in handy when I need to get into or out of tight places."

"How does one change from a man to a wolf?" Mary was trying to understand what she was getting into.

"It happens when the need arises, love…like a force of nature."

"I believe I am ready to embrace your world…" Mary trailed off, as she thought about having to drink blood; this was something she still struggled with.

"I will make you happy, Mary…I promise you."

Mary giggled and jumped from the bed. "I know you don't eat…but I do. If you require a tireless lover, then I must be fed."

"And what kind of English delicacy does my love fancy?" Dracula asked, already getting dressed.

"Surprise me."

Dracula moved to the door, but Mary followed him as though afraid he'd never return. "Mary…why have I never felt like this before? Have you cast a spell on me?" Dracula asked holding her face in his hands.

"This is how it feels to be in love…I guess."

"Mary, I will never let anyone or anything come between us. I will love you as long as there is blood running through my veins…and I will never let anyone hurt you again."

"No one can be safe from everything, can they?" Mary said somberly.

"What did I just say, Mary…I will never let *anything* happen to you."

He almost didn't leave, so overwhelmed was Dracula by her musky scent. Her heartbeat thundered in his ears; the vampire already felt himself a part of her. Dracula finally pulled himself away and stepped outside to take a breath of cool night air. He hummed a tune that was stuck in his head as he walked toward the baker's shop, blissfully unaware he would never see his love alive again.

Mary closed the door behind him and moved to her tiny dresser, pulling the drawer all the way out. She opened the secret compartment where she kept a tiny silver cross on a piece of twine. Mary held it to her chest and closed her eyes, as she thought of her mother in heaven. Naturally, Mary could not wear her cross when Dracula was near; soon she wouldn't be able to wear it at all. Happiness had come to her in a handsome stranger who promised her a better, if somewhat darker way of life. As she finished dressing, Mary heard someone tapping on the door and thought Dracula had forgotten something. She ran to open it without a second thought, despite the neighborhood.

Her visitor was a pretty young girl of about twelve with arresting dark eyes and skin like ivory. The fog was heavy but Mary could clearly see the girl shivering from the cold.

"Hello, miss," Eva said in her best cockney accent. "I lost my mum and was hoping I could come in and get warm for a minute...it's so cold out here."

"You poor dear...please come inside." As Dracula observed, Mary had a kind heart.

Eva slipped inside, careful to conceal the hunting knife she hid underneath her long skirt. Mary offered the girl a chair while she heated water for tea. It was a hovel at best. The room stank of smoke and stale gin, and the bed was nothing more than a cot. Eva studied Mary as she placed dried tea in a strainer. This woman was no great beauty, and didn't appear well-educated either. Despite these facts, Mary Kelly had somehow managed to capture her lord's heart; Eva was determined to end this sorted love affair, tonight.

"How did you end up in this neighborhood, child?" Mary asked, setting a cup of hot tea on the table.

Eva smiled with eyes gone devil black, as she leaned forward. "I came to see you, Mary." Mary was surprised the girl knew her name, and suddenly wished she hadn't answered the door.

"I've been following you for a long time now," Eva continued, losing her cockney accent.

"Why would you do that...do I know you?" Mary asked confused.

"No...but you know my father...maybe a little too well!" Eva's voice turned to ice.

"*Who* are you?"

"My name doesn't matter…but my face is the last thing you will ever see," Eva replied. She advanced on Mary, who was unprepared and without means of defense.

Mary backed up and fell upon the bed, half dressed and at the mercy of a child who was wielding a knife with incredible strength. When Eva plunged the knife into Mary's abdomen the first time, she felt as though her body was splitting in two. A scream caught in her throat, as blood poured from her nose and mouth. Another flash of the blade cut clean through her right kidney. A feeling of weightlessness took over, and then mercifully, everything went black. High above the blood-soaked bed now; Mary could see her ruined corpse. Eva continued to cut and mutilate her remains until she was so unrecognizable, police had to assume it was her corpse based on a drunken boyfriend's identification.

Fearing Dracula's return was imminent, Eva prepared to go; as she was leaving, Eva hung Mary's silver cross on the doorknob. A small mirror above Mary's dresser would serve as her entry back into the Otherworld. Though Eva would have liked to explore Whitechapel further, her clothes were now covered with blood. Incapable of remorse, Eva wore a smug smile as she re-entered the Otherworld through a haze of colored light, deciding she enjoyed killing very much. She stripped off her soiled clothes as soon as she passed through the portal; Eva never noticed Prince watching her from behind a stack of pilfered library books.

CHAPTER 53 - A COWARDLY END – LONDON - (NOVEMBER 10, 1888)

In his dream, Jack's hands were covered with blood, making him wake with a start. Every time he closed his eyes, his mind was tormented by faces of his victims; Jack felt certain he was going mad. The newspapers called Mary Kelly's killing a massacre, but Jack remembered nothing at all about the night before; he was puzzled, because he didn't normally target redheads. Jack took notice of Mary around the same time he began stalking Elizabeth Stride in late September, but never considered her as a potential victim. Despite what authorities believed, Mary's killing didn't fit his profile; he believed killing a woman in her home was a cowardly act. Holding his aching head, Jack thought about the bizarre offer from a self-proclaimed vampire, but knew he couldn't possibly take anything that was said seriously. In the past twenty-four hours, Jack had begun to realize the last thing he wanted, was a life without end. Best to keep a low profile, Jack thought to himself, as he stole furtive glances out a window in the dilapidated boarding house. He could hear police whistles in the street below as they stopped pedestrians, questioning anyone who looked the least bit suspicious.

Jack moved to the mirror and studied his haggard face. His complexion was gray and he was desperately in need of a shave. As he stared at his reflection, Jack was repulsed by the despicable man he had allowed himself to become. He took out a straight razor and laid it down with shaking hands. Jack was so disgusted with himself, he could barely face his reflection. How can I go on living this way? Jack began to weep as he picked up the razor, holding it across his arm. He turned away in disgust, because he didn't have the guts to go through with it. What a pitiful man I am. Suddenly, Jack felt like he would suffocate unless he got some air. He grabbed his coat and muffler against the cold, and walked purposefully toward the riverbanks as an idea began to form.

Despite a dense fog, he observed the police were no longer in sight; perhaps they had gone home for dinner. He was hungry and couldn't remember the last time he had eaten but thought, *what's the point?* Jack pulled up his collar against the biting wind. A few boys were having a snowball fight and it made him nostalgic for the innocence of childhood. He passed them and headed toward the bridge he had crossed at least a hundred times, since moving to the neighborhood. The Thames River was a black sheet of ice, but certainly not yet safe enough to skate on. Jack realized he might die of a head injury from hitting the ice, before he had the chance to drown; either way was fine with him. Scotland Yard detectives were closing in on him, and it was only a matter of time before he was caught. Jack would have the last laugh by beating them to the punch. Once he was gone, the mystery of Jack the Ripper would never be solved. This one fact gave him a small measure of satisfaction, as he prepared to plunge into the frigid waters below. Jack stepped up onto the railing, grabbing a tree branch for balance. As he moved his foot forward, he heard one of the boys call out, "Hey, mister!"

Knowing time had run out for procrastination, Jack jumped into the frigid waters of the Thames; as expected, his head cracked through a thin coating of ice, before plunging into the black water below.

CHAPTER 54 - A SCORE TO SETTLE - WHITECHAPEL DISTRICT - LONDON - (NOVEMBER 1888)

Dracula ran blindly through the streets of Whitechapel, filled with a hatred he could barely contain. He lost all composure when he saw her mutilated body. His love was gone, and he could not save her! Mary's killer carved her up so badly; there was no way to bring her back to life. His love had been ripped apart, and Dracula was going to make certain Jack paid with something dearer than his life. The night grew quiet, as Dracula scoured the cobblestone streets looking for the man who had stolen his one chance for happiness. Determined to hunt Jack down, Dracula searched his favorite haunts, but he was nowhere to be found. Shoving his hands into his pockets, Dracula headed toward the river, to a place Jack was known to frequent. The wind howled as he got closer to the water and then, like an answer to his prayer, Dracula spotted a group of young boys gathered by the bridge. Two boys were pointing toward the water below, as they spoke in excited voices. "Look, mister! That man just jumped into the river!"

Dracula ran to the railing and saw Jack flailing his arms in the water. His declared enemy was trying to violate the verbal contract he made and now, he was apparently trying to drown himself. So, Jack was a coward after all! He had chosen the easy way out, but Dracula was not about to let that happen.

"Jack…you son of a bitch! I'm coming for you!" Dracula screamed. He climbed up on the railing and dove into the Thames. The icy water had no effect on a vampire, but for a human being, death from hypothermia could occur quickly in water this cold. Dracula had to act fast! He swam to Jack's floating body and rushed to pull him from the river. The seasoned vampire had his own ideas about how justice would be served. Dracula yanked Jack's upper body out of the water as he gasped for air. "You'll not get off that easy, my friend." Dracula dragged Jack to safety, pulling him onto a rock large enough to hold both of them.

Jack remained breathless and still unable to speak, as Dracula loomed over him; his eyes red with murderous rage. In that moment, Jack found his fear as he stared into eyes that were no longer human. Dracula flashed a menacing smile, as he prepared to take his revenge.

"Please...just let me die," Jack pleaded.

"Dying's too good for you!"

"I didn't kill her...I swear...," Jack's voice was cut off, when Dracula punctured his larynx and began gulping his blood; he was careful to stop drinking while Jack's heart was still beating.

Dracula sliced open a vein in his forearm, and forced Jack to drink from him. Jack's eyes snapped open as he began to shake with violent spasms; his limbs twisted into a knot and his skin took on a most unnatural hue. Jack writhed and moaned as the transformation took hold; the pain was different for everyone. Dracula hoped he was in agony.

Jack lay still when it was all over. His skin tone had changed to pale gray, and the sharp angles of his face were more pronounced. Dracula slapped him hard across the chin, and the fledgling's eyes opened wide; Jack the Ripper was now a creature of the night. The seasoned vampire wore a sadistic smile; Jacks eyes were glowing like polished rubies. Finally, more than four hundred years after he himself became a creature of the night, Vlad Dracula returned the favor and made a vampire of his own.

Chapter 55 - Jack - The Otherworld

Jack opened his red eyes to complete and utter darkness. Am I dead? I can feel coldness all around me so, maybe I am buried underground, he thought. But, where?

"Wretched beast...rise up now and see your new world," Dracula spoke harshly. Jack stood up and his vision improved greatly; he faced Dracula in his wolf-like form, and then realized he was a wolf as well.

"Is this my punishment then...to be a wolf for all eternity?" Jack asked silently. They were now communicating with only thoughts.

"No, we will fight as wolves to the death...that is your punishment," Dracula challenged.

"I did not kill her," Jack argued, as Dracula lunged at him with claws extended.

The two battled while continuing a silent argument about Mary's death. No matter how many times Jack denied taking her life, Dracula would not let up. Attracted by the commotion, Akos flew in circles around them, but kept a safe distance. Nikos advanced, shouting for them to stop but they kept on fighting; two huge beasts rolling around in an apparent fight to the death. "You cannot kill him!" Nikos shouted, as he watched their fierce struggle.

"He killed my Mary!" Dracula roared in a half-wolf, half-human growl.

"Vlad...this was not our plan. We need this fledgling to start our work!"

Dracula's found it impossible to accept the loss of his love without taking vengeance. Jack lost his footing as Dracula charged, prepared to take full advantage of his opponent's weakness. As he pounced, Jack assumed his human form and Dracula did the same, determined for a fair fight. Back in human form, the two vampires were breathless and collapsed to the ground; their eyes still burning with anger.

"I made you and I can take you down, Jack!" Dracula's threatened. Nikos tried to break up the fight by standing between them.

"We need each other for our cause....petty differences do not matter now."

"You call killing my love, a petty difference?" Dracula shouted with fists clenched.

"I told you a dozen times, mate. I didn't kill her. That kind of killing is not my style."

"I cannot trust this man, Nikos!" Dracula declared.

Prince and Rory, drawn by the noise came to investigate; Akos immediately flew to Prince's extended arm.

"Where have you two been anyway?" Nikos asked, trying to change the subject.

"Rory and I found something important in Linden Hall Library... it's a tunnel that leads right to the metro...it's also connected to an abandoned tube station. It's everything Dracula requested...a safe place to house the future colony. Most of the tube stations are connected to one another...this will allow multiple routes for escape." Dracula was impressed and motioned for Prince to continue with more details.

"We found a tunnel under the library that appears to be closed off in one direction, toward Trafalgar Square. We found a basic floor plan, and it looks like a section of the tunnel was cordoned off for some reason. If we find the space habitable and secure, we will have found a home for your progeny. Who would ever think to search for your kind *underneath* the streets of London?"

"Great work, Prince." Nikos said, giving the boy a pat on the back.

"The kid's right, you know." Jack stood up, quite happy to be in his human form again.

"Right about what?" Dracula responded impatiently.

"The metro...the library, it's all connected...why there's a virtual city under the streets of London...and it actually *could* be made into a suitable home."

"Don't listen to him...he doesn't know what he's talking about!" Dracula snapped.

Nikos ignored his lord and countered, "Do you really think our fledglings would be safe in an underground tunnel?"

"Sure, mate. But I'm not just talking about a tunnel...I'm talking about a whole city block of living space, quite suitable for our kind. A town without sunlight." Jack was already warming to the idea.

"Kind of like your own tunnel town," Rory added, with a nervous laugh.

Jack, who was not one for social graces, blurted out, "Who the hell are you?"

Prince put a protective arm around Rory. "We are companions to Count Dracula...but are not vampires. We refer to ourselves as earthbound spirits."

"What a motley crew this is," Jack replied, looking around. "What is this place of darkness?"

"This is the Otherworld. It has been home to us for centuries of human time. When we are here, there is no passing of time, no danger of exposure and...most important, here there is no need for a vampire to feed," Nikos explained.

"I thought maybe it was some kind of library or something...there are books everywhere."

"This place will always be a refuge, but we need a physical location to establish a colony as our numbers grow. This is our safe haven, a place where we connect as a family. Eva is one of us too...she is not here right now."

"Eva...is she a vampire?"

"No, she's a child like the others...and off limits to you," Dracula snapped protectively.

Prince hated being referred to as a child and quickly changed the subject. "Well, what do you think about our idea? Imagine the convenience of housing fledglings...right under the noses of unsuspecting Londoners." Akos tipped his head from side to side, as if he were following the conversation.

Dracula's anger began to subside as he reluctantly acknowledged, this was the most viable option. He would still have to establish himself legitimately; this meant procuring a gentleman's residence within London. Wherever they lived, access to the London Underground was essential. The metro tunnels offered protection from sunlight and easy access to potential victims. Once the vampire population started to multiply, other methods of obtaining sustenance would be necessary;

daily killing would expose their presence and use up too many human lives. Nikos had been investigating the emergence of blood banks throughout the London area; everyone warmed to the idea of accessible sustenance, it was simply a matter of re-directing shipments. Dracula immediately warmed to the idea, and was already considering how they would store it.

The vampire rubbed his chin, hating to admit he needed Jack's help. "I concede...this could work for all of us. Jack, how well do you know the metro system...the stops, storage areas and the like?"

"I know the metro like the back of my hand. If you want my opinion, the old Kings Cross Station is our best bet...much larger than Trafalgar Square. I can show you where it is, mate."

"Stop calling everyone *mate*," Nikos interrupted. "You are addressing Count Vlad Dracula, crowned Prince of Wallachia!"

"Fine, I'll call him count. Now, when do I get to kill someone?" Jack asked.

"When I say so!" Dracula snapped.

Dracula turned back to Prince and Rory. "Go, explore this further and bring us floor plans for the library...I have every confidence you two can break into the archives of Linden Hall. Either way, go and find anything that gives us a better idea what's down there...and take that damn bird with you!"

Without another word, the two dashed off to the portal so they could return to Linden Hall and start their research. Akos flew over their heads clearly delighted to be a part of their great adventure.

Chapter 56 - Eva's Secret Journey - Windsor Hotel - NYC - (December 31, 1899)

The Windsor Hotel in Midtown Manhattan was one of the most elegant hotels New York City had to offer. The Windsor was for the elite, with luxurious furnishings including imported tapestry rugs, priceless works of art and Tiffany glass chandeliers in every common area. It was a place where high society gathered to celebrate special events, weddings, baptisms and holidays. Famous people from all over the world were scheduled to attend tonight's New Year's Eve party. Eva did her homework when she picked this wonderful place. Newly opened, everything was shiny and brand new, making her feel like royalty once more. The Windsor Hotel was evidently *the place* to be, if you wanted to make the society pages. Eva had carefully selected a location in the heart of New York City, to witness the beginning of a new century. She felt guilty for sneaking away, but the thrill far outweighed the consequences. Standing in the grand ballroom with happy people dancing and laughing all around her, Eva began her love affair with New York City. With a tingle of excitement, she navigated the growing crowd of gaily dressed men and women with relish. She was wearing a royal blue gown, she purchased from a newly opened store called *Bergdorf Goodman*; the dress made her feel like a princess. The band played a beautiful waltz, as Eva's moved gracefully across the dance floor; her long gown trailed behind her like a calling card.

Once Eva grasped her full potential for time travel, she developed a constant desire to find new and exciting places to visit. The thought of a century coming to an end filled her with breathless anticipation. Eva felt stifled by Prince and Nikos, because of their superstitions about the future. The others could spend the next eleven years doing what they wanted; Eva couldn't wait any longer to see the twentieth century. She had chosen her location well; New York City had it all. Excitement. Glamour. New Year's Eve was a dress-up night that came only once a year. Eva was enamored with fashion and all things glamorous. To her, there was nothing more exhilarating than watching the progression of women's clothing, as she traveled through time. This guilty pleasure was the only thing that distracted Eva from her innately evil nature.

The night passed in a rush of sound and color, as Eva moved through the crowd; she never remained in one place long enough for anyone to engage with her. Tonight, she didn't feel like dancing, and before long, her wristwatch declared a new century would be arriving very soon. On cue, the music picked up and Eva listened as the countdown to midnight began. People around her appeared to hold their breath, as the clock chimed the midnight hour. Screams of joy filled the air, as a blizzard of colored confetti fell from the ceiling. As Eva listened to the clock's chime, she felt nothing. For her kind, the passing of time was quite irrelevant. Eva's last thought in the year 1899, was that she regretted not having anyone to kiss.

An elderly gentleman came up and tapped Eva's arm. "Excuse me; miss," the stranger interrupted. "How could a lovely young lady like you be unescorted?" Eva smiled and turned to face a rather large man, on the other side of fifty; he had a strong jaw, full beard and a rather pallid complexion. The stranger abruptly took her gloved hand and kissed it.

"I'm afraid my escort was called away...but he insisted I stay and enjoy myself...so here I am." Eva hoped he didn't plan to make advances.

"Happy New Year! Let me introduce myself. I am Bram Stoker... *the* Bram Stoker," he repeated.

"Well, very nice to meet you, Mr. Stoker. My name is Eva Bathory. I apologize but I don't recognize your name."

"Why, I'm the author of Dracula, of course! Is it possible, dear lady, that you have not read my book?" he asked incredulously.

"I am sorry, I have not. Is it a new book, sir?" He had her interest now.

"I will get you a signed copy straight away." Stoker snapped his fingers, and a balding man appeared out of nowhere.

"Run to my carriage, Duncan, and secure a copy of my novel for miss...er..."

"Bathory, Eva Bathory." She was certain he recognized her family name.

Eva had no choice but to wait for the book. She knew how important it was to read what this author had written about Dracula. Too much information based on fact, could compromise their position in the future. Eva's instinct to protect her lord was strong, and she guarded his secrets fiercely. Bringing back a copy of Bram Stoker's novel might be just the peace offering she needed, when Dracula discovered she had seen the millennium without him.

Bram held out his arm. "Dance to celebrate the New Year?" he asked, and Eva could hardly refuse. The dance seemed to go on forever, until finally Eva spotted poor Duncan returning with the book. Her dance partner stopped in his tracks, making a big production of signing his masterpiece. He blew on the wet ink after he signed his name, and handed the book to Eva.

"Thank you, Mr. Stoker. I will make a point of reading your story at my earliest opportunity."

"It's a vampire story, you know...it all started in the fifteenth century..." Bram began but Eva interrupted.

"Please forgive me, Mr. Stoker, my carriage is waiting downstairs," Eva lied, backing away toward the door despite his protest.

"But my carriage can take you home. Will you not allow me the pleasure?" Bram Stoker asked hopefully.

"Good sir, you are too kind...but alas, my driver waits...," her voice trailed off as she ran into the crowd, where he lost her in a sea of colored taffeta.

Chapter 57 - Dracula Rewritten - London, England - (November 1896)

As a flickering gaslight burned, Bram Stoker labored over the pages of his latest novel about a vampire from Transylvania. He was nearing the climax of a scene, and was so intent on his subject matter he neglected to make dinner for himself. Laying down his pen, Bram looked up to find a man standing in the doorway of his study. The stranger wore a long black cape, but he did not speak or move. Bram was apprehensive, but not afraid.

"Sir...by what authority do you accost me in my residence?" Bram bellowed.

"Good evening, Mr. Stoker. I understand you are writing a book right now...what they call a novella." Dracula made no attempt to apologize for barging in on the writer.

"Who let you in?" Bram demanded, as he rose from his seat.

"Forgive me, your wife was leaving as I was getting ready to ring the bell...I told her I was a business associate, so she let me in."

"State your business, sir!"

"Why, I've come to talk with you about your story," Dracula explained, advancing into the study without invitation.

"And why would I want to discuss my book with you?"

"Well, Mr. Stoker...that's the interesting part. You see, my name is Count Vlad Dracula."

"Now see here, I am in no mood for jokes!" Bram shouted angrily.

"I assure you, I am not joking," Dracula replied, moving closer with eyes that had begun to glow. Dracula removed his spectacles, and Bram looked right into the red eyes of the devil himself. He tried to keep the desk between them, as panic set in. Dracula is not real, he thought to himself. This can't be happening. A vampire in London. Impossible!

"I mean you no harm, Mr. Stoker. We just need to discuss your novella and a few changes I would like to see." Dracula smiled warmly, taking a seat to face a dumbfounded Bram Stoker; in the dimly lit room, their conversation felt surreal.

Bram studied his face, still smooth and handsome, with eyes that penetrated his very soul. "But you can't be...I mean, the original Vlad Dracula...he died in 1476."

"You should know better than anyone...that a vampire never dies."

"Vampires...why everyone knows vampires aren't real...the whole concept of such creatures was born of fear and superstition!" Bram declared excitedly.

"Again, this is simply not true," Dracula said with a broad smile; revealing razor sharp teeth.

"Father in heaven, bless me, Lord Jesus," Bram whispered, crossing himself for protection.

Dracula laughed, "That will not help you...but fear not, I have not come here to harm you or your family...yet."

"Why do you visit me here...are you going to help me finish writing my story?" Bram spoke with undisguised sarcasm.

"Actually, that's exactly why I'm here."

Bram stood up again and started pacing the floor, no longer afraid Dracula would harm him. "This makes no sense! I wrote a story *loosely based* on Vlad the Impaler...something to excite women and make men fearful of the night." Bram spoke rapidly as he tried to make sense of things. How could his fictional character be sitting in front of him; Vlad Dracula was killed in the fifteenth century!

Dracula continued as though there were nothing unusual about his presence. "Here's how it will work...I will tell you some basic facts about vampires. Think of it as an interview of sorts. You, in turn, will amend sections of your book where too many secrets have been revealed. You must add another character...perhaps a love interest for the count..."

Bram stomped his foot in anger, his face beet red. "This is preposterous! How dare you try and tell me how to write my book!"

Dracula rose to his full height, and his eyes took on a malevolent glow; Bram felt his blood run cold. "Let us not forget, Mr. Stoker... this is *my story!*"

"You speak as though you've read it. How do you know you won't like the story as I have told it?" Bram asked, trying to reason with his nocturnal visitor.

"I *have* read it...that is the reason I am here tonight."

"But how can that be…when I haven't finished writing it?" Bram was clearly rattled.

"You completed your novella in 1897…I procured a copy on New Year's Eve, signed by you in 1899."

"What…that's impossible. Are you some sort of time traveler or something?" Bram asked indignantly.

"Mr. Stoker, we are getting off topic. I need some changes to the direction of your story…a vampire must protect his secrets, as I'm sure you understand. By the way, I never sleep in coffins…too stuffy. You can leave that part in your story. Oh, and mirrors…that nonsense about vampires not casting a reflection, an ingenious concept but unfortunately misguided. As a vampire, I have no soul…but cast a reflection using my life force. Actually, all vampires can. So…you can leave that misleading detail in your story, too."

Bram squirmed uncomfortably in his seat, wondering how he could be talking to a vampire about a book he claimed to have read at some date in the future. "You really mean to tell me how to rewrite my story?"

Dracula ignored his comment. "I think we need a beautiful and rich heiress as a love interest for Dracula…she should have beautiful red hair and be quite spoiled in nature. This woman is young and still pure…but she exudes sexuality. Let's give her a name that describes her…something like Olivia, or perhaps Lucinda…," Dracula trailed off.

"You're quite serious then…you're going to force me to edit my novella to your liking?"

"That's the plan," Dracula shot back smugly.

"And if I refuse to do as you ask?"

"Is your wife in good health, Mr. Stoker?" Dracula asked, as his smile disappeared.

"You bastard…don't bring Florence into this!"

"That is entirely up to you."

Bram lowered his head in defeat, shuffling through papers on his desk until he found a blank page. The author wet the tip of his pen and let out a deep sigh of resignation. "I like the name Lucinda…let's call her Lucy for short, shall we?"

"Thank you. Your book will do very well, Mr. Stoker."

Chapter 58 - Jack the Vampire - London - (December 1888)

When his throat was opened up, Jack did not feel any pain. Because his nerve endings were numb from the cold, he transitioned without feeling anything but intense nausea, and then there was nothing. It took a few days for Jack to get his bearings, as he struggled to comprehend the changes in his body and his mind. Twice already, Jack had tried to eat human food only to become violently ill. He still felt hunger, but Dracula explained this feeling would eventually go away. He warned Jack that vampires cannot tolerate human food, with the exception of raw meat or fish. Dracula also explained it was lethal for a vampire to drink from a corpse. The only way to avoid the risk was to stop drinking before the victim's blood turned cold. Jack needed guidance and Dracula grudgingly accepted his responsibility, as a father. Jack felt a weakness in his limbs as they walked toward his favorite neighborhood, to hunt like the predators they were. Tonight, the fledgling vampire would feed alongside the one who made him. His mouth watered at the thought of tearing into human flesh. Jack was still getting used to the taste of human blood, but when it came to killing, he was a natural.

The backstreets of Whitechapel were fairly empty, as they turned onto Farrant Street. The fog was especially thick, and a faint scent of burning opium hung in the air. Dracula could feel Mary's presence everywhere; there was no escape from it. Her face appeared as he gazed up at the night sky where they had once shared a fabulous flight together. Mary's absence cut like a knife; she was dead and beautiful no longer. The streets of Whitechapel had lost their allure for a vampire, whose heart had been broken.

"Do you mind if I ask why you keep coming back to this place?" Jack asked. Two women of the night passed them, and Jack turned his head in appreciation.

"This neighborhood was the first place I visited one random night; since then, I come here...when I chose to hunt human prey."

"But, why Whitechapel? Hell, we could go anywhere...even years from now, where no one knows who we are! A fresh start in a new place *and* a new time!" Jack exclaimed as he adjusted his red spectacles on the bridge of his nose. Dracula covered his face for a moment, as though trying to wipe his sadness away.

Jack decided to focus on the hunt. "So, who do we target?"

"Look up ahead. See that drunken sot up there rounding the corner?"

Jack's eyes were keen and his sense of smell even better. He could smell cheap scotch and it was not appealing. "Not him...how about one of those lovely prostitutes we just passed? Now that...I could really enjoy."

"Very well...I'll wait here," Dracula didn't want to be tempted; his responsibility tonight was to Jack.

"I think I'll go for the blonde." Jack tipped his hat, and stepped into the street.

Dracula hissed at him, "Discretion, please...no souvenirs!"

In the shadows Dracula waited patiently, having already fed on bottled blood. He felt it was important to be well fortified in case Jack got into trouble. Dracula's primary concern was to make sure Jack wasn't seen or detained by police. As he watched Jack disappear into the darkness, Dracula realized that staying around Whitechapel so close to the timing of the Ripper killings was a bad idea. After tonight he would take Jack hunting on the moors, instead of an area where they might be recognized. The piercing scream of a woman, announced Jack had made his first kill. He ran toward the noise to determine whether intervention was needed, then realized there was only one scream. Where was the other woman? Did she run away? Did Jack have them both?

Dracula's questions were answered the moment he caught up to them. Jack stood against a brick wall with a blonde on his right arm, her neck splayed open. Her blue eyes no longer saw anything as she slumped against her killer. In Jack's left arm, he held a brunette with a hand over her mouth to muffle her screams. The young girl's brown eyes darted back and forth, as she tried to understand what was happening. For a moment she almost believed Dracula was coming to her rescue; when he flashed a set of sharp teeth, the girl understood her nightmare was just beginning.

Jack smiled and pushed the frightened girl toward Dracula. "If she is half as sweet as her blonde friend, you are in for a real treat." The girl tried to run, but was instantly restrained by Dracula's gripping hold. He had never killed a woman but right now, he had a more human need.

Jack studied him with a knowing smile. "If you're going to kill her anyway, why not enjoy a ride first."

Dracula's loneliness overcame him, as he dragged the brunette into a corner out of Jack's sight. Pushing her face first against the wall, he ignored her whimpering cries as he fumbled with his clothes, determined to take what he wanted. It took only moments for Dracula to lift her skirts and force himself deep inside her. When Mary's face appeared, his thrusts became more forceful as he tried to dispel the dull ache in his heart. Knowing he couldn't let her go, the ruthless vampire sunk his teeth into her neck and began to literally suck the life out of her. Dracula drank until her blood began to cool, and she collapsed to the ground. He stepped over her corpse and realized he had broken his promise. He had killed a woman. Vlad Dracula felt neither satisfaction, nor remorse. The two vampires left the alley and found their way back to the main street, where gas lamps made the night a little safer. Clothes straightened, they looked like two old friends out for a late night constitution.

"Feel better now?" Jack taunted. Dracula smiled in reply, as his walking stick tapped the ground in measured increments.

"I have to thank you for what you have done," Jack said, taking Dracula by surprise.

"How is that?"

"You actually did me a favor. You turned me into one of your kind... probably saved me from going to prison...and as an added bonus, I get to live forever!"

"I still haven't made up my mind about you, Jack. I made you, and it is my duty to groom you in the ways of our kind, but you'll have to earn my trust."

"Are you my vampire father now?" Jack asked only half-serious.

"I have the ultimate obligation to you...I must teach you about the new powers you possess. As your father, I must defend you with my life, if the occasion demands it. A vampire must have others like him because…ours is a life of loneliness." Dracula tried to explain, that which he did not fully understand himself.

"So, all of you living in this place of mirrors…are like a family?"

"I guess you could say we are a family of sorts. Nikos has been my right hand for centuries of human time. Prince was once royalty… he and his brother were murdered in the fifteenth century. Rory has only been here a short while, but seems a perfect companion for young Prince. Eva, she is a different story altogether…and certainly not who she seems to be." Dracula tried to give Jack a better understanding of the history they shared together.

"I know about Eva. Nikos told me. She was a countess you had a passionate affair with…in the sixteenth century. He claims she returned as a younger version of herself. An interesting story to be sure…" Jack trailed off.

"It is a true story. Eva is a precious flower to be protected," Dracula responded tersely.

"What was she like in bed?" Jack asked, ducking his head to miss the punch Dracula tried to land.

"Don't you ever ask me anything like that again!"

"I just wanted to know how she likes it," Jack continued shamelessly.

Dracula grabbed the collar of Jack's shirt, his face only inches away. "If you go near her, I will lock you in a pit underground, until you shrivel and die from lack of blood! Do you understand?" Dracula released Jack, knocking him to the ground before turning away in disgust.

"Does this mean our hunting lesson is over?"

Chapter 59 - Birth of Adolf Hitler - Braunau Am Inn, Austria - (April 20, 1888)

The Dark One had been restless for a long time now. Waiting for Dracula to fulfill his destiny had been a tedious and frustrating experience at best. The faithful vine spent its days and nights guarding the portal to the Otherworld, spending most of its time in dreamless slumber. Something important was happening; the malignant growth could feel it as the day gave way to night.

"Wake up...something amazing has happened," the Dark One hissed. The vine stretched itself into wakefulness at the sound of its master.

"Another is born this night like the other one...perhaps with a heart more evil than that of our Lord Dracula."

"Who, master...who is born this night that could matter to us?"

"They'll call him, Adolf. I can already feel his presence all around. A budding force that will soon become a storm of epic proportions! This one's heart is black as pitch...his blue eyes, a gateway to evil."

"Do you wish me to go see this infant...to care for and nurture him as I did Count Dracula?" the vine asked hopefully.

"No...nothing like that. Contact must only be made after the colony has been well established beneath the streets of London," the Dark One explained.

"What do you ask of me then, master?"

"Be my eyes and ears, as I work to recruit the whore killer to our ranks. He is still a fledgling but over time...I will mold him into a worthy servant to our cause. It is he who will bring this child into our legions...but that will be many years from now."

"Will the child be as powerful as Lord Dracula?"

"Perhaps, even more."

"How do you know these things, master?"

"Like Dracula, his coming was foretold. The child will be raised to hate all but the most perfect of the human race. He will grow to be a great leader and his course will lead the world into great battles.

During a great war...Hitler will annihilate millions in the name of racial purification, while his devout followers view him as a deity."

"Will he become a vampire, master?"

"Now you are beginning to understand."

Baby Adolf was not thinking about vampires as he lay in his wooden cradle, waiting patiently to be fed. He did not know yet what evil was or that he would become a world leader, responsible for the extermination of six million Jews. This night, he was a helpless child, yet a dark presence had already begun to spread within the very depth of the child's being. The infant had a round face, alabaster complexion and piercing blue eyes that seemed wise beyond their years. His full head of black hair nearly covered his ears and his fingernails were so sharp, he scratched his mother's face the first time she held him. While most newborns cry quite often, this child remained silent, as his beady eyes moved back and forth trying to focus on his surroundings. Apparently, Adolf's vision was nearly perfect already, as he began to document every detail of his world.

His middle-aged aunt and older sister whispered just outside the doorway to his nursery; baby Adolf could hear every word. "I'm not holding him...he was born with teeth!" declared his older sister, Paula.

"A sure sign of the devil," his aunt replied, crossing herself.

"At least you won't have to feed him. I suspect nursing is going to be rather painful," the plump aunt quipped with a loud chortle. Paula looked at the baby one last time and shivered, as a sudden chill made her blood run cold.

Chapter 60 - The Otherworld

Dracula returned to the Otherworld from his night of hunting with Jack; he planned to go directly to his quarters so he could be alone. There was no question about it, the time had come to start their colony, but not within a tired old century. Ideas were old-fashioned and disease still ran rampant throughout London neighborhoods. They needed to go far enough ahead in time for man to have made more advances in transportation, and where old world superstitions wouldn't stand in their way. Dracula was adamant he would establish himself as Romanian royalty; he planned to change his name to Count Vlad Draco. If anyone made the connection to Vlad Dracula, he would insist there was no relation to the infamous character in Bram Stoker's novel. He trusted Nikos to establish a legitimate identity so he could integrate himself into London society. Dracula had warmed to the idea of targeting a more modern time, perhaps even 1936, as Prince suggested due to the coronation of his blood relative, Prince Edward VIII. They all agreed Eva and Prince would be presented as Dracula's niece and nephew; Rory seemed content to be a family friend. They still hadn't made a definitive plan about Jack, since Dracula refused to name him as a family member; such details could be addressed later.

Dracula approached Nikos, Prince and Rory who were studying a detailed map of the London metro system, to determine exactly where abandoned tunnels were located. Rory was working up a diagram of the area they planned to target as their underground refuge. As Dracula watched them, he began to feel optimistic about their future. Eva had just returned from the Metropolitan Museum of Art in New York City. Her face was flushed with excitement as she ran to tell everyone about the Egyptian artifacts she got to hold in her hands.

"Where's Jack?" Nikos asked, looking over his spectacles at his old friend.

"How should I know?" Dracula said more harshly than he intended. Before Nikos could respond, Jack stumbled through the portal, still trying to get used to the flashing light.

The first thing Jack noticed was Eva, dressed in a burgundy velvet dress that hugged her curves. Could this charming woman really be a mere girl of twelve? Jack refused to believe it, as he licked his lips in appreciation. Her breasts were small but he was a leg man anyway. Dracula moved between them, as Jack stepped toward Eva to introduce himself. As always, when a man reacted to Eva's beauty and accepted her for a woman, she was willing to flirt with them shamelessly.

"Since no one will properly introduce me, my name is Jack...aka Jack the Ripper...mysterious killer and the terror of London...at your service," Jack finished with an exaggerated bow.

"I am Eva Bathory, descended from the Hungarian royal family," Eva replied, holding out her hand for Jack to kiss.

Eva jumped up excitedly clasping her hands together. "Let's all go to the finest hotel in all of London and celebrate the new millennium together!"

"You mean skip ahead in time so we can see the twentieth century begin?" Prince asked.

"Can we actually do that...skip ahead right now...all of us?" Rory asked eyes wide with excitement.

Dracula warmed to the idea himself. Anything to get out of Whitechapel. "It appears we are soon headed to a more modern London...so why not say goodbye to the old century first!" Due to Eva's clandestine visit to see the new millennium, Dracula was willing to cast his superstitions aside.

"Can we do it anytime we want?" Prince asked hopefully.

Nikos replied, "Of course we can...just ask Eva. She has already seen the new millennium...from the Windsor Hotel in New York City!"

"Who cares about New York City! Let's all of us dress up and crash a New Year's Eve party, right here in London!" Eva declared.

Everyone had a sparkle in their eyes at the idea of a grand New Year's Eve party. To spend the evening in a brightly colored place with dancing and music would be a vast and welcome change from the solitude of the Otherworld.

"Splendid idea! I am ready for a change of scenery," Jack replied in agreement.

"What party should we attend?" Prince asked.

"Why…the annual bash at the Carlton Hotel, of course," replied Eva, as though the location should have been assumed.

Although looking forward to celebrating with the others, Jack was preoccupied with resolving the ongoing problem with Mr. Stoker. It was up to him to protect Dracula's secrets, so he slipped away quietly when no one was paying attention. Jack would return in time to greet the millennium with his new family, but there was something he needed to take care of first.

Chapter 61 - An Ultimatum for Bram Stoker - London - (October 1897)

Bram put down his pen and rested his tired elbows on the desk. His manuscript was ready for the publisher; he was finished with what he considered a masterpiece. He had an appointment to drop it off at his publisher tomorrow. Due to the time of year, it had already grown dark outside. Bram went to the window and raised the shade as he looked up and down his street, eyes searching for something he couldn't define. He felt uneasy and wouldn't relax until his manuscript was in the hands of his publisher. Putting on his waistcoat, Bram buttoned up in front of a standing mirror, and was startled when he saw a man standing at the entrance to his study. Bram whirled around and was confronted by a tall, thin man, dark hair parted in the middle and eyes as cold as ice.

"You didn't do what my master asked, did you?" Jack asked, moving closer to Stoker.

"I don't know what you're talking about...how *dare you* come into my home uninvited!" Bram exclaimed, trying to hide his terror.

"And the count asked you so nicely, too."

"I wrote *my book* as I saw fit...which is *my* right," Bram replied defensively.

"Mr. Stoker...please call your wife downstairs," Jack commanded.

"What has she got to do with this?"

"Call her, Mr. Stoker," Jack said more harshly, he was losing patience.

"Please don't bring her into this," Bram pleaded.

"I won't ask again...call her now!" Jack repeated, almost shouting now.

"Florence..." Bram called weakly.

Bram's wife was very dutiful and responded right away, joining her husband in the parlor. "Yes, dear...oh, I didn't know you had company," his wife immediately detected the terror in her husband's eyes.

"Mrs. Stoker...Florence, please come with me into the kitchen," Jack said in a calm voice. Bram followed keeping a safe distance.

"Now, Mrs. Stoker, please sit down at the table," Jack said pointing to a round table in the corner. She hesitated for a moment, and then moved to sit down as he asked.

"Mr. Stoker, where do you keep the kitchen knives?" Jack asked.

Bram hung his head and started weeping. Not waiting for an answer, Jack started opening drawers, dumping their contents on the floor in frustration. When he found the knife drawer, he retrieved the largest one he could find. Florence was on the verge of tears, but unwilling to give him the satisfaction of showing her fear.

"Place your left hand on the table, please," Jack commanded in a steely voice.

"Don't do it, Florence!" Bram warned but Florence did as she was told, wiping her sweaty palms on her flowered skirt.

"That's a lovely wedding band you have there," Jack said, lifting her ring finger to inspect it more closely.

"You can take it...go head. Please take it and leave us alone!"

"I could take your ring...but I'm afraid it's not quite enough."

"Lord Jesus, protect us..." Bram prayed with folded hands. Jack raised the knife and Florence closed her eyes, so she wouldn't see her blood spilling all over their kitchen table. Bram screamed, "NO!!!!" as the knife came down hard, but Jack had merely cut into the table inches from her hand. Seeing her chance, Florence pulled her hand away.

"Change the book as you were told or the next time I visit, your wife will be missing more than just a finger!"

"But...I have deadlines, there is no time..." Bram protested.

"Go visit your publisher and buy more time!" Jack shot back, then turned and walked through the front door he had left open.

Once again on the street, Jack smiled smugly and realized that for the first time he could ever remember, he had done something for someone else from which he would not benefit at all. Maybe he was trying to get on Dracula's good side or perhaps, it was an attempt to make up for Mary's death in some small way.

CHAPTER 62 - NEW YEAR'S EVE - HOTEL CARLTON - LONDON - (DECEMBER 31, 1899)

Prince and Rory arrived first, entering the Carlton Hotel through a mirror in an upstairs hallway. Dressed in fashionable clothes, the two easily passed for children of the hotel's wealthy clientele. The clock chimed the nine o'clock hour, as they entered the grand ballroom where the sound of music beckoned them further inside. Crystal chandeliers hung from the ceiling; Rory counted twenty of them in all; never in her lifetime had she seen anything so magnificent. A Viennese waltz played in the background, as couples moved gracefully across a polished wooden floor. Prisms of colored light adorned party guests with a veil of festive splendor, as Prince took Rory's hand and led her to the dance floor.

Dracula and Nikos made their entrance shortly afterward, followed by Eva, who strutted proudly in her emerald green gown, complete with elbow length satin gloves.

"You look lovely tonight, Eva," Nikos said with a genuine smile.

"Thank you. Tonight, I will be a debutant...and you will both be my uncles!" Dracula smiled and kissed her cheek.

"Where is our friend, Jack?" Dracula asked with a raised eyebrow.

"Out hunting, perhaps?" Nikos offered.

"Not like him to miss a party," Dracula said absentmindedly; he had already spotted a striking blonde who appeared to be unescorted.

Nikos was left standing alone as he took in the glorious vision of sequined gowns and men dressed in formal wear, all gathered together to celebrate the passing of another year. Young and old seemed serene and carefree as music enhanced the sense of anticipation in the room; it seemed everyone was happy another year of time had passed. They were another year older and that much closer to the grave, yet, they were still filled with joy. Tonight, more than ever before, Nikos was mystified as to why human beings celebrated the passing of time.

Turning his mind to more serious matters, Nikos recognized they had some important decisions to make about where and when they would settle in London. Prince was pushing for the year 1936, because one of his descendants would be celebrating a coronation he hoped to attend. Through extensive research, Nikos and Prince confirmed that by this time, mankind would advance greatly. Horse-drawn carriages would be replaced by motorcars, and electricity would provide a way to turn the nighttime into day. By 1936, advances in medicine had made the world a much safer place. As a result, people were leading longer, healthier lives. Through careful management of his master's funds, they would be in a position to secure a small estate outside London. The location had to be strategically placed and modified to accommodate a vampire's unique needs. Shuttered windows and security fencing were a must. Guard dogs were also under consideration, and all of this was costly. Fortunately, Nikos had worked discreetly to ensure the vast fortune Dracula had amassed was invested and protected. In order to live within the human world, they would need to establish identities that couldn't be easily challenged. Nikos wasn't worried; the human world was filled with unscrupulous people who could provide the documentation they required. It all came down to money, and they had plenty of that. They also needed to appear human in every way, so, naturally they had to purchase a home and establish themselves within their community. The object was to earn the trust of their neighbors by assuming the role of a dignified European family. Presenting Count Draco as a reclusive art dealer would allow the vampire to maintain a certain distance from the general population. Everything was in place to leave the nineteenth century behind. They all decided that 1936 was as good a choice as any. History books stated this to be settled and peaceful time in London. Wars would surely come, but no one wanted to find out something like that ahead of time. That is, no one except Eva.

Dracula watched as Nikos spun Eva around the dance floor. At times like this, it was difficult to believe she had once been a royal tyrant. Jack was missing in action, but Dracula couldn't have cared less; he had an endless stream of beautiful women to dance with. His current dance partner was a saucy one with generous curves and a long elegant neck. As he admired her ample breasts, Dracula realized a very human need was taking over. He pulled her close and nuzzled her neck. When she did not resist, the vampire knew he had a sure thing. Eva watched them from across the room with a seething fury, determined no one could have her lord, if she could not. She did not mind a woman giving herself to him but she would not allow Dracula to fall in love again. Eva would let him have his fun tonight; if he chose not to kill his human plaything when he was finished, she would take matters into her own hands. As if reading her thoughts, Dracula left the dance floor in search of a more private place.

For Dracula, tonight was all about satisfying his growing lust and saying goodbye to Whitechapel, with all its painful memories. His dance partner's name was Victoria, but he had already forgotten it by the time he took her from behind. Tonight, there would be no romance. He was here to enjoy the carnal pleasures only a woman could provide. The moment the act was done, the vampire was up and dressed again, anxious not to miss the climax of the evening's festivities. Never one to linger after sexual encounters, Dracula quietly left the room.

Victoria dressed and attempted to fix her makeup before returning to the party. She smiled at herself in the mirror, pleased with her reflection. Her face was flushed and her full lips were the color of pomegranates; Victoria had been blessed with natural beauty, and was still naive enough to believe she would stay that way forever.

A young girl's reflection approached the mirror from behind. It was Dracula's niece, but her eyes were full of malice. Hadn't she locked the door? Victoria turned around to meet Eva face to face. Dracula had introduced them earlier in the evening.

"I see you like to dance," Eva said sweetly.

Victoria relaxed a little. "Yes...everyone should dance on New Year's Eve...I'm sure it's a law somewhere."

"I think you like to do other things as well...," Eva said, moving a step closer.

The smile evaporated from Victoria's face, as she backed into a corner of the room. Fear gripped her as her blood ran cold. This was no child; this was a thing of pure evil.

"I think you should leave now," Victoria said, sensing she was in real danger. She reached behind her for a letter opener she'd left on the dresser. Her fingers touched the edge, but Victoria couldn't quite grasp it.

Eva began her ranting. "He belongs to me and only me!" Eva held the knife behind her back; her other hand caressed Victoria's face.

"Yes, of course...he is your uncle," Victoria replied nervously, pushing Eva's hand away as her fingers inched a bit closer to the letter opener.

"He is much more than that. We were once lovers!" Eva growled.

"But...he's your uncle!" Victoria finally got hold of the letter opener and without hesitation, plunged the blade into the girl's shoulder. Eva saw her opportunity and dropped to the floor, her reaction all part of a nefarious plan.

For a fleeting moment, Victoria thought she had beaten her attacker, until the girl suddenly recovered and pounced on her. A scream caught in Victoria's throat as Eva's knife entered her stomach. She doubled over and fell to the floor, eyes wide with surprise. Her screams were stifled as blood spurted from her mouth; Eva continued stabbing Victoria in blind rage. She finally threw down the knife, satisfied the girl was no longer a threat. Checking her wristwatch, Eva shed her blood-soaked dress and hid it under the bed. Frantically, she ran to the closet and pulled a red taffeta gown off the hanger, then fled the room in her undergarments. She had just enough time to change.

In the grand ballroom, the excited crowd grew more boisterous. Champagne bottles were already popping all around them; some revelers just couldn't wait until midnight. Couples were kissing, as free-flowing champagne loosened up everyone's inhibitions. The music died down a bit as preparations for the final countdown to midnight began. Eva spotted Prince and Rory in the crowd, and met them in the middle of the dance floor. Nikos and Dracula arrived minutes later and Eva smiled when they all came together. The only one missing was Jack. Where was he? As if on cue, Jack slipped in through a mirror, just fifteen minutes before the old century gave way to the new millennium. Eva saw him first, as he entered through the double doors; Jack crossed the dance floor and took her hands in his.

"Did you not like the green dress?" Jack asked, but Eva just shrugged without responding.

Nikos and Dracula approached with Prince and Rory close behind. It was less than five minutes to the new millennium. The countdown began, and all that mattered was the celebration of a new century. The modern world waited, and so did the future of an ancient vampire and his legions. On the last night of the nineteenth century, they made a solemn promise to protect each other until the end of time.

Tired of being confined indoors, Eva convinced everyone to meet on the rooftop for one last look at a night she didn't want to end. The cold air was refreshing as, they gazed at the snow-covered rooftops below. Ahead was a time of uncertainty, yet, one full of promise and adventure. London was Dracula's home and had been for a very long time. Surely, traveling ahead just a few decades couldn't make much difference. It was time to leave the nineteenth century and Whitechapel behind.

Dracula raised his glass to the sacred night. "To the fair city of London, we salute the new millennium!"

Eva stepped forward, raising her empty glass. "To the millennium… and the fashion of a new century!"

Nikos shrugged because he had no glass so, Jack took the floor. Stepping onto the chimney stack to elevate himself above the others, Jack raised his glass. "A new century awaits…the new world is ours for the taking!" He smashed his glass against the wall, noting the scowl on Dracula's face.

Dracula assumed his bat-like form, and became instantly airborne. Jack followed suit. Within moments, they were all flying above the breathtaking London skyline.

"Last one back to the Otherworld is a lame duck," Prince taunted, as he held Rory's hand to keep her steady. They flew past a bright white moon; six black dots of no significance. Such was their impact on a soft velvet night that would yield to the dawn of a new generation.

THE MODERN
WORLD

PART II

Chapter 63 - The Dark One

The Dark One had waited with inhuman patience for Dracula to start his colony of undead servants; it was driven to help contaminate the city of London with a species of civilized vampires. The evil entity was fire and ice, its frenzied mind in constant conflict; even for the undead, it was a powerful force to be reckoned with. It scorned the very concept of religion and was repulsed by human frailty. As Satan's spawn, it felt no compassion and could not be reasoned with. The Dark One's only purpose was to ensure Dracula fulfilled his destiny.

The vine stirred as it felt the Dark One's presence; it had become weary of a world behind mirrors. "Evil friend, it is time for you to join your lord and his entourage outside London…a place they call Makefield Manor."

"Master, I am ready to do your bidding." The vine had already begun to untangle itself from the gateway to another realm. The vine dug deep underground in search of a new adventure; like a determined hound dog, the vine followed Dracula's scent and the beating of his dead heart. A surprising hunger for the taste of blood began to gnaw at the vine, as it tunneled a clear pathway with amazing precision.

The Dark One took one last look around the dark timeless place. It would join them in the twentieth century; the evil entity had its own role to play. Someday soon, humans would become slaves to creatures of the night, and would feed them without protest. The ghosts who clung to Dracula now were easy enough to manage; and then there was Eva, who was already well acquainted with the Dark One. The two vampires and the blood countess would prove useful, even if they needed a little convincing now and then. Each was instrumental in the formulation of its master plan; should the evil entity encounter any objections, the Dark One could be very persuasive.

Chapter 64 - An Artist Named Vincent - London Underground - (January - 1936)

When he first woke up in the afterlife, Vincent van Gogh touched his right ear. He took a deep breath when he found it still intact, which was strange, since he cut it off himself with a razor. *All who are maimed in life become whole again.* The artist didn't remember who told him that, but after he died, he got his right ear back. At least it was there when he happened to pass a mirror, which wasn't very often. It took a while, but the artist eventually accepted being a ghost; it was peaceful and quiet which suited him just fine. Vincent closed his eyes as he recalled his last painful days on earth. Fact was Vincent had killed himself, plain and simple. Life had become too much of a burden, and constant rejection of his art, too difficult to take any longer. Barely able to make his rent, Vincent felt himself drowning in a sea of hopelessness. In frail health, the artist struggled with severe depression when summer came early to Arles. Everyone within city limits, suffocated under an oppressive heat wave. By the third week of June, the temperature had been over ninety degrees for ten straight days. Vincent's studio was located above a vegetable market and the unrelenting heat made the nights unbearable. He no longer had a desire to paint into the wee hours of the morning, and the artist feared something had died inside him.

By mid-July, Vincent van Gogh had run out of inspiration, and could see only darkness in the years ahead. His normally rugged face had become haggard and pale; he was only thirty-seven, but Vincent wore the face of a much older man. One rainy night when storm clouds hovered over the town of Arles, Vincent lost his final grip on reality and did the unthinkable. The artist picked up his gun and shot himself. Most historians agree absinthe and poor nutrition likely contributed to his struggles with mental illness. Vincent believed himself completely sane; he'd simply lost his will to live. During his last days on earth, the artist began to believe anything was better than a life without meaning, and he welcomed the sleep of death.

After his demise, Vincent remembered being cold, then falling into a deep sleep. He felt no pain. Maybe this was all there was, a quiet blackness from which one did not awaken. The only problem was, Vincent did wake up and understood at once, this was another life. He felt an ominous presence that made him uneasy and wondered if it was Satan, come to claim his soul. The artist had, after all, committed the ultimate sin by taking his own life. The artist hung his head in resignation, resolved to accept his fate, however difficult this new and strange existence might be. After a period of time, Vincent realized no one was coming to claim his soul; the price of his grave sin was to be left alone for all eternity. A loner by nature, the artist had to admit he could have gotten worse. Literally caught between the living and the dead, Vincent tested his limits and quickly discovered he could move about within the living world. He also realized he could choose his own home of sorts, just about anywhere he wished. People could see him, but no one knew he was a ghost, making it easy to blend in with humans. He had no loyalty to Arles; most of his friends and family had turned against him by the time of his passing, so there was no reason to return. Right now, Vincent craved privacy and a quiet place to resume his painting.

In this new life, Vincent wanted to live in a place with memories, and where he felt accepted. Vincent recalled the happy years he spent in London, painting portraits near Trafalgar Square. In those days, he found plenty of locals willing to pose for him in exchange for a meal. Vincent loved the people of London, and honestly believed he would enjoy going back to the one place that had embraced his work. With surprisingly little effort, the artist found his way to the place he used to paint, only to discover an abandoned tube station that had been closed for more than twenty years. Vincent looked around appreciating the spaciousness, something he never had as an artist in Arles. Desperate to find a place he could call home, Vincent decided to create a makeshift studio underground, where he could continue his work in the afterlife.

After he had been dead a few days, Vincent realized he no longer felt hungry or cold, and this was certainly a pleasant change. Naturally, he would need supplies to set up a studio; because he was a specter, locked doors couldn't keep him out. It was a simple matter to enter business establishments after hours, where he helped himself to the supplies he needed. Vincent eventually made himself at home in London, moving about the streets as he made quick sketches for future reference. The artist made a point of offering genuine smiles to everyone he met. After living in London for over a year, the artist discovered that middle-aged men, who walk with a limp, are often treated with courtesy and respect. The artist's extensive vocabulary and genteel way of speaking also went a long way. No one ever asked where the oddly dressed man lived, and he never spoke unless someone asked him a direct question. Vincent made sure to address police and other officials with a friendly smile, and was careful not to let anyone discover where he lived. And so, Vincent lived in his makeshift studio as the new century dawned and human time continued to pass, with one day running into another. The artist painted furiously year after year in an effort to recreate some of his former works, using only his memory for reference.

The year was now 1936, which he discerned by snagging abandoned newspapers. The actual date didn't matter to Vincent; for ghosts, time was meaningless. Yet, something inside him made the artist want to know how much time had passed since the day of his death. Vincent was stunned to realize he had been living underground for more than forty years and, thus far, he remained undetected. He stared at the canvas in front of him; it was almost finished, but not nearly as good as the one he had painted in Arles. Since coming to this solemn place, the artist stopped painting people altogether, concluding portraits were something he did in his *other* life. In his studio, Vincent sometimes found himself rendering a flower that suddenly evolved into the soft bud of women's lips; whenever this happened, the artist quickly smeared fresh paint across his work, creating a stormy sky he dappled with crows in flight. Black birds had always haunted him, and still did. "The black birds of death," Vincent said to an empty room.

Vincent picked up a brush, plunging it into a mixture of raw sienna and yellow ochre, swirling the paint in tiny circles until it was blended to perfection. Vincent had worked in darkness all his life, so living under Trafalgar Square was a perfect place for a doomed ghost to continue painting. Like most ghosts, Vincent was able to see well in dark places, having a natural illumination by which he could create replicas of lost works, many now hanging in museums. Amsterdam had been his home, but the place Vincent van Gogh found true happiness, was in the heart of London, where he could hear the sound of Big Ben chiming in the distance. London was a city of mystery and dark history, but what Vincent loved most, was the solitude he found within the deepest recesses of the London underground.

Silence was what mattered to Vincent most, as he worked to hone his skills by painting day and night. The artist picked up a wide sable brush, as the sound of footsteps approached the door to his hidden chamber. It was not uncommon for metro workers to pass through the abandoned tube station Vincent called home. As he approached the door, he saw the doorknob turning back and forth, but the lock would not budge. Vincent returned to his canvas, confident the threat of being discovered had passed.

"Good sir, what is this place?" Prince asked from behind him. Vincent spun around to confront a tall man and two children.

"How did you get in here?" Vincent demanded.

"We mean no harm. We are looking for the Kings Cross Station," Rory said boldly.

"Who are you?" Vincent asked.

"My name is Rory Revere," she said, holding out her hand.

Vincent took her hand, but did not let go. "And why do you barge in on me at my place of residence?"

Jack stepped forward wearing his black top hat, and bowed politely. "My name is Jack Druitt. Forgive me for asking, but how can an abandoned metro station be your home?"

"This place doesn't exist, according to modern maps...so I have claimed it for my own."

"Are you a homeless person?" Prince asked.

"No more so than during my human lifetime," Vincent said with a sigh, leaving more unanswered questions.

"Are you trying to tell us you're a ghost?" Jack asked with a doubtful look.

"I could say the same of you, who penetrated my chamber through a locked door."

"Touché, good sir...you are correct...none of us are human. So, what are you?" Jack inquired once more.

"I don't know. All I know is that I moved from a life of suffering, to one of peace and quiet. I no longer eat or need to sleep...all I do is paint here in solitude...it suits me just fine." Vincent returned to his work, trying to ignore them.

Prince glanced around the room in awe at the volume of canvases strewn about. They hung on the walls or were stacked knee deep in corners, all breathtaking and full of vivid color.

"How do you get your paints and brushes?" Prince asked, as he inspected the sunflower painting more closely.

Vincent ignored this question and responded, "Kings Cross is two stations left of this one...going northwest. This place was once the old Trafalgar Square Station."

"I know these paintings!" Prince exclaimed when it finally clicked.

Rory looked more closely at a large canvas of wheat fields and a hectic blue sky. She was looking for a signature, but there was none. No signatures on any of his works, yet they were so familiar.

"You're Vincent van Gogh!" Prince declared.

"Posh, my boy...I most certainly am not!" Vincent declared, now painting more furiously.

"Yes...yes you are! It all makes sense now. You killed yourself in 1890...I've read about you in history books. Wait, why isn't your ear missing?" Prince continued to insist this man was indeed the famous artist. Vincent put a hand to his right ear, and began laughing hysterically.

"Why is he laughing?" Rory asked a bit confused.

Vincent finally recovered and dropped his brush into a paint-laden palette. "Go on now, little ghosts. I am a busy man with lots to do." Jack didn't even know who Vincent van Gogh was, and frankly didn't care. They had the information they needed, so it was time to go. Jack and Rory passed through the door first, but Rory lingered for a moment watching the red-haired man swirl colors on his palette.

"Go on now, little bird...fly, fly away..." Vincent said, flapping his arms at the air.

Chapter 65 - Makefield Manor - London - (April 1936)

Makefield Manor was one of the finest country houses London had to offer; it was conveniently located just outside Central London. With a few modifications, it would be accessible to the metro system through a carefully designed underground escape tunnel. The modest manor had been designed and built by a distinguished architect, Captain Francis Fowke, who was certain the grand structure would become a historic landmark in the years to come. Unfortunately, his untimely death meant the captain's investment never really paid off, and as luck would have it, the home became available. Without hesitation, Count Vlad Draco's generous offer of cash was immediately accepted. The manor was constructed of brick and sandstone, providing impenetrable, maintenance-free security. The house was grand, yet not too overstated. It was elegant and secure; a physical living space where they could congregate. With funds from his estate, Makefield Manor would provide Dracula with all the comforts of home, something he had not experienced for a very long time. The human world was a place where years passed quickly, people got old and eventually died. There was no escape from it, the human curse of aging; their decision to settle in a world of time would make it impossible to ignore this reality.

Nikos warned they would need to stay on the fringes of society; Londoners were an inquisitive lot, and might wonder why the European count and his family appeared to age very slowly. Because of this, Dracula planned to conduct most of his affairs through written correspondence organized by his loyal solicitor, Nikos Fabri. Dracula inspected every window to confirm they were shuttered and bolted behind the heavy brocade curtains. He climbed the stairs to inspect the second floor, as they continued discussing future plans.

"The additional tunnel you requested will be finished before the beginning of May, so we're right on schedule." Nikos explained, following Dracula up to the second floor.

A hidden passage to the metro guaranteed a foolproof escape from the manor. Using a map Eva pilfered from the library, Dracula studied an intricate maze of underground tunnels. A few ran parallel with the metro system and would be easy to access. Nikos hired two men to dig a narrow tunnel from Trafalgar Station to the back entrance of Makefield Manor. Dracula agreed with the plan, but insisted the workers were a liability; Jack stepped up and agreed to make them *disappear,* but he planned to drain them first.

Dracula focused on the details of his ornately furnished bedroom. Everything he requested, including imported fabrics for draperies and bedding; Nikos had done an excellent job. Dracula moved to a window that had been opened to the moonlight. For the first time, the lights of London in the twentieth century shined more brightly, than the stars above.

"This window should never be left open," Dracula said tersely.

"Sorry, I overlooked it, Vlad," Nikos replied, but Dracula had already left the room.

Finding his lord pacing by the front door, Nikos took one last look around confident the house had been properly armed against intrusion. Nikos retrieved a brown envelope from the table and handed it to Dracula. "I have procured identities for all of us, including Eva and Prince. I thought it best to use his given name, Edward."

"And Jack?" Dracula asked opening the envelope.

"There's one in there for him. I used, Jack Druitt. He's got a wild streak, though…I expect we won't see him much."

Dracula suddenly thought of something. "And, what about clothes for everyone? I mean…items that were purchased recently… not ten years ago."

"The best your money could buy, Vlad," Nikos replied with a hint of sarcasm.

"And what about our blood supply…that is all in order, I assume?" Dracula inquired, nearly forgetting this very important detail.

"Safely stored in the wine cellar…at least sixth month's worth. The cool temperatures of the cellar make it unnecessary to have ice delivered. We can't risk the prying eyes of curious delivery men." As usual, Nikos thought of everything.

"Very good then," Dracula responded, satisfied the house was nearly ready for occupancy. Nikos locked the carved oak door and they stepped out into the cool April evening. The two followed the stone walkway together in silence, until they reached the front gate.

When they reached the sidewalk, Dracula stopped for a moment. "Listen, Nikos…what do you hear?"

"What is it, Vlad?"

"The sound of horses in the street…it's completely gone. Nothing but a memory now." Dracula seemed disappointed.

Nikos sniffed the air. "Can't say I miss the smell of their manure."

"Not sure I care for the smell of petrol any better," Dracula replied weakly; the vampire needed to feed. Nikos watched in silence as the count assumed his rodent form and flew into the night.

As he walked in the cool night air, Nikos marveled at the dramatic evolution of architecture in a city that had changed greatly in a relatively short period of time. He was continually amazed at the many advances of mankind. There were cars and buses to take people from one place to another; London was a city in constant motion. Gone were the gas lit streets of Victorian London; here electric streetlights illuminated every corner. As Dracula had observed, horses were no longer used for transportation. In the twentieth century, horses and beasts of burden were mostly found in the countryside or on farms. Nikos admired the shiny red car up ahead; his lord required an automobile for appearances, so he took the liberty of picking one out. Nikos had settled on a brand new Packard, and he intended to be Dracula's chauffeur.

Chapter 66 - A Frightening Premonition - Clock Tower of Big Ben - (May 28, 1936)

Jack circled the huge clock in his human form, as the bell rang in the eleven o'clock hour. Eva flew close behind him, savoring the rush of wind blowing through her hair. At times like this, Eva didn't mind being a ghost at all. Jack lowered his arms as he prepared to land on the clock tower's roof, signaling Eva to do the same.

"The Thames is glowing tonight...more beautiful than any sunrise," Jack observed. They sat together legs dangling from the rooftop.

"So much beauty in the world and so many who want to destroy it," Eva replied.

"What's on your mind...you seem worried?"

"What makes you think that?" Eva asked.

"It's written all over your face."

"The future holds no guarantees...there's always a chance of..." Eva trailed off.

"Bad things are bound to happen," Jack said abruptly. "You know something, don't you?"

"Jack...please don't ask me to reveal something you'll regret knowing."

"Been poking around in the future again, huh?"

"Please spare me the lecture. I've heard it all before. It's dangerous to go too far ahead in time...too many risks and all that."

"Dracula is a superstitious man...he fears the consequences of carelessly skipping through time."

"I know...I know...I could become trapped and be lost forever. I've heard the warnings enough times believe me," Eva argued.

"Come on, Eva...tell me about the future," Jack was becoming impatient.

"Jack...please don't ask..." Eva closed her eyes, trying not to see the flames behind them.

"Eva, look at me," Jack said gently, turning her head toward his.

Eva's face took on a haunted look as she gazed into Jack's hungry eyes. He is a vampire so he can see what I see, Eva thought; she would let her visions reveal the truth. Jack watched as her eyes turned black as pitch. A feeling of intense heat came between them, followed by Eva's vision; a wall of fire consuming London Bridge and Westminster Abbey. Eva finally pulled away from Jack covering her eyes, but the horrifying vision lingered.

"Eva...what did I see?"

"War, Jack...war is coming to London and it won't be pretty."

"When? Where?"

"I went ahead in time just to see if anything significant had changed...and now, I wish I hadn't."

"How can you be so sure?"

"You should read the papers once in awhile, Jack...things are already brewing."

"Quit stalling for time. What did you see?" Jack grabbed her by the shoulders.

"All right, a few nights ago I came here...but, in the year 1943... London was burning, Jack. Fires were everywhere and I became so frightened...I left and decided to keep the discovery to myself."

"Maybe the fire started some other way..."

"War *is* coming, Jack. I can feel an evil presence working its way into the very heart of London."

"Wars are inevitable...but we don't have to worry..." Jack trailed off.

"Always worried about your own skin, right," Eva teased and he couldn't deny it.

"Don't worry so much...the manor house can withstand anything." Jack stood up to brush off the seat of his pants.

"Leaving already?" Eva asked.

"Yes, my dear...I have a pressing need that you cannot satisfy."

Jack was airborne in moments, and Eva watched him disappear into a night that had become suddenly still. She felt a wave of nausea as the night sky transformed into a wall of fire; in her vision, Eva heard people screaming as the city of London burned to the ground.

Chapter 67 - Coronation of Edward VIII - Westminster Abbey - (May 29, 1936)

Prince Edward studied himself in the mirror as he dressed for the special event. Chronologically, he was twelve years old; this fact was difficult to reconcile when he gazed into the face of a man-child. Prince looked at his hands, still smooth and childlike; when he rubbed his chin, there was only a downy layer of facial hair. Sadly, his reflection would never change. Though humans believed, never growing old was a good thing, he knew better. Looking like a child often meant being treated like a child. Prince straightened his tie and stood back to get a better look; he was pleased, except that his hair was terribly out of style. Unable to change the length, his only recourse was to wet it down and tie it back in a pigtail. The style looked good on Dracula, so it should work for him. Behind him stood Rory, dressed in modern clothes for the first time ever. She was a vision of loveliness, delicately laced with apprehension. They stood in front of the mirror that would take them to Westminster Abbey in the year 1936.

"You truly look like a crowned prince now!" Rory declared.

"And you, look like a princess," Prince replied. "We'll go ahead of the others."

"Won't we be a little early?" Rory asked.

"There's something I need to do." Colored lights flashed, and deposited them in one of the most historical places in England, Westminster Abbey.

"How do we know what year it is?" Rory asked, taking in the magnificence of stained glass windows more beautiful than anything she had ever seen.

"Listen to the crowd below! You can hear people already gathering for the big event. This is it! Our new life begins this day in 1936." Prince took her hand to lead the way.

Prince and Rory made their way through elaborately decorated hallways, as memories of his childhood came flooding back. Both a church and a fortress, this historic landmark had protected many royal families, often providing sanctuary during times of conflict. It had been centuries since Prince had been inside the place where he himself once lived. The outside had notably changed, due to modernization and because of a devastating fire in 1834.

Footsteps echoed and were headed their way. "Come with me…we need to find the back stairwell. I'm certain we aren't supposed to be in this part of the abbey." Prince pulled her into a dark corner, allowing two security guards to pass.

"Where exactly are we going?" Rory whispered.

"My brother is buried in this place…my bones are too."

Rory understood now; Prince wished to visit his final resting place. Surprisingly, the stairway Prince sought was still there; when they reached the top step, he heard his younger brother counting out loud for a game of hide-and-seek. When they reached Henry VII's Chapel, Prince knew they had found the right place. Before long he located what he was looking for; Rory felt a shiver run down her spine, as she read what was written, wondering what it must be like to visit the site of your own burial.

"Edward…," a voice whispered. Rory turned with a start and came face to face with the ghost of Edward's brother. It could be no one else; his sea blue eyes penetrated her very soul.

"My name is Prince. Edward is dead!" Prince snapped, turning away from his brother's spirit. Guiding Rory away from a place with too many memories, they moved toward the great hall where a growing crowd gathered.

They moved swiftly past marble statues of former kings and queens. Try as she might, Rory was unable to ignore the mournful wailing of wandering ghosts that echoed in her ears; she knew Prince heard them too.

"I wonder where Jack is," Prince commented, as they reached the main chapel.

"Maybe he hates churches or…maybe he's insulted he wasn't invited to ride with *Uncle* Vlad," Rory replied with a chuckle.

"Oh, yes…Uncle Vlad and Cousin Eva…they must make their grand entrance tonight. Nikos will be driving that slick new Packard…I wonder when he found time to teach himself to drive," Prince said with a snicker.

Preparing to make the short drive to Westminster, Nikos was grateful he had procured official passes ahead of time. The last thing they needed was a problem on the night they all planned to make their London debut. Tonight's celebration was a golden opportunity for Count Draco to be introduced into London society; it was crucial that everyone played their part to perfection. Nikos looked at his pocket watch; it was time to put on his chauffeur hat so his lord could arrive in style. Eva was thrilled to play the wealthy niece of the eccentric count; naturally, she wore the most inappropriate dress she could find. Seated in the sleek red Packard, Eva felt like a princess as she spread her velvet dress across the upholstered seat.

Dracula glared disapprovingly at her plunging neckline. "You are supposed to be thirteen years old, Eva," he hissed.

Eva ignored his comment. "Prince and Rory...have they gone ahead?"

"Yes, Prince wanted to visit the chapel first."

"And, Jack?" Eva asked raising an eyebrow.

"Hunting I expect, but who knows?"

The coronation concluded yet, still no sign of Jack. Dracula was irritated but not surprised; Jack seldom arrived on time for anything. As the vampire waited for the others on the stone steps, he welcomed the night air, glad to be outside the confines of a church. Dracula began to feel his strength return and with it, a burning hunger; he would need to feed soon. He was about to leave for the moors, when Jack came running up the steps wearing a rumpled jacket and a limp necktie.

"I'm sorry...I ran into traffic," Jack said breathlessly as he reached the top step. Dracula responded with a nasty scowl. Next to Jack stood a scrawny pale-faced teenager, with hard blue eyes and a cocky smile.

"And who the hell are you?" Dracula asked fixing his eyes on Jack's new friend.

"I'm Jericho," he responded, as if that explained everything.

Chapter 68 - Jericho - Whitechapel, London - (May 28, 1936)

Jericho was not even his real name. He hadn't answered to the name, Michael, since he was a toddler. The boy had been on the streets since the age of thirteen, and was used to fending for himself. He never knew his father; this fact made him become obsessed with every possible candidate. From the time he was old enough to wonder who his father might be; Jericho had already tried on a hundred fathers. Their images floated in his dreams, faces with bright smiles and kind eyes filled with joy when they were reunited. Daylight came and with it, the nameless faces he could call father. Days turned into years, yet Jericho was no closer to discovering who his father was. Even when he finally gave up the search, Jericho still sought the love he had been denied. Without making a conscious decision, Jericho had taken his pain and turned it into a sustainable living. He was a handsome boy, and used his looks to charm his way through life; both men and women responded equally to his beauty and unique sexual aura.

Jericho had been a beautiful child; his jet black hair and alabaster complexion affected a startling reaction from people everywhere he went. As he grew older, Jericho noticed men were drawn to him, and soon realized this could be used to his advantage. When he was old enough to embrace his sexuality, Jericho found solace in the company of wealthy men who became substitute fathers, at least for one night. Who knew London was full of men who would happily pay good money for sex? How could making a living get any easier? Jericho didn't think about the future. He didn't have to. He was seventeen, with a body and face people craved. Despite having been with a few women, Jericho found he preferred the company of men. London gentlemen with means were usually willing to make sure Jericho had a hearty meal before being serviced; on occasion, he was even offered a comfortable bed for the night. Not bad for a homeless person. The boy's humble dwelling was an abandoned storage facility beneath London Bridge; it had once been used to stash excess salt and gravel. It was not much, but it provided shelter and a place to keep the few belongings Jericho owned. A clever boy, he spent most nights in the heart of London, mostly high-end neighborhoods, but Jericho loved slumming. It was not uncommon for him to frequent Whitechapel, the place where he was born. The neighborhood had been made famous when a gruesome murder spree horrified London citizens during the late 1880s. All the victims were prostitutes and the killer never apprehended; this fact fueled a continued interest in the elusive killer known as Jack the Ripper. Jericho was convinced there was no neighborhood with a more sinister past. The grizzly murders credited to Jack the Ripper changed London history forever, and turned Whitechapel into a rather morbid tourist attraction. Jericho also felt a connection to the place where his parents fell in love; Whitechapel had history and held an allure that kept him coming back for more.

On the very same night, Jack found himself restless and bursting with energy as his natural hunger grew. The blood-starved vampire gave in to his craving, taking on his bat-like form as he flew toward a neighborhood he knew well. What would Whitechapel look like today? How much did his maniacal crime spree affect the future of his old stomping ground? Would local residents even be talking about the Ripper murders anymore? It had been nearly fifty years of human time since then. It didn't matter, Whitechapel had been his home for a very long time, and he felt like going back. Jack reasoned a quick visit could do no harm; there was certainly no chance of being recognized so far into the future. Jack became airborne and headed toward the familiar streets of his checkered past, determined he answered to no one.

Reaching his chosen destination, Jack gracefully slid into his human form, and perused the streets of his former hunting ground. It was definitely cleaner than he remembered, likely due to the elimination of horse carriages. The second thing he noticed was the smell, or lack of it. Gone was the pungent odor of horse droppings and garbage in the streets; to someone with an acute sense of smell, this was a tremendous improvement. Walking up Dorset Street, memories came flooding back of a murderous rage and the trail of bloody corpses he often left unrecognizable. Jack averted his eyes and abruptly changed direction, nearly bumping into a young man who was leaning against an ivy-covered wall.

"Got a light, guv?" asked the stranger, stepping into the amber glow of a streetlight. Jack took one look at Jericho's chiseled face, and his dead heart quickened.

With a sweep of his wrist, Jack offered a light; the flame flickered on the boy's perfect face. He had high cheekbones and a forced smile; it was clear the boy worked to keep his true self hidden. Perhaps the most arresting thing about this boy was his startling blue eyes. He had the pale skin of someone who spends a lot of time indoors, and perhaps on their knees. Without even trying, this boy held a promise of raw sexuality, and Jack found himself drawn to it like a drug. Surely, someone like him made his living on the streets, selling what God had given him.

"Name's Jericho," the boy said, with the guarded voice of someone who trusts no one.

"M. J. Druitt…but everyone calls me Jack," He replied, trying not to smile too wide, lest his teeth be revealed.

"Don't live around here anymore …just like to visit now and then," Jericho replied. He inhaled deeply, letting smoke snake out the side of his mouth.

"I used to live here a long time ago, myself."

"My mother lived a few blocks away, until she passed away. They were going to send me to an orphanage somewhere in Oxford, so I left home. I was thirteen…and been on the street ever since. Not meant to be a sob story…just my story."

"How old are you?"

"Seventeen…had a birthday last month."

"How old are *you*?" Jericho asked with growing ease. This man was well-dressed and seemed quite harmless. Maybe this would turn out to be a good night after all.

"Older than I look," Jack replied; telling the truth was not an option, at least not yet.

"Perhaps…but I think you are a man of many secrets," the boy replied, as he stroked the fabric of Jack's cape.

"What kind of a name is Jericho, anyway?" Jack asked, generally curious.

"My mother's nickname for me…since I was very young. Apparently there was some famous battle or something…I don't know, but the name stuck," Jericho explained; the boy took one last drag on his cigarette, before flicking it away.

"It suits you," Jack replied, touching the boy's cheek as he gazed into eyes he could get lost in.

"What are you doing here tonight?" Jericho asked, tired of small talk.

"Actually, I like to visit the site of the Ripper murders," Jack said. He was already dying to taste the boy's sweet blood.

"And what could something that happened that long ago mean to you?" Jericho asked.

"Let's say I knew the victims…every one of them."

Jericho was temporarily taken aback, unsure what he meant. "But… how is that possible…I mean…it happened almost fifty years ago."

Jack's ears thundered like a freight train, as he tried to control his hunger. He needed to feed, he wanted to taste this beautiful boy and he wanted to possess him for all eternity. It was time for him to make a vampire of his own! It would be so perfect; he would have his own companion, someone he could take under his wing and travel through time with. This boy was so young and fresh, everything Jack could never be. Losing all composure, Jack prepared to take what he wanted. Sensing danger, Jericho backed away, but Jack pinned him against the wall. He nuzzled the boy's neck, savoring his unique scent and felt him start to relax. Jack understood now; the boy thought Jack just wanted to have sex with him. He actually did, but a more pressing need gnawed at his gut.

"I'm afraid I want more than that tonight. You see…I'm Jack!" His voice broke off, as he plunged his teeth into Jericho's neck. The boy yelped and tried to pull away, but quickly understood he was no match for the well-muscled stranger; he let his body go limp, leaning into the man he believed would be his killer. Oddly, there was little pain, but he could feel his body heat being drained out of him. Jericho was suddenly weary of servicing wrinkled old men, and of London's brutal winters. If he had to die tonight, then let it happen on the streets of his old neighborhood. These were Jericho's last thoughts before everything went black.

When he awoke, Jericho had the distinct taste of copper in his mouth; his lips were dry as parchment. At first, he thought he was dreaming, but then he remembered being attacked in Whitechapel. He was in a dark place and could feel soft bedding beneath him; the room had no windows so he couldn't make anything out. Jericho understood the risks associated with his lifestyle; however, nothing prepared him for someone like Jack. If he was being held prisoner, he could feel no restraints. As he lay in the darkness, Jericho began to recall details about the strange gentleman with a black cape.

"Wake up, boy," Jack hissed.

Jericho tried to determine where the voice was coming from and whether or not he was in any danger. "Is this a dream?"

Jack paused for a moment then responded, "Vampires don't dream boy...this is more like a nightmare."

"Am I dead?"

"No...you are undead," Jack replied, and then he turned on the light. The boy lay on the bed, still covered with a combination of Jack's blood and his own. His eyes were fearful, but still held the cockiness Jack found so attractive.

"What is this place?" Jericho asked, sitting up to take in his surroundings. The room was well furnished so he had been right; this was a man with means.

"Not important right now. Do you know what you are?" Jack asked with a cunning smile.

"Of course...a homeless boy...but I'm still alive...right?" Jericho struggled to understand his circumstances.

"Let's say this is a different kind of life...a place where no one can hurt you...and almost anything you wish can be yours for the asking." Jack chose his words carefully; he didn't want to frighten his fledgling vampire.

"This place is a lot nicer than where I live now." He looked down at his blood covered clothes in dismay. "Why am I covered in blood?"

"As I already explained, you are undead...like me. If I need to spell it out…you are a creature of the night." Jericho grabbed his neck as his memory returned; despite the amount of blood on his clothing, he had no wound.

Jack handed the boy a wine glass, without explaining it was fresh blood pilfered from Dracula's wine cellar. At first, the boy pushed the glass away, until the smell of copper assaulted him; his burning need took over as he gulped down its contents then wiped his mouth with the back of his hand. So much for any hesitation about drinking blood, Jack thought.

"I always thought vampires were the stuff of legends."

"Come on now, we have much to do…let's get you cleaned up. You'll find a change of clothes on the chair behind you."

"Where are we going?" Jericho asked.

"A coronation ceremony," Jack replied, as he began removing the boy's soiled clothing.

"We're going to Westminster Abbey? I didn't think vampires could enter churches."

"Falsehoods like these are common…but misguided. You will soon learn what your limitations are."

Jericho stood unashamed with his back to Jack, using a wash basin to clean the blood from his face and hands. His body was sheer perfection, as only the young are; the seasoned vampire craved his touch as he watched the boy clean himself. Unable to restrain himself any longer, Jack approached the boy from behind, putting his hands on Jericho's slim shoulders.

"Do we have time?" Jericho asked, turning around to face Jack with a provocative smile.

"What did you have in mind?"

"I only want to thank you for taking such good care of me," Jericho replied, as he began to unbutton Jack's shirt. Jack's immediate response was to drop his trousers to the floor.

Chapter 69 - An Ultimatum - Makefield Manor - (June 1936)

The wine cellar at Makefield Manor was where Dracula felt most comfortable, close as it was to an ample supply of human blood he attended much like a collection of fine wines. Windowless with only one secure entrance, the room provided a safe place to congregate even during daylight hours. Living in such close quarters with humans, it would be important to feed with extreme discretion. Killing every night would become impractical; there were only so many criminals and homeless people, even in a large city like London. The room was composed of whitewashed brick which gave the room an inviting soft glow. Gaslights were strewn about the room in favor of electric lighting; Dracula insisted the original lamps be preserved as tribute to a bygone era. Nikos had taken a few overstuffed chairs from the upstairs parlor, so they had a comfortable place to gather. The previous owner had left an oversized table and chairs from the eighteenth century; this served as a place to lay out maps and documents that would help them navigate modern London. A large map of London's metro system hung on the wall; colored pins marked the area surrounding Trafalgar Square.

Prince and Eva spent a great deal of time perusing libraries; they pilfered books with the expertise of a cat burglar. Lately, they had become obsessed with gathering various editions of Bram Stoker's Dracula novel, along with newspapers and copious volumes on vampire and werewolf folklore. Nikos enjoyed reading through them, always looking for a new piece of information. Eva had also obtained half a dozen books on Jack the Ripper; she knew Jack would enjoy them.

Nikos was engrossed in a leather bound first edition of Bram Stoker's novel. "You know, Vlad… this Renfield character is fascinating. He's declared insane and locked up like an animal…but still remains loyal to the count."

"Yes, a rather pathetic villain don't you think? And the bug eating… who came up with that story line?" Dracula replied distractedly.

"No matter…thank goodness I am nothing like that fellow," Nikos responded with a chuckle; he laid his book down, sensing Dracula had something on his mind.

Dracula stood up, pacing back and forth as he pondered what to do about Jack and his unpredictable behavior. "That son of a bitch does whatever he wants...never thinking about the consequences!" Dracula spat his words as he poured a glass of his reserve.

"Jack's spontaneous decision to make a vampire...was certainly ill-advised."

"Ill-advised...now *that* is an understatement!"

"Vlad...he is still adjusting to life as a vampire. Surely, we can embrace this new boy and guide him in the right direction." Nikos tried to remain neutral.

"That boy is a liability, more so because Jack cares for him!"

Nikos countered, "Is it such a bad thing for Jack to have a companion...someone he has to protect and fight for?"

Dracula smashed his wine glass to the floor, spinning around to face Nikos. "Jack only cares about Jack!" Nikos rushed to get him another wine glass; he wasn't surprised to learn Jack was gay.

"I've always suspected Jack preferred men...I just don't think he knew it. A man like that must have an utter loathing for women...it explains why he kills with such savagery," Dracula mused, as he sipped from a new glass.

"I do not understand men who have disdain for the fairer sex. From what I can recall...the touch of a woman was one of life's great pleasures."

"Well, we have no idea where he is now. Probably running through the streets of London declaring his love for a derelict teenager, who has no idea what he's gotten himself into," Dracula paused to drain his glass. "Jack needs to understand that making a vampire comes with a certain amount of responsibility!"

"I don't think Jack understands what he has become yet...how can we expect him to teach another?"

"All the more reason to track them down as soon as we can," Dracula was concerned about more spontaneous vampires being made.

"And what if Jack wants to live his own way and by his own rules?" Nikos challenged.

"He made a promise to all of us, damn it!"

Chapter 70 - A Partnership of Evil - London - (August 1936)

The Dark One's hiss sliced the night, stopping Jack in his tracks as he headed toward the white lights of London Bridge. Scraping the gravel with his foot, Jack turned and ducked behind an iron fence.

"Do not fear me...I know what you are and embrace your wickedness."

"Come out and show yourself! I don't negotiate with someone I can't see," Jack replied, his eyes darting about nervously.

"You do not need to see me in order for us to converse."

It was very late and Jack was alone, in a less than ideal part of town. "I generally like to look my opponent in the eye," he countered.

A sinister laugh pierced the night. "I never look anyone in the eye... but don't worry. We are on the same side."

"What do you want from me, then? I'm searching for a friend and the night is waning fast."

"The young girl...Eva, perhaps?" The Dark One was toying with Jack; he knew exactly where he was going.

"How do you know Eva?"

"Eva and I are well acquainted. We have a rather long history together. I knew her as a woman...on her deathbed I granted Countess Bathory's wish to be young again."

"You've got my attention...go on."

"I came to talk about something entirely different, Jack. For some time now, I have been watching a prodigy to evil...he is an enemy to England and appointed guardian of the Aryan race. Surely, you have heard of him...Adolf Hitler, Germany's dark prince."

"I know who he is, but what does a malicious dictator have to do with me?"

"Why, it's quite simple...this man should become a creature of the night. A heart and mind so innately evil should be preserved for all of time. Don't you agree?"

"The man sounds like a lunatic...besides, Dracula and I can pick our own recruits!"

"You fool! Dracula may have granted you eternal life...but I can take it away!" The Dark One's voice thundered.

"How do you know who I am?" Jack asked meekly.

"I know everything about you, Jack...and now, you are a creature of the night. Every choice has a consequence."

"I did not choose this life...it chose me."

"And here you are...a creature of the night with the gift of eternal life. Did you really believe this came without responsibilities?"

Jack thought it best to go along. "Okay, let me get this straight. You want me to entice Germany's dictator, Adolf Hitler to embrace vampirism. I assume you want *me* to turn him?"

"Yes! But...Hitler is a complex and formidable man...the best approach is to stroke his giant ego. Once you gain his trust, you can explain the perks of what we offer." The Dark One laid out his plan, as though it were a simple task to recruit a world leader to redirect his entire system of beliefs.

"You have a lot of confidence in me."

"I've watched you for many years, Jack; as a man and a vampire. Evil like yours is delicious to observe. What I've truly enjoyed is watching you execute murder with the precision of a surgeon."

"I try..." Jack was at a loss for words, as the Dark One continued.

"You know what I enjoy the most, Jack? The blackness of your eyes...when you're hacking your victims to pieces."

"Never mind that...let's talk more about what I have to do." Jack glanced nervously at his pocket watch; the moon was already sitting lower in the sky.

"Flattery first...then intimidation, Jack. The man will respond to nothing else. I believe you can earn Hitler's trust...but you must utilize your special talents. His two weaknesses are fear of losing control and physical pain. What makes him such a viable candidate is his military acumen. Unfortunately, his fear of capture will make him consider a cowardly act...when it becomes evident Germany will lose the war."

"How do you know so much about the future...how could anyone know the outcome of a war that hasn't even started yet?" Jack didn't know what to make of this nefarious presence. Could this all be true? Was England really going to war with Germany?

The Dark One ignored his question and continued, "*Your* assignment is to prevent Adolf Hitler from shooting himself! As a vampire, his inherently evil nature will finally have a chance to shine."

"So, when am I supposed to approach him?"

"There is time yet. A great war is coming first and it must play out. Hitler will only agree to your offer when he's backed into a corner."

"And you're sure about all this?" Jack asked.

"Mark my words, Jack. Germany will surrender and Hitler will take his own life...*unless* he's turned before that happens."

"I'll need a discreet way to penetrate his camp...a mirror, perhaps." Jack was already working things out in his mind; he knew he faced a great challenge.

As if reading his mind, the Dark One hissed, "A piece of cake for you, Jack."

"If what you say is true...and Hitler plans to kill himself; why not take a glimpse ahead to find proof... a newspaper clipping or death announcement...something like that."

"Not on your first visit, Jack. It's never a good idea to play all your cards at once."

"Too bad we can't turn him now...and save London a lot of grief."

"Hitler's war is necessary to our cause! War feeds the darkness of the human spirit, Jack. Its bittersweet melody brings out the worst in human nature...and feeds the souls of all who are lost to heaven. Someday soon, German bombs will fill the skies and silence the playful laughter of children in the street. How I long to hear their mournful cries, Jack."

"How can you be so cavalier?"

"Don't be a sentimental fool! Human beings are expendable. As a vampire, you and your kind cannot be easily killed...let's focus on the task at hand."

"Ah-h-h yes, building Dracula's legions," Jack replied with undisguised sarcasm.

"There is something festering between you."

"Dracula likes to hold onto grudges...and I'm getting tired of trying to please him."

"I have been with the one who made you, since the day he was born...I know more about him than anyone else."

"Like what...tell me something I don't know," Jack challenged.

"I happen to know Dracula's grudge against you is based on a falsehood..."

"What kind of falsehood?" Jack demanded truly baffled.

"The red-haired woman...Mary Kelly"

"What about her?"

"Dracula thinks you killed her...but I know you didn't."

"Her death is the reason he'll never trust me."

"Is it trust you seek...or Dracula's approval?"

"His approval doesn't matter to me at all," Jack lied.

"It's quite evident your relationship is strained."

"Yeah, so what...I don't get along with most people."

"Don't you believe things would improve, if you were able to recruit a strong and valiant candidate? The Fuhrer has been in military service for most of his life...his experience would be invaluable as your numbers grow."

"Maybe you're right..." Jack trailed off. He had never considered this.

"When the time comes...you must bring the Fuhrer to London... but, not as a man, Jack. You must make him a vampire."

Jack became angry. Who was this malevolent presence, anyway? What if he refused to do as he was asked? "And...what if I go to Dracula instead...and let him decide whether Hitler should join us?"

"You idiot! Dracula would ruin everything if he knew! This is not up for debate. Do what I ask...*or* suffer the consequences!"

"You can't kill me...I'm already dead. What can you possibly do if I refuse?"

"I recommend you do it for yourself, and for those you love!"

"What do you know about *who* I love?"

"I know all about your new fledgling."

"You leave Jericho out of this!" Jack replied angrily.

"I certainly will...the moment Hitler's blue eyes change to red."

"Just exactly who and what are you?"

"I am the ultimate enemy to mankind...I have seen ancient

192

civilizations flourish only to crumble in ruins, including some not mentioned in history books."

"You're not going to give me a real answer, are you?"

"There are no real answers, Jack…only theories…"

Jack felt the wind pick up, and instinctively knew the dark presence was gone. He Glanced at his watch and realized he had lost more than an hour of precious night. He longed to see Jericho again, and planned to take him to the moors; there was no better place to get lost. The moorlands of England were filled with mystery and intrigue; romantic tales of wandering ghosts and rabid dogs helped to make it an ideal retreat from the human world.

Chapter 71 - A Home Under London Bridge - (August 1936)

They were waiting for him when he returned, often huddled together reading tattered books by candlelight to pass the time. The children had become dependent upon Jericho, especially during winter months when food was scarce. Greeted by five smiling faces, Jericho realized that after years of searching, he had finally made his own family. The children, ages seven to fourteen had been living with him for over a year now; as the oldest, he had taken them under his wing. During the daylight hours, the younger ones pilfered fruit and bread from street merchants and they managed to keep from starving. Oliver worked as a newsboy, selling newspapers in neighborhoods many wouldn't frequent after dark. The two older boys had become adept at landing odd jobs, which helped with anything else they needed. At night, Jericho left them to sell his many attributes; Oliver and the twins were led to believe he worked the nightshift. Together, they found community living under London Bridge; despite being quite frigid in winter, it served them well.

After he was turned, Jericho knew a thirst greater than any he had ever known. His knees were weak and he had a hollow feeling in his stomach that felt nothing like hunger. Jack left him without explaining much of anything; Jericho was forced to return to the only home he knew. Jack promised to come for him after he "smoothed things out" with Dracula, leaving him no choice but to wait. It had been months since Jack made his promise to return; Jericho had learned in his line of business, there were never any guarantees. To quench his burning thirst in those first few nights as a vampire, Jericho killed several rats and a feisty alley cat. He was not made for killing human beings, so he continued living this way as he waited patiently for Jack to return. As summer droned on and Jack stayed away, the fledgling began to doubt his vampire was coming for him.

On a brutally hot August night when the air was thick enough to stir, Jericho was desperate to feed and made a mistake he would later regret. Hunting had been a bust; the fledgling vampire was unable to find any rats; because of the heat they had gone deeper underground. Feeling too weak to go on, Jericho went home without feeding; he was foolish enough to believe his hunger could be ignored. Reaching the backside of London Bridge, Jericho struggled to ignore the gnawing pain in his gut. The two older boys saw the hunger in his eyes and kept their distance. The twins ran to greet him; he took in their intoxicating scent, and it made him swoon. When he looked at the children, Jericho saw a way to keep them connected forever. In the end, this realization was what drove him to do the unthinkable; before the night was over, Jericho had tasted each of his children, unknowingly changing them forever. Henry and Rupert tried to resist, but Jericho's will was stronger, and they finally surrendered their necks to him. He was careful not drink too much, stopping in plenty of time. The children were not harmed and feeding from them meant he would have no need to kill humans; to an inexperienced fledgling, this solution made perfect sense.

Jack abandoned Makefield Manor on the hottest night of the summer; determined Jericho was what he wanted and his only chance for true happiness. Trying to shake off his conversation with the evil entity, Jack located the well-worn pathway leading to the iconic bridge. By the time Jack reached his destination, he was much later than he expected. Would Jericho still be living here? Whenever Jack thought about the beautiful dark-haired boy, his dead heart skipped a beat. Following the directions Jericho provided, Jack entered the partially hidden doorway and quickly adjusted to the darkness. To his great surprise, Jack was greeted by his fledgling vampire and five children, who he immediately determined were supplying Jericho with blood. If only Jack had warned him about the power of a vampire's craving, but now it was too late; Dracula would certainly blame Jack for this fiasco.

Jack had spent the past few months at Makefield Manor, trying to defend his right to make a vampire of his own; Dracula remained adamant the teenage vampire be trained, and then left to his own devices, insisting there was no place for the boy at Makefield Manor. As August neared its final days, Jack gave up the fight and left to find the boy whose touch he craved more than laudanum.

As he stood in the abandoned structure Jericho called home, Jack understood he was in danger of being saddled with five children who were nothing but an additional liability. "I thought you lived alone." Jack said finally.

"And just who are you?" Henry demanded.

"I'm Jack...introductions all around?"

Jericho introduced his family to Jack. "Henry is the oldest, fourteen... Rupert is thirteen...Oliver with the cap over there just turned nine and the twin girls are seven...meet Alice and Audrey," Jericho concluded, as the two girls curtsied.

Alice stepped forward and held out her hand. "We are twins and Oliver is our older brother." Jack took her hand and felt its warmth; she felt human yet, she was not.

"Jack," Jericho whispered pulling him away from the others. A few candles provided the only source of light. The children appeared to be sleeping on makeshift beds made of straw; it made Jack sad, but truthfully, his only interest was in the boy loved.

"Do you understand what you've done?" Jack hissed angrily.

"They let me drink from them. It doesn't hurt them and it gives me what I need," Jericho explained.

"There are more sensible ways to feed."

"I can't kill humans, Jack...I just can't," the boy said, pulling away from him.

"This is my fault. I didn't take time to teach you what you had a right to know. These children belong to you now." Jack said.

"That's what I want, Jack. They are the only family I have...and I intend to keep them."

"These children are caught between worlds...it means they'll never age," Jack explained what he had been taught by Dracula himself.

"I still don't understand the problem."

"These children are still flesh and blood. They need human food and are susceptible to human illnesses." Jack was surprised at what he remembered.

"They're no worse off than they were before," Jericho replied defensively.

"And the fact that they'll never grow up...that doesn't bother you?" Jack asked, gently pulling the boy a little bit closer, so he could take in his delicious scent.

"I saw it as a way to keep my family...they used to stay because they wanted to. Now, they are a part of me."

"I don't want you to stay here. Come away with me." Jack was anxious to convince Jericho to leave his old life behind.

"I can't just leave them here to fend for themselves."

"If I help you find a new place for them to stay, will you come with me...even for just a little while?" Jack pleaded.

"Winter's just around the corner. We have to find them shelter from the cold. It's not like they can spend their life riding the metro system every night to stay warm," Jericho said jokingly.

Jack's mind raced with thoughts on how they could rid themselves of the children. He wasn't completely heartless; they deserved at least, to have protection from the elements. Naturally, they couldn't expect children to ride the metro all night, but what about somewhere underneath the street? Maybe they could take shelter in an unused storage unit or, better yet, an abandoned tube station. Luckily, Jack knew of just such a place.

Chapter 72 - Vincent van Gogh - Old Trafalgar Station - London - (August - 1936)

Despite being underground, Vincent knew night had fallen. The sounds of daytime were filled with a rhythmic pounding and the hum of human voices that meant business. Nighttime sounds were different; they were more musical and filled with laughter. An occasional police siren was the only reminder, the night invited criminal activity. Vincent was working on a landscape, clearly frustrated by his inability to capture the beauty of the Thames. Although time was meaningless to a ghost, Vincent could still feel the length of a day; lately he had come to realize his punishment was utter loneliness. At first, he craved solitude as he furiously created hundreds of paintings, a lifetime's worth; but still, he was not truly happy. Perhaps he had no right to happiness; after all, he had committed the gravest of sins.

The artist's only friends were two misfit children and a pet falcon. Ever since his hideaway had first been discovered, Prince and Rory had become regular visitors. Although Vincent had initially been annoyed by the intrusion, he now looked forward to their company. Jack visited now and then and seemed particularly fond of Prince. Dracula's visits were less frequent, but he always took time to comment on the artist's latest works. Vincent understood they were both vampires, and while Jack played his role to perfection; Dracula seemed much more human, unless he was angered. Vincent found them interesting and reasoned; vampires were no threat to him.

"I really like your latest sunflower painting, Vincent…it's your best one yet!" Prince commented, running his hand along the edge of the canvas.

Rory was amazed at the volume of paintings Vincent had created; she thumbed through stacks of completed canvases finding each one unique, yet familiar. Vincent's larger paintings were hung up, covering dark water-stained walls; others leaned against the wall half-finished. Akos fluttered about the room looking like a frazzled art collector, assessing the value of Vincent's work. At first, the artist chased him away but eventually, they became friends; it was not uncommon to find the falcon perched on Vincent's easel.

Footsteps echoed in the corridor making Prince pause; Vincent looked up from his work and waited for the intruder to pass them by. Jack barged through the metal door and took Rory's hands, spinning her around like a dance partner. He stopped abruptly to flash Vincent a bright smile. Vincent wasn't fooled by Jack's jovial demeanor for one minute. He knew trouble when he saw it; this man, or whatever he was, meant trouble with a capital "T."

Jack nodded at Vincent; the vampire clearly had something on his mind. "Mr. van Gogh, good to see you again."

"What brings you here? I assure you the children are in good hands."

"I have no doubt…this is a perfect place for children…"

Before Jack could explain himself further, a young dark-haired girl walked through the doorway, pulling along an identical twin. They both stood wide-eyed as they took in the bizarre makeshift art studio. "Is this going to be our new home?" Alice asked Jack.

"I hope so, Alice…I like it!" exclaimed her sister, Audrey.

"Home?" Vincent asked knitting his eyebrows together.

"Well…you see…they have nowhere else to go, Vincent."

Henry and Rupert followed the girls inside, but Oliver lagged behind; once inside, the boy gaped at a room filled with magnificent oil paintings that exploded with energy. Oliver approached Vincent who was still holding a brush full of paint. "Will you teach me how to paint like this?"

Vincent could feel his heart tighten; there was something more than hunger in the young boy's face. He bent down closer to the boy, whose eyes were tinged with red; behind him, the twins watched him with eyes that were no longer human. "Jack…what are they?" Vincent croaked.

"They are not vampires… and have no need to drink human blood," Jack explained. Vincent realized all five of them were of the same species.

"But…what do they eat?" Vincent asked.

"They still eat human food, Vincent…they just need shelter from the cold and a safe place to sleep every night. Just think…you would have five new subjects to paint! I mean, don't you ever get tired of painting landscapes and sunflowers?" Jack was a born negotiator.

"I don't do portraits anymore," Vincent replied tersely.

Jack coaxed Oliver closer to Vincent; his clothes didn't fit and his face was dirty, but Oliver was still a handsome boy. "Look at this face, Vincent…yours to paint for all eternity."

"Such responsibility…I don't know."

"Vincent…they have nowhere else to go," Jack pleaded, as he backed toward the doorway to make his escape.

While Vincent was contemplating his next move, Jack assumed his bat-like form and left to join his love on the moors. He would teach Jericho about the simple pleasures associated with being a vampire, like the joy of flying. Yes, the first thing Jack would teach Jericho was how to fly, both as a bat, and in his human form. They would fly and hunt through the night, and when daylight threatened, they would seek their cave to wrap themselves around each other and embrace the unnatural sleep of the undead.

CHAPTER 73 - MAKEFIELD MANOR - (MAY 1937)

Nikos sat in the dimly lit room reviewing ledgers and paying household bills. It was a startling change to live in the human world of time and all its trappings. To maintain an estate such as this, involved a complicated and creative method of financial maneuvering. Naturally, the personas they had established for Count Draco and his family were entirely fictitious, despite the seemingly legal documents verifying their identity. With Britain on the verge of a possible war, government officials were becoming more vigilant in confirming every London resident had proper documentation. What worried Nikos most about their circumstances was how easily their fraudulent documents could be challenged, if inspected too closely.

Dracula sat across from Nikos watching his loyal friend study an array of documents spread out on the weathered table. Books had already started to accumulate everywhere, as Prince and Rory procured history books from various libraries; Eva made a habit of pilfering leather bound copies of Dracula, along with anything new she could find about Jack the Ripper.

Nikos looked up over his glasses to find his lord studying him intently. "What is it, Vlad?"

"It has been nearly nine months since Jack and his plaything disappeared."

"There has been no recent criminal activity that remotely resembles vampire killing. Whatever he's doing, Jack is keeping a low profile." Nikos countered.

"Where the devil could he be, Nikos? We've searched just about everywhere...Jack and his fledgling, have simply vanished. What if he has chosen another city, or worse yet...another time?"

"Good! Let him be someone else's worry. At least he is staying out of trouble. Frankly, I have other concerns," Nikos retorted with a furrowed brow.

"Such as?" Dracula asked clearly distracted.

"Our plan is floundering, Vlad. If Jack continues his absence much longer…"

Dracula cut him off. "Actually, I believe the time has come to make assumptions that Jack no longer shares our vision."

"So, you agree we need to consider an alternative plan?"

"I have been exploring another angle…one I think will work very well."

"All right, then…tell me about your *master plan*."

"I think we're both in agreement that our goal is to make vampires with ethics, character and reasonable wealth…"

"Vlad…I think we also need to consider turning others…who are not so well endowed. We should have a certain amount of loyal fledglings that can blend in with the masses, while keeping an eye out for trouble. For example, it might be wise to recruit employees who work in the metro; the job is underground…making it a safe environment for vampires to work by day. Just a suggestion…" Nikos trailed off, knowing there was more to Dracula's plan.

"Of course…we'll likely need more than a few unscrupulous individuals for what I have in mind…but the wealthy and powerful will be our primary targets. Wealthy men live guarded lives; they encounter envy in almost everyone they meet. Men of means also have a vested interest in protecting what they have achieved. Luckily, most have at least one secret that could destroy them, if it were exposed. The answer to our recruitment dilemma is: blackmail!" Dracula revealed his plan with a wicked smile.

"Blackmail?"

"Yes…it's such a simple solution…I can't believe it took me this long to figure it out." Dracula began pacing back and forth as he explained his strategy.

"Kindly indulge me with a few more details, will you?" Nikos replied.

"Anyone can be bought for the right price…I've yet to meet a judge or police official who didn't have at least one skeleton in his closet. Keep in mind…we won't have to turn everyone we recruit…some will serve a better purpose by staying human. Having someone from Scotland

Yard in your back pocket, is a most effective way to stretch the tiresome limits of the law."

"I can't believe I'm saying this, but your plan might work. Have you decided how you will initiate contact with chosen candidates?" Nikos asked now fully engaged.

"I see no reason to treat our proposition as anything other than a business deal," Dracula continued.

"So, we're going to sell vampirism?"

"No...no, the product we're selling is *eternal life*."

"Many will turn you down at first...that is, if they even believe you at all." Nikos tried to be realistic.

"I expect that but, I'm confident we'll bring them around..."

"And how can we prevent someone from going to the authorities?"

"Because...the men we target will have too much to lose, by doing so."

"And how will we gather dossiers on those we want to recruit?" Nikos asked.

"Honestly, I was hoping you could help with that. I'm sure Prince can assist, too...it's time we stopped treating him like an errand boy."

"And what about Jack...do we keep searching for him?"

"Fuck, Jack! He can go to bloody hell, for all I care!"

Chapter 74 - Eternal Sleep - North York Moorlands - (July 1937)

A steady breeze drifted across the moors, creating a soothing melody in the early morning hours before dawn. No other place in the world could rival the captivating beauty of the English moorlands; it was home not only to human ghosts, but all manner of unnatural beings. The black wolf had ruled the North York Moorlands for centuries; these ferocious beasts were the main reason few dared to cross them once the sun went down. Some actually believed the moors harbored werewolves; Londoners could be a superstitious lot, especially in light of the famous Sherlock Holmes story. Tonight, the wolves were louder than usual, a guarded response to the scent of a beast that did not belong.

The black wolf didn't frequent this part of the moors very often, but tonight it had been called to a very special mission. The moon disappeared behind the horizon, as the sky changed from deep purple to a tranquil shade of blue; night was fading fast. The massive beast stood on a cliff carefully concealed behind a patch of coarse bracken. Its ears were poised to hear and obey the commands of a presence far more powerful than he.

"You must take him from the cave...let the sun burn him up...only then, will our vampire return to fulfill his destiny."

The wolf waited patiently for the sun to come up over the horizon, its only mission, to serve the one who claimed dominion over a terrain that had remained unchanged for a thousand years. The cave was less than a hundred yards away but the wolf didn't move, sensing the sun needed to rise a bit higher in the sky. The beast slowly approached the entrance to the cave; it stopped for a moment and sniffed the air, recalling its master's words, "Take only the boy."

Inside the cave, Jack and Jericho were settled into the daytime slumber only vampires know. They had spent most of the night hunting together, their bodies moving in perfect harmony as the boy quickly learned the savage pleasure of tearing flesh with his teeth. Even in his twilight slumber, Jack could feel the boy's presence and it calmed him.

Jericho was gentle, kind and didn't judge Jack on how he had lived his human life; the boy's love was unconditional. Here on the North York Moors, Jack had finally found peace. He didn't care about destroying the world, making new vampires or any of the things that were expected by Dracula. Jack discovered he was quite willing to hunt red deer, sheep and rabbits for an eternity, as long as Jericho was beside him. Whenever he thought about returning to the manor, Jack realized he had never really belonged.

Jericho bolted from his sleep shaking and breathless; he had a sixth sense something was wrong. The boy carefully untangled himself, leaving the one who made him lost in peaceful slumber. Jericho stood up and stretched his arms above his head willing himself awake; he suddenly caught the scent of a sinister presence lurking outside. Jericho was about to wake Jack when he heard the low, menacing growl. He needed a weapon! The boy grabbed his hunting knife, as a huge black wolf entered the cave. It was an ugly brute with matted fur and rotting yellow teeth. Jericho cried out as the wolf pounced and knocked the boy to the ground, sinking its sharp teeth into his thigh. Jericho screamed in agony, stabbing the air frantically with his knife, but quickly realized he was no match for the massive beast.

Jack jerked awake and tried to grasp what was happening. He watched as a black wolf savaged his beautiful boy; Jericho's face was already a mask of death. Now fully awake, Jack understood the beast meant to bring the boy into the sunlight. Jack took hold of Jericho's extended arm, but the wolf tore the boy from his grip. Morphing into a wolf, Jack tried to even the odds, but knew it was already too late. The wolf reached the entrance to the cave and as Jack looked on, it dragged Jericho's milk-white body into the searing rays of a blazing summer sun. Jericho's beautiful blue eyes were full of surprise, as he flailed his arms in desperation. The sun was merciless; Jack screamed as Jericho's tender skin began to burn, turning his beautiful naked flesh into a mass of sores and blisters. Jack beheld his love's murder as he returned to his human form, helpless to do anything to save the boy, without sacrificing his own life. For a brief moment, Jack considered running out into the sunlight; it would be a just end to his miserable existence. But, he could not do it. He would not do it. Coward that he was, Jack chose to remain in the safely of his cave; so unwilling was he to give up the only life he had. Now starting to sizzle, Jericho became an unrecognizable heap of scorched flesh and bones. Jack fell to his knees in anguish, as his beautiful boy was reduced to smoke and ash.

The ferocious wolf continued to stand its ground; it watched the boy's bones burn, and then scattered Jericho's ashes to the wind with its hind legs. As Jack watched his dreams die, he finally understood what people meant when they talked about the world turning black. He stepped back further into the cave, nearly tripping over Jericho's leather boots. Jack scooped them up into his arms, and finally gave in to the wracking sobs he had been suppressing. His love had been sentenced to a fiery demise, and he had allowed it to happen; Jericho's death was his fault and his carelessness had cost him dearly. Tears streamed down Jack's face, burning his skin as they fell, but he didn't care. Something inside him snapped. He felt hatred and lust for human carnage, such as he had never known in his human life. He would never give his heart to anyone again; from now on, he would kill for sustenance and for pure enjoyment. From inside the cave, Jack studied the nefarious beast; it was cleaning its paws with utter satisfaction, as if gloating over the kill. Jack instinctively knew this was no ordinary wolf; it had been sent by someone to do this awful thing. Jack was determined he would not be the only one to suffer.

With Jericho gone, the moors had lost their magic and Jack resigned himself to return to London. As soon as the sun set, he would begin his journey back to Makefield Manor; Jack had nowhere else to go. He would return to Dracula and work hard to be agreeable. He would not make accusations and would be discreet in his inquiries, but one way or another, Jack was going to make somebody pay for killing the only person he had ever loved.

Chapter 75 - Jack's Second Show - Central London - (August 1939)

Oliver loved being a newsboy. The work was easy and the pay decent, perhaps one of the best jobs for young boys in London. Now that he understood he couldn't age, the boy realized he would never outgrow his favorite job which suited Oliver just fine. Today's paper had big news of another brutal murder in Whitechapel; the victim was a pretty young prostitute, whose body was missing several organs. Her mutilated corpse was found on Farrant Street, leaving Scotland Yard scrambling to find even one clue as to the identity of the ruthless killer. Many wondered if they had a copycat killer on their hands; the newspapers had already dubbed him, the *Ripper Killer,* which, of course, was impossible.

Oliver was too young to know anything about the original Ripper murders, committed during the summer and fall of 1888; however, there were plenty of Londoners happy to divulge details not found in history books. Many Whitechapel residents had grandparents who were alive when the gruesome murders occurred; throughout the years, firsthand stories had been carried down to the next generation. This new wave of murders had the public on edge, as Scotland Yard detectives struggled to find a solid lead. Nightly patrols, especially around Whitechapel, had been doubled. Although it was not public knowledge, several male officers were being used as decoys; the plan was to outsmart the vicious killer when he tried to strike again.

When Jack first returned to Makefield Manor, he expected anger and accusations. Instead, he was pleasantly surprised to receive a warm welcome from both Dracula and Nikos. They filled him in on what he had missed, as though he'd only been gone for a weekend. For the time being, Jack embraced Makefield Manor as his home; at least he could be with those of his own kind. It was also nice to have a roof over his head again, and to have something other than wild game to feed on. No one inquired about his young fledgling, and Jack was grateful; the loss of Jericho was something he refused to discuss. Jack was brought up to speed on Dracula's latest plan for the recruitment of vampires, and he assisted where it was required. Unable to prove Dracula had been responsible for Jericho's demise, Jack turned to killing in an effort to dull the monotony of a life without purpose. It worked for a while, but eventually his inner demons took over.

When he first started killing again, Jack adopted Whitechapel as his personal hunting ground; he knew the streets like the back of his hand; surprisingly, over the years not much had changed. Once he made his first kill, a Mary Kelly look-alike, Jack was back in his element and ready to give Scotland Yard another run for their money. There was something very gratifying about teasing law enforcement, so Jack made a habit of leaving something behind, like a handkerchief or other personal item. He was pretty sure the detectives assigned to the case had figured out by now, his "souvenirs" were nothing but dead ends. Jack loved the challenge of staying one step ahead of law enforcement, and realized how much he had missed the excitement of it all. Killing by night and sleeping by day in his private suite of rooms at Makefield Manor, Jack generally avoided the others, and was careful to keep his more gruesome nighttime activities a secret.

Jack tried to find contentment at the manor, but struggled against a burning rage inside; he was consumed by guilt and regret at his failure to protect his fledgling. The problem with eternal life is that you spend most of it lost in regret. For Jack, life had become an endless stream of never-ending days and nights so tedious, he cursed Dracula for the cruel sentence of a life without end. In the early hours before dawn after returning from his nightly pursuits, Jack lay in the darkness and keenly felt the hollowness of his existence. Consumed by a crushing loneliness, Jack longed for the solitude of the moorlands and a beautiful blue-eyed boy named Jericho. As he slipped into twilight slumber, Jack felt a tingling in his fingertips as he stroked the boy's translucent skin; the sensation quickly evaporated, and with it came a coldness from which there was no escape.

Just as Jack began drifting off to sleep, Oliver left the comfortable makeshift bed he shared with his two sisters, and prepared to pick up newspapers to sell later that morning. Oliver liked their new home and enjoyed watching the eccentric artist paint his colorful canvases. Most days he spent above ground earning what he could on the mean streets of a city getting ready for war. His was a difficult life for such a young boy, but Oliver didn't mind; it was the only life he had ever known. The money was fairly good and helped contribute to food; although, since becoming a black swan, Oliver had lost much of his appetite. Jack came to visit them at the old Trafalgar Station regularly; he felt as though he owed Jericho that much. Oliver was always ready for even the smallest assignment; he was small, quick and able to blend in when necessary. Fact was, young children were often invisible to adults, making it easy for them to navigate places without being noticed. Sometimes he was asked to eavesdrop on conversations and other times, Oliver merely picked up or delivered packages. One night, Jack asked him to follow a police captain as he frequented a strange place Oliver knew wasn't meant for children. The women he saw standing outside were garish looking, with their painted faces and scantily clothed bodies. When they spotted Oliver watching them, they beckoned him across the street saying things that made him blush.

Henry and Rupert were hostile toward Jack; they blamed him for what happened to their friend. Alice and Audrey, on the other hand, were crazy about him and that made all the difference. Oliver had been on his own for most of his life and only cared about one thing, protecting his younger sisters. If his sisters liked Jack, that was good enough for him. Oliver accepted his makeshift family and never questioned his responsibility; with them, the boy had a sense of belonging.

As the early morning sun temporarily covered the rooftops of London in butterscotch, Oliver adjusted his newsboy cap and prepared to start his day. The diligent young boy sighed deeply as he hoisted the worn canvas bag onto his bony shoulders, and headed toward the groggy streets of London. Once stationed at his usual corner, Oliver dropped the heavy bundle to the ground. He held up a fresh newspaper and cried out, *"RIPPER KILLER STRIKES AGAIN!"*

Chapter 76 - Watching the Skies - Central London - (August 1939)

Despite a certainty England was on the verge of war, there was little anyone could do but wait. London citizens went about their daily lives, depending on the press for the latest news. Some started hoarding staples, especially tea; no Londoner could be expected to do without this essential beverage. There was talk of evacuating children before the German bombs arrived, but understandably, parents were hesitant to do so unless it was absolutely necessary. If there could ever be an example of *calm before the storm*, this was it. London citizens lived cautiously within a temporary bubble of safety, as Hitler purposely delayed his rain of bombs to a time when Londoners least expected it.

Jack spent most of his nights alone, hunting where he knew Dracula would never go. The two conversed when it was required, but there was no longer any camaraderie between them. Jack had been asked to make two vampires. One was so terrified, he wet himself; the other got such a violent case of the hiccups, Jack had to knock him unconscious so he could turn him. Now that Jack had spent a period of consecutive time in the human world, he observed time passed with excruciating slowness. The fury of Jack's killing began to quiet; he killed less frequently, but there was still a hunger burning inside him. Consuming blood from wine bottles didn't interest Jack much; in a pinch maybe, but not on a regular basis. For him, Dracula's approach to vampirism was a bit too civilized. Jack liked to drink from human flesh itself, so he could savor its sweet pulpy texture.

The seasoned vampire liked his independence, and had no intention of submitting to Dracula's will; everything would change once he began his partnership with Adolf Hitler. The Dark One had presented a challenge and Jack was just pissed off enough to accept; in fact, he couldn't wait for the bombing to start, so he could make his move to recruit the fearless leader of Germany. Jack had already worked out the details of his master plan; Hitler spent his time directing subordinates from a secure bunker in East Prussia. Jack's best approach would be to confront the Fuhrer when he was alone. He was fairly certain Hitler would initially refuse his proposition, and in fact, Jack quite expected it. It was the second visit that would rattle the Fuhrer; Jack planned to deliver proof Germany would lose the war. Eva promised she would find something to help him and Jack insisted their plans be kept from Dracula. Truthfully, Eva thought the whole idea absurd and never even considered telling anyone.

Despite having fed well, Jack lay in the darkness wide awake; adrenaline pumped through his veins like a freight train. He had just returned from a night of hunting and his fingers still tingled with the feel of his favorite knife. The woman had begged for her life, as eye makeup ran down her doughy face; in her last moments, she looked like a demented clown. On her knees, the whore whimpered like a dog, until Jack could take no more and finally opened her throat. Lately, Jack had begun to detest human beings and their disgusting frailty.

The room was dark and silent as his bloodlust quieted, but only because he knew tomorrow would bring another chance for carnage. As Jack felt himself drifting into twilight slumber, he heard the Dark One's serpentine voice whisper, "It's time to check the papers, Jack."

Chapter 77 - England Goes to War - Berlin, Germany - (September 5, 1939)

Adolf Hitler loved the idea of war. Exploding bombs and splattered blood were regularly featured in his nightly dreams; he found the idea of war more erotic than pornography. Unfortunately, thoughts of bloodshed also left the dictator with a constant struggle to control spontaneous erections. The Fuhrer was fastidious in both his dress and person, always making sure his uniform was wrinkle free; his trademark mustache was also properly waxed and trimmed. Framed in the gilded mirror like a picture portrait, the dictator savored the news he had just received this morning; British Prime Minister, Neville Chamberlain, had officially declared war on Germany. Just two days before, Germany had taken Poland; things were going well. As he stood buttoning his shirt, Hitler made a mental note to bring out one of his reserve bottles of wine for dinner tonight with his girlfriend, Eva Braun.

Hitler belched loudly; he believed suppressing natural bodily functions led to digestive problems. As he adjusted his collar, the dictator stared into harsh blue eyes he felt commanded fear and respect. Adolf Hitler knew exactly who he was, and never doubted for one moment Germany would be victorious. If all went according to his plan, the United States would be engaged in warfare before the decade was over. By the time the U.S. entered the war, Hitler would have made great strides toward eradicating those of inferior nationality; the Fuhrer was obsessed with preserving the integrity of the Aryan race. As he made plans for his busy morning, Hitler admired his reflection. He made a common practice of reciting speeches in front of his mirror, to ensure his words conveyed the message he intended. As he spoke, the bathroom mirror began to fog. When Hitler wiped it with his towel, a tall thin man was standing behind him; the terrified Fuhrer spun around, only to find himself alone.

"Over here, Fuhrer," Jack taunted, bouncing his voice around the room. Remaining invisible on his first visit had been the right choice. He had learned from past experience, this was quite unsettling to human beings and easily gave him the upper hand.

"I have a gun!" Hitler challenged.

"Do you really plan to shoot what you can't see?"

"How did you get in here? This bunker is concrete and without windows." Hitler was livid that his safety had been compromised.

"I mean you no harm, Fuhrer…I only wish to talk."

"I have nothing to say to you!" Hitler bellowed; calling his guards, as he fired his pistol erratically until the chamber was empty.

Jack laughed out loud as Hitler stood dumbfounded, and holding an empty gun. Hitler's guards burst through the door, and found Hitler calmly picking up bullet casings from the floor. Unwilling to admit shooting at an invisible man, Hitler lied and said he had been target shooting. The guards who heard the Fuhrer's cries of alarm knew better, but no one questioned Adolf Hitler if they expected to stay alive.

As Jack flew into the night in his bat-like form, he realized the Dark One had been right; Hitler really was a terrible coward.

CHAPTER 78 - A KILLER'S RAGE - CENTRAL LONDON - (AUGUST 1940)

The moment just before he killed them, was what Jack enjoyed the most. It wasn't the fear that excited him as one would expect. What excited him most was seeing how desperately his victims clung to any hope at all, they might be spared. It was a certain expression in their eyes. They all had it during their final moments, but women especially; they were soft, weak and repulsive. Women were the scourge of humankind, only necessary for procreation. With every woman he killed, Jack's pain buried itself a little deeper. When he was asked, Jack assisted Dracula with the recruitment of new vampires and went along with plans as directed. Most nights, he roamed the streets of Whitechapel; when the mood struck him, Jack made vampires of his own determined he had every right to do so.

Tonight, he felt driven by more than hunger, as he walked a familiar neighborhood he had committed to memory. Jack embraced a sudden rush of cool air, as he led the tall brunette toward a vacant corner where no streetlight burned. The young woman was a bit drunk, and noticeably stumbled as they walked beneath a moonless sky. Jack's chest thundered as he took in the scent of her perfume, it was strong, but not potent enough to disguise the coppery smell of her blood. She was telling a story Jack wasn't even listening to, as they reached a brick wall partially obscured by overgrown shrubbery. Pulling her arm, he brought the woman deeper into the bushes. She gave him a crooked smile, holding out her hand for payment; Jack instantly complied then kissed lips that, after tonight, would never speak again.

Jack liked to play psychological games with his victims sometimes; tonight, he was feeling particularly sadistic. "What if I told you I had the power to let you live forever?" Jack asked looking deep into her chocolate brown eyes. She was a real beauty except for her teeth; he almost regretted killing her, but only for a moment.

"Sounds lovely, but I doubt I'll even make it to forty," the whore replied with a nervous giggle.

"Well, you know what they say, after forty…it's all downhill," Jack replied playfully, his eyes starting to glow.

"I get it now…this is a game, right? I'm supposed to say I'll do anything to have eternal life…and there goes my chance for heaven." The prostitute tried to appear lighthearted when inside, she was beginning to taste her fear.

"Heaven? How could someone like *you* go to heaven?"

Indignant, the prostitute began to pull away sensing danger. Stalling for time she replied, "Damned or not, I am smarter than I look… believe me!"

"And a smart woman like you wouldn't be stupid enough to get herself killed…now, would you?" Jack held her arm firmly; he was ready to pounce.

The whore's face went deadly pale, as her breath quickened. She was certain he could hear the pounding of her heart. "If I didn't know better…I'd swear you mean to murder me." Her statement ended in a whisper, as she looked into the face of evil.

"Well then, my lovely lady…you really *are* much smarter than you look." Jack's red eyes shined, as he sunk his teeth into her open neck and warm blood filled his mouth with liquid joy.

Jack felt rejuvenated as he drank his fill and thought perhaps, he would send Scotland Yard a souvenir of this one. The prostitute squirmed and made a pitiful mewling sound, like something other than human prey as she slipped into unconsciousness. Nearly drained, Jack lowered her body to the ground; she resembled a sleeping princess, as she lay at his feet with her hair spread all around. He bent down on one knee, pulling a hunting knife from his belt as he hovered over the lifeless corpse. He marveled at the flawless face he would leave unmarred; Jack was focused on a more private part of her anatomy. Slowly pushing up her flowered skirt, he admired his victim's long legs, then sliced off her underwear and deftly began his work.

CHAPTER 79 - INSPECTOR POOLE - SCOTLAND YARD - (AUGUST 1940)

Inspector Charles Poole was in a lousy mood, and made no effort to disguise it. It was pouring outside and he hadn't seen the sun in days. He tapped his red pencil nervously as he looked out the window; the weather matched his disposition. The desk clerk dropped a package wrapped in brown paper on the inspector's desk. "This was dropped off by a young boy in a cap...a few minutes ago," he said turning to leave.

"Did you get the boy's name?" Inspector Poole asked.

"Sorry, inspector...he just dropped it at the front desk...then disappeared before anyone could ask."

Inspector Poole waved the clerk away and examined the package more closely; it was addressed to Scotland Yard, but not to him directly. The package looked harmless enough, but he could detect an unpleasant odor; and then he noticed the red stain on his desk blotter. Inspector Poole knew blood when he saw it. Carefully, he used a letter opener to break the seal; inside was something that had once been very much alive. The newspapers will have a gruesome story for tomorrow, he thought, as he pushed away what remained of his lunch.

The following morning, as expected, every London newspaper contained a front-page story proclaiming Jack the Ripper had come back from the dead. The story also included the contents of a note accompanying the foul-smelling parcel delivered to Scotland Yard. The note read as follows:

"There once was a killer in London

Who everyone learned was named Jack

Now near a half century later

Jack the Ripper has finally come back!"

Jack R

Inspector Poole nursed a tepid cup of tea as he read the newspaper the day after his grim discovery. He put the crumbled paper aside in frustration, and pulled a brown folder that lay open closer to him. The file looked older than the others, and rightly so; it was the original case file for the 1888 Ripper investigation. The inspector pulled a few strings to get the file; he thought digging through the case file might help determine what kind of person this "copycat" killer might be. Of course, he didn't believe Jack the Ripper had come back from the dead, but that didn't mean he wasn't dealing with someone equally dangerous. He skimmed through the file, until he found sections of interest from which he took copious notes. As far as he was concerned, the case should have been solved; Inspector Poole had always believed sloppy police work had been the reason the Ripper was never caught. The big question was: how closely would this new killer mirror the crimes committed in the previous century?

Inspector Poole adjusted his wire-rimmed bifocals, as he compared the original Ripper killings against a string of murders committed over the past twenty-four months. Scotland Yard was clearly embarrassed they had no viable suspects; now, this homicidal maniac was taunting authorities by sending gruesome packages and cryptic notes, just like the original Jack the Ripper. This killer is engaging in a game of cat and mouse, the inspector thought; and he was absolutely correct. Charles Poole believed it was significant the murders started in Whitechapel. This could mean there was some connection between whoever the real Jack the Ripper was, and the current killer. Could it be a son or other family member perhaps? Lately the killings had expanded to areas outside Central London; and then, there were the recent killings on the moors to consider. Could there be more than one killer afoot, he wondered. The inspector was a very thorough man and never ignored even the slightest detail. To his trained eye, the most curious thing about the murders was the lack of blood remaining at the crime scene. In addition to the murder of prostitutes, police had discovered fourteen bodies in the North York Moorlands within the last twenty-four months, three times what it should be. Without exception, every one had identical wounds on their necks; none of the original Ripper victims had neck wounds like these. There had been no reports of wild animals on the loose. He refused to believe wolves lived on the moors, despite stories to the contrary; jackals maybe, but not wolves. In his opinion, people who claimed they saw wolves were either intoxicated, superstitious or both. The frustrated inspector tapped the file with his pencil and spoke out loud without even realizing it, "What am I missing here?" The phone rang startling the inspector from his reverie.

"Inspector Poole?" a voice asked apprehensively.

"Yes...to whom am I speaking?"

"Miles Stuyvesant here," answered an old acquaintance he knew from boarding school.

"Hello, Miles...what can I do for you?"

"Well, it's a rather delicate matter...are you alone in your office?"

Inspector Poole got up to close his office door. "I can assure you complete privacy...now, please tell me the reason for your call."

"An associate of mine recently had an unexpected visit from a Nikos Fabri. You know who he is?" Miles asked.

"No."

"He is solicitor and business associate of this rather eccentric Count Draco. You know who I mean...that wealthy chap from Romania or someplace like that," Miles explained.

"He keeps a low profile, as I understand."

"Well, that may be, but this anonymous friend of mine told me something rather interesting the other night...I found it quite disturbing. My friend claims he received the strangest invitation to dinner with Count Draco. He had the distinct impression this...Nikos Fabri wouldn't take no for an answer, so he accepted."

"So, what happened?" the inspector asked, as he ruffled through loose papers in front of him.

"A few nights later, Nikos picks up my friend and drives him to the Blue Orchid restaurant over near Piccadilly Circus. You know the place...horrible food...cute waitresses," Miles veered off topic, something he was well known for.

"So, your friend gets to the restaurant and then...," Inspector Poole prompted Miles to continue.

"Yes...he arrives at the Blue Orchid and about ten minutes later, this Count Draco shows up offering business services. Specifically, he states he can promise eternal life...in exchange for keeping a secret only he knows about my friend." Miles paused to catch his breath.

"So, your friend believes he was being asked to do something against his will?"

218

"Something like that…honestly, when my friend first told me about this…I thought he was overreacting and probably had one drink too many. You know how that can be," Miles replied.

"And this friend, I assume he made it home safely?"

"Yes, he did…but…" Miles was cut off.

"No crime has been committed here. Tell your friend this was simply a practical joke of some kind. The count donates generously to charities and regularly attends the theater. I understand he is also legal guardian to a young niece and nephew…I believe he resides just outside the city." Inspector Poole was anxious to get back to the Ripper case file.

"Bollocks, Charles! I should think you of all people, would know *blackmail* is against the law!"

"*Blackmail*, you say?" the inspector sat up straight, giving his caller undivided attention.

"Of course, I need to protect my associate's privacy, but he tells me the count's offer was made under the premise that refusal was not an option. That sounds like blackmail to me. I have no idea what my friend's secret is…but that doesn't matter. Blackmail is illegal!"

"What exactly was the count asking your friend to do in order to protect his secret?"

"This you're not going to believe. The count told him he would need to drink human blood."

Inspector Poole froze as Miles continued to ramble on; he couldn't let his old friend know an alarm had just gone off in his mind.

"I can certainly place a call to the count to see if I can get to the bottom of what is going on…maybe learn a little bit more as to what his *business services* entail. I'll ring you up again after I investigate further."

"Thanks, Charles. I really appreciate this very much."

Inspector Poole hung up the phone, gratified his recent suspicions about the goings on at Makefield Manor might actually have merit after all. For the past few weeks he had been looking into the activities of Count Draco and his houseguest, Jack Druitt. He had been unable to obtain evidence of a legitimate corporate business license of any kind, yet; the two men were obviously conducting some sort of business between them. He scribbled down the name Nikos Fabri and would need to research him further; Charles had not considered the man anything more than a servant. The inspector had learned from his sources, the count's young nephew had been seen in the company of street urchins and apparently didn't attend school, despite his young age; concern for the boy's education was a legitimate reason for a friendly telephone call.

There was something else bothering him this morning; it gnawed at him as he pushed his cold tea aside. Inspector Poole was a bit of a history buff and spent much of his free time in the local library. Lately he had been researching royal families throughout Eastern Europe. Because he was so well read, the inspector felt certain there had never been a family by the name of Draco in Transylvania or Romania, despite the credentials the count and his family presented when they were granted access to live in London. There was, of course, the infamous house of Dracul which spawned the horror classic by Bram Stoker, but that story was pure fantasy. The real Count Vlad Dracula and his brother Radu had perished in the fifteenth century. Uncovering the count's real identity could turn out to be a missing link in his quest to stop a killer. One thing Inspector Poole knew for sure; if there was anything illegal going on at Makefield Manor, he would uncover it. The wealthy European count may have charmed London society, but the inspector was an extremely perceptive man, and prided himself on knowing when someone was not who they claimed to be.

As if reading his thoughts, the desk clerk dropped an airmail letter on the inspector's desk, and then quietly slipped away. Inspector Poole snatched the envelope up and carefully slit the end with his engraved letter opener; he couldn't wait to dig into these documents to learn more about Count Draco and the mysterious Jack Druitt. The inspector had made a chart showing the timeline of unsolved murders, starting with the Whitechapel killings. As he suspected, the recent sadistic crime spree started shortly after the count and his entourage took up residence in London.

Charles chewed on his pencil, unaware he was even doing so. He thought about the strange call he had just received, which added yet another level of complexity. Could the attempted blackmail be connected to the recent string of murders? Was someone killing in Ripper fashion just to throw Scotland Yard off the trail of what they were *really* up to? There just had to be a connection between the murders and this blackmail scheme! The timing all made sense; the count arrived in May of 1936 and the first murder in Whitechapel occurred shortly thereafter. Some might believe the timing of these events were a mere coincidence; however, Inspector Charles Poole did not believe in coincidences.

Chapter 80 - The Blitzkrieg - Central London - (1940-1941)

As the Dark One predicted, war did come to the city of London. Despite the official declaration, the streets remained fairly quiet as citizens held their breath in anticipation. People moved about at a notably quicker pace while carrying on with their everyday lives, full of obligations and mundane tasks. As the year progressed without incident, London citizens followed newspapers and radio broadcasts closely; awaiting the shower of bombs that could arrive at any time. It was a common sight to see parents hustle children through the streets, as they glanced warily at the sky above. If not brave, Londoners were at least masters at preparation; before the bombing ever started, the city of London already had the appearance of a nation at war. Air raid drills were practiced nightly and shelters were set up throughout the city for refuge. Blissfully ignorant of what lie ahead, Londoners worked by day and watched the sky by night, waiting for the heavens to explode.

On a brisk autumn morning in mid-September 1940, the first rain of German bombs finally did arrive; despite all their preparations, Londoners were still taken by surprise. The first victim was seventy-year-old Edward Conroy, whose body was impaled by a V-1 bomb while his wife made breakfast on the last day of her life. Neighbors heard the blast and ran into the streets to discover, war had indeed begun. Hitler's strategy was to hit London and hit it hard; and so, the bombing began. Bombs didn't discriminate. Bombs exploded and killed victims at random, and with extreme cruelty. Mary Simpson discovered this in a very personal way, when she took her six-month-old baby for a walk in his pram; it was the same morning Edward Conroy was so brutally ripped from his earthly life while waiting for breakfast. It was the sound Mary heard first; her eyes were round with fear as she tried frantically to determine where it was coming from. Pushing the pram faster, she headed toward a public house to take shelter. A flash of light took her vision, and then shrapnel took her life; a V-1 bomb split both her and the sidewalk in two. There was nothing left of Mary Simpson or her baby, except the infant's left arm, which lay abandoned on the sidewalk, still nestled inside a woolly sleeve.

Initially the bombing occurred only during daylight hours; by December, the German military changed its strategy and started showering London citizens with V-1s and V-2s at night. Many sought tube stations for underground shelter; families used makeshift hammocks strung across railroad tracks for children to sleep on, after the tracks were switched off each night. The number of homeless increased with each passing week; countless businesses closed or were destroyed, leaving many with an unexpected taste of life on the streets. Food rationing escalated, which caused some to hoard supplies while others opened their kitchens to those in need. Many London households took to sleeping in one room, lest they be separated during an explosion. The formerly peaceful nights were filled with the piercing sound of air raid whistles that warned of impending attacks; German bombs continued to fall like autumn foliage. The city of London resorted to nighttime blackouts to save energy, and to make it more difficult for bombs to reach their chosen targets. Businesses continued to operate when they could, but closed up by late afternoon while the sky was still bright. London streets were mostly abandoned by dusk, as everyone prepared for the bombing to resume. Night after night, German bombs lit up the sky as an entire city seemed to hold its breath, in the seconds before impact. Most mornings the color of dawn was a smoky gray as sporadic fires burned; another piece of London was reduced to an ugly pile of rubble.

By December 1940, Londoners reluctantly began evacuating their children; some parents decided to tough it out, refusing to be separated from one another. Countless children were orphaned; some even forced to watch their parents die in a most violent way. It was not uncommon to see homeless children living outside; another painful reminder, that war was hell. By the beginning of 1941, the city of London had lost its luster; London residents had begun to look as gray as the rubble they lived in. Everywhere one looked, the devastating effects of constant bombing had taken its toll. Churches throughout London were full every Sunday; people prayed for peace and tried to remain faithful during an extremely difficult time.

By the fall of 1941, Londoners had fallen into a pattern of dodging danger, as they went about their daily lives. Most followed the newspapers and radio, desperate for any word as to when the bombing would cease; Londoners were anxious to rebuild their lives and their city. By Thanksgiving, tensions were running high, and the United States appeared to be losing its battle to remain neutral. Aggressive actions of the Japanese changed everything, and ultimately forced America to take sides. On December 7th, in the early morning hours, the Japanese bombed Pearl Harbor, catching everyone by surprise. Word of the attack reached London, along with a declaration of war from President Roosevelt; the United States had officially entered World War II.

Nikos held the newspaper in his hand, as he looked out his hotel window; a smoky haze hung in the air, nearly blocking out the sun. Christie's Auction House was nothing but a burnt skeleton; against the morning sky, it appeared menacing. Although adorned with a few simple wreaths to celebrate the holiday, Buckingham Palace failed to brighten his mood; the structure was covered by a layer of soot, affecting a rather sinister look. From his window, Nikos watched with amusement, as a determined milkman who had lost his truck continued his route; he was toting a metal cart, climbing over piles of bricks and other debris. With a soiled uniform and smiling face, the milkman kept his routine because he had a family to feed.

Nikos glanced toward the Tower of London, noting it had remained unscathed; despite several direct hits, the ancient structure still stood proudly on the horizon. Hitler deliberately made targets of historic sites; his ultimate goal was to crush Britain's spirit, and force Prime Minister Chamberlain to surrender. Fleet Street, home of the newspaper industry, survived the bombings with minimal damage; many wondered if this was intentional. After all, it was headlines that incited fear, with photos of exploding bombs and faces of despair. Newspapers were a lifeline to London citizens, who devoured any information available; as the war continued, families began to understand the true meaning of loss.

Nikos heard a knock on the door, noting his visitor's promptness with satisfaction; punctual men were often reasonable, and less likely to be excitable. Chief Inspector Pennock entered the hotel room, making every attempt to assume the upper hand in their conversation.

"Mr. Fabri, I am only here because I found your telephone call intriguing. I must speak frankly; I'm not a man who responds well to practical jokes." The chief inspector spoke in a gravelly voice, surely meant to intimidate.

"Thank you for coming, and for the record...I never make jokes." Nikos reached out to shake the officer's hand.

"I don't shake hands with people I don't trust. I'd like to know why the mysterious Count Draco sends his solicitor to conduct meetings on his behalf."

"A fair question. The count has a rare skin condition...it is exacerbated by sunlight...we realize that evening meetings may not always be convenient. I'm authorized to speak on his behalf...I assure you."

"All right, then...now about your call. You mentioned something about a son...rather odd, since my wife and I have no children. Why don't you tell me what this is *really* about?" The chief inspector removed his hat, and began spinning it around by the brim.

Nikos reached into his pocket to retrieve a brown envelope and handed it to Pennock. The chief inspector opened the package carefully, as though the contents were fragile. Inside were a letter and a photograph that fell to the floor. The chief inspector bent down to scoop it up; his eyes told Nikos everything he needed to know. The man was holding a photograph of his six-year-old son; product of a one-night stand that happened before he was married. He couldn't tell his wife about Benjamin. He was a man of power and influence, it would be quite impossible to declare he had a bastard son. It would ruin him!

"So, tell me...what is it you want?"

Nikos smiled and said something completely unexpected, "What would you say if I told you the count wants to offer you a chance to live forever?"

"Well, I'd say you're crazy! Now, what do you *really* want for your silence?" The chief inspector was starting to get pissed off.

"Nothing that is not already yours to give. We don't want money, Chief Inspector Pennock. All we require is a willing partnership."

"Okay...I'll bite. What kind of partnership?"

"One that keeps your little secret quiet," Nikos replied, as his smile disappeared.

"Why don't you call it what is, then...blackmail, plain and simple!" Pennock spat angrily.

Nikos ignored the accusation and continued, "Count Draco would like another meeting, a discussion over dinner tomorrow night, where he can explain what we offer. I will pick you up at your residence tomorrow evening at 6:00PM sharp. I do not yet know what restaurant the count prefers, but no matter...I will be driving you there." The chief inspector replaced his hat, deciding it was best to be agreeable.

"This is not a proposition you can walk away from, Chief Inspector," Nikos said, as he pocketed the envelope, noting Pennock had kept the photograph.

CHAPTER 81 - INSPECTOR POOLE - (OCTOBER 1940)

Inspector Poole had been slowly seething all day. Three separate attempts to reach the European count by telephone had been unsuccessful; to the inspector, this was the ultimate insult. Behind closed doors, he studied a pile of letters and documents; unfortunately, they brought him no closer to solving a wave of brutal murders, he was certain had something to do with Count Draco and his associates.

"So, the mysterious Count Draco thinks he can ignore me, does he?" Charles said out loud in utter frustration, trying to determine his next move. As the inspector began packing his attaché case with files to take home, his eye caught something he had overlooked; for a moment his heart skipped a beat. Underneath the Ripper case file was a list of numerous suspects, as assembled by Scotland Yard back in 1888. He had skimmed the list before, but never really looked at it closely until now. Inspector Poole slapped his head and let out an almost sinister laugh, as he read a name he hadn't noticed before: Montague John Druitt aka M. J. Druitt.

He snatched the list from his desk; Inspector Poole felt like an idiot for missing something so obvious. Count Draco's houseguest and business associate went by the name Jack Druitt; as far as he was concerned, "Druitt" was not a very common surname. Could this Jack Druitt be a descendant of the original M. J. Druitt? The inspector picked up a magnifying glass, as a thought came to him. Squinting at a document whose ink had faded, he jotted down the date of birth for M. J. Druitt, August 15, 1857. Next, Charles inspected the birth certificate for Jack Druitt; his birthday was August 15, 1902. The deeper he dug, the more Inspector Poole believed he should be looking more closely at Count Draco's houseguest. Referring back to his notes, he confirmed M. J. Druitt committed suicide by drowning in November of 1888; roughly the same time the Ripper killing spree ended. The inspector felt certain he had found something worth investigating; this case had evolved into something well beyond what he imagined.

Inspector Poole decided then and there, the time had passed for polite engagement; he would be ignored by the eccentric count no longer. Makefield Manor was harboring secrets, and he intended to expose them. Shoving the Ripper case file in his overstuffed case, the inspector decided to make a house call. The sky was already dark when he left his office; colder weather would be here soon and with it, London's dark shroud of winter. The chief inspector took the metro across town, and got off at Kings Cross Station; he was determined to walk the remaining distance. Every man deserved the opportunity to explain himself, and that is exactly what the inspector would offer. He finally reached the ornate gate that led to Makefield Manor; of course, it was locked. Charles had no choice but to climb the six-foot fence; an unscheduled visit might catch the count off guard. He considered taking his attaché case, but didn't want to risk it; the inspector stashed it out of sight behind a stone pillar, where he could retrieve it later.

The back of the house possessed none of the grandness of the front entrance. The first thing the inspector noticed was that every window was covered by sturdy metal shades; it was like nothing he had ever seen before. No one kept a fortress like this, unless they had something to hide. He felt his breast pocket to confirm he had his Scotland Yard identification and with surprising agility, scaled the fence. He made a clumsy landing that knocked him backwards onto a pile of damp leaves; he felt pretty smug, until he heard the sound of barking dogs. Charles was forced to climb a nearby elm tree and was trapped; his feet dangled from a branch, as two massive Dobermans barked incessantly below.

Nikos Fabri came into the yard carrying a sword; the man was dressed in rather old-fashioned clothing. The inspector was taken aback at the burly man's choice of weapons. Nikos glanced up at the inspector, keeping his weapon drawn. "You there…identify yourself immediately… or I will sic more than just my dogs on you!"

"Inspector Poole…Scotland Yard," Charles croaked, tossing his identification to the ground.

"Come down, then and state your business." Nikos lowered his sword as the inspector disengaged himself from the elm tree, while trying to maintain his dignity.

"Are you the one they call Nikos Fabri?" Charles asked.

"Indeed, I am…and you are…Inspector Poole of Scotland Yard, who happens to be trespassing…by the way," Nikos replied, returning the inspector's wallet.

"Yes…I am. Please pardon me. I've been trying to arrange a meeting with Count Draco for several weeks now…he won't return my telephone calls or respond to written correspondence." The inspector explained, keeping a wary eye on the dogs.

"Well, then…I guess we should take care of that right now. Please follow me."

Inspector Poole was happy to be admitted unannounced, despite his clumsy entrance. In his experience, the first few minutes of an interview spoke volumes as to a person's guilt or innocence. "Would Mr. Druitt also be available, Mr. Fabri? I would very much like to speak with him, too."

"Unfortunately, Mr. Druitt is out of town…perhaps, another time."

The grounds were more extensive then they appeared from the street, and the inspector couldn't help but admire the work they had done. Entering a side door, the two men descended a winding staircase into utter darkness and a bone chilling cold. They came to a stop in front of a huge metal door; Nikos pushed the door open and led Charles into a comfortable wine cellar. Seated at a huge table piled with dozens of books and newspapers, was Count Draco. The vampire's chiseled face and piercing green eyes bore right through the inspector, but Charles was not easily intimidated.

"Inspector Poole…I could smell you coming, before you had a chance to violate my property," Dracula spoke with the most menacing voice he could muster.

"Count Draco…I *have* come to Makefield Manor uninvited…but only because my previous requests for a meeting have been ignored."

"I am a busy man, Inspector Poole."

"Ah-h-h, that is exactly why I decided to pay you a visit. It's about your business, Count Draco. I can't seem to locate a legitimate license of any kind…and find myself curious as to what kind of services you offer. Perhaps, you can enlighten me."

"Have I broken any law?" Dracula asked in a steady voice.

"In all honesty, I'm not really sure…hence the reason for my visit."

"And what kind of questions do you have, inspector?" Dracula asked. The vampire stood up and began pacing the room, while sipping a glass of what appeared to be red wine.

"How do you know Jack Druitt?"

"Easy question…he is a business associate and personal acquaintance. We've known each other since we were boys. I'm sure Nikos told you already…Jack is out of town…but I will be glad to answer any questions I can." Dracula tried to keep things cordial.

"Count Draco, are you familiar with the Ripper murders in Whitechapel, by any chance?" As he waited for a response, Charles discreetly observed his surroundings. The books scattered about drew his attention; several were about Jack the Ripper.

"Naturally, I've heard of the Ripper, who hasn't?" Dracula could scarcely deny it, when books on the subject were strewn about. Damn Nikos, and his obsession with book collecting!

"Are you aware Scotland Yard has another psychotic killer on their hands? The modus operandi is eerily similar to…"

Dracula cut him off, "Inspector, I find myself a bit perplexed here. Exactly, what is the *real* reason for your visit?"

"As I explained to Mr. Fabri, I find myself unable to secure information as to what kind of business you…and your associates are conducting. Perhaps, you can provide some clarity."

"By what authority do you scale my fence, upset my dogs, and violate my residence?" Dracula was shouting now, as he stood over the inspector's chair.

The inspector rose to his feet, determined not to give the count the upper hand. "By the authority of Scotland Yard!"

"Very well…my associates and I offer consulting services to local businessmen. Frankly, I'm at a loss as to why you barge in here talking about murders, I know nothing about!"

"Count Draco…let me get to the point. I am looking for two things here; documentation of a corporate business license…and the whereabouts of your associate, Jack Druitt."

"I will have Nikos procure these documents…he will need a few days, because they are not here. I don't know where Jack is, but…maybe I can help. What do you want to know?"

"Where did you meet him?" The inspector didn't expect the truth.

His eyes drifted again to the collection of books; there were numerous volumes on vampires, including several editions of Bram Stoker's *Dracula*. Maybe his suspicions had merit, after all.

"Whitechapel." Dracula realized his mistake too late.

"I thought you and Jack were boys together...how could that be, when you've only been in London for a few years?"

Dracula felt cornered, but maintained his composure. "Jack and I went to private school together. His parents were geologists and spent a few years at a dig in Romania."

The inspector let out a hearty laugh. "You're smooth...I'll give you that. I don't believe a word of it...not for a bloody minute."

"It doesn't matter to me what you believe; I am not Jack's keeper."

"Count Draco...I couldn't help but notice you have a decided interest in vampires."

"Well...I am from Romania, after all...it is an interesting aspect of our native history. Certainly, there is no crime in that?"

"You think you're so clever, don't you?" The inspector was beginning to fume.

"Clever, how so?"

"This house you maintain like a fortress...your obvious interest in Jack the Ripper *and* a poorly explained interest in vampires. I know you're hiding something, and I intend to find out what you're up to!"

Dracula came at him so abruptly; the inspector was caught off guard. The angry count picked the inspector up by the neck; their faces were just inches apart, as a deafening silence filled the room. "You have no idea who you're dealing with, inspector," Dracula growled; he was no longer concerned with acting human.

Charles Poole had never been so afraid in his life. As he looked into the eyes of evil, a gruesome vision appeared; he was tied to a stake as vultures attempted to pluck out his eyes. The terrifying vision lingered, even after Dracula released him.

"You'll forgive me, Inspector Poole...but I have a rather pressing engagement. Nikos will see you out." As Charles watched with his mouth agape, the vampire vanished inside a cloud of vapor.

Chapter 82 - A Boy Named Charlie - Empire State Building - NYC - (October 31, 1945)

For Eva, the Empire State Building was something magical; certainly worth skipping ahead a few years to see; especially on such a beautiful October evening. Completed in 1931, the majestic structure had a hundred and two floors, and an observation deck that offered a spectacular view of the Manhattan skyline. Located in midtown on Fifth Avenue between 33rd and 34th Streets, the building's construction forced the original Waldorf-Astoria to move its location to a site on Park Avenue. It was glamorous and alive, a welcome change from living in a war-ravaged city. Eva was dying to spend time in a more modern world; her favorite American city was Manhattan. She had already visited several times, always skipping just a few years ahead; stealing a glimpse of the future was half the fun of being an earthbound spirit!

Tonight, there was an All Hallows Eve Ball at the Waldorf-Astoria; Eva planned to enjoy the nightlife of a modern American city. October 31st always had a certain feel she supposed only a ghost could appreciate. All that mattered tonight was having fun and leaving thoughts of war behind, if only for a little while. Eva had grown weary of waiting for the war to end; Makefield Manor had almost been hit twice, and the bombing never seemed to let up. There were no more starry nights to gaze upon; instead, London's decimated skyline resembled the gaping mouth of a prizefighter. With each passing day, Eva could feel the glimmer of a modern city calling to her, on the gentle winds of a future time.

From the observation deck, Eva beheld a cloudless night sky adorned with thousands of tiny diamonds. The view of Fifth Avenue below was breathtaking; block after block, brick and glass buildings lined the streets, their windows sparkling like spun gold. The heavy traffic below moved about like a force of nature; the sound of beeping horns keeping rhythm with the night. Without a doubt, New York City had a life of its own. Eva wanted to settle here, and was determined to convince the others to agree. Tomorrow, she would return to London with newspapers for Nikos and Dracula; they needed proof the war would last far longer than anyone expected. It was time for a fresh start; there was no compelling reason to remain in London. Why not, America?

As the yellow cab pulled up in front of the hotel, Eva realized she didn't want to go inside yet; it was such a perfect autumn night. She paid her fare and moved away from the crowd, searching for a rear entrance. Eva drew a cigarette from her purse and leaned against an ivy covered fence; nicotine had no effect on her, but smoking kept her hands busy.

A young boy was concealed in the shadows; he didn't know what to say to such a beautiful girl. Finally getting up the courage, he asked, "Got an extra one, by any chance?"

Eva gasped in surprise; a young boy emerged from the bushes; she guessed he was twelve or thirteen. Something in his brown eyes appealed to her; Eva handed him a cigarette with a genuine smile.

"I work in the kitchen," the boy explained. Eva watched as he executed three perfect smoke rings to impress her.

Eva studied the boy's profile; he was certainly too young to be smoking. "Why aren't you working?"

"Tonight's too beautiful to be stuck inside."

"I know what you mean…October nights *are* special," Eva said dreamily.

"I won't be here for long…I'm on a quest to see the world. If I have time, I'd like to try a hundred jobs on for size. I don't mind hard work… but, it's not easy to get hired when you're only twelve."

"I *knew* you were too young for cigarettes!"

"And I suppose you think makeup and high heels make you look like a woman. They don't fool anyone…certainly not me." Eva should have been insulted, but she wasn't; he was incredibly charismatic for someone so young.

Eva decided to change the subject. "What do you want most out of life?"

"That's easy…freedom to pursue my dream."

"What dream?"

"To be a professional musician."

"Well, this is America…you have the right to pursue any dream you want."

"Not at my age…I have no rights at all."

"What brought you to New York?" Eva asked.

"Well…I recently parted ways with a place called Gibault and let's just say…I'm never going back."

"Gibault…is that like a private school?" Eva asked sweetly.

The boy laughed, "Private school…that's a good one."

"Don't you have a home…where's your mother?"

"I don't know where she is. Gibault was my home for the past two years…until about a month ago."

"Why did you leave?"

"Because home shouldn't be a place where they beat you into submission…and lock you up at night."

"I am sorry." Eva hated to think of him in such a place.

"Don't be…as soon as I have a little more money saved up, I'm headed for California. I write songs, you know. I'm going to buy a guitar and make my music famous someday." Eva smiled; the boy was still young enough to have such dreams.

"But, how will you get there?"

"How I reach the West Coast is all part of my journey. The people I meet…the places I see. I believe my life has already been mapped out, exactly how it's meant to be. Meeting someone like you tonight is a perfect example. I don't know why we were brought together; in time all will be revealed."

A steady breeze picked up and Eva suddenly felt like flying. The night was so lovely; she didn't want to go inside. "Would you like to see something amazing?" Eva took his hand in hers.

The boy stubbed out his cigarette. "I'm game."

"What about your job?" Eva asked.

"If they fire me, I'll find another one."

"Come on, then!"

"Where are we going?" the boy asked.

"To Central Park, of course…hurry!"

As they ran toward the park, they ran into a group of inebriated adults wearing disheveled Halloween costumes; All Hallows Eve was their only chance to be someone else. They reached the street, crossing against traffic as angry cabbies raised their fists in anger. The two ran like the children they were, as cool night air invigorated them. The boy was out of breath by the time they reached the entrance to the park.

"Where to now?" he asked, still trying to catch his breath.

"We're going to the top of the Empire State Building!"

"From here?" The boy was clearly puzzled.

Eva gently pulled the boy behind a stone wall, where no one could see them. She closed her eyes and grasped his hands, as the ground began to vibrate. The wind picked up and a funnel of dead leaves engulfed them, swirling frantically around as they were lifted into the air. When the boy looked down at his feet, he realized they were being carried by the wind well above the rooftops. At first, he thought it merely a fluke of nature, but quickly realized they were actually flying! Eva held his arm, as they flew over late night traffic on Park Avenue; the boy was mesmerized and as Eva watched him, she felt him to be a kindred spirit.

She guided them back toward Fifth Avenue, and to New York City's tallest building. Breathless and euphoric, Eva slid into position landing gracefully on the observation deck. The boy touched down hands first, making an unplanned summersault.

"That was incredible!" The boy shouted, raising his arms to the night.

"I thought you'd enjoy it."

"So, who exactly are you?"

Eva let out a peel of laughter, and replied cryptically, "I'm exactly what you came looking for tonight."

"That certainly explains it."

"It was the wind...it only happens in October." Eva attempted a rational explanation, sensing his unease.

It started to rain, and the spell was broken. "I guess I should go and see if I still have a job," the boy said awkwardly.

Eva didn't want him to leave; she found herself smitten by this dark-haired boy. She didn't even know his name. "Wait...my name is Eva..."

"Yes, I know...I've seen you here before," the boy replied.

"I don't believe you ever told me your name," Eva said.

"Didn't I?"

"No."

"Name's, Charles…Charles Manson. My friends call me Charlie."
With that the boy skipped away, before she could say anything more.

Eva stood alone as rain rolled off her human form; it was unable
to penetrate a body without substance. The rooftop felt barren once he
had gone. She had never made it to the party, but her heart wasn't in
it anymore.

There was still one more thing she needed to do; using the fire
escape, Eva made her way back to the street in search of a newsstand.
She procured a copy of the New York Times, and tucked it under her
arm. The desk clerk was asleep when Eva slipped quietly past him; she
returned to her room and shed her gown, leaving it on the bed for a
chambermaid to find.

Eva was pleased with what she had gathered in such a short time;
she had procured an illustrated volume of Dracula, along with two more
books about Jack the Ripper and a Time Magazine. At the bottom
of the pile were the most valuable items of all; two newspapers with
confirmation of Hitler's death, along with details about the end of
World War II. Eva hoped these would convince Dracula, it was time
to get out of Europe altogether. London had lost its appeal; Eva knew
it would take decades to rebuild the city to its former grandeur. Packing
up the books and newspapers in her satchel, Eva moved to a full-length
mirror. Bidding a fond farewell to the year 1945, Eva put her hand to
the glass, and passed through the colorful lights of the Otherworld.

Chapter 83 - Eva and Dracula - The Otherworld

Dracula was waiting for Eva when she returned with her bundle of books and newspapers; he sat alone reading from a well-worn copy of obscure poetry. Eva thought poetry about the most boring thing ever invented; she considered poetry a poor attempt at romanticizing the pathetic human condition. When she saw Dracula reading peacefully the old desire returned, taunting Eva with images of what she could no longer have.

"I only have one question for you," Dracula said, looking up from his book

"Not, where was I tonight?"

"No."

"What is it, then?" Eva said, placing her bundle on an overstuffed chair.

"I just want to know why you insist on disappearing," Dracula noted her makeup and gown, and then added, "posing as a full-grown woman is a dangerous game."

Eva ignored his comment. "Look at what I brought back for you... news about this endless war."

"Really? Let me take a look." Dracula softened a little; it was hard to stay angry with a petulant child.

Eva retrieved the newspapers and magazine, handing them to Dracula. "Here's proof this war won't be over until 1945!" Dracula read the headlines, noting the dates to confirm Eva was correct.

Dracula pulled Eva close; even now, after all this time, a spark of passion still burned. "Eva...what am I going to do with you? You travel to New York City alone...tell no one where you're going. Is this how you want to spend your life...skipping through time, in search of the ultimate adventure? Dressing like a woman doesn't make you one."

"You forget...I know much about being a woman," Eva replied, pulling away.

"It must be difficult to be trapped inside a child's body but...surely, you understand the risk of masquerading as an adult. Believe me…to most you're just a precocious little girl wearing makeup. Anyone who pretends to accept you as an adult is merely being indulgent!"

Eva felt rage building up inside her; everything he said was true. Although she rarely cried during her human lifetime, Eva began to tremble as her twelve-year-old body became wracked with sobs. She buried her face in the crook of his arm; her tears continued to fall, until she had nothing more inside.

Eva finally stopped to wipe her eyes. "On my deathbed, I cursed your name and offered my soul for a chance to gaze upon you once again…but not as a child. I was coerced into a role I never intended to play."

"And I intended to make a companion of Mary Kelly…but a vicious killer had other plans…" Dracula trailed off.

"Yes…and now we both know the heartache of a love that is out of reach."

Dracula turned to the second page of the paper; there was a shocking photo of London Bridge on fire. He picked up a second newspaper and there it was, an official declaration the war was over! Underneath the headlines, was a photo of Adolf Hitler; the dictator had apparently committed suicide, rather than suffer the humiliation of defeat.

The ancient vampire was ready to consider leaving his beloved city behind. "Maybe we *should* think about leaving London. Let's go back and talk it over with Nikos. I think we have all the proof we need to convince Jack and the others too; London no longer feels safe. I don't know about you, but I'm tired of sharing the night with German missiles."

"We should relocate to New York City!" Eva exclaimed.

"New York City is one possibility," Dracula replied noncommittally. Eva packed her satchel and prepared to return to Makefield Manor; there were many important decisions to make.

Chapter 84 - Something about Virginia - Rodwell, England - (March 28, 1941)

If she had known suicide by drowning was such a messy business, Virginia Woolf would have chosen a more comfortable method; a handful of pills in a nice warm bed were certainly a more comfortable way to die. As she walked heavily into the river, the pockets of her husband's overcoat filled with rocks, Virginia had no regrets. The writer's life had been a continuous stream of ups and downs, as she fought the insanity living inside her. The water began to pull her in deeper; Virginia wondered if her life would really flash before her eyes, as everyone claimed. When the water reached her chest, she let the current take her; Virginia kept her eyes closed, so she wouldn't see the world slip away. Her life had been a sad one; despite a devoted husband, the prolific writer had always been an island unto herself. When depression seized her, Virginia became lost in it. The sun stopped shining and the world became smaller; Virginia's random thoughts were slowly driving her mad, and there was no escape from it. Trapped inside a brilliant, yet tortured mind, Virginia considered the unthinkable; she decided to drown herself in the Ouse River. Virginia was gasping for air now; she was lightheaded and beyond feeling any pain. Hypothermia set in and her limbs grew numb, as her lungs filled with muddy water. As death loomed, Virginia realized there was nothing remotely glamorous about drowning. The last thought Virginia had in this life, was remorse for taking her husband's overcoat.

For the longest time, Virginia felt nothing; when she finally opened her eyes, there was only darkness. Her body was floating in water, but that was all she could ascertain. Her husband's overcoat had been taken by the current, along with her goulashes. She kept her eyes closed until she heard voices; two boys were night fishing nearby. London Bridge was clearly visible on the horizon; how far had she traveled? Virginia grabbed hold of a rock and pulled herself out of the water.

"I told you I saw someone swimming in a nightgown!" one of the boys shouted to his friend. Virginia's hiding place had been discovered. As the boys came running toward her, Virginia saw only one option; she jumped back into the frigid water and swam into a black pool of uncertainty.

CHAPTER 85 - AN EXTRAORDINARY PROPOSITION - (APRIL 12, 1941)

Henry had a graceful build and creamy unblemished skin, but he could never be as beautiful as Jericho; his former love had no equal. Jack watched the boy as he strutted purposefully across a narrow street, to an area Jack knew well. London was full of places like this, streets where love could be bought with the understanding, it was momentary. Henry had no trouble finding paying customers; he had a pleasant face and a smile that put his client's at ease. The night's earnings had been fair and would provide for a family he had chosen, not the one he was born into.

The streets were sparsely populated this time of night, but Henry didn't mind; he enjoyed his solitude and felt most at home when walking in familiar neighborhoods. Lately, his hearing had become acute. Since becoming a black swan, Henry could hear things most humans could not. He heard children whispering secrets in the dark, and the voice of a young mother singing a lullaby. He passed the bakery shop, and picked up the sound of the baker's wife working warm dough between arthritic fingers. He kept walking until he passed the Red Lion public house, where a game of late night pool was being played. The tap of a cue stick and the playful clack of colored balls, were comfortable sounds; they kept Henry grounded in the human world, even as the blood of a murdered vampire coursed through his veins. Jericho's life as a creature of the night had been cut short, in a most brutal way. Henry had loved him despite what he was, but he swore an oath never to become a vampire.

As his favorite corner came into view, Henry realized someone was tailing him. He had been followed before; sometimes it was nothing more than a stumbling drunk, who had lost his way. Henry stopped abruptly and listened to the night. It was deadly quiet, and he knew that was not a good sign. "Show yourself!" Henry said to the empty air.

Jack had cut the corner, and was now ahead of him; he came out of the shadows to reveal his presence. "It's Jack." Henry relaxed, but just a little. He didn't trust Jack one bit.

"Henry, why do you walk the streets selling your body to wrinkled old men?

"I do what I have to..."

Jack moved closer. "Join me, Henry. I can give you what most would kill for...a life without end...and the ability to stay young forever."

"I have no desire to drink blood, thank you very much," Henry snapped, and began to walk in a different direction.

"Come on, Henry...you're already halfway there. Let me be the father you never had."

"I had a father. He died and I don't need another," Henry replied, keeping his back turned against Jack.

"Drink from me, boy...and you will never know cold or hunger again. I will show you things beyond imagining. Let me into your heart, Henry...you'll never regret it." Jack was desperate for company in his solitary world.

Henry turned to face Jack, determined to stand his ground. "Because of you, Jericho is dead. Now get away from me, you foul thing!"

"But I loved him, too. What happened had nothing to do with me." Jack's thirst for Henry's blood became unbearable.

Henry began walking faster, hoping Jack wouldn't follow. When he reached the next block, he started to relax; convinced Jack had finally given up his pursuit. Henry turned and headed back toward Trafalgar Square, unaware Jack had expected him to do just that. It happened so fast, he had no defense. Jack was on him before he could resist; within seconds the vampire's jaw was locked onto Henry's exposed neck. Henry felt his life force slipping away; when he tried to scream, he found his voice was gone. Dragging the boy off the street, Jack continued to feed, pressing Henry against a brick wall; the boy had no choice but to submit to his will. Tearing open his shirt, Jack used his sharpest fingernail to create an opening on his chest so his fledgling could drink. Henry tried to twist his body away, but Jack was persistent; he pulled Henry to the wound. Henry finally succumbed; he was no match for the seasoned vampire. As Henry drank, he felt lethargy take over, accompanied by a feeling of weightlessness. Henry's body dropped to the ground, convulsing violently as his human body began to expire. Jack had seen this all before; this time, he planned to stay and teach his new fledgling how to survive. Jack believed this was a second chance for him to do things right. Henry could never be what Jericho was to him, but Jack felt it was time to have a partner.

Henry lay on the ground, eyes staring up at a sky that never looked so beautiful. He could feel Jack's blood inside him, and although he wanted more; Henry would not yield to his true nature. Jack pulled the boy to his feet, and the two locked eyes; Henry was still adjusting to the sensation of becoming a newly-made creature of the night. It saddened Jack to see such hatred in his young fledgling's eyes, but he believed Henry would eventually come around.

"You see, my boy…it wasn't all that bad now, was it?" Jack asked through bloodstained teeth.

"I curse the day you were born…if I could kill you now, I would!" Henry screamed.

Jack had not expected this reaction, and was temporarily speechless; a passing car startled them and, Henry bolted into the darkness. Jack stood mutely on the vacant street corner; he was baffled that anyone would turn down the offer of eternal life. He shrugged, deciding his fledgling would have to figure things out on his own, after all.

Chapter 86 - Vincent's Muse - Old Trafalgar Square Station - (April 25, 1941)

Akos was perched on Vincent's easel as he watched Prince mixing pigment in a most graceful motion. The bird, of course, did not understand a thing about painting; he stayed because Vincent kept sunflower seeds in his pants pocket. His life as a specter was much the same as his earthly life, only now, the bird ate for pleasure. Ignoring the bird's incessant squawking, Prince worked skillfully on a landscape, as Vincent observed his apt pupil with obvious delight. The boy had amazing talent!

"You have the magic inside you, Edward." Sometimes Vincent called him Edward; Prince had grown tired of correcting him.

Alice and Audrey watched from a blanket on the floor, where they had made themselves a picnic of discarded food. Sharing a tattered book, they whispered to each other in a language only twins can share. Rupert came in from his nightly wandering, plunking down a burlap sack. At only thirteen years old, his features were already hardened by life on the streets. He nodded to Vincent, and then bent down to kiss the twins; it was something he did every time he returned, as though he might never see them again.

"Did you find Henry?" Audrey asked hopefully.

"Not yet, poppet...I'm sorry," Rupert replied with a defeated expression. He moved to deliver a tube of raw sienna paint he pilfered for Vincent.

"Thank you, kindly," Vincent said, already opening the tube.

The mood had become somber since Henry's disappearance. The boy had been missing for more than two weeks; Rupert had been unable to find his friend anywhere.

"And, where is Oliver?" Rupert asked.

"Left to pick up his papers already." Prince replied distractedly.

Rupert moved to a makeshift kitchen area, where they stored their meager food supply. He was famished, but always careful not to eat more than his share. Fortunately, Prince and Vincent required no daily sustenance, which helped their provisions last longer. Selecting the butt end from a stale loaf of bread, Rupert moved to the corner and he threw his tired body down onto a pile of comfortable blankets. Tired from walking all night, Rupert began to feel drowsy and soon drifted off to sleep. Alice and Audrey had also fallen back to sleep, having tired of books they long ago memorized. They had all become a family of sorts, but there was still something missing; although the words were never spoken, they all longed for the love and comfort only a mother could provide.

As a very unorthodox family made the best life they could underneath the streets of London, Virginia Woolf was just beginning to understand she had reached the afterlife. She wasn't sure how long she had been swimming, before landing on a riverbank exhausted. Her hair and clothes were still wet, but at least she no longer had to swim. Virginia spotted a warehouse building in the distance; she hurried toward it, hoping to stay out of sight until daylight. At first, the place appeared abandoned, until she noticed light coming from somewhere *beneath* the floor. Virginia descended the stairs, apprehensive about what she would find, but curious enough to continue. As she got closer to the source of light, it seemed to draw her in. Would she find others like herself?

Virginia pushed on the door, surprised to find it unlocked. Once inside, she immediately recognized that people were living down here. And then she heard the voices, children's voices.

"Hey, how did you get in here?" Audrey asked, pointing to a woman wearing a damp nightgown.

Prince nearly dropped his paintbrush, as Akos flew in frenzied circles. The woman did not speak; but she and Vincent locked eyes from across the room.

Alice gasped at the ghostly vision, immediately uttering a word she had almost forgotten, "Mummy?"

Chapter 87 - Jack's Progeny -
Whitechapel District - (June 1941)

Blood…need blood…must kill to survive. Find blood and drink it. You must find it before the sun comes up. Blood will take away the hollow feeling. Find blood now! The fledgling vampire's thoughts were primal. Never in his short life had he been so hungry, yet the sight of food made him ill. His teeth almost seemed to vibrate inside his mouth, as he drooled like a rabid beast. The night was nearly over and still, he had not satisfied his natural hunger.

Henry had to feed or he was doomed. With his acute hearing, Henry picked up the scent of a tomcat. The animal froze at the sight of two piercing red eyes, quickly assessing it was cornered. The tomcat crouched low to the ground in a futile attempt to appear menacing. Green eyes met red, as the vampire began to slowly circle his prey; Henry was determined to hypnotize the feline creature into submission. The gray tabby extended its claws, arching its back in anticipation of battle. Henry's hunger became unbearable; the fledgling vampire was experiencing physical pain. The tomcat growled as the vampire revealed his razor sharp teeth, and then accepted its demise underneath a yellow moon. Henry savaged his prey, drinking hungrily until the tomcat's feet stopped twitching, and its tail hung lifelessly in the moonlight.

Watching from a distance, were two young fledglings; their rat-like eyes burned with the wickedness of what they had become. Turning away in disgust, the taller boy commented in a guttural voice, "It seems alley cats are becoming scarce these days…now I know why. I hear tabbies taste best but, what do I know? No self-respecting vampire feeds on alley cats!"

"No way! I actually killed *two* humans the night I was turned…I was really hungry. The one who made me…claimed he was a homicidal maniac from the nineteenth century. His only advice was to avoid sunlight." His companion let out a chortle of depraved laughter.

"I run into more and more like us every night. I know what we are, but…why were we chosen?" the taller boy asked, not expecting an answer.

"I don't know…but it can be a lonely life. I'm glad we found each other."

"We best get underground now…dawn already brightens the horizon."

Chapter 88 - An Audience with the Fuhrer - Berlin, Germany - (July 1941)

Adolf Hitler was in a distinctly foul mood today. In some respects, the war was going exactly as he planned however; the Fuhrer was frustrated by America's refusal to engage. While the ongoing offensive with Britain was going well, Hitler was dismayed by the determination of the British people. After almost a year of incessant bombing, London citizens remained strong and resilient; the Fuhrer was clearly disappointed things were dragging on for so long. He had expected the offensive to last less then six months. It was astounding how much the British people could withstand, while remaining steadfast and true to their country, and their crown. Families separated from their children, widespread hunger, joblessness and a city in ruins. What else would it take?

The Fuhrer finished shaving, satisfied with the symmetry of his trademark mustache. He turned to find a German officer standing in the doorway. Hitler could not remember hearing him enter, and felt certain he had locked the door. The soldier saluted with a cap swung so low, Hitler couldn't see his eyes.

"A letter, Fuhrer...a most urgent document," the soldier spoke in perfect German.

"Do I know you?" Hitler stepped forward, deciding to let the intrusion slide because he wasn't one hundred percent sure about the door. He snatched the envelope from his hand, and tore it open. His eyes grew wide when he saw a newspaper clipping, with an apparent photo of his corpse.

Hitler reached for his pistol, but Jack's expression made him hesitate. "Touch that weapon, Fuhrer...and your life will end today."

Hitler knew he was cornered. He stared at the newspaper clipping in disbelief. "What kind of treachery is this?"

Jack took off his hat. "Perhaps a proper introduction is in order."

"How did you get past my guards?" Hitler demanded.

"All in good time, Fuhrer...all in good time," Jack replied, as he motioned toward Hitler's desk. It was time to stroke the man's ego, if they were to make any headway.

"I am sure you have questions, Fuhrer. Let me say...first and foremost, I have the utmost respect for you as a leader, and as a proponent of purifying the human race."

"This newspaper clipping...how did you manage it? It's obviously a fake," Hitler challenged.

"Quite authentic, I assure you. By the way, name's Jack. Thought you should know the name of your new partner."

"Partner!" Hitler stood up, and drew his weapon.

Jack reached across the desk and grabbed the Fuhrer by his lapels. "Don't test me," he growled, disarming Hitler and shoving the pistol in his pants. Hitler sat back down, and tried to maintain his dignity; the Fuhrer could have called his guards, but he wanted to hear more.

"What kind of partnership are we talking about?"

"Now, that's much better, Fuhrer. Let's talk about how this is going to go, shall we?"

"What do you want?" Hitler began to think the man was a spy; how else could he have penetrated his bunker?

"What I propose, is merely a slight variation of your master plan... to preserve the Aryan race. I know you wonder where this is going...so please, indulge me." Hitler sat in his chair stone-faced and impossible to read.

"I'm sure by now you've figured out there is something shall we say, *otherworldly* about me. For instance, the first time we met was in your bathroom mirror..."

"It *was* you!" Hitler's interruption was met with an icy stare.

"I'll keep it simple. I am a vampire, nosferato or creature of the night...whichever you prefer. Surely, you're familiar with Romanian folklore in this regard?"

"Ghost stories used to frighten women and children," Hitler scoffed.

"Stories...yes, we do have a colorful story. You've no doubt heard of Count Dracula from Transylvania...or Dracula, as he is named in a book written by Bram Stoker. I would be surprised if you had not heard of it."

"I am vaguely familiar with the story."

"Fair enough, but I'm here to inform you...vampires are very real.

The real Count Dracula did not die in 1476, as history books would have us believe. Bram Stoker's novel had some truth to it…but I can assure you, Dracula is alive and currently living in London." Jack could see Hitler was becoming intrigued.

"How, you may ask, did I become involved? Count Dracula plucked me from my human life and gave me a better one…"

"So, how old are you?" Hitler wasn't sure why he chose to ask such a question; it somehow seemed important to know more about his strange visitor.

"Not that old…not compared to the one who made me. In my human life, I was a psychotic killer. I once terrorized the streets of a little town called Whitechapel. I'm sure you've heard of Jack the Ripper…well, here I am!" Jack bowed, as Hitler's jaw fell open. He watched as the Fuhrer's eyes darted around the room; he was looking for another weapon.

"Jack the Ripper and Dracula are vampires! More fairytales," Hitler exclaimed defiantly; Jack's anger finally came to a boil.

Tired of talking, the vampire jumped up from his seat; he came around the desk so fast, the Fuhrer had no time to act. Jack gripped Hitler's neck, nearly cutting off his air supply. "I can see you still need convincing." Hitler kicked his feet, unwilling to give up without a fight.

Jack put his lips to Hitler's ear. "It's so much better, when you don't fight it." Jack plunged his teeth into the Fuhrer's neck, drinking from one of the most evil human beings the world would ever know. The vampire drank just a little, before shoving him back into his seat. Straightening his jacket, Jack returned to his chair and continued his story, as though they had just shared a cup of tea.

"So, now you know who I am and why I'm here. We need a man of your caliber to join us…someone who shares the vision of establishing a superior race." Hitler rubbed his neck, it had already stopped bleeding.

"There is nothing to fear…my blood will heighten your senses in a delightfully unnatural way. Can't you already feel the difference inside you? The change has already begun. When you are turned, you will have more power than you ever imagined."

"What kind of superior race are we talking about?" Hitler asked, struck by a surge of energy that made him fidget in his chair; something indeed was happening to him.

"Count Dracula and I plan to build an army of others like us. In the human world, we are outnumbered...but that won't be for very long. We seek to fill the world with our kind, a race that feeds on human blood and owns the night. We aren't so very different from you, Fuhrer. You strive to purify the human race...our kind plans to enslave them!"

"I don't understand where I fit in," Hitler replied looking confused.

"We have followed your illustrious career...and believe you have much to contribute. There will eventually be armies of others like us... and they will need a leader. Your extensive military background will be a tremendous asset...as we expand our numbers throughout North America."

Jack studied Hitler's eyes, and could see he was starting to get through; it was time to go in for the kill. Reaching inside his coat pocket, Jack retrieved another document. It was a page from the New York Times, declaring World War II was over. The article further detailed the defeat of Germany and the death of Hitler. He threw it on the desk, giving the Fuhrer a moment to digest it.

"Another forgery!" Hitler exclaimed without conviction.

"You know better. It's real and so is your impending defeat. Germany will lose the war...and you will die an abysmal failure. Don't you see what a waste it would be to kill yourself?"

"I would never kill myself...that's against God's law."

"Newspapers and history books don't lie, Fuhrer."

"Newspapers with dates that haven't happened yet. Do you really expect me to believe that in addition to being a vampire...you can also time travel?"

"The truth will be revealed in good time...but, that bite on your neck is real now isn't it?"

"So you all drink blood, then?" Hitler asked.

"Yes...it keeps us alive."

"Would I have to drink blood, too?" Hitler asked his stomach turning at the thought.

"You will learn to love the taste...I promise," Jack declared with his most cunning smile. Hitler noted his wound was already scabbed over.

"You will heal even faster once you become one of us."

"And, do I *really* get to live forever?"

"And beyond," Jack said, as he stood up to leave.

"What about the war?"

"It must continue to its inevitable conclusion...until the pivotal moment when you begin to consider taking your life."

"I already told you, I would never do that!" Hitler almost spat the words.

"Look into my eyes, Fuhrer. You'll see that everything I've told you is true." Hitler tried to look away, but found he could not. His mind exploded with visions of a defeated Germany, including the horrifying sight of his bloodied corpse.

"A little more convincing than a newspaper now, wasn't it?" Jack said with a sneer. Hitler was so rattled; he was temporarily at a loss for words.

Hitler finally snapped of it, just in time to see Jack vaporize before his eyes. Hitler's mind raced as he tried to make sense of his conversation with a man named Jack, who claimed to be a vampire; a vampire who had information about the future. How could this even be possible? It had to be a hoax. The telling documents Jack had brought with him were gone, but their images were burned upon the Fuhrer's memory.

Hitler suddenly felt in need of fresh air. Moving from his desk, he called for an impromptu inspection of his troops. Once outside his comfortable office, the Fuhrer could instantly feel something inside him had changed. He could hear voices, but when he looked around no one was speaking. German soldiers stood in perfect formation, their faces void of emotion; the Fuhrer found himself replaying his conversation with his enigmatic visitor. As Hitler moved through the endless rows of well-groomed soldiers, he could hear a sort of chatter that was difficult to decipher. Hitler came to a halt when he reached a soldier who had neglected to fasten his chin strap; he smiled, always happy when he had a chance to correct someone. The soldier fastened his chin strap; followed by a salute he hoped would compensate for his oversight. Hitler removed one of his brown leather gloves, slapping the soldier several times until his cheeks were a bright red; the soldier accepted his punishment in silence. Hitler moved on to an–acne faced soldier with steel gray eyes.

"Stinking killer of babies...I hope you rot in hell." The words had not been spoken out loud, but Hitler heard them. The man had not moved a muscle, of that, the Fuhrer was certain. Unwilling to look like a fool, the Fuhrer continued further down the row of perfectly dressed soldiers.

"How does it feel to murder helpless women and children?" another voice asked. Hitler turned his head, but once again, there was no indication words had actually been spoken.

Unnerved, the Fuhrer dismissed the men without further inspection. Commanding Officer Himmler stood behind the Fuhrer, relieved to have the inspection over so quickly. Himmler raised his arm in salute, but Hitler ignored him and headed back toward his bunker. As he passed his commanding officer, Hitler heard a voice say, "What a joke this guy is...that mustache makes him look like a damn fool." Hitler turned around to glare at Himmler. It couldn't be. His second in command would hardly dare make such a derogatory remark. Himmler stood at attention, as if expecting another command. Hitler held his gaze for a moment, and then finally looked away.

Hitler was clearly rattled and anxious to be alone, so he could figure this out. Hurrying past another set of guards, the Fuhrer resisted the temptation to cover his ears so he couldn't hear anything else. Inside his bunker once more, Hitler let out a deep sigh of relief. Official documents required his immediate attention, but his mind could not focus on anything but what had just happened. The Fuhrer was shaking with excitement, as he slowly understood something had profoundly changed him. He had been bitten by a man claiming to be a vampire; could this mean he was no longer entirely human? Absentmindedly rubbing his neck, Adolf Hitler sat down at his desk to absorb the startling realization he was able to read minds.

Chapter 89 - Dracula in Real Time - Central London - (August 1941)

It was a secret pleasure he indulged whenever he could. Since the invention of moving pictures, Dracula closely followed movies about himself, amazed at how a simple novel by Bram Stoker evolved into a parade of what, in his opinion, were poorly made films the public seemed to adore. As the real Count Dracula focused his attention on the screen, he was fascinated by the ignorance of a film producer who insisted on casting a bug-eyed Hungarian actor named Bela Lugosi; his performance was more comical than scary. The credits began to roll, but Dracula remained seated; being last to leave the theatre ensured he was never blindsided by the unexpected.

Walking into a warm summer night, Dracula wrinkled his nose when the acrid smell of smoke filled his nostrils. As he walked silently across St. James Square, Dracula noticed many local businesses were closed, due to damage and a lack of paying customers. Jermyn Street was littered with bricks and other debris, setting a perfect stage for its defeated residents. London was no longer beautiful; it was now just a shadow of the magnificent city it had once been. For Dracula, the magic was gone, replaced by a painful realization it was time to leave his beloved city behind.

Tonight, Dracula found himself in desperate need of solitude; a pale orange moon provided the only splash of color in a sky without a single star. The ancient vampire closed his eyes and found himself drawn to the moors. Walking now with a definitive purpose, Dracula headed toward the only place where there was no need to disguise his true nature. Cutting across an open field, Dracula assumed his bat-like form and took flight. The moors called him like no other place on earth; the night wind welcomed as he prepared to land on a well-placed rock. In the distance, he could see the outline of London Bridge, a black shadow against the sky. Most of the city was under a blackout; illumination only made buildings a better target for German missiles.

Surrounded by the steady hum of crickets, the vampire savored a calmness only the moors could provide. Dracula heard a wolf cry out, and sniffed the air to determine its distance. The snap of a branch disrupted his reverie; he caught the scent of a red deer, and it made his mouth water. An experienced hunter, he sprang from his comfortable perch and stalked what he knew would be easy prey. The doe went down without a struggle; Dracula ripped open her throat and fed like the wild thing he was. Wiping a hand across his mouth, Dracula returned to his rock and discovered a black wolf waiting for him. Like a runaway dog, the wolf ran to his master, and sat at his feet as if asking, "Where to now?" Dracula reached down to scratch the beast behind the ears, and he responded with a growl of contentment.

As the wolf happily licked blood from Dracula's hands, a blinding light appeared behind them; Dracula abruptly turned around, prepared for a confrontation. As the light began to dim, the ancient vampire saw a woman standing a few feet away; she was not just any woman, it was his Mary.

"Vlad..." Mary's voice sounded like silk.

Dracula reached out to touch her, but pulled back when his hand went clean through her. Suddenly, the ruthless vampire was terrified. As a vampire, Dracula avoided all things holy, just as he spurned natural light. Whatever this vision was, it could not be trusted. Bright sunlight had nearly killed him in the past. But the ancient vampire was fearful of sunlight for another reason; to Dracula, God *was* sunlight, and part of a world to which he could never belong. Dracula knew his judgment day would eventually come; it was truly what he feared most. After living for hundreds of years, Dracula feared very little, but his religious roots ran deep. When he saw Mary Kelly's ghost, he believed his judgment day had finally come. How could he face his God, as the wretched thing he had become? To Dracula, this was unimaginable. He was a prince of darkness, but it had not always been so. In his human life, Dracula had been a warrior who fought tirelessly for Christianity, effectively swearing his allegiance to the church of his God. Prince Vlad Dracula had tortured and killed Turkish soldiers by the thousands, all in the name of Christendom. What did he get in return? What was his reward? A queen he loved sentenced to rot in hell, with no chance for redemption. Was someone like him even worthy of redemption? Dracula already knew the answer. He was a vampire, a killer of innocents and a drinker of human blood. He was an abomination, and certain hell awaited him. This couldn't be his Mary. This was a ruse of some sort; Dracula would not be bested by a ghost, no matter how beautiful.

"What sort of trickery is this?" Dracula asked, backing away from the ghostly vision.

"Vlad...there is a world of light waiting...you only have to choose it."

Dracula covered his ears and screamed, "Speak no more...your false promises mean nothing to me!"

Mary moved toward him and although he wanted to pull away, her mere presence was intoxicating. Dracula became lost in Mary's golden brown eyes and her translucent freckled skin. She seemed so real, even though he knew she was not.

"I want to help you...I want us to be together..."

"How can that be? I am doomed to rot in hell!"

"You can turn away from evil, Vlad...it is your choice to make," Mary said softly, holding a transparent hand to his cheek. "God forgives those who ask for it."

"Mary...I am a vampire and will always be. To walk away from what I need to survive...is to sacrifice my life. Is that what you want?"

"It is the noblest sacrifice anyone can make," Mary replied, trying to make him understand.

"How can you ask this of me...how can I be expected to put humanity before my own needs?" Dracula realized how selfish he sounded. Mary took his hand in hers; Dracula studied her profile, determined to commit every detail of her face to memory.

"You once promised me a better life," Mary said softly.

Dracula dropped her hand. "The life I was going to offer you was nothing but a curse. It is a blessing you were killed...before I made you what I am, believe me."

"I couldn't have gone through with it, you know. I was going to tell you that night, when you came back with dinner...but you never came."

"I shouldn't have left you, Mary." Dracula turned his body away trying to hide his tears, but Mary took him in her arms. Dracula fell to his knees in anguish, and surrendered to his grief; his body became wracked with sobs as he considered his wretched life. The ancient vampire truly believed there was no hope for him. No afterlife. No glorious and purifying light and *absolutely* no forgiveness. As a vampire, he was doomed to a life in darkness; Dracula was certain he would never have a place in God's kingdom.

"The choice is yours to make, Vlad."

Dracula got control of himself, and showed his red eyes to the woman he once loved. "Look at these eyes, Mary…they are the eyes of the devil himself!"

Mary reached out to him, but Dracula would have no more of it. As Mary watched, the vampire took on his wolf form and moved toward her in a menacing way. Her presence began to dim, and then she vanished inside a cloud of shimmering smoke.

Leaping off the comfortable rock, Dracula resumed his human form and landed in a patch of hair grass. The black wolf followed, always ready for a new adventure. Almost immediately, Dracula picked up a scent that was distinctly human, but there was something else. The black wolf smelled it too, as they traveled in silence under the cover of low hanging trees. The pungent stench of swamp water temporarily masked the scent of their pursuer; but the sound of footsteps was getting closer. A twig snapped behind them and then another to their right; as natural predators, both recognized there was more than one human prowling about. Dracula took cover behind a patch of tangled branches; he was determined to remain in place. The seasoned vampire did his best fighting when the element of surprise was involved; Dracula would let his prey come to him.

The whistling sound passed his ear, before Dracula could determine where it came from; he didn't have to wait long to find out. The black wolf was down; an arrow had pierced his heart. Dracula cursed because he had no weapon. A half-dressed teenage boy emerged from the trees, and fell upon the wounded beast. As Dracula calculated his next move, an older boy with red eyes came into view, carrying a bow. These were not teenage boys, at all; Dracula watched as they savaged the dying wolf, desperate to drink its blood before the heart stopped beating.

Dracula took in the distinct scent of fledgling vampires; these weren't made by him. The older one looked familiar, but Dracula couldn't place him. Lost in a feeding a frenzy, the boys were oblivious to his presence.

The older boy finally looked up to take a furtive look around; Dracula got a closer look and knew who was responsible. Once again, Jack was doing as he pleased; rogue fledglings were a threat to all vampires! The boy scanned the trees with vacant eyes; he didn't see anything but his own primal needs. Jack had turned Henry, and left him to survive in the wild; the boy was only fourteen!

The angry vampire screamed Jack's name at the top of his lungs, following the echo of his voice as it resonated like an amateur choir called to midnight practice. Anxious to avoid a confrontation with the teenage fledglings, Dracula spread his arms and gracefully took flight.

CHAPTER 90 - THE NEW YORK
PUBLIC LIBRARY - (MAY 1967)

Eva was always happy to have a mission. She and Prince had been traveling regularly to New York City, as they worked to build a new life in America. Eva marveled at the freshness of America, such a contrast to the ancient cities of Europe. In America, everything seemed so well-scrubbed; it was a vast improvement over the dingy stone fortresses of London, already crumbling with age. The people of New York City were stark contrasts to the conservative demeanor of London citizens, fighting a war in their own backyard. Here in America, people dressed in a more casual and almost provocative, way; Eva couldn't help but notice that many young women had abandoned their brassieres altogether. Most astounding was the diversity of New York City residents; for the first time ever, Eva saw a wide range of people, many with skin quite different from her own. The most beautiful were the dark-skinned people, with smiles that lit up their faces as they walked the streets of Midtown Manhattan. The origins of New York City immigrants during the 1960s were almost too many to name; Eva thought they were all wonderful.

Prince and Eva had both done thorough research on New York City in the 1960s, so they were not entirely surprised by what they saw. On the surface, the diverse city appeared to be in sync and its citizens tolerant of one another, but that was not always the case. As Prince and Eva continued exploring what would soon be their new home, they began to understand the effect racial tensions had on their chosen city. Just two years before, Malcolm X had been assassinated and since then, racial tensions had escalated greatly. Upon his death, African Americans hailed a new leader of the civil rights movement; Martin Luther King.

When they reached Fifth Avenue, the library came into view. Eva remembered the lions from previous visits; Patience and Fortitude glared at her with recognition as she crossed the street.

"Race you up the steps!" Prince said, bolting toward the entrance.

When they reached the top step, they were chastised by a uniformed man. Ignoring him, they ran between the columns, feigning an impromptu game of hide and seek. Experience had taught them the importance of acting like children when others were watching. The New York Public Library was truly a magnificent place; Prince was beyond delighted to be living underneath a building where books would literally surround him. The decision to reside in New York City had been much influenced by Eva, who always had Dracula's ear. After careful consideration, Dracula agreed it made sense to not only leave Europe, but to skip ahead in time for a fresh start all around. The library itself was placed within Bryant Park, a green space where people could feel the grass under their feet. The main selling point for both Dracula and Nikos had been convenient underground access to the 42nd Street Station; this would guarantee a secure escape route if the need arose.

As they walked through the main entrance, Eva and Prince lost their smiles. They strolled nonchalantly toward the information desk, where an elderly man was engrossed in a worn copy of *War and Peace*.

"May I help you, children?" the wrinkled man asked in a condescending voice.

"We are looking for your historical section…American history, that is," Prince replied.

The man's eyebrow arched, as he leaned down to take a better look at them. "American history…right down that corridor…then take the stairs to the second floor. Mind your fingerprints on the books now!"

They weren't looking for books. Today, their quest was to find their way into a long-abandoned storage facility beneath the library itself. After carefully studying the building's floor plan, Prince calculated the approximate location of book vaults and planned to find a way in. Prince confirmed most of the storage vaults had been vacated decades ago; what a perfect place to house a growing fledgling population.

"This way," Prince whispered, pulling Eva behind a marble pillar. An elaborate candelabrum covered in cobwebs made him feel right at home. Prince cleaned it off and lit the candles with his finger; sometimes it was fun to show off.

Eva followed behind until they came to a rusted metal door that appeared securely bolted. Seeing no other option, they walked through the door and found themselves inside a cave-like structure. As they

260

adjusted to the dark, Prince could feel his excitement build. He was certain they were getting close. Cobwebs hung above them, dangling just low enough to caress their faces; Eva had to comb them out of her hair along with several spiders. Prince was so intent on his purpose; he ignored the cobwebs that clung to his clothes, making him look like a walking corpse. Eva wrinkled her nose at a damp, musty smell that grew stronger, as they inched their way along a narrow tunnel that seemed to go on forever.

It was Eva who spotted it first, an obscure iron gate she felt certain would take them beneath the library. Prince yanked on the badly rusted handle not expecting it to open, but it did. The opening was too small for them, so Prince stepped through the wall and found Eva had already beaten him to it. The stairs were steep and in a state of disrepair, but Prince was quick to point out what looked like an elevator shaft. No longer powered by electricity, they had to manually work the pulley to lower themselves down to the first level; they found thousands of crumbling books that filled wooden shelves so bowed, they made the whole wall appear to be smiling at them. Neither of them heard the books chattering quietly, as they tried to make sense of their unearthly visitors.

Chapter 91 - A Strange Visitor - Old Trafalgar Station - (November 1941)

Dracula was fuming when he reached the center of Whitechapel, just after sunset. This time of year the nights were long; this gave creatures of the night boundless energy. Dressed as a proper London gentleman of the 1940s, Dracula stood out as he walked past several public houses filled with drunken rabble-rousers; he reasoned humans needed to anesthetize themselves to endure living in a war-ravaged city. This was Jack's turf and he hoped to find him while he was still angry. How could he turn Henry at such a young age? Dracula wondered if the boy had submitted to Jack willingly, then realized that was too much to expect of a cold-hearted killer. Henry should have been given a choice! Now, he was roaming the moors like a savage, and for this, Jack took no responsibility. There was no denying Jack's guilt this time around; Henry reeked of the vampire who made him. He slowed his pace slightly, as he passed Miller's Court; it held such powerful memories. Dracula quickly moved on, convinced Jack was somewhere else tonight.

Vincent was still trying to understand how a night-gowned woman had found their secret hiding place. She had gray eyes too big for her narrow face, but they were captivating. Virginia's curly hair hung about her shoulders, still damp from the water. In her dressing gown and bare feet, Virginia looked like a young girl. At least this is what Vincent saw, when he beheld Virginia for the first time. There was something about the woman that moved him; a face like hers made him want to start painting people again. Virginia moved to a table where a single lantern burned; her face was illuminated to reveal the ghost she was.

Rupert jumped to his feet, feeling unexpectedly protective of their visitor. The woman appeared rather sad, as though searching for someone. He moved closer to inspect their otherworldly visitor; she was definitely not a vampire. Moving closer still, Rupert studied her soulful eyes, only to become lost in them. He asked her name, gently taking her hand which was surprisingly warm.

"My name is Virginia. What is this place?" she asked, surprised at how well her dead spirit could see in the darkness. She would never wear glasses again!

Vincent dropped his paintbrush and moved closer to their spectral visitor, placing a blanket over her shoulders in a gesture of modesty. "Virginia...this is a special place...if you've found your way here, there must be a reason."

"I went into the river...it was so cold and then I just couldn't swim anymore..." she broke off as the painful memory took her speech away.

Prince left his easel, and like the others, wanted to help this woman understand she was beyond the human world now. Alice and Audrey stood by, anxious to learn more about their strange visitor. Although the twins understood she was not their mother, they wanted her to stay.

"Are these your children?" Virginia asked Vincent.

He laughed heartily and answered honestly, "They were not born to me, but they are my responsibility now."

Virginia put her hand out to the twins, and they immediately stole her heart by burying their faces in the folds of her nightgown.

"Well, that settles it then; it seems you've found a new home," Vincent declared.

Their conversation was interrupted by the sound of anxious footsteps outside the thick metal door. Vincent was expecting Jack, but when the door burst open, a well-dressed vampire stood in the doorway with a scowl on his face. Count Dracula was pissed off about something.

"Where's Jack?" Dracula asked with a snarl. Virginia ducked behind the table, frightened by the angry vampire who hadn't even noticed her.

"What's wrong?" Prince asked boldly unfazed by Dracula's temper.

"Sorry, Vincent...I just need to speak to him." Dracula softened, when he realized the children had gone into hiding.

"I don't understand this nonsense between you and Jack. You're always at odds with one another," Vincent replied.

"We are only angered by the actions of those we love." Virginia surprised them by speaking directly to Dracula.

"And who are you?" Dracula asked harshly

Vincent dropped his paintbrush and moved to Virginia's side. "She is my new muse, and will be staying with us from now on."

Alice and Audrey came back into view; Dracula grinned as he

retrieved a small sack from his coat pocket and held it out for them. Alice ran to grab it, dumping its contents on the floor.

"Yo-Yo's!" exclaimed Alice. Audrey ran to claim her own, flashing Dracula a sunny smile.

"See now…there's no reason to be afraid of me now, is there?" He could feel their trust beginning to grow each time they saw him. Audrey ran to hug him, and Alice followed suit as Jack entered the room. Dracula pulled away and turned to face Jack; he had to keep his anger in check.

"Jack!" Prince called out, clearly happy to see him.

Jack got down on one knee and the girls went running into his arms, giggling as he lifted them into the air. Suddenly, Dracula's anger evaporated. He needed Jack in the days ahead. There was so much to do before they left London, and he couldn't do it alone. The vampire decided to shelve his anger, convinced a change of scenery would give him a new perspective.

Jack stood up and faced Dracula, one vampire to another. Although they couldn't read each other's thoughts, they somehow understood each lived by their own set of ethics and this would likely never change.

"I hear the moors are crawling with red deer this time of year…what do you say?" Jack said finally, breaking the ice.

"Maybe another time," Dracula replied, unwilling to let Jack off that easy.

CHAPTER 92 - LEAVING LONDON BEHIND - MAKEFIELD MANOR - (DECEMBER 15, 1941)

It was a rare night at Makefield Manor; for a change, they were all together. Nikos sat at the head of the table where he took command of their plans, including the practical things required to live in a more modern time. Their plan was to make a new home in the heart of New York City, more than twenty-five years into the future. They all agreed Dracula could ill afford to take any more chances with Scotland Yard; it was best to get out of London while they had the chance. In a big city like Manhattan, they could get lost in anonymity. Rory was thrilled to be finally going to America, the country her father had fought so hard for. Everyone regretted leaving the manor house behind; Dracula hated the idea of giving up real estate. Subletting an apartment, even a penthouse overlooking Central Park, was well beneath his standards; a man of status should own property. Eva absolutely refused to live underground; she was already focused on decorating ideas for Dracula's penthouse.

Jack was anxious to relocate to New York City, too, but for entirely different reasons. In a new place and time, Jack believed he would have more freedom to do as he pleased, and eventually hoped to branch out on his own. He had not forgotten about his final showdown with Adolf Hitler, determined he could travel back in time to complete the task. His plan was to arrive minutes before the Fuhrer was about to shoot himself; Jack grinned as he thought about his nefarious plan to alter history, in a most profound way.

"Everything is in order, Vlad," Nikos mumbled, jotting something down in his journal.

"Good work," Dracula replied, as he studied blueprints of the library.

Rory suddenly thought about the black swans. "What about Vincent...and the children? We can't just leave them behind."

Dracula knew they faced a difficult decision. "We can take Vincent with us, because he is a ghost...no different from you or Eva. Virginia, too. The problem is going to be the children...it's complicated."

"They are family! They have to come with us!" Prince declared.

"Agreed…but there is only one way…I think we all know it." They all stared at him with blank faces; they had no idea what he was talking about.

"The children are flesh and blood…but not entirely human. If we want to take them with us, they must become like me…like Jack." Dracula felt his voice choke. Making juvenile vampires was against everything he believed, but there was no other way. After the initial shock, Prince and Eva recognized this as a logical and necessary step.

Rory remained silent, her body trembling with rage; she was horrified at what they planned for these innocent children.

"What's wrong, Rory?" Prince asked, noting her distress.

"Wrong…what's wrong?" she shrieked, her face contorted with rage. "You're all evil!"

Prince was taken back by her anger. "You don't understand…."

"How can you talk about turning innocent children into vampires? It's incomprehensible. Why is this necessary? Why can't they stay here with Vincent?"

Dracula tried to explain, "Rory…please, I know this is difficult, believe me. I'm no killer of children…but Vincent and the children would be better protected if they came with us to America."

"But these are *children*…and now you want to make them bloodsucking killers!" Rory responded angrily.

"Rory," Prince moved to take her hand, "If we leave them behind, they remain vulnerable to illness and starvation. Our way allows them a better chance of survival." Rory dropped his hand, pulling away from him as though repulsed by his touch.

"My dear girl, if there was another way, I would choose it. I am sure Vincent will agree it's for the best, too," Dracula replied patiently.

Rory was about to continue her protest, when she felt the ground shake and fell backwards into her seat; a missile exploded in the street above them, even underground, the sound was deafening. Smoke filled the room as they scrambled to grab whatever they could, then headed to the tunnels. They had to get to Vincent!

266

Chapter 93 - A Narrow Escape - Central London - (December 15, 1941)

Eva and Prince held fast to one another, as they moved through the underground tunnel beneath Makefield Manor. Prince had concerns about timing; the book vaults were not quite habitable, but Dracula insisted they could make it work. Rory ran a few paces behind them; she always felt left out, whenever Eva was around. Dracula and Jack ran ahead; the destination was Kings Cross Station, as previously arranged. When they were all accounted for, they proceeded up the stairway into a dark December night, filled with fire and smoke. Prince blinked when he realized the night sky was literally raining books; pages torn from decimated books fluttered in the air like oversized snowflakes.

Rory and Eva stood aghast, as they beheld what remained of Holland House Library. The library received a direct hit by a German missile, leaving parts of the building exposed to the elements; the resulting effect of bomb's impact made the library appear it had been turned inside out. Leather bound volumes of classic literature littered the snow-covered street; pages filled with the enduring words of Byron and Keats lay on the ground, already beginning to disintegrate. Famous plays by Shakespeare and Marlowe were shredded, and commingled with classic children's tales like *The Velveteen Rabbit* and *Peter Pan*. A group of children gathered on the sidewalk, reading picture books as though this were an everyday event. Even Dracula and Jack paused to observe the bizarre scene, taking cover under a dilapidated awning.

Dracula charged Nikos with keeping the others together, while he and Jack went to rescue Vincent and the children. When they reached the familiar door to Old Trafalgar Station, another ominous rumble shook the ground above them. Vincent was working on a painting when Dracula and Jack came through the door.

"Vincent...listen to that. We have to get you out of here, NOW!" Dracula commanded.

"I'm not leaving."

"It's not safe…you might not be mortal, but what about the children? Don't you care about them?" Dracula asked.

Jack tried to help plead their case. "Vincent, this whole storage unit is in danger…think about the children. You must come with us!"

"How will that work? You said yourself…they're only half-human. If I agree…what happens to them?"

Dracula stepped closer to Vincent, and spoke softly, "Vincent, they have to become like us…like Jack and I…but I promise…it will only hurt a little."

Vincent's eyes brimmed with tears; the artist nodded his head as Virginia put a hand to her mouth. The children would become vampires and need to drink blood; it was a horrifying thought.

Rupert exploded with anger and screamed, "I'll not be a part of this! It's bad enough Henry went missing…now you want to make vampires out of Oliver and the twins…you're both monsters!" Rupert ran toward the door and into the night, before anyone could stop him.

"I'm sorry, Vincent…there's just no other way," Dracula said again, as another explosion sounded above; the bombs were getting too close for comfort.

Oliver stepped forward, his newsboy cap slightly askew; the boy posed his question bluntly, "Are you going to have to bite us first?"

Dracula bent down to look Oliver squarely in the eye. "Yes, but only this one time…and never again."

Audrey moved closer to her brother and asked a question of her own, "Is it going to hurt?"

"No," Dracula lied.

Oliver took his sisters by the hand, and brought them to the corner where they slept. Dracula followed and Oliver turned to him. "Please bite me first, so I can show them how to be brave."

Dracula studied the boy's face with anguish; he didn't want to take away his humanity, but there was no other choice. The vampire turned his back on the others and took Oliver into an embrace, sinking his teeth into the boy's neck. To his credit, Oliver merely flinched and seemed surprised it was over so quickly. Virginia ran to the far corner of the room, unwilling to witness any more. Vincent turned back to his easel; he could not watch what was happening to children he had come to love.

Audrey approached him with tearful eyes, and surrendered her neck to him; he bit her in the tenderest way he could. Alice followed next, letting the vampire taste her blood, but kept her eyes closed until he was finished.

"What about Rupert?" Audrey asked, rubbing her neck wound.

"I don't think he's coming back, Audrey."

Oliver stepped forward, pointing at Dracula. "Now we have to drink your blood, don't we?"

Alice and Audrey were horrified by the thought of drinking blood. Dracula knew this would be difficult for them, but it was necessary to make them his own. Rolling up his sleeve, Dracula used a sharp nail to open a vein in his arm for Oliver. The boy moved to drink without the slightest hesitation; he was a brave boy indeed. Vincent turned to watch them, anguished at the choice they had to make. Oliver stopped drinking and dropped to the ground, his body flailing like a fish out of water. Virginia let out a scream, as the boy moaned in agony; his human body was dying. After a few minutes, his complexion turned deadly pale and a toothy smile spread across a face completely transformed. The boy stood at least two inches taller, and his face had lost every bit of its childish innocence.

Alice turned to run from Dracula, but he quickly scooped her up and whispered in her ear, "I just need you to take one tiny sip...and then it will be over." Alice gave up her fight and drank from her father. As Dracula held her tightly, her human body began to die; convulsions turned her small body into something grotesque. Finally, Alice became still and fell into a deep sleep. "It is nothing to worry about...she will wake up in her own time," Dracula reassured the others.

Audrey hid behind Virginia, her fear so great she became incontinent. "I don't want to drink blood...I don't want to..."

"What you're doing is inhumane!" Virginia cried, as she attempted to shield the child from him. Dracula snatched the child from Virginia, and coaxed her in to a deep sleep; he knew it was dangerous to leave Audrey in such a vulnerable state, but there was no time to turn her now.

Dracula tried to explain his actions. "It's the only way to take them with us." The roar of another bomb exploded above, and this one brought a ceiling beam down; Vincent's easel was crushed, along with the stool he had just been sitting on.

"Come...we need to go, NOW!" Jack moved to gather the children's overcoats and boots.

Oliver's eyes were glowing red, as his natural hunger began to burn; Dracula pulled out a leather pouch and handed it to the boy. "Drink... it will take away the burning in your gut." The young fledgling grabbed the pouch greedily and began to drink in huge gulps until Dracula took it away.

"Now...we must leave." Dracula took command; the time for maudlin thoughts had passed and would serve no purpose. He motioned to Jack, who picked up a sleeping Alice; Dracula grabbed hold of Audrey and they made their way above ground.

"Where are we going?" Oliver asked.

"We need to locate a private place with mirrors; it's the only way we can make our journey to America. Storefronts are boarded up...but I'm sure we can find a way in. We need to meet the others at the tube station first...hurry," Dracula urged.

"I know a place...Crestwood Hotel. It's only a block from the station...I'm sure there are plenty of mirrors inside," Oliver was anxious to be of assistance; supercharged with vampire blood, the young fledgling felt invincible.

"Okay, lead the way, my boy," Dracula replied, playfully knocking his cap to the ground. Oliver almost bent to pick it up, but then decided it was time to abandon childish things. It took them no time at all to reach the street, where they were reunited with Nikos and the others.

"Where to now?" Prince asked, nodding at the sleeping twins; but no one offered an explanation.

"Follow Oliver...we are going to that hotel over there...it has lots of mirrors," Dracula commanded. Prince understood their plan now.

The girls continued to sleep like the dead, as Big Ben stroked the ten o'clock hour. Jack and Dracula carried the twins as Oliver pointed to the hotel in question. Nikos darted across the street first, looking both ways for any sign of V-1 missiles. Vincent held Virginia's arm; they walked briskly as she tried to comprehend how they could get to New York City from a hotel lobby. Prince and Eva, their clothes covered in soot, sprinted ahead to the other side of the street. Oliver and Rory joined them on the sidewalk; Jack was close behind holding a sleeping Alice.

Dracula was the last one to cross with Audrey in his arms. A bomb exploded directly above them; Audrey woke as she was savagely ripped from his grasp, just seconds before his right arm was severed. Blood gushed from the wound, bringing Dracula to his knees, as he tried to staunch the bleeding. Nikos ran to Dracula's aide; he worried about a life threatening loss of blood. Dracula felt no pain, but was momentarily disoriented; Nikos removed his belt to create a makeshift tourniquet.

Oliver ran toward Audrey's broken body through a cloud of suffocating smoke; all hope vanished when he realized half her face was gone. His sister was lost to him; Oliver wanted to scream, but found he couldn't. He closed his eyes trying to picture Audrey's smile, anything to obliterate the ghastly vision of her disfigured face. Overcome with grief, Oliver threw his body across his sister's corpse and started wailing, as Rory attempted to drag him back to the sidewalk.

Dracula had already stopped bleeding; fully recovered, he bent down to retrieve his severed arm from the ground. Putting his arm in position, Dracula watched with satisfaction as the tissue came to life, and his arm reattached itself. A vampire lived with many curses; tonight, Dracula was thankful for a vampire's natural restorative powers. Dracula helped Rory get Oliver to the sidewalk; he tried to comfort the boy, as he faced his own guilt over the little girl's death. Audrey's death was his fault; he should have forced her to drink. Dracula had left the child vulnerable; for this, he would never forgive himself.

Once again focused on their mission, Dracula took Alice from Jack; he stepped discreetly over Audrey's mutilated body without looking down. Alice finally woke and looked into the eyes of her new father; the young girl felt a craving she could scarcely comprehend. Pulling what remained of his blood supply from his vest, Dracula fed her slowly; he didn't fail to notice she continued sucking long after the blood was gone. With renewed urgency, Dracula recognized it was time to get to the Otherworld, before anything else went wrong. When they located the Crestwood Hotel, they were surprised to discover an unlocked door. The lobby was empty except for a night watchman; he took one look at Dracula's bloody clothes and tried to stop them. Not known for his patience, Jack silenced him by snapping his neck; it was often his habit to kill first, and ask questions later. Tonight, Dracula was grateful for Jack's no-nonsense approach. Locating a large mirror by the door, Dracula quickly gathered everyone together as the glass began to glow like a brilliant rainbow. Within seconds, they were securely delivered to the Otherworld, where safety was guaranteed.

Outside the Crestwood Hotel, a lone figure remained on the street as the flashing lights of the Otherworld slowly extinguished. The vampires would pay dearly for their crimes, and for taking away all he had ever loved. He cringed when he thought of young Oliver and the twins; they had been turned into something grotesque. He tempered his anger and began to formulate a plan for revenge on the master vampire who had started it all. His enemies may have eluded him for now, but he was no fool. Rupert knew where they were going; more importantly, he knew *when* they were going. He was in no rush; Rupert would remain in London and bide his time. He had no doubt, the ancient vampire and his crew had left a good number of pesky fledglings behind. He would start with fledglings; any creature of the night was fair game to him. In fact, Rupert could think of no nobler calling, than killing every last vampire in the city of London.

CHAPTER 94 - RORY'S FIGHT FOR HONOR - NEW YORK PUBLIC LIBRARY - NYC - (SEPTEMBER 1967)

Rory's only escape from life in a modern city was the rooftop. She had been exploring one day and stumbled upon an attic room at the rear of the library, just below the rooftop. There were two dormer windows; one was boarded up tight, but the other was unlocked and opened with very little effort. Up here, Rory experienced an inner calm she didn't feel when around the others. Since Audrey's death, she had been struggling with her conscience, pulling away from Prince whenever he tried to talk about it. The rooftop had become her place of serenity; a comfortable retreat where Rory could be alone with her thoughts.

They had been settled in New York City for several months now; despite her love of America, Rory missed London and its oddly tangled streets. Ancient bells chimed a melody New Yorkers often became immune to; tonight, the sound made Rory homesick for London. She had abandoned hair clips, and now let her chestnut hair flow freely. Once they arrived in America, Rory let go of her old-fashioned clothes and embraced the fashion of a contemporary time. She wore bell bottom jeans and boots with a higher heel, to make her appear taller. Her black turtleneck sweater felt soft against her skin; Rory didn't wear it for warmth, she just wanted to blend in. On her finger, Rory wore the ring her father, Paul Revere, had given her before she died; it remained a constant reminder of her earthly life.

Rory was troubled by recurring visions of the night they left London; vivid images of Dracula turning children into vampires haunted her, even as she tried to forget. A gruesome vision of Jack snapping the neck of a security guard flashed before her eyes; Rory could still see the astonished look on the poor man's face; his life was snuffed out just for doing his job. Human lives were meaningless to creatures of the night. Tonight, Rory Revere realized she could no longer make peace with the nefarious lifestyle Prince had convinced her to embrace. She loved him, but had lost all respect for Dracula; in her mind, vampires were sadistic killers with no soul. Rory was also disturbed by how the children had changed since drinking Dracula's blood. Oliver's sweet face had become something sinister; he resembled a street urchin one might find in a Dickens novel. The most astounding transformation, however, was in young Alice. Her eyes had turned fiery silver, with flecks of red; they were the eyes of evil. The girl rarely smiled and her bloodless lips were tinged with blue, as though she had stayed out in the cold too long. Rory avoided them both; certain they could read her thoughts.

As she enjoyed the cool night air, Rory wondered why she had chosen such malignant company. What would her father think if he knew she consorted with creatures of the night? She still believed in God, never once questioning why she remained earthbound. When Rory was a child, she went to church every Sunday, and always believed something wonderful followed her earthly life. Has God abandoned me? Rory listened as the church bells rang again; suddenly, she knew what to do. If God wouldn't come to her, she would go and find him.

Breathless with excitement, Rory stood in awe before the most magnificent cathedral she had ever seen. There were many churches in London, but none like this. Since coming to New York City, the bells of Saint Patrick's Cathedral had provided a distant comfort, but Rory had never gone inside, fearful she was no longer welcome. She mounted the stone steps, completely mesmerized by stained glass windows that filled the night with glorious color. When she reached the massive door, Rory swallowed her fear and ventured inside. There were several parishioners in attendance; some clasped rosaries to their breast in silent prayer; others lit candles to honor deceased loved ones. The soft glow of candlelight showcased a host of beautifully carved marble statues. Rory found an empty pew and got down on her knees to pray; when she closed her eyes, Rory saw her father's face. Not the Paul Revere who rode a horse through Concord and Lexington to warn the British were coming; she saw the father who once tended her in sickness, a father she had loved fiercely. "Help me father...I am lost." Rory looked to her earthly father for guidance, despite being in a house of God.

"I am listening...," a voice answered from behind a marble pillar. Rory's eyes snapped open; she jumped up from her seat and spun around, but no one was there. Maybe coming here was a mistake; the smell of incense suddenly became so unbearable, Rory had to step outside.

Rory felt better once she took a gulp of fresh air. She jogged down the steps casually looking about, convinced someone was watching her. Could Prince have followed her? When she reached the sidewalk, Rory turned back toward the library. Someone caught her attention from across the street; the stranger was positioned underneath a streetlight, and he looked familiar. Rory crossed the street and finally saw his face. She gasped and said his name out loud, "Rupert?"

The boy moved closer and Rory recognized the boy she once knew; he looked much harder now. His lips were cruelly twisted, and his dark eyes seemed incapable of compassion. Rupert was dressed almost exclusively in black leather; a conspicuous bulge in his pocket told her he was carrying a weapon. His boots were also black leather, with pointed metal tips she was certain could do serious bodily damage. Rupert had been thirteen years old in 1941, when she saw him last; yet, he had not aged at all. How was that possible?

"Don't I look good for my age?" Rupert asked, reading her thoughts.

"Stay away from me...I hate vampires and everything they stand for!" Rory spat, then turned to walk the other way.

When Rory reached the corner of 40th Street, she scowled; Rupert was waiting for her in front of the library. How did he get so far ahead of me, she wondered.

Deliberately ignoring him, she entered the library and made her way to a hidden stairway few knew existed. When Rory reached her attic room, she locked the door and climbed out the dormer window. Once again on the rooftop, Rory questioned her decision to leave London; why was she compelled to keep company with creatures of the night? She did not want to live this life anymore, but knew only she could change it. Rory's thoughts were interrupted by a scratching sound. When she turned around, Rupert was sitting on a chimney stack with a cigarette dangling from his lips.

"I told you...I want nothing to do with your kind. You're all cursed and I'll not be part of it!"

"And what do you mean exactly by...*your kind*?" Rupert asked defensively.

"Vampires...bloodsucking baby killers!"

"I'm no vampire...and for the record, I hate them as much as you do," Rupert replied.

"Then, how come you haven't aged? By my calculations...you should be close to forty by now, and look at you!"

"Ah-h-h...I guess that will take some explaining. You see, while it's true I am not a vampire, the blood of one runs through my veins...it was not by my own choosing, I might add. After I was bitten...I discovered a plus side to being infected. Vampire blood apparently keeps me from aging."

"Why are you here...some sort of vengeance?"

"You're smarter than you look," Rupert replied.

"Was that your voice I heard in church earlier?" Rory asked. She didn't really want him to go; it had been such a long time since she had spoken to anyone remotely human.

"I had to get your attention somehow. I didn't realize you would skitter away like an alley cat."

"When I agreed to come here, I didn't really understand what Dracula and Jack were. They turned innocent children into vampires, Rupert!" Rory said angrily.

"I know."

"Something has to be done...we can't let vampires keep doing this."

"I couldn't agree with you more," Rupert replied.

"So, what exactly does that mean...you're already doing something about it?"

Rupert let out a hearty laugh, nearly losing his balance atop the chimney stack. "Not officially, I'm afraid...but we've been very successful."

"That doesn't really tell me much," Rory retorted hands folded across her chest.

"So, no need for me to sugarcoat things, then?" Rupert asked losing his smile.

"Tell me!"

"Well then, I guess you could say...I'm a bounty hunter of sorts. To be more specific, I dedicate myself to eliminating the walking dead from the streets of Manhattan. Once in a while, we go into Brooklyn...

big problem there, for some reason. There are others like me…together we have accepted the task of removing every last vampire from the face of the earth."

"Go on."

"Right now…I am trying to locate Count Dracula's lair. He and the Whitechapel killer…are the ultimate prize! But I digress…I suppose you're wondering what I've been doing for the past twenty-five years."

"The thought had crossed my mind." Rory found his appearance disturbing, but was gratified to find someone who shared her hatred of vampires.

"Until very recently, I was living in London. Over the past two decades, my associates and I have killed hundreds of rogue vampires, saving London from a scourge of bloodsucking monsters."

"Will you try and kill me?" Rory asked, taking a step away from him.

"Why would I kill, what isn't alive? You are just a misguided ghost, who has chosen to remain earthbound far longer than was intended." Rupert spoke as if these were given facts.

"How do you know these things?"

"I know the evil vampires do. They kill without regard for human suffering. They take what they want and discard blood-drained bodies like so much garbage, or maybe…they make monsters of innocent children and sentence them to a life of cannibalism." Rupert could see he was getting through.

"They let Audrey die, Rupert…they left her mutilated body in the street," Rory said softly.

"Then, why do you stay with vampires who prey on children?" For a moment Rory felt as though her heart would explode, as she recalled the vision of Oliver grieving over the corpse of his sister. Over the years, Dracula and Jack had done horrible things and would continue, if they weren't stopped.

Rupert moved closer, taking Rory's hand as he explained his role in eradicating the vampire community. "We call ourselves the Van Helsings…I assume you've read Stoker's novel. We honor the fictitious vampire hunter by taking his name for our cause." Rory nodded for him to continue.

"We take vampires off the streets...people like your friends, who kill without conscience...and with absolute cruelty."

"I won't lead you to them...I can't betray them like that."

"I would not ask this of you. We actually enjoy picking them off one by one, as they hunt for what every vampire craves. Bottled blood can only go so far..."

"Bottled blood just means fewer corpses...it doesn't change what they are," Rory replied bitterly.

"If you come with me tonight, I will show you a whole new world...I can teach you how to fight a force of evil that has plagued mankind for centuries."

"And what about Dracula...what if he comes after us?"

"I promise you...I will kill them both... the false Romanian prince and the wretched mutilator of women. It will be a glorious victory when they are finally banished from the planet."

After a moment of silence, Rory asked an unexpected question, "Does it hurt when you kill them?"

"Only when they fight back."

CHAPTER 95 - DRACULA'S PENTHOUSE - CENTRAL PARK SOUTH - NYC - (SEPTEMBER 1967)

Eva enjoyed spending time with Dracula in their lovely penthouse apartment; Nikos had negotiated the rental using an assumed name. Carefully retrofitted with blackout shades and heavy brocade curtains, the sun didn't stand a chance to intrude. Dracula was rarely here during daylight hours, but Eva found the apartment a delightful place to live. The sun had finally set as Eva lit candles and opened a bottle of Dracula's special reserve. Nighttime changed the aura of the lavishly decorated apartment completely. Eva pulled up the shades and welcomed the cool night air, along with a spectacular view of Central Park.

Tonight, she was troubled about Jack's plans for Hitler. Eva realized too late, the future of America could be at risk, if she allowed Jack to go through with his plans. She had read up on the German leader, Adolf Hitler; historians declared him one of mankind's most wicked villains. Now long dead, Jack was planning to alter history by going back in time to save him; he planned to make him a vampire. Not only was such an action reckless, it was strictly against Dracula's code of ethics; there could be dire consequences in tampering with historic events. She had procrastinated long enough; it was time to come clean to Dracula about Jack's plans. Eva looked at her diamond-studded wristwatch; Dracula was fashionably late, as usual.

Eva moved to a hallway mirror, where a little girl's face greeted her; she was a pretty child, but would never grow to adulthood. A little makeup enhanced her features, but it was still a child's face looking back at her. The curtains flickered as a cool breeze filled the room; as if by magic, Dracula was standing behind her. Eva closed her eyes, longing to be a woman again, and to feel a man's hands caressing her body. Her eyes snapped open; Countess Bathory, the woman, gazed back at her. Dracula looked on in disbelief; he saw it too. Eva was overcome with a wave of desire as Dracula swept her off her feet and carried her to the bed; Eva shed her robe and began tearing at his clothes, fearful Dracula would change his mind. Her lord was naked, as he beheld his countess in all her splendor; the ancient vampire had forgotten how lovely she was. He buried himself in her creamy smoothness, navigating a body he had committed to memory. Dracula took in her intoxicating scent as he prepared to mount his prize; her legs opened to him, as she recalled every intimate moment they had ever shared together. The illusion held, as Eva's womanly body responded to the only man she had ever loved; Dracula whispered her name as they moved together in a dance of passion as old as humankind.

A flash of lightning washed the room, and in that moment, the spell was broken; Eva was but a child again. Dracula pulled himself away, turning his back on the sight of Eva's childlike body. Lightning flashed again, followed by a hollow clap of thunder; the storm was right above them now. Neither spoke as the rain began to fall. Now fully dressed, Dracula came to sit next to Eva; she had covered herself, embarrassed by her prepubescent body.

"I'm sorry, Eva...I shouldn't have...," Dracula spoke just above a whisper, as he stroked her tousled hair. Eva leaned against him and they were quiet for a long time, the sound of rain filling the void that ensued.

"It was not your fault...I saw it too. For a little while, I somehow reclaimed my womanhood...in those moments, you were all I wanted."

Dracula leaned forward and kissed her fully on the mouth. "I still love you, Countess Bathory...and I always will."

Eva smiled and jumped up to retrieve her clothes from the floor. Dracula helped himself to a glass of Type O blood, his personal favorite.

"I'm not sorry," Eva announced once she was dressed again.

"It will remain our secret...a rare opportunity to have once more, what has been lost. If only there had been a second chance for Mary."

Eva frowned as the conversation turned to Mary Kelly. After all these years, Dracula still yearned for someone who wasn't her. Eva decided to change the subject. "I have something to tell you...it's about Jack."

Dracula emptied his glass then poured another. From a comfortable leather chair, Dracula listened patiently to Eva's words; his eyes grew angrier by the moment, as heavy rain drowned out all but the sound of her voice.

CHAPTER 96 - THE FINAL SHOWDOWN –
BERLIN, GERMANY – (APRIL 30, 1945)

When Dracula saw Hitler for the first time, the Fuhrer was contemplating which weapon he would use to end his miserable life. The ruthless dictator had waited as long as possible for Jack to show, but he never came; Hitler finally concluded it had all been hoax. His pistol lay on the desk, loaded and ready to fire, but the Fuhrer struggled to find the courage to use it. Killing others was easy, firing a weapon into your own temple, not so much. He considered using his father's saber, but decided gutting himself was too messy. As a last resort, Hitler could always take cyanide; it would be painful, but quick. He favored the gun; in his mind, poison was a woman's method of suicide. Anxiously glancing at the door, the fallen leader knew time had nearly run out.

Dracula had quietly entered the room as mist moments ago; he enjoyed watching Adolf Hitler's anguish, as he contemplated his method of suicide. Dracula would wait until the deed was done; if necessary, he would stop Jack from interfering. Who knows, maybe Jack wouldn't show. Hitler continued toying with the gun, keeping his eye on the door as the minutes ticked by with painful slowness. When the clock struck the noon hour, Jack came through the locked door and faced Hitler; he had a loaded weapon, and was willing to use it. The Fuhrer pointed the gun at Jack's chest; he needed to weigh his options carefully. If he killed Jack, there was no way out. What if his strange visitor was really who he claimed to be? Was he willing to give up his only chance to get out of his predicament? Something had changed in him since Jack had bitten him. The Fuhrer felt younger and more virile; on occasion, he had even been able to read minds. Surely, these things were a sign Jack was not entirely human.

Jack decided it was time to call the Fuhrer's bluff. "Go ahead, Fuhrer…shoot me; I told you, I'm already dead."

"A half hour ago I administered poison to my wife. She couldn't shoot herself…so I provided a more merciful way." Hitler spoke less harshly, but kept his gun aimed at Jack.

"Yes...I know, and if history is correct, you even poisoned your beloved dogs...poor things," Jack replied. Hitler's eyes glistened with something like remorse.

"Why have you come at the eleventh hour? I thought you weren't coming at all," Hitler barked, lowering his weapon.

"Better this way...no time to change your mind then, eh?"

Jack moved toward the Fuhrer to fulfill his promise, just as Dracula appeared. Before Hitler could react, he had been knocked to the floor, gun flying from his hand. Jack was startled by Dracula's appearance; at first, he thought he had come to help, but soon realized he was mistaken. Before he could explain himself, Dracula tackled Jack to the ground and stuffed a handkerchief in his mouth. Using a drapery cord, Dracula tied Jack securely to a chair.

"How did you penetrate my bunker? Are you like him?" Hitler asked.

"Ever more powerful than he, Fuhrer."

"What's to stop me from calling my men...you'd be dead at my command," Hitler said bravely, despite being seated on the floor without a weapon.

"Fuhrer, I know you'll find this hard to believe, but...you're already dead."

"You *are* like him," Hitler said nodding toward Jack. "He speaks in riddles, too."

"The fact is...you died this very day more than twenty years ago... by your own hand."

"Nonsense...I had a deal with Jack...he offered me eternal life." When Hitler said the words out loud, they seemed ludicrous.

"We've no time to waste...I need you to fulfill your destiny...as it is written in history."

"Will you not spare my life?" Hitler pleaded for mercy.

"So you can be tortured and imprisoned? Isn't that the reason you administered deadly poison to those you love...and only moments ago, had a gun to your head?" Dracula was becoming impatient. Perhaps, he had misjudged the man; he was either a greater coward than Dracula realized, or just trying to manipulate his way out of a death sentence.

"It's true…I did contemplate suicide and…perhaps it *would* be better this way…"

"Good…now all I need you to do is shoot yourself in the head, and I'll be on my way." Dracula helped the Fuhrer up and gave Hitler back his gun.

"And what if I don't? What if I just shoot you, instead?" Hitler held the gun with a shaky hand.

"You already had your chance, Fuhrer." Dracula could scarcely believe this pathetic man could have been responsible for the deaths of millions.

Dracula was done playing games; it was time to show Hitler who he really was. Dracula opened his mouth to reveal a set of sharp teeth. The vampire's jaw began to stretch, and the snap of breaking bones was audible; Hitler felt certain he was going insane. The Fuhrer fired his weapon as all that was human departed and a massive black wolf towered over him.

"You promised me, Jack," Hitler whined, putting the gun to his head; tears streaming down his face. The Fuhrer whispered a silent prayer, as he wiped sweat from his brow; the wolf would kill him unless he fired. Hitler had run out of time. His finger pulled back and he heard a click; the bullet exploded into his brain. There was little pain and to the Fuhrer's surprise, he was still alive. With one eye open, Hitler watched as Dracula assumed his human form. The fallen Fuhrer began crawling toward Jack's chair; he tried to pull himself up, as he implored Jack to keep his promise.

"Come now, Fuhrer…take your death like a man…or I may have to finish it for you," Dracula said, placing a foot on Hitler's prostrate form. The Fuhrer's body convulsed, as his brain finally gave up its fight; even in death, Hitler held fast to Jack's ankles.

Jack worked the handkerchief from his mouth and spat it on the floor. "He could have been a great ally for us…I had our best interest at heart."

"You've never done anything, except to serve yourself," Dracula said angrily.

"So, what now…are you taking me prisoner?"

"What I do will now is on behalf of all our kind. Even to a vampire, Adolf Hitler was an abomination."

"Come on now…untie me, will you?" Jack pleaded, as Dracula picked up Hitler's saber.

Dracula anguished over the decision he had to make; there was no other way. Jack was dangerous. Jack could not be trusted. Jack had to go. For a fleeting moment, Jack detected a trace of empathy; but then, a curtain closed and there was only blind rage. Dracula slashed at Jack's abdomen with Hitler's saber; the wounded vampire watched in horror, as blood poured from his body. Dracula's rage was fuelled by his long-standing grudge against Jack; he continued his vicious attack until Jack was eviscerated. Jack could feel his life force draining, as he clung to the intoxicating allure of the human world. Saturated with Jack's blood, Dracula finally came to his senses and flung the weapon across the room. At last, Mary's death had been avenged; Jack the Ripper was truly dead!

The sound of thundering footsteps approached; in a matter of minutes, Dracula would be discovered. He pulled Hitler's corpse away from Jack and laid his body on the floor beside the desk, carefully placing the pistol in the dead man's hand. The metal door burst open, just as Dracula turned to mist. By the time the guards unlocked the door; Jack's remains would be nothing more than an unexplained pile of ash. As he left the shadow of another time, Dracula felt confident history had been left undisturbed.

Chapter 97 - The Dark One

The demise of Jack the Ripper was definitely *not* part of the Dark One's master plan. The evil entity should have realized Dracula would eventually exact his revenge on Jack. The count's obsession with a prostitute from Whitechapel was difficult to comprehend; Mary Kelly had been nothing more than a common streetwalker. Dracula had been so blinded by lust, he couldn't see who she really was; now, the vampire had appointed himself judge and jury. Killing Jack interfered with the Dark One's plans; the vampire's reckless actions had to be rectified at once. It was time for the countess to pay for her night of carnal pleasure, by saving Jack.

Eva laid naked on the comfortable king size bed; she was thinking about Dracula's touch as she carefully replayed every moment of their spent passion the night before. She didn't understand what had happened, but found herself wishing for a repeat performance. It was getting lighter outside; Eva waited lazily for the calming warmth of sunrise. She opened her eyes as an impending darkness made her jump up to cover herself, as though someone was watching.

The Dark One spoke in a reptilian voice, "Young one...I have granted your dearest wish...now it is your time to meet my demand."

"My wish?" Eva stood up to make a tunic of the bed sheet.

"Now, don't insult my intelligence by being coy."

"How so?"

"To be a woman...to finally entice the vampire into your bed. Did the experience not meet your expectations?"

"He came to my bed of his own choosing..."

"Do you really believe that?"

"What do you want from me?" Eva asked impatiently.

"Much."

"The sun has risen...isn't it time for your kind to slither back to the hole from which you came?" Eva replied.

"Be careful, young one...I can take you from this life in an instant and leave you in total blackness, where no one will ever look at you again…as a woman or a child. Or perhaps, you would like me to arrange for your vampire to be hypnotized every time you wish to seduce him."

"It was you, then…but why?"

"I'm not here to discuss that…something has happened that interferes with my plans."

"What do you mean?"

"Because of you, Dracula has killed Jack!"

"Not Jack…he wouldn't…he went to stop him from doing something terrible, but…Dracula would *never* kill him."

"I assure you, he is quite dead…and that's where you come in. I'm no longer interested in an association with the Fuhrer… but Jack is another matter." The Dark One paused when Eva started crying.

"Is he really dead?" Eva asked, wiping her eyes with the palms of her hands.

"Yes, but you can save him. Right now, Jack's body is tied to a chair inside Hitler's bunker. Next to him, you will find the as-yet-undiscovered body of the fallen Fuhrer. You will only have minutes before Hitler's guards break down the door. You must bring blood… and restore Jack back to life. Do you understand?"

"And, if I do this…you will allow me to reclaim my womanly form?"

"Save Jack first…and I will consider your request."

Eva dropped the bed sheet to the ground and dressed quickly. She knew exactly when Dracula had targeted the showdown with Hitler, and prayed she would be able to save Jack. She was angry that Dracula had taken such drastic action; why had it been necessary to kill him? She was now forced to go against her vampire, something she rarely did. She would revive Jack and let Dracula figure out how he had managed to come back to life. Eva couldn't wait to see his face when Jack showed up, alive and well.

It was cold in Berlin this time of year; but Eva didn't worry about how she was dressed. If all went according to plan, the only other person she would encounter was Jack. As the Dark One pointed out, she would have very little time to get in and out of Hitler's bunker. Eva retrieved two liters of blood from the refrigerator, and stuffed them inside her jacket. She moved to a hallway mirror; the glowing entrance to the Otherworld welcomed her, unaware of her important date with history.

Chapter 98 - Halloween – Times Square - (October 31, 1967)

Alice loved the idea of Halloween, even more so, since she became a nocturnal creature. Tonight, Uncle Vlad promised to take her to the annual Halloween parade in Times Square. Alice had grown weary of dark winding hallways and dusty books that reeked of a time gone stale. There was nothing of interest to her in books any longer; she absorbed them much too quickly. As a new vampire, Alice was still learning about her powers and her limitations. She was disappointed Jack would not be joining them; he had been gone for several weeks now. She had chosen to dress as a witch, her lips painted black to create a most gruesome look. Dracula came up from behind; Alice spun around for him, so he could inspect her costume.

"The scariest witch I've ever seen," Dracula said, taking her small hand in his. His love for Alice was unconditional; he had affection for Oliver, too, but the feeling was different. Alice was innocence defined; in her, Dracula found his purpose. Guiding and protecting this lovely child of the night was what mattered most. Dracula also took comfort in knowing Alice was of his blood; she would never betray him. Over time, she would become more adult-like in her words and actions, the same as Prince. For now, Dracula enjoyed the child who still lived inside.

"Why isn't Uncle Jack coming to the parade?" Alice asked again.

"I already told you...he decided to live somewhere else for a while. I'm sure you'll see him again...when he gets tired of stalking small game in Central Park."

"You know where he is, don't you?" Alice could be relentless.

"Of course not...why would I lie to you?"

"You two had an argument right before he left...I heard you. What were you fighting about?"

"There are many things beyond your understanding," Dracula replied tightly.

"But I wanted Uncle Jack to see my costume," Alice whined.

"Maybe he'll show up later. Come on, let's go have some fun."

Alice held tight to Dracula's hand as they navigated their way to the heart of Times Square. Alice loved being part of a glimmering city; there was a special magic in the air, as hundreds of people celebrated the last night of October. Revelers roamed happily about in colorful costumes, as a tired moon peeked through the lingering clouds of an All Hallows Eve. The brisk weather provided the perfect backdrop for a night when goblins roamed the streets; most were simply humans in costume, but Alice spotted more than one of her kind. The others were already waiting for them on the corner beneath an amber streetlight; Dracula keenly felt the void left by Jack's absence. Perhaps, his actions had been too extreme, but the ancient vampire still believed Jack was dangerous. Deciding to chase thoughts of Jack from his mind, Dracula returned his attention to those he had sworn to protect.

Times Square was a magnificent place to congregate. It was bursting with energy; tonight, it shined brighter than any star ever could. Never had Alice seen so many people; the crowd moved together in harmony, as if somehow prearranged. Storefronts were illuminated by the neon lights of *Woolworth's*; above, bright white lights flashed the words, *Bonds Clothing*, as though its message was of great urgency. On the next corner, people filed out of a *Regal Shoes Store,* carrying colored bags. They passed a farm stand loaded with pumpkins that spilled onto the sidewalk. Alice wrinkled her nose as the acrid smell of roasting chestnuts turned her stomach. The sounds of traffic created a rhythm to which pedestrians eagerly adapted; cities were like that, especially ones that stayed open all night. Cabdrivers honked incessantly against the throng of people entering Times Square. Dracula motioned them to follow him, past a red neon sign advertising something called *Coca-Cola*. Church bells chimed the nine o'clock hour and right on schedule, the All Hallows Eve Parade began its journey down Broadway. Alice clapped her hands with excitement, as the first float passed by; a giant mouse named *Mickey*, threw handfuls of candy into a crowd of adoring fans.

Dracula watched the parade with feigned interest; his eyes darted back and forth, always looking for someone who didn't fit in. He knew there were vampires in New York City; some he had personally sired, but there were others who could pose a threat. To complicate matters, Prince had recently encountered a group of so-called vampire hunters;

the gang was apparently hell-bent on killing creatures of the night. Dracula hoisted Alice onto his shoulders, as he scanned the crowd for anything unusual. He had to admit he was starting to enjoy living in New York; the cool night air was invigorating. A large float passed before him in a blur of color, as Dracula's keen eyes spotted someone in the crowd. The vampire locked eyes with a hooded stranger directly across the street; the seasoned vampire immediately sensed danger. The stranger's eyes were almost luminescent; something about his stance seemed familiar, but Dracula couldn't place him. He crouched down on his knees to pull Alice off his neck; when he stood up again, the hooded man had vanished. The parade continued for another half hour without incident; Dracula relaxed as the crowd cheered, and the sound of music filled the night. Alice began to look tired; Dracula picked her up again, and they made their way back to the subway station.

As he descended the subway steps, Dracula noticed writing on the tiled wall that had not been there earlier. He reached the bottom step and read the message written in red paint; it was a direct threat. Dracula was astute enough to recognize Bram Stoker's fictitious character, a sworn enemy to vampires. Fictional characters don't scrawl threatening messages on subway walls. Whoever did this was very real. Dracula reached out to touch the wall; the paint was still wet.

Alice read the words aloud, "Death to all Vampires…Van Helsings. What does that mean?"

"I'm afraid…it means we have a new enemy."

CHAPTER 99 - HALLOWEEN – RUPERT - (OCTOBER 31, 1967)

He could smell them as they crossed the street. Sweet little Alice was now one of their kind; her face now tainted by the savagery of craving human blood. And there he was, Count Vlad Dracula a.k.a. *Count Draco*; he held the little girl's hand as they moved through the crowded intersection. The Romanian vampire's translucent skin glowed in the moonlight, as he walked serenely down Broadway; the vampire carried himself as though he owned the night. He was the personification of evil, disguised behind a face that was impossibly symmetrical. The boy pulled his hood forward, as he caught the lighter scent of fledgling vampires. Young Oliver exuded a musky odor that screamed *I am no longer human.*

Rupert's keen eyes surveyed the crowd, searching for the mutilator of women; Jack was nowhere in sight. Where on earth could he be tonight? No matter, there would be time to deal with him later. Besides, Dracula was the ultimate prize. He spotted the others walking in a group; Eva walked with Oliver, and Prince followed behind. He felt an unexpected wave of sadness when he saw Vincent and Virginia; they had always been so kind to him. He wondered why these earthbound ghosts chose to keep company with bloodsucking vampires. Once upon a time, he had been part of this unconventional family; until Dracula stole them away.

Rupert moved into the shadows as they passed, and only Alice turned around. They locked eyes and Rupert put a finger to his lips. Alice flashed him a very human smile, but said nothing to the others. He moved behind them, and waited underneath a streetlight for Harry Pepitone. He was late, as usual. Rupert glanced at his watch and frowned. If he didn't show soon, it would be too late.

Harry Pepitone finally tapped Rupert on the shoulder. "Sorry I'm late...where is he?"

"Up ahead, about a block or so. You'll see a gentleman wearing a cape...a very tall man with a walking stick. He has a little dark-haired girl with him."

"So, I compliment this Count Draco on his dress…and try to get him to accept the role of Dracula in a play I'm directing, correct?"

"Harry…he's getting away. Just offer him the role for now…I'll be in touch soon to explain our next steps." Rupert watched as his accomplice deftly weaved his way into the crowd.

Count Draco was a very vain vampire. Rupert stressed this to Harry, but there was really no need; the man knew all about actors and their egos. Harry had no idea Count Draco was anything but an actor; Rupert's plan would allow him time to learn more about his adversary. His ultimate goal was to uncover Dracula's vulnerabilities, and end his deadly reign of terror. A vampire who had survived this long would not be easy to take down, but Rupert was up to the challenge. The key was in finding the vampire's lair. At first, Rupert believed it was located somewhere within the library, but after a thorough search by several operatives, there appeared to be no evidence this was so. The next place they scoured was the 42nd Street Station; they searched for hidden doors and passages, but everything was locked up tight. Rupert didn't understand that ghosts and vampires could pass through doors, even ones that had been locked for years. A few Van Helsings had actually been quite close to Dracula's lair; they just didn't know how to get in.

Rupert doggedly trolled midtown each night, hoping to get a glimpse of the elusive vampire; before long, he discovered the count's preference for Central Park. One night, he followed him as he headed toward the zoo; he was fascinated when Dracula unlocked the gate with a wave of his hand. The vampire kept a steady pace, tapping the ground with his walking stick before he took each step. When Dracula approached the lion cage, the great beast rose up from a dead sleep, and let out a ferocious roar; in response, several monkeys grunted loudly, pounding their chests in unison. As the vampire moved on toward a group of larger cages, two gray wolves stood at attention; Dracula reached through the cage to pet them. Rupert detected a purring sound and watched the animals bend their heads, as though bowing to a king. The vampire hunter understood he faced a formidable enemy; the man had been born in the fifteenth century, and managed to survive several attempts on his life. He would make no mistakes with this one. Rupert understood that bleeding out a vampire was not enough; a misconception like that could get you killed. To properly dispose of a vampire, the body must be burned and the ashes scattered to the wind.

Naturally, Harry Pepitone had no idea he was helping the leader of the Van Helsings catch a vampire. The man was nothing more than a willing pawn; his only flaw was asking too many questions. Rupert kept him around anyway, reasoning it would be a shame to lose a good stooge, whose only vices were gin and loose women.

Chapter 100 - Alice in Tunneltown - New York City - (December 1967)

Alice watched Prince put finishing touches on a portrait of Oliver; she had to admit, it wasn't half bad. Since Rory's mysterious disappearance, painting was all Prince seemed to do. Vincent worked alongside him; he had been painting mostly portraits since coming to New York City. Virginia had finally convinced him to abandon sunflowers and wheat fields. He had painted her at least a dozen times; several hung haphazardly from a wire Prince strung around the room. Sometimes Vincent painted Oliver and Alice, when they were willing to pose. They made a game of wearing different outfits they fashioned from old curtains and bed sheets. Vincent's finished works successfully captured their ethereal spirits, but he always made a point of rendering them with human eyes.

As the year came to an end, Vincent's mood darkened; he began painting nefarious-looking strangers with undefined features and vacant eyes. Eventually his work evolved into canvases that were hauntingly macabre, yet captivating. Virginia became increasingly disturbed by their content; fearful Vincent might be seeing future events and putting them to canvas. The artist refused to believe his paintings were prophetic, but admitted to having spontaneous bursts of inspiration. His new muse called to him from the darkest recesses of his mind, controlling the very strokes of his paintbrush. His newest painting was drying on his wooden easel. The canvas showed a well-dressed Negro man on a hotel balcony; he appeared to be preaching to an adoring crowd below. At first glance, one didn't notice the rooming house in the background; but it was impossible to miss the silhouette of a man holding a rifle. Vincent couldn't explain why he added such a sinister presence; he confided to Virginia he was frequently surprised at the content of his finished work.

Virginia couldn't make her mind up about living in New York. It was certainly a much meaner city than London; here, people seemed to look right through you. As she scribbled random thoughts in her journal about life in a modern city, Virginia realized how much she missed taking care of *human* children. A vision of Audrey filching chocolate from Vincent's pocket flashed through her mind, and with it came a wave of sadness; Audrey always had such a sweet tooth. Virginia studied Alice in the dim light; she looked nothing like a child anymore.

"Who is that Negro man supposed to be?" Alice asked, taking an empty stool behind Vincent.

"He is a man of great importance...if you read a newspaper, you would know his name...Martin Luther King, Jr.," Vincent replied impatiently.

"Well, then...who is the other man holding the rifle?"

"Why do you ask so many questions, child?"

Alice lost interest and directed her next question to Prince. "Where do all the other vampires stay, Prince?"

"They are of no concern to you."

"I only wanted to know where they sleep."

Alice spun around on the stool, trying to make herself dizzy; Prince finally put his hand out to stop her. "Why won't anyone talk about the sleeping bats?" she persisted.

"Vincent's right...you *do* ask too many questions!" Prince said impatiently, turning back to his easel.

"Do you think Uncle Vlad keeps them locked up somewhere here, in Tunneltown?" Alice asked.

"Tunneltown?" Virginia asked, looking up from her journal.

"Well, that's what I call it...with all its winding tunnels..."

"Come and sit with me...we can play hearts," Virginia offered, shuffling a worn deck of cards.

"I'm tired of that game...I want to see the Christmas lights...or maybe take a carriage ride like tourists do." Alice never got to go anywhere this time of year; Dracula hated Christmas, and planned to spend most of December on the moors.

"Can't I just go out for an hour?"

"Dracula won't allow you to go out alone...come on now, we're trying to concentrate," Prince hissed.

Nikos entered the room with Oliver right behind; the boy held Akos on his extended arm. "Nikos is teaching me falconry...we just came from Central Park...it just started snowing!"

Alice wanted to walk through Central Park in the snow; why did she need a chaperone every time she left this place? She was bored beyond endurance and dying to be outside. Alice moved away from the others, while they were distracted by the speckled bird's newest tricks. No one would notice she was missing, until she'd already made her escape.

Her first stop would be Columbus Circle; she couldn't wait to see Fifth Avenue lit up for the holidays! Within the well-traveled subway station, Alice spotted others of her kind; they occasionally made eye contact as if to assure, she was never alone. Many of Dracula's children found employment underground, operating concession stands and other similar occupations. Vampires like these were made to serve as appointed guardians of the vampire colony; Alice knew she was always safe in this neighborhood.

The heavenly scent of fresh roasted cashews permeated the air, as Alice passed a concession stand; it was run by a vampire who gave her a wink of his eye. She desperately craved the salty-sweet crunch of a favorite food she could no longer eat; what Alice really needed, she wouldn't find here. The juvenile vampire hungered for something more primal; she was sick of drinking bottled blood. Alice kept on walking, but her hunger became harder to ignore. She reached *Bloomingdales,* and marveled at two giant hand-carved nutcrackers, standing guard outside. A black limousine pulled up to the curb; the passengers eased out as though they hadn't a care in the world. The woman was a blonde who appeared lost inside her chocolate mink, a tasteful declaration of obscene wealth. On the next corner, a Salvation Army band played tarnished trumpets, as a white-gloved man rang a bell to solicit donations. As Alice continued uptown, a light snow began to fall, and the night suddenly became magical.

At last, Alice reached the center of Columbus Circle; this was a very upscale neighborhood. Straight ahead was the famous Plaza Hotel; the grand marble staircase appeared to await the footsteps of royalty. Impeccably dressed bellmen stood at attention, as though guarding a fortress. Alice sucked in her breath then turned toward the street; several hansom cabs were waiting patiently for paying customers. The drivers wore black jackets and top hats, making Alice homesick for

London; she crossed the street to get a closer look. Alice approached a white mare with turquoise eyes; the horse reared up, nostrils flaring in alarm. Alice backed away and started across Fifth Avenue; the snow was coming down more steadily now.

A red hansom cab approached the crosswalk, drawn by a magnificent speckled horse; his eyes instantly locked eyes with hers. The frightened beast rose up on his hind legs, dumping the driver and his fare-paying passengers into the busy intersection. The horse stood his ground in the middle of Columbus Circle, as traffic came to a screeching halt. Two police officers cautiously approached the frightened animal; he reared up, disengaging the harness and bolted into oncoming traffic. The sound of car horns and breaking glass pierced the night, as several cars slammed into each other. By this time, more police were on the scene; most, were trying to redirect traffic. Alice was frozen in place, as an ambulance whooshed by; the young vampire realized she had somehow caused this accident.

"You best not stand around like that...they'll come after you," a sweet voice said from behind her.

Alice turned to see a girl of about nine or ten, she had snow-white hair. "What do you mean...the police?"

"When you live on the street, you learn to keep a low profile. In this neighborhood...there's little tolerance for vagrancy." Her voice was melodic, and she had arresting eyes; they were baby pink. As if to confirm the strange girl's warning, Alice saw two unformed men with raised nightsticks heading their way.

The girl took her hand. "Come on...time to run!" Without another word, the girl yanked Alice directly into traffic. A cabbie cursed at them out the window; he had missed them by inches.

The girls reached the sidewalk, and Alice realized the strange girl was taking her into Central Park. By this time of night, foot traffic was scarce; even more so because of the weather. The snow came down harder as they moved deeper into the park; after a few minutes, Alice began to relax. A blanket of fresh snow created the effect of a magical kingdom; park benches became padded white thrones, and a deserted playground turned into a thing of wonder. Antique lanterns lit the main pathway through the park; the girls stayed within the cover of trees until they were certain no one followed. The night was beginning to get colder; Alice didn't feel it, but could see the girl shivering beneath her thin coat.

The white-haired girl began to slow her pace, allowing Alice the opportunity to study her more closely. She had a slightly asymmetrical face; her mouth only curled up on one side when she smiled. Her pink eyes were those of a white rabbit; her waif-like hair was in need of brushing, but the color suited her. Alice had been without the companionship of someone her own age for a long time; something about this exotic human drew her in.

"What's your name?" Alice asked, holding out her hand.

"Semele."

"Do you live in the park?"

"Yes, a few of us do...behind the zoo. It's easier to find food there. I get the impression you're not exactly homeless, are you?" the girl asked, observing Alice's warm coat.

"No...not homeless exactly," Alice replied. All she could think about was the lovely girl's pulsing neck. Hypnotized by the subtle journey of blood underneath Semele's skin, Alice finally understood who she was. The truth was both thrilling and frightening, at the same time.

"There is something about you..." Semele broke off, as the streetlight revealed the juvenile vampire's reptilian eyes.

Semele was unable to move, and not sure she even wanted to; there was an ethereal quality about the dark-haired girl, she found captivating. Semele had been on the street for three long years, and had never met anyone like Alice. With the snow falling all around, the night seemed surreal, and alive with possibilities. The fledgling vampire moved closer to study her eyes; this girl was a misfit too. Semele suddenly felt paralyzed; Alice had taken control of her mind. It took only moments to uncover all there was to know about an albino girl forsaken by her family; it was all there, inside the world behind her eyes. Semele was surprisingly relieved to reveal her darkest secrets, without having to utter a word.

By now, Semele realized what Alice was; surprisingly, she wasn't afraid. Life on the streets had been hard; as a girl, she was especially vulnerable. Maybe Alice had a home, and possibly an extra winter coat.

A well-dressed vampire girl wanted to feed from her. So what? Semele had seen people do much worse, just to stay alive.

"Please don't hurt me," Semele whispered, as she started to unbutton her coat.

Alice moved to stop her. "I would never hurt my friend." She gently took the girl's bony wrist in hers; when she touched her lips to the girl's soft skin, Alice finally understood what she was hungry for.

Chapter 101 - Jack's Revival - Berlin, Germany - (April 30, 1945)

When the first drops of glorious blood began to penetrate his abandoned corpse, Jack opened his red eyes and saw Eva standing over him. His first instinct was to kill her, for the traitor she was. His eyes darted back and forth, as she fed him slowly from a plastic bag. As he drank, Eva watched his eyes become more human, and more like the Jack she loved.

"Traitor!" Jack croaked, as he tried to push her away.

"No, Jack…I am here to help you…now drink," Eva replied, coaxing him to drink more.

As he drank, the vampire felt himself being gradually restored; human blood was just what Jack needed. Gradually, the blackness of death fell away; he was alive once more! Jack studied Eva's familiar face, convinced she was an enemy. When his strength finally returned, Jack lunged at her; Eva was thrown to the ground, his hands around her neck. She couldn't be killed, but Eva was devastated Jack thought she would betray him. She had come to save him!

Dracula had left moments ago; there was no time to waste. The sound of thundering footsteps announced it was time to go. Jack rolled off Eva, as though suddenly coming to his senses. He helped her to her feet, and they both began to evaporate; they were still partially visible when Hitler's guards broke down the door. It didn't matter though; everyone was staring at the body of the fallen Fuhrer, who had just blown his brains out.

Chapter 102 - Life Imitates Art - New York City - (April 4, 1968)

Standing in front of his dressing room mirror, Dracula thought about the new vampire movie he saw last night with Prince, Oliver and Alice; they all shared his fascination with horror movies. The film they attended was called *Dracula, Prince of Darkness*. It was a British film starring Christopher Lee, as himself. Prince thought he played a better part than Bela Lugosi, and Dracula agreed. Dracula was amazed at the popularity of vampire movies, all spawned by Bram Stoker's novel, the very one Dracula helped the author involuntarily edit.

When Dracula accepted the offer to play himself at a local theatre; he did so in order to learn more about the Van Helsings. He played his part so well; Harry Pepitone refused to believe he had never acted before. Dracula rather enjoyed playing himself; he didn't need the money, but he took it to avoid arousing suspicion. The truly unexpected perk was his unlimited access to beautiful and adoring women. Dracula combed his hair in the mirror, feeling especially smug about tonight's prospects; it was a packed house.

"Count Draco...you look smashing tonight!" Harry Pepitone said, as he barged into the dressing room.

"Kind of you to say...now, if you don't mind..." Harry cut him off.

"You know, it's amazing how popular our show has become and...it's all because of you. I don't know how I came to find you...but I'm glad I did."

"I believe you flagged me down at the parade."

"I guess that's true, but you were already dressed for the part...how could I cast any other?"

"Yes...well, I appreciate that." Dracula could hardly be rude.

"You know, it's rather interesting about your name," Harry said looking down at the floor.

"How do you mean?"

"I mean...you're playing a vampire, and your name is Vlad Draco. Doesn't that seem rather improbable? Almost sounds like a fictitious name...," Harry persisted.

"I find your insinuation insulting," Dracula growled, but Harry pressed on.

"Just 'cause I pay you in cash…don't mean I shouldn't know your *real* name…after all, I'm still your employer!" Harry had no idea he was in danger.

Dracula moved closer to the man, as if sizing him up. Harry tried to stand tall, but Dracula still towered over him. "Let's assume you're right… and Draco is an abbreviation for Bram Stoker's vampire…Vlad Dracula. If we follow your train of thought…I could be Vlad Dracula, himself. But wait…how can that be? Count Vlad Dracula has been dead for centuries… or has he?" Harry's smile disappeared; Dracula's eyes had begun to glow.

"Now…Mr. Pepitone…I have a show to do…any more questions?" Dracula's red eyes had evolved into the yellow eyes of a wolf. Suddenly, Harry's feet seemed glued to the floor.

"No, sir," Harry croaked. He backed toward the door holding his precious neck, as though that would save him.

When Dracula headed home later that evening, it was well after midnight. It was the time he liked best, when a city told its own story. The ancient vampire could detect the patter of rodents moving underground; the bowels of the earth were home to rats and they were challenged by no one. Dracula believed the same was true of Tunneltown; it belonged to his children and all who were like him. Tunneltown housed the future of his kind, and protected them from killing sunlight. Alice had named their new home, and Dracula realized the name was perfect.

Dracula passed a newsstand and picked up a copy of the New York Times. Of course, he had heard about the assassination of Martin Luther King, Jr., earlier that evening, but he hadn't had time to read about it. When he unfolded the newspaper, Dracula blinked in amazement; the black and white photograph of the civil rights leader giving a speech, was nearly identical to Vincent's painting. The details of the photograph were eerily similar and impossible to ignore. Dracula tucked the paper under his arm, and walked toward his penthouse. He met with Eva faithfully, once a week; lately, Dracula sensed a growing tension, and wondered if she suspected what he had done to Jack.

Chapter 103 - Return of a Killer - New York City - (July 1968)

She was a dark-haired beauty, with flawless skin he couldn't wait to taste. She moved gracefully through the neighborhood, confident and sure. She passed a balding man; he turned around for another glimpse of her from behind. This was no tawdry middle-aged hooker; this woman was of a different kind, and the vampire found her irresistible. Her eyelids were artfully tinged with blue; she surveyed the night, always on alert for any sign of trouble. Jack stayed out of sight, as he continued stalking her through the narrow streets of Greenwich Village. He knew she was a high-end prostitute; she wore stylish clothes and had perfect white teeth. Jack watched her hips sway seductively, as she turned onto Prince Street. Jack was pleased to find his prey so young and pretty; it would be so satisfying to carve her into something grotesque. He tingled at the thought of her glorious blood; tonight, Jack the Ripper would be resurrected.

There was nothing remotely human left of the angry vampire; he had spent the last few months moving through various neighborhoods within Manhattan. Eventually, Jack found Greenwich Village to be his personal favorite; it was where he spent most of his time. To Jack, it was an upscale version of Whitechapel. He avoided midtown and most areas of Central Park; he wasn't ready yet, to let his enemy know he had survived. When Jack chose to hunt wild game, he frequented remote areas of upstate New York; it wasn't the moors, but it would do. The Catskill Mountains were loaded with white-tailed deer and coyotes, most living on the outskirts of obscure towns like Hudson and Chicopee. His personal preference was a quaint little town, called Sleepy Hollow; no one would think to look for him here. Away from the city, Jack felt better and began to formulate his plan for revenge. Tonight, he planned to make his first "Ripper-like" killing. It would be the first step in announcing a psychotic killer had returned from the dead. One way or another, Vlad Dracula was going down for what he did. He had ruined Jack's plans for Hitler; worse yet, he had taken a fellow vampire's life!

On one occasion, Jack encountered two Van Helsings, but they passed him by without incident; the vigilante group generally targeted vampires who misbehaved. Jack wondered if he could cut a deal with Rupert; together, they stood a better chance against Dracula. Jack's vengeance would not be complete, until he personally severed Dracula's head. His own father had killed him; it was against nature and could not go unpunished. Jack even considered joining forces with the Van Helsings to fight against his own kind. He could help reign in rogue fledglings, and assist with recruiting new members. Once he defeated Dracula, Jack would make a lot of enemies; it made sense to work *with* the gang, instead of against them.

Jack had to admit, it was nice to see a clear night sky; one thing he didn't miss about London, was the fog. He lost sight of the woman for a moment, and then caught a glimpse of the long legs he'd been admiring all evening. She had stopped to talk with a portly man, who whispered in her ear. The hooker threw her head back to emit a feminine peal of laughter, as the man led her behind a brick wall. Jack knew it was time to act; she was his prize tonight! He was upon them at once; before either could react, Jack snapped the fat man's neck. The woman tried to bolt, but Jack was too quick; he pulled her close, putting a finger to her lips to stifle her scream.

"We can do it here, against the wall…if that's how you like it, honey," Jack said. He ripped open her low cut sweater, as silver buttons flew into the air. Jack buried his face between her exposed breasts, taking in her musky scent. He felt the woman exhale with relief; she thought all he wanted was her sex.

"Please, don't hurt me."

"What is your name, my lovely?"

"Charlotte…I have a place where we can be more comfortable." The woman's voice shook with fear; her only chance of escape was to remain calm.

Jack slammed her hard against the wall, as he held her throat. The prostitute's eyes grew wide with terror. "You're going to kill me, aren't you?" she asked, as a single tear ran down her cheek.

In response, Jack sunk his teeth into Charlotte's neck; she tried to scream, but was silenced by the sting of Jack's knife.

Chapter 104 - Flying Free - Empire State Building - NYC - (September 1968)

Eva sat with Dracula on the observation deck of the Empire State Building. Below them, a crowded city moved at a hectic pace, as though unable to do anything else. Eva had been following the latest construction project; it began last month in the financial district. Apparently, there were two buildings going up, that would surpass the height of the Empire State Building by at least ten floors. Newspapers were calling it part of a *World Trade Center.* The Twin Tower construction project was expected to take at least five years; Eva was already making plans to skip ahead in time to see the end result.

Eva held on to her anger about what Dracula did to Jack; there was no justification for such brutality. How could Dracula kill so savagely, and without remorse? For the first time ever, she feared him. They were a family. They were supposed to protect, not *kill*, one another. Eva began to wish they had never left London. She missed the sound of Big Ben filling the air with the soothing tone of a bygone era; Eva even missed the undeniable mystique of London fog

As the first signs of autumn appeared, Eva detected a growing distance between herself and Dracula. She had once loved him with a passion that nearly drove her mad; these days, it was Alice who claimed Dracula's heart. She sighed deeply, wishing she were somewhere else.

"The night sky is bright with man-made illumination...I'm not sure I like it." Dracula attempted to fill in the awkward silence.

"The price of living in a more modern time," Eva replied distractedly.

Dracula studied Eva's profile; she knew Jack was alive, and he was fairly certain she had something to do with it. "Looks like Jack, is back in action... he's targeting upscale hookers this time around," Dracula said trying to extract a confession.

"Uh-huh," Eva said, refusing to meet his gaze.

"...four killings in three months...all prostitutes, no less. Papers say the last one was mutilated...it has to be Jack!"

"Of course...who could miss his perverted calling card?"

"I wonder who rescued him…" Dracula mused, as he turned to face Eva.

"I had to! I couldn't leave Jack bleeding to death!" Eva screamed, she'd been holding the truth in long enough.

"I saved the world from certain disaster!" Dracula exclaimed, grabbing her by the shoulders.

"I don't care… he was my uncle, and you left him to die!" Eva shot back, as she wriggled free.

"You know what kind of man Adolf Hitler was! I was making sure a source of innate evil stayed in his grave. Jack would have unleashed a madman on the world. Is that what you wanted?"

"You didn't have to kill him! You tore apart the only family I've ever known…and I hate you for it!" Eva shrieked. Before he could stop her, Eva took flight and disappeared into the night.

Dracula slumped against the guardrail in defeat. It seemed no matter what he did, those he loved always turned against him. Behind him a door opened; Dracula turned around, ready for a fight.

"Excuse me, sir…I don't know how you got up here…but the observation deck is closed now." In no mood to argue, Dracula muttered an apology and headed toward the stairs.

"No, sir…those doors are locked." The boy stepped back as Dracula's cape flashed; the strangely dressed man jumped off the metal railing and was gone. The boy approached the guardrail and observed traffic humming along; there was no body! Where had the man gone?

High above the dumbfounded security guard, Dracula held fast to the building's antenna. He chuckled to himself; no one ever thought to look up. The night air felt good against his face as he scanned the horizon. Across the Hudson River, stood the iconic Statue of Liberty, proudly holding her faithful torch. As he watched a tug boat drag across the black night water, Eva's angry words reverberated through his mind. The tension between them had been building for a long time; Dracula sensed Eva was ready to break free. He had no choice but to let her go, but the ancient vampire couldn't imagine life without her.

Chapter 105 - The Dark One

Eva continued using Dracula's penthouse during daylight hours; she always left well before sunset. At night or when the weather was bad, Eva favored sneaking into movie theatres; she thoroughly enjoyed escaping to a celluloid world. As she laid on Dracula's king size bed, Eva ran her hands down her childlike form with bitter regret. This was her punishment; to be trapped inside a child's body for all eternity. She rolled over onto her stomach as the sun poked its sleepy head above the treetops in Central Park. Eva watched, as sunlight turned the entire room the color of orange sherbet; at times like this, she was thankful not to be a creature of the night. As she lay between Egyptian cotton sheets, Eva thought about making a fresh start, but where?

"Young one…," a familiar voice hissed.

Eva pulled a pillow over her head and moaned, "Go away."

"I come to you with a proposal…one I am sure you will find interesting."

"What, more false promises you won't keep?"

"Do you remember a young boy named Charles? You met him at the Waldorf Astoria…during one of your escapades. He worked in the kitchen and got fired for leaving in the middle of his shift…"

Eva thought for a moment, and then it came to her. "Charlie…the boy I took flying! I wonder what happened to him."

"What if I told you he lives in the sunny place of your dreams… California?"

"Go on…"

"This boy is a man, now…he would be about thirty-four. In pictures he is quite handsome. He has a quick mind…one most suited to evil. I am sure if you went to him, he would be happy to see you."

"Is he rich?"

"No…he has endowments much more valuable…we need a replacement for Jack. Don't you agree?"

"Maybe, Jack just needs time to get over his grudge," Eva replied.

"Let me worry about Jack...I need *you* to go to California...to present the ultimate offer."

"What, exactly...is he doing in California?"

"Amassing a group of loyal followers to fight his war against the establishment; another misguided attempt by humans to dominate one another. Once Manson's turned, he will yield to greater priorities."

"Why him, and not a man of wealth and status?"

"He's the perfect candidate...troubled childhood...a loner...and yet, he has amazing charisma. Manson doesn't yet know he has been chosen for a life of carnage. Once he is turned... Charles Manson will understand fate brought you back together for a reason."

"Who will turn him? Dracula would never agree to do it."

"Let me worry about that...let's talk about your role in all of this."

"Does Charlie have someone...a girlfriend?" Eva asked, suddenly curious about the boy she met only once.

"He has many women living with him, but no one who truly holds his heart. Maybe, you can change that. Think about it...you are Dracula's favorite no longer. What do you really have left to hold you here?" The Dark One had her full attention now.

"Absolutely, nothing," Eva replied sadly; she wondered how a grown man could be expected to fall in love with a twelve-year-old girl.

"Manson lives with his makeshift family on an old movie set...a place called Spahn Ranch. It's located in Los Angeles County...the Manson family takes in anyone who embraces their ideology, especially girls. You'll need to visit a used clothing store first; you'll stand out otherwise." Eva picked up a pillow and threw it in defiance, against her unseen visitor.

"You are angry...why?"

"You ask me to seduce your next vampire, but leave me trapped inside a half-baked body...and you want to know why I'm angry?" The Dark One emitted a sinister laugh in response; its presence was already fading away.

Eva felt extremely resentful of the Dark One's demands; it had already cost her a friendship with Jack. The former countess was growing tired of being a pawn in the evil entity's nefarious schemes. No longer looking forward to the day ahead, Eva pulled the comforter over her head and fell into a deep sleep.

It was late afternoon when Eva woke; the room was almost completely dark. The sheets were hanging off the bed, and Eva was tangled in the mess. She kicked her feet to shake the covers off; in the dim light, her legs looked too long. Eva stretched out her arms; they looked longer, too. She put her hands to her chest; for the first time in hundreds of years, she had fully developed breasts. Heart pounding, Eva jumped up from the bed and fumbled for the light, running to a full-length mirror. Staring back at her was a perfectly sculpted woman of twenty-two; Countess Bathory had regained her womanhood! Eva marveled at the beauty of her former self, as though seeing it for the first time. Her delicate face was flawless in the early evening light; below were the perfect breasts she remembered, with nipples that quivered when a man touched them. Eva cupped them protectively for a moment, as though afraid they would be taken from her. Her white belly was slightly curved, but firm; Eva couldn't resist running her hands over the swell of her new hips. When she touched her most private place, she remembered all the pleasure it had known. Eva danced her way to the open window; she wanted to run naked through Central Park, like a woodland nymph. Her body had been restored, and the former Countess Bathory planned to use it well. The Dark One had kept its promise; Eva would keep hers, too.

Eva fumbled around for clothes that fit; she ended up wearing one of Dracula's dress shirts, and a pair of his trousers. In no time at all, Eva was dressed and out the door; making her way into the glorious night. It was a perfect autumn evening; the scent of burning leaves and pumpkins lingered in the air. Because she had no shoes that fit, Eva walked barefoot to the 59th Street Station. No one seemed to notice her lack of shoes; this was New York City, after all.

Chapter 106 - The Van Helsings - Greenwich Village - (November 1968)

Jack was huddled in a doorway; his sharp eyes focused on the street ahead. He was waiting for the fearless leader of the Van Helsings; it was time they became re-acquainted. An industrious street vendor advised Jack, the gang leader could be found here on Wednesday nights. Apparently, Rupert had a gambling habit and was known to play into the wee hours of the morning. Jack planned to approach Rupert before he had a chance to make it inside; they needed to have a very candid conversation about what was in everyone's best interest. The night was a bit foggy; for a moment, Jack imagined himself back in Whitechapel. The traffic was letting up, but it didn't matter; Jack stood where he couldn't be seen. He picked up the sound of someone nearby. He heard a footstep, followed by another; each crisp as a McIntosh apple, and then there was silence. Jack heard something click; it was time to make his move. He could smell Rupert before he saw him; the gang leader moved under the streetlight; Jack could barely recognize the boy he once knew. Rupert's eyes now resembled those of a ferret, his skin was gray, and he wore a permanent sneer on his bloodless lips.

"What do *you* want?" Rupert growled; he was holding a pistol.

"I only want to talk, Rupert. I have an idea I believe will serve us both."

"You wouldn't be alive if I didn't know you…my men are all around." Rupert moved closer to Jack, and patted his coat pockets.

"I have no weapons," Jack said, as they sized each other up.

Rupert let out a whistle; several sinister looking gang members made their presence known. "As I said…I'm seldom alone…I think you know my girlfriend." From across the street, a girl stepped into the crosswalk; Jack couldn't believe Rory had taken up such company.

"Rory is with me now…a match made in heaven," Rupert said, pulling her close; Rory would not meet Jack's eyes.

"Jesus, Rupert…she's only twelve years old."

"You know chronological age means nothing to creatures like us."

Jack abruptly changed the subject. "I'm here because we both share a common goal...the destruction of a certain vampire...by the name of Vlad Dracula." Rupert's eyes glistened with interest.

"Why should I make deals with vampires? I should just kill you right now!" Rupert made a poor attempt at being tough.

"I know where he lives and...how to draw him out!" Jack exclaimed.

"Tell me where he keeps the fledglings!" Rupert demanded.

"I won't expose his lair...there are others living there I wish to protect. What do you want with a bunch of misplaced ghosts and a few homeless kids, anyway? Dracula's your prize, Rupert. All we have to do is lure him to a place where we have the advantage. I can help you trap him. My only stipulation...I get to sever his miserable head!"

"I can live with that." Rupert was not a fan of such gruesome tasks.

Jack continued with his persuasive argument. "I know him better than anyone...his mind...his heart...and I know how to take him down!"

"Why change loyalties this late in the game? What makes a seasoned vampire turn against his own kind?"

"He betrayed me in the worst possible way...all because of a whore named Mary Kelly!" Jack spat, then quickly composed himself."

"Spare me the details...I couldn't care less. We both want the same thing...so, how do we draw him out?" Rupert wasn't sure if Jack could be trusted.

"Vlad Dracula is a man of honor...there is only one way. I will challenge him to a battle."

Rupert cut him off, "Like a duel?"

"Just like that...Vlad Dracula has much to account for."

Chapter 107 - The Otherworld

Prince and Nikos returned to the Otherworld from time to time; they liked to rummage through books and newspapers as they discussed the past. This place was mostly used for time travel now, but they still visited on occasion to bask in the aura of a simpler time. Prince cradled a well-worn volume of Charles Dickens, as he re-read his favorite story, *A Christmas Carol.* Something about the stingy old man being saved by a trio of well-meaning ghosts, made Prince think more deeply about his own purpose; even more so, now that Rory had disappeared. Nikos dropped his pen and sat back in his chair. Prince looked up from his reading; his friend had something on his mind.

"All right...let's get it out...what's on your mind?" Prince asked, putting his book aside.

"I think Jack's lurking around...it's just a feeling I can't explain."

"Come on...why would he return after all this time?" Prince replied indulgently. He and Nikos knew what had happened with Hitler; they both agreed Dracula had no other choice. The only thing they didn't know was whether Eva's extended absence was due to Dracula's actions.

"Perhaps, he's ready for a showdown...you know he holds onto a grudge."

"Does Dracula expect Jack to challenge him to a battle?" Prince had seen vampires fight before; it wasn't pretty.

"It can be no other way. Jack wants to settle the score...that's his beef. For Vlad, it's more complicated. He broke the vampire code by killing Jack; a victorious battle would put an end to any further speculation about the validity of his actions." Nikos seemed quite certain of Dracula's ability to defeat his would-be challenger.

"Why, a fight to the death, Nikos?"

"That's how it's done with creatures of the night. Vlad is a very traditional man, despite his occasional attempts at modern dress." Prince snickered and picked up his book again; he turned the page to a lovely illustration of Ebenezer Scrooge, begging for his life beneath the ominous shadow of his own grave.

Chapter 108 - Dracula's Lair - Tunneltown - (November 1968)

Nestled far beneath the busy streets of Midtown Manhattan, lived the first generation of well-fathered vampires, most courtesy of Count Vlad Dracula. They rested well, secure in the knowledge that here, the afternoon sun was rendered powerless. They hung upside down from the rafters above; oversized bats breathing the dust from thousands of books no one would ever read again. The fledglings huddled together in a twilight sleep; their bony arms across their chests, as they dreamed of tearing human flesh. In the peaceful bosom of pitch darkness, the children of Dracula patiently waited for the moon to beckon them into the hungry night.

Don Baker was one of three research librarians employed by the New York Public Library; this afternoon, he had the unfortunate task of retrieving a volume of John Milton's poetry from what he liked to call, *the bowels* of the library. A longtime employee, Don was one of very few, who knew about the storage vaults underneath the library. It took Don twenty minutes to locate the door; it was hidden behind a bookcase full of obscure textbooks.

By the time Don climbed down two flights of narrow stairs, he was out of breath. He cursed as he fumbled with a flashlight, while trying to unlock the door. His key fit, but the lock was stuck from lack of use; he jiggled it until it finally pushed open. Don made his way into a vast book vault grown stagnant with time; this was the last place he wanted to be on a Friday night. He reached for the light switch, but couldn't find one; this section of the library had never been updated with electricity. All he had was a flashlight, and he couldn't remember the last time he'd changed the batteries. Don made his way to the back wall; archived poetry volumes were stored alphabetically in a gray file cabinet. He felt his stomach flip, as the pungent odor of mildew and rotting flesh assaulted him; something must have died in here, he thought.

Anxious to get away from the horrible odor, Don moved more quickly; the hairs on the back of his neck started prickling as he approached the cabinet. He heard a skittering sound above him, but deliberately ignored it; it was probably just a few bats. Don opened the drawer, smiling with relief when he found what he was looking for; he tucked the book under his arm, without bothering to close the drawer. Don hustled toward the exit; the door suddenly looked very far away. He heard the skittering sound again and another noise, like the sound of flapping wings. He finally shinned his flashlight into the rafters; an unspeakable force of evil waited, with its mouth wide open.

"Holy Mother of God...," Don whispered. He dropped his flashlight and fell backwards onto the floor, still clutching the book. He heard them come for him; it was a blessing his flashlight was out of reach. Don Baker lay motionless, as a dozen fledglings pounced on him and drained every last drop of blood from his body.

Chapter 109 - The Final Showdown - Central Park Zoo - NYC - (December 1968)

On a brutally cold December evening, it finally came; confirmation Jack was very much alive. It came in the form of an anonymous letter, left with the cashew vendor. In his brief note, Jack proposed a duel of sorts, but without weapons; he wanted a fight to the death, using brute strength only. Dracula read the note twice then tucked it into his breast pocket. Jack had chosen the zoo at midnight; his tone inferred he expected to be victorious. It could be a trap, Dracula reasoned, and even expected; he wasn't worried, because he had allies of his own. Dracula was more than ready to take Jack down; this time, he would make certain there was nothing left of his body to save.

It was just before midnight, as Nikos and Prince moved quietly toward the perimeter of the zoo. Akos stayed hidden in the trees above; the falcon's job was to make sure Dracula wasn't ambushed. The two spoke in whispers as they waited for the midnight hour. Suddenly, they heard the sound of someone moving toward them. Nikos cocked his pistol, aiming at the cluster of trees a few feet away. Prince drew his faithful sword, thrilled at the opportunity to actually use it. A young girl with snow-white hair came out of the clearing; standing behind her, was Alice.

"Alice!" Prince called out. Alice grabbed Semele's wrist, and they ran back into the trees. Afraid to draw attention to themselves, they had no choice but to let her go.

Jack found the leader of the Van Helsings already waiting for him in a clearing. He and Rory were dressed in black, their faces void of emotion.

"Punctual...I see," Rupert said, a cigarette dangling from his mouth.

"I've been waiting to settle this score for a long time," Jack replied.

"We're as ready as we'll ever be...Rory's got a plan."

"We don't need a plan...I just need back up from your goons if I run into trouble," Jack snapped angrily.

"Listen...the girl has a plan...something to catch him off guard.

After that, he's yours." Jack wanted to protest, but the look in Rupert's eyes changed his mind.

They made their way to the zoo's main entrance, and easily scaled the fence. Most of the animals were quiet this time of night; wolves adapted by feigning sleep. Jack had chosen to battle near the wolf cages, because he felt their strength and kinship. Once Vlad Dracula was defeated, Jack would claim dominion over these and all wolves. His vampire heart ached for revenge, as vivid memories of Dracula's savagery flashed before his eyes; Jack would never forgive the one who made him.

Dracula watched their approach from a huge oak tree. While the ancient vampire was not surprised to discover Rupert was a Van Helsing, he was crushed to see Rory had turned against him, too. He dropped down from the tree, and made his presence known; at first glance, Jack didn't appear to have a weapon.

"I thought it was just you and I...a fair fight, remember?" Dracula glared at Rory with a look of betrayal on his face. "How could you side with a gang of vampire killers?"

Rory didn't see anything but her hatred for Dracula. It happened so fast, the vampire was caught off guard; Rory squirted a water pistol at Dracula's face. Holy water singed the vampire's skin, but he recovered quickly; the unintended side affect, was that Dracula assumed his wolf-like form.

Dracula jumped onto Jack's back, taking a chunk out of his neck; Jack howled in pain as he flung the wolf away. Dracula charged again, his teeth dripping with Jack's blood. Jack leaped into the air and grabbed hold of a tree branch; Dracula came at him again, but Jack kicked him away. Nikos and Prince arrived as Dracula got to his feet. Rory was running at him with a wooden stake; it was clear she meant to kill him. There was no time to intervene. Everything depended on Dracula's agility. Prince held his breath as the stake appeared to move in slow motion, before plunging into the vampire's shoulder. It was not a deadly strike; but it took Dracula down long enough for Jack to get the upper hand. Jack pounced on the wounded vampire, and took a bite out of his shoulder; Rupert whistled for his gang members to come in for the kill.

Under the cover of a rhododendron bush, Semele and Alice watched the deadly battle and felt helpless. The caged wolves behind them growled and hissed as they tried to escape their manmade cages; Alice decided it was time to even the odds. With lightning speed, she disengaged the lock, using a brute strength she didn't know existed. The larger wolf was first to push the door open; the others followed as the frenzy of battle triggered the killer instinct raging inside them. Dracula was down, and so beaten, he had resumed his human form. Rupert snatched Prince's sword and tossed it to Jack, so he could make the killing blow. As he raised the sword to take Dracula's head, he briefly hesitated; and it proved a costly mistake. A gray wolf caught Jack's arm in mid-air and severed it; his hand still grasped the sword he had been holding. Jack rolled onto the ground in agony, trying to stop himself from bleeding out. Like the coward he was, Rupert watched from behind the safety of a well-placed boulder.

The largest wolf overpowered one of Rupert's crew, and swatted him to the ground; the terrified boy looked up at a gaping mouth of evil, before everything went black. Two gray wolves fought over the remains of another boy; he lay face down in the dirt, most certainly beyond feeling any pain. The other Van Helsings had scattered, including Rory. Dracula had finally regained his strength, and now stood over Jack. He had permanently lost his arm; the wolves had devoured it. The bleeding slowed and color began to return to Jack's face. Police sirens sounded in the distance, as Dracula helped Jack to his feet. There were no more grudges to hold onto; it had to end tonight. Jack pulled away from Dracula in anger, as Rupert finally came out of hiding.

"This isn't over!" Jack screamed. The sirens were getting louder, as they raced up Fifth Avenue toward the zoo; it was time to go.

When Dracula reached the busy sidewalk, he surveyed the area to determine if he was being followed. Nikos and Prince had taken Alice in the opposite direction toward Tunneltown. Dracula spotted three police cruisers parked across the sidewalk ahead. The sound of a multiple ambulances confirmed the unfortunate victims would soon be discovered. Curious pedestrians craned their necks, as a hoard of police officers and paramedics swarmed Central Park. Dracula couldn't wait to read the newspapers tomorrow.

Nikos held Alice in his arms; she rested her head on his shoulder, still shaken by what she had seen. Prince walked beside them robotically, he was crushed by Rory's defection. He could still see the look of hatred in her eyes; it was something he would never forget. Prince couldn't believe he had been so blind, and vowed never to trust anyone again. Neither one saw the white-haired girl as she skillfully tracked them all the way back to Tunneltown, without ever being noticed, not even by Alice.

Chapter 110 - The Manson Family - Spahn Ranch - Los Angeles County - (May 1969)

Just as Nikos predicted, Eva went ahead in time, but not too far. The Dark One directed her to a place in Los Angeles County, during the month of May in 1969. Newspapers and television stations were buzzing about the upcoming *Woodstock Festival*; it was scheduled for August in a remote area of upstate New York. Maybe, after she satisfied her curiosity about Charlie, Eva would have time to attend what many claimed was going to be an historic event. Eva returned her thoughts to the boy she remembered; the Dark One was right about one thing, Charles Manson definitely had charisma. Suddenly, Eva felt a tinge of excitement at the thought of meeting Charlie, the man. Would he find her womanly curves appealing? Eva wondered what he looked like now; was it possible he would even remember her? She would find out soon enough.

Eva took the Dark One's advice, and picked up a few things from a secondhand clothing store. She was able to get fairly close to Spahn Ranch, using the Otherworld portal; Eva targeted a roadside diner called, *The Greasy Spoon*. It was just a few miles away from her destination. Using a cracked restroom mirror, Eva entered the year 1969; she managed to escape without being noticed, by climbing out the bathroom window. As she walked on the narrow dirt road toward the ranch, Eva slowly let herself slip into character. This wasn't a time to act like nobility; Eva had to forget everything about who she used to be. Here, she had to act a bit naïve about the world, and must appear to embrace the so-called "hippie movement." Eva brought few belongings, and had a well-rehearsed sob story about an abusive boyfriend.

It was very warm, so Eva wore only a sleeveless top and denim shorts; she had become an expert at blending in. A battered pickup truck plowed by, leaving Eva in a cloud of dust; when the dust cleared, she saw the driver had pulled over. Eva didn't understand he was offering a ride.

A skinny old man finally got out of the truck. "Well, girlie, do you want a ride or not?" Eva needed no further invitation; she hopped up into the front seat, stowing her backpack between her legs.

"Name's George Spahn," the leather-skinned man said with a gravelly voice. He wore a white cowboy hat, and looked as weathered as the terrain he lived in.

"*Spahn* as in *Spahn Movie Ranch*...do *you* own the place?" Eva couldn't believe her luck.

"Yep...that's me...I assumed that's where you're going...you never said where you was going," George replied.

"I guess I didn't...did I?"

"Well...not much out here besides them there mountains," George said, pointing out the window.

George explained proudly that his ranch was still a working horse farm. He confessed that he was barely making ends meet, until Charlie and his family came to stay with him. George believed in the barter system; it worked in his father's time and was good enough for him. The girls helped with household chores and cooking meals; Charlie and a man named "Tex" helped with the horses and other farm chores. A few hours of honest work was all George asked, in exchange for free room and board; he confided to Eva, that he also enjoyed the company.

"My name is Eva." She realized she'd never told him her name.

"I gotta ask, are you a runaway?" George kept his eyes on the road as he waited for a response.

"No...too old for that."

"You're never too old to run away...just easier to catch," George replied with a loud chortle.

"I'm looking for someone..."

"You're looking for Charlie, ain't ya? All the pretty ones are," George said, patting her bare knee.

"It's nice to have young people around...I like hippies and the whole free living thing." George seemed to need conversation.

"I'm not sure I know what you mean," Eva replied. Her comment sent George Spahn into a fit of uncontrollable laughter.

"You know, I like a woman with a sense of humor."

They rode in silence the rest of the way, as Eva observed the barren terrain; this was certainly not the California of her dreams. They finally pulled off the road, and Eva found herself in the middle of an abandoned western movie set; the Dark One had been right about that.

"Here we are now. It looks deserted but...they're around here somewhere...probably congregating in the barn." The old man ambled out of the truck.

"What are they doing in there?" Eva asked, taking in her bizarre surroundings.

"Here comes my sweet thing," George said. A petite girl with hard blue eyes and mousy brown hair came out to greet them. The girl whispered something in the old man's ear; he gave her bottom a squeeze, and then headed toward the house.

"My name is Eva." She didn't think a last name mattered here.

"No one calls me by my given name...just call me Squeaky."

"I met Charlie many years ago...I was hoping he might remember."

"I guess it all depends on how much acid he did that night," the girl named Squeaky replied with a forced smile.

"It was a long time ago."

"I think he already started. Come, I'll take you." Squeaky took her hand and they moved toward the barn; even from outside, Eva could hear Manson's powerful voice. The girl directed Eva to a rickety ladder which led to a hayloft, providing a perfect spot to observe.

The first thing Eva noticed was that most of Charlie's followers were women, young and attractive women. Most sat on the floor in clothing not much better than rags; even her secondhand clothing was an improvement over what most were wearing. Charlie, the man, bore almost no resemblance to the boy Eva remembered. The boy she knew had soft brown eyes and a sweet smile. The man speaking to a captivated audience had piercing dark eyes and seemed angry, despite a constant smile. His face was largely concealed by an unkempt beard; his lifeless brown hair hung to his shoulders. Charles Manson donned a simple gray robe, just long enough to dust the tops of his bare feet. He had a commanding voice and spoke with much animation, flailing his arms about to further engage a crowd who seemed to hang on his every word.

"I've spoken to all of you before, about who Hitler really was. He was not the evil villain you've have read about in school...not at all. Classroom textbooks are filled with nothing but lies and deception.

They tell us nothing about the greatness he aspired to…even he knew the American dream would eventually crumble…"

"Kill the pigs…kill the pigs…," two dark-haired girls chanted softly, until Manson's glare silenced them.

"Our greatest enemy gets stronger every day. The establishment is trying desperately to preserve a way of life that died a long time ago. A civil war is coming…it will be the salvation of our cause. The pigs have turned their backs on the youth of America…and anyone not like them!" George Spahn had just entered the barn, but he could not see her.

"Tell us more, Charlie," sounded a chant from a group of three girls who clung to each other.

"God will tell us when to rise up our weapons against the rich…and make them pay for their sins in human carnage!"

"How much longer? When can we take up our weapons against them?" asked a lone voice; Eva realized Squeaky had spoken.

Charles Manson looked up, and his eyes locked on a stranger who looked familiar. "How many times have I told you all…time is a man-made illusion? *God's* timetable…is the only one that matters!"

"Amen," chanted the crowd.

"My children…that is all for today. Make no mistake, the United States government is at war with its youth…and they will win, unless we fight for what is rightfully ours!"

Eva remained in the loft, as she pondered how best to approach Manson. She was suddenly nervous about meeting him face to face. What if he didn't believe, she was the girl who took him flying? Maybe it wasn't necessary. Eva was tasked with only one thing; making Charlie fall in love. Love or lust, it really didn't matter; either had the ability to enslave a man, if only for a little while.

She looked down at the dispersing crowd. A group of women with unkempt hair shuffled toward the door, their movements slow and deliberate. Manson had a powerful hold over them; the boy she took flying might be a preacher, but he was certainly not affiliated with any church.

"How did you know where to find us?" a voice whispered from behind her. Eva turned to find her Charlie, grown into a man she didn't recognize.

Chapter iii - Inspector Niles Poole - Scotland Yard - (June 1969)

Inspector Niles Poole had been doing this job for a very long time; there wasn't much he hadn't seen. From the time he was old enough to sit on his father's knee, all Niles ever wanted to do was work in law enforcement. His father, Charles, had passed away recently at the age of ninety-three. Since his father's death, Niles had taken an interest in a very cold case; the same one that made Charles Poole a stranger to his own son. Growing up, his father had always been distant. Niles believed it was largely due to the Whitechapel murders, and his obsession with avenging the Ripper's victims. Niles heard Jack's name in his sleep; it was the only thing his father ever wanted to talk about, right up until the day he died.

On the desk in front of him, was a well-worn leather briefcase that had once belonged to his father; ever since Niles opened it, he wished he hadn't. His father was a fanatic when it came to Jack the Ripper; it destroyed his parent's marriage, and kept friends at an uncomfortable distance. Even as he reached his ninth decade, Charles Poole lived and breathed the Ripper case. The file in front him, was a copy of the Ripper case file; the original file had been lost during the Blitzkrieg. At first, Niles was reluctant to dig into the nineteenth-century crime spree; once he began, the inspector was hooked. The mysterious case would forever be a black mark in London's colorful history. During the investigation, his father focused much of his attention on Mary Kelly; he remained convinced her killing was personal. On the surface, Niles had to agree; her killing was different from the other Ripper victims.

Niles sorted through a second folder; there were a handful of cryptic notes, and other documents regarding vampires. His father had put together a handwritten dossier on Count Vlad Dracula *a.k.a. Count Draco*. He quickly devoured the information, and pocketed a charcoal sketch someone had rendered of the mysterious count. Next, was a photograph of Makefield Manor, the established residence of Count Draco and his family. A scribbled notation indicated Jack the Ripper also lived at the manor for a period of time; naturally, this was impossible. Niles also found a well-preserved newspaper clipping about Makefield Manor, confirming it was destroyed by German bombers in 1941.

Niles reflected on his father's farfetched tale about encountering "supernatural beings" at Makefield Manor. His father's dissertation went on to claim Jack the Ripper and Count Draco were living vampires! There were even details about a wine cellar stocked with human blood. He stopped reading for a moment; how could anyone believe Jack the Ripper was alive and consorting with vampires? Although not a superstitious man, Niles did believe in vampires. But not the kind of bloodsucking monsters found in horror movies; these men drank human blood as part of their killing rituals. Because Niles had a brother living in New York City, he had been following a rash of unsolved murders in lower Manhattan; the victims were all prostitutes and their subsequent mutilation *did* have an eerie resemblance to the Ripper killings. Obviously, it couldn't be the same killer; Niles believed a copycat killer was looking to make a name for himself. The ruse appeared to be working; *The New York Times* and *The Post* had officially dubbed him the "Ripper Killer."

Pushing the case file aside, Niles pulled a stack of newspapers closer; he was searching for a back issue of *The Post*. He wanted to take a fresh look at the Central Park Zoo killings, last year. Niles plucked out the December issue, without upsetting the pile. The inspector picked up a cream-colored envelope anonymously delivered, earlier today. Inside the envelope was a letter and a color photograph, he believed were meant to draw him into a trap of some kind. The photograph was of a medieval sword, small, like something for a young boy; on the back was written: *Sword of Prince Edward V circa 1483.* He took up the note and read it for the third time:

Dear Inspector Poole,

We know you want to rid the world of evil, just as we do. Here are some facts currently known only to high-ranking officials of law enforcement, regarding the wolf attack in Central Park last December:

* This sword was handcrafted for Prince Edward V, and went missing from Westminster Palace in 1483. It suddenly showed up at the Central Park Zoo; the very same night the wolves attacked and killed two teenage boys. The

sword had blood on it, but neither victim had a single knife wound. Who else do you think was there??

* At the murder scene (yes, murder) there was a bloody wooden stake left by one of the assailants. The blood type was neither human nor canine! Those wolves didn't start this. They were driven to kill by someone who left the scene. You know who controls wolves, Inspector Poole? Vampires do. The police want the public to believe they are safe and keep the ugly truth hidden. But I know the truth, and now, so do you.

The one you seek is living in Midtown Manhattan. Come to our fair city, and we can tell you more about who he really is. Come and all your questions will be answered. You owe your father that much.

When Niles first read the letter, he couldn't help but be intrigued. If Jack the Ripper was still alive, he would be an extremely old man; *unless* his life had been prolonged by some unnatural force, like the bite of a vampire. Niles had a sick feeling in the pit of his stomach. How could he apprehend an adversary that wasn't human? If Jack the Ripper had really been made a vampire, the city of New York had no idea what they were dealing with, but he did. Niles had been hearing about vampires and Jack the Ripper his whole life; it was time to put an end to it. His mind raced, as he pondered how this Count Draco fit into the picture. Niles could feel the pull of excitement as he contemplated his next move. Closing up the file, the inspector realized he was exhausted; Niles couldn't remember the last time he took a day off.

Chief Inspector Max Tillerson was a reformed chain smoker; he got through his day by sucking on lollipops. His boss looked up from his newspaper with sagging, bloodshot eyes, "What is it, Poole?"

"Hey boss, you know how you're always after me to take vacation time?"

"Yeah…what of it?"

"Well…we're not really busy this time of year, so I thought…"

"Just give your case files to Jenkins and get outta here."

Niles couldn't believe his boss didn't ask where he was going. As if reading his thoughts, the chief inspector added, "I hear New York City is a nice place to visit this time of year. Do me a favor…come back before I have to chase after you." Inspector Niles Poole shook his head; there were no secrets at Scotland Yard.

324

Chapter 112 - In a Dream - Spahn Ranch - Los Angeles County - (July 9, 1969)

When people asked Charlie how his ideology evolved, he would always say God spoke to him in his dreams. Manson also claimed he found inspiration in music, particularly The Beatles and their hit song "Helter Skelter." For Charlie, the song summed things up; the lyrics spoke to him in a way no other song did.

Charles Manson slept in a shabby room at the farmhouse with George. It gave him the privacy he needed when he meditated, which was often. His "meditation" was generally another name for Charlie's frequent hallucinogenic journeys on acid; he was on a quest to reach the very core of his inner consciousness. Charlie believed he was capable of becoming a divine being, and merely had to uncover his potential; he had total faith that God would lead him in the right direction. He had been born with a kind of sadistic charisma that made it easy for him to control others; Manson was a master at intimidation. Fact was, Charlie was a man of small stature, and wasn't very brave when confronted with a physical challenge; being a leader really worked for him. Manson truly believed it was up to him to get things started; it would be time soon to make those rich pigs pay, the ones living in their high-end homes strewn about Bel-Air and Beverly Hills. Although Charlie understood killing would be necessary, he planned only to guide the others; he believed his role too crucial for him to partake in something as risky as a ritual killing. Adolf Hitler, who was Manson's hero, often had others do his killing, convinced it was not always necessary for leaders to be soldiers as well.

Charlie looked out the window and watched, as three of his girls drew buckets of water from the well. He looked more closely and realized one of them was Eva, the strange girl who clearly didn't fit in. Charlie hadn't recognized her, as Eva expected; her only course of action was to insist she shared his vision, and had come to Spahn Ranch to join him and his family. The others seemed to accept her, eventually, he did too. Manson watched the girls intently, as they finished up; they had gotten all wet and were giggling like school girls. She was a pretty one; in the morning sunlight, something about her seemed familiar. He followed her graceful movements as she disappeared from view.

George rapped loudly on the door. "Charlie!"

"Yeah, man...what time is it?" Charlie asked in annoyance.

"Time to get your skinny ass out of bed, and help me feed the horses." Charlie groaned, but got up to pull on his pants; he looked in the mirror and barely recognized his own image.

There was another knock on the door, Charlie scowled. "Shit, George...give me a minute!"

"It's not George," Eva said, as she pushed the door open.

"I know you've been deliberately ignoring me...I think you and I need to talk," Eva said, closing the door behind her.

"I can't sleep with all of you," Manson replied arrogantly, as he pulled on a t-shirt.

"Is that what you think...that I'm upset because you haven't taken me to bed?"

"I have no time for emotional outbursts...leave me now!" Charlie snapped, turning away from her.

"You forgot everything, didn't you, Charlie? How you told me about escaping from a place called Gibault...that I later discovered was a reform school."

Charlie turned back to face Eva; it was impossible for her to know such a thing. He moved across the room, and looked into her eyes; Manson blinked, when he saw himself flying high above the Manhattan skyline. "Who are you?" he whispered, almost afraid to know the answer.

"The girl who took you flying over Central Park...a long time ago," Eva replied. Charlie's face softened, as he remembered the young girl wearing too much makeup; she had become a woman.

"It's really you, then?" he asked, taking her face in his hands. Without further hesitation, Eva kissed Charles Manson, and he slowly slipped into a dream.

Chapter 113 - The Dark One

The Dark One felt the heartbeats of hungry fledglings, as the sun set over Bryant Park; hundreds of bat-like creatures opened their eyes, as the promise of absolute darkness called to them. Departing in an amazingly uniform manner through unused coal chutes, the army of bats soared high into the sky, gracefully forming a tight circle, before disbanding to feed. The sound of flapping wings pleased the Dark One; Dracula's children served Satan, and no one else.

Although encouraged by a steady increase in the vampire population, the Dark One observed that under Dracula's regime, things were becoming a bit too civilized. Where was the carnage? Newspapers were clamoring for another gruesome story; the nightly news was hardly worth watching anymore. Why had the killing stopped, and where was Whitechapel's wounded puppet? The Dark One missed the headlines about mutilated corpses; one could always count on *The Post* for gory photos. Damn it, the Dark One missed Jack! Ever since his injury, Jack had gone into hiding and no one knew where. The Dark One put thoughts of Jack aside, and reflected on the budding romance between its protégé and Charles Manson; so far, it was going well.

Charlie and Eva seemed madly in love to others, and at first, they were. But, by late-July, they began to fight about everything; even their coupling seemed like a battle for dominance. Manson didn't like strong women; Eva wasn't about to bow to anyone, so they struggled to find balance. As the month of July came to an end, Eva became disenchanted; she feared Charlie had destroyed his mind by taking so much acid. Others in the family whispered about it, when they didn't know she was listening. Everyone thought he was coming unhinged, but no one would dare defy their leader. Charlie explained the family would need to stay off the radar, once the pigs were dealt the justice they deserved; the plan was to hide in their cave until things blew over. Whenever Eva tried to discuss the basis for his ideology, Charlie would just say, "Helter Skelter...man...just listen to the song." She had listened to it several times, but the song made no sense to her at all.

Eva believed herself in love with Charlie, which is why she stayed. Over the past week however, his talk of ritual killing accelerated; Eva knew he was planning something deadly. The night before, Charlie spent the night in his cave, explaining he and Tex needed to bring their stockpile of weapons down from the mountain. In the past few weeks, they had been going there more frequently. One morning, Eva finally confronted Charlie about his plans, and he admitted they were targeting a home in Beverly Hills; they needed to send a message by killing a few "rich pigs." He gave no names or any other information, so Eva had no idea who they were. She pondered the concept of random victims; she had always killed people she knew, and always in a fit of rage. Would Charlie himself do the killing, or would the others? In her opinion, he didn't seem very brave. The first week of August arrived with an unexpected heat wave, as Eva began to question the success of her mission. In her mind, Charlie wasn't going to be coaxed to New York City or anywhere else.

It was late morning, and Eva was delightfully lost inside a twilight dream, when the Dark One made its presence known. "Why do you always disturb my slumber?"

"He will ask you to be part of it, you know...the killing, I mean," the Dark One said, as Eva brushed her unruly hair.

"I didn't come here to be part of something like this! What is the point of killing a few rich people anyway?" Eva understood she was in love with a man she really didn't know, and yet, to be with him was so exhilarating.

"He means to make a statement...he'll need to be turned right after the crimes are committed, or it will be too late." The Dark One attempted to stir the inner pot of wickedness, living inside an evil specter it had known for centuries.

"You speak as though this is an easy thing...how can you expect *me* to convince him to leave a family of faithful worshippers?"

"You came because I commanded...not to test the limits of your newly acquired sexuality. Don't think you're anything special...to Manson, you're simply the flavor of the week."

"You're wrong! We share a special bond...he can't possibly feel for

328

the others, what he feels for me." Eva wanted desperately to believe her own words.

"What you *share*, countess…is a carnal bed. I must say…I find the acrobatics very entertaining."

Eva threw a shoe across the room. She had fallen for Charlie, without realizing what a complex man he was. Eva saw the way he looked at the other girls; she was fairly certain at least one of the family's young children was fathered by him. Could it really be possible, he had given up all the other girls just for her? In her heart, Eva knew it was unlikely.

"You don't know him like I do…when we're alone together and he takes me in his arms…there is no one else."

"Intercourse between a man and a woman…is often a loveless act."

"He loves me…and he lusts for me…"

"Yes…Charlie has plenty of lust in him, countess. On that point, we can readily agree. After all, he sure keeps busy up in those caves." The Dark One baited its hook cautiously.

"What do you mean?"

"You think he and Tex are the only ones up there all night?"

"But he loves *me*."

"Manson is not a one-woman man…never was."

"You can't prove that," Eva said, then instantly regretted her words.

The room went dark as a vivid picture flashed; Charlie and Tex were in the cave, but there were others, all women. Like a television show, the Dark One played the painful footage; Eva felt compelled to watch, as her love for Charlie began to slowly crumble. In the vision, Charlie was wearing his dingy robe as Tex came into view; he was naked and stood next to a young girl Eva had never seen before. They joined a group of scantily clothed women seated in a circle, no one looked familiar. As Charlie began to speak, all eyes were fixed on him; at times, he really did look like a man of the cloth.

"It is nearly time for our redemption…children. Our actions will rock the establishment on its ass, and we will be waiting to show the world a new way."

"We believe, Charlie…we dream of being part of the new world," a waif-like blonde chanted; her eyes were glazed over by whatever drug she had taken.

"Everything I have promised will come to pass...just as God promised...but we must be patient. He speaks to me, children...and asks that you honor my body as my word," Charlie said in his most commanding voice; he let his robe fall to the floor, and Eva observed he had a full erection.

The girl with Tex stood up first and went to sit at Charlie's feet, like an obedient dog. Charlie put his hands on the top of her head and continued, "God speaks through me and has promised we will be rewarded for our actions. Behold my divining rod, through which all God's words are uttered...it should be worshipped and adored." Charlie grabbed the dark-haired girl by her hair, and forced himself into her mouth.

"Don't show me any more..." Eva cried, covering her eyes with her hands.

"She certainly seemed to enjoy herself, didn't she?" The Dark One had a very cruel sense of humor.

"I thought what I shared with Charlie was real...and special..." Eva trailed off.

"Very real...and very temporary."

Eva was hot. "Tell me then...why do we want to recruit someone who abuses women, under the guise of a false prophet?"

"Men have been abusing women since the beginning of time... if that mattered, we would have no heroes. I am losing my patience, countess. I want Charlie to join us...and I want *you* to start cooperating with my plan."

"He has no inclination to leave the West Coast...I think it was a mistake to come here."

"I didn't ask you to think!" the Dark One hissed.

Eva sat on the edge of the bed, feeling powerless and a little bit afraid. With a deep sigh, she decided to play along. "I suppose you know who he plans to kill?"

"My dear countess, I know everything. Now, if you'll give me your full attention, I just might overlook your insolent behavior."

CHAPTER 114 - A DIVINE INTERVENTION - (AUGUST 6, 1969)

The room was filled with fire and smoke; Eva gulped for air out of instinct. She rose from the burning bed, desperate to find the door. Her feet felt heavy, like she was walking in quicksand. Eva found the door and pushed it open, but there was only blackness; she took a step and tumbled down a deep hole, just like the one Alice found, only this one led to hell. As she continued falling, Eva finally understood the meaning of absolute abandonment. No friendly moon or twinkling stars to light her way; Eva was suddenly overcome with the very human need to find comfort. She felt a chilling breeze, followed by a familiar voice that often haunted her dreams.

"A world of blackness awaits…I thought you should get used to it." Eva felt the need to say her name out loud.

"Mary Kelly…"

"The one you killed…but not the only one."

"The one Dracula still loves." No one knew it better than she.

"Eva, they're going to kill a young woman and her unborn child… an innocent baby," Mary whispered urgently.

Eva clapped her hands over her ears, trying to block out Mary's words. Another vision flashed; a bloodied corpse, with a tangled mane of golden hair. It didn't matter if Eva closed her eyes, she could clearly see the dead woman was heavily pregnant, and it made her feel sick.

"How many more lives, Eva…or should I say, Countess Bathory?" Mary's growing anger changed her voice into something terrifying.

Eva had stopped moving; ahead were the front gates of her ancient home, Sarvar Castle. At first, she was excited, until she realized the castle was in ruins. She walked toward the castle entrance, noting the doors were hanging from their hinges; her magnificent courtyard had been reduced to nothing but crumbling marble. Eva stood on the stone pathway, as a little blonde-haired boy came out to greet her; when he got closer, she felt suddenly afraid. The boy looked up at her with dull,

331

gray eyes; he was dressed in a woman's cotton nightgown, and it was covered in blood.

"Are you hurt?"

"I am killed…I wear my mother's nightgown…it is my death shroud." Eva watched in horror as the little boy's face turned into something grotesque.

A lovely young girl came out of the castle calling after the boy. When she got close enough, Eva recognized Theresa, the servant girl she had ordered killed centuries ago. Eva closed her eyes as she was assaulted by a vivid image of Theresa being burned alive. A man dressed in rugged clothing approached, and she easily recognized Desio Vas; he had unknowingly sacrificed himself so Dracula could live again. Behind him, a dark-haired woman of about twenty appeared, and Eva remembered her, too. She was the one Eva slaughtered in a jealous rage, before helping herself to one of her evening gowns. She wanted to run, but there was no escape. More young girls were coming out of the dilapidated castle, now; they moved toward her, with mean eyes that became at once, judge and jury. Eva turned away from her accusers, unable to look at their hateful faces any longer.

"We're all here, countess…and we'll be waiting for you…" the boy said, with sharp teeth that weren't there before. She was surrounded by all of them now; they were angry and began clawing at her with blood-stained hands.

Eva let out a yelp and woke up in a knot of bed sheets; she was soaked with Charlie's sweat. He lay curled up in a fetal position; he was shivering despite the fact his skin was slick with perspiration. Eva reached out to touch him, and then quickly pulled her hand away; her boyfriend had begun to repulse her.

Chapter 115 - Dracula's Penthouse - Central Park South - (August 8, 1969)

Dracula had been spending more time at his penthouse apartment since Eva's departure; her absence left him with a void he couldn't deny. He had tried to adapt to spending time at the Statue of Liberty to enjoy some nighttime solitude; but due to twenty-four-hour security, he was constantly being chased away. The penthouse at least offered him a comfortable privacy; it didn't feel like home here though, not without Eva. Dracula still loved Countess Bathory, in whatever shape she assumed. Yes, he had loved Mary Kelly, too, but for very different reasons. He had loved Mary for her wholesome beauty and her gentle nature, but, how well had he really known her? Because she was so savagely murdered, Dracula idolized her memory, often forgetting who she really was; a woman who took money for sexual favors.

When the ancient vampire really thought about it, there was no valid reason for him to love someone like Mary Kelly, but he had. It was very puzzling that he could love two women who were nothing alike. Eva was self-absorbed and had an evil streak, but was fiercely loyal; Dracula believed she still loved him, no matter what she said in anger. From the first time he met Countess Bathory, Dracula found her wanton sex drive so very exciting, especially in a time when most women were quite reserved in bed. Dracula felt his old desire returning, as he remembered nights when passion seemed almost more important than feeding. The ancient vampire could almost feel her warm body moving beneath him; his chest ached with longing for what had once been. Dracula wanted to believe Eva would return when she grew tired of her clandestine adventure; but, as each day passed, he became less convinced she would return.

Dracula's thoughts turned to Alice, who was slowly pulling away from him; she had matured quickly, and was already starting to act like an adult. It started the night she brought the albino girl to Tunneltown; it was a blatant declaration that she would choose her own way to feed. Semele was a sweet girl and they accepted her, but Dracula knew there would be more; his instincts proved correct. Dracula tried to discourage Alice from bringing kids to Tunneltown; but once they were inside, Virginia and Vincent were adamant they should stay. It started with the twins, Mary and Maude; Alice thought it would be a novel idea to befriend another set of twins. Unfortunately, Alice tired of them quickly and soon brought home two others, Susie and Sarah. By far, Dracula's favorite was a tiny girl named Jill; she had golden hair and eyes that sparkled like polished emeralds. All of them had been homeless, and near starving when Alice found them. She brought them to Tunneltown, where they had plenty to eat; in turn, they provided Alice with the sustenance she required. The ancient vampire battled with Alice for insisting on fresh blood; but finally gave up, deciding it was better than letting her develop a taste for killing.

Nikos knocked softly on the door; Dracula only answered after looking through the peephole, an invention he rather liked. It was always a comfort to see his old friend, but he was not another vampire with whom Dracula could share a glass of his reserve vintage. Dracula could tell by his expression, Nikos had something pressing on his mind.

"Vlad…we need to talk." Nikos seemed out of breath as he spoke. Dracula uncorked a fresh bottle of AB negative, not bothering with the pretense of using a wineglass.

"I ran into Harry Pepitone…boy, is he pissed that you just up and left the show…asked me if I'd seen you around."

"Well…what could I do, after the mess we made in Central Park? It seemed like a good time to drop out of sight. Don't worry about Harry… he paid me in cash and has no idea I live here."

"We were lucky with him. Most establishments won't do that… every transaction has to be documented now. America's fascination with credit cards creates another problem…unless we can find someone to forge the documents we need to create legitimate identities."

"I agree, my friend…living in the modern world has its challenges. Soon, hotels and restaurants will require credentials we don't have. Let's go ahead and find someone to work on our little problem…we need authentic-looking birth certificates, at the very least. If we don't catch up with modern technology, we'll all be forced to hide underground… and I've had my fill of that."

"Vlad...there's something else. Harry told me he was visited by a Scotland Yard detective...his name was Poole."

"*Poole*...how could *he* still be alive?"

"It's his son, Vlad. Niles Poole. Apparently, he is still digging into the Ripper murders, if you can believe that. He told Harry he thought Jack the Ripper was still at large...I assume he meant a copycat killer."

"Jack. I swear, Nikos...that man will be the death of me!"

"Vlad...I'm afraid you can't stay here anymore...it's just too risky. I found you a comfortable room at the Doral Hotel...it's on East 39th Street. No view of Central Park, I'm afraid...but, we can pay by the month in cash, no questions asked."

"And...what about Poole? We need to get rid of him."

"Don't worry about it, Vlad...I have this under control."

"Of course...I can always count on you," Dracula replied, as he drained the wine bottle and went to get another.

Exactly one hour later, in Midtown Manhattan, a yellow checker cab picked up the distinguished English gentleman in a London Fog raincoat; the man asked to be taken to JFK Airport. He spoke to the cabdriver who asked questions about England, and they talked like old friends as they worked their way through rush hour traffic. Next to him, was an overstuffed briefcase filled with everything available on the oldest murder case the inspector had ever worked on. They came to a railroad crossing as the light turned red; the man scowled because he was already running late. Looking up from his newspaper, the inspector locked eyes with the cabdriver in his rearview mirror. In that moment, his life flashed before him in a wave of heart wrenching emotion.

"I'm really sorry, inspector," the cabby said; he hit the gas and deliberately crossed the railroad tracks in front of an oncoming commuter train. Inspector Poole never felt any pain at all; the yellow cab exploded on impact, along with the original Ripper case file.

Chapter 116 - Murder on Cielo Drive - Beverly Hills - (August 8, 1969)

In his dream, Charlie was flying; the weightlessness of it was far better than any drug he had used, of that he was certain. The girl beside him was glowing, as they sailed effortlessly through the night air; from high above the rooftops, the boy saw a whole new world. Charlie always knew when he was dreaming; he didn't want to wake up from this one. With the touch of her hand, the dark-haired girl reached into his very soul. Charlie closed his eyes, as the burning hatred of all who had ever wronged him, temporarily vanished. His stomach flipped with joy, as his mind was set free; until the girl let go of his hand. Charlie reached out to her, but all she kept saying was, "Wake up, wake up."

"Wake up, Charlie…wake up!" Eva was shaking him.

Charlie sat up with a jolt; Eva held him back so he didn't get up too fast. "I dreamed I was flying…," he said, frowning as he looked around the tiny, wallpapered room.

"Too much acid, Charlie…it's going to fry your brain. I thought you would want to get ready for tonight by remaining somewhat coherent."

"What time is it?"

"4:30…you slept the day away…and you still look like shit," she said, punching him playfully.

"I just need some coffee…I'll be fine," Charlie replied, stretching his bony arms over his head.

"Don't you ever worry about killing brain cells?"

Charlie leaned over to kiss her dismissively. "Experimenting with mind-altering drugs has helped me discover who I really am. You should try it sometime…it might loosen you up."

"Sorry…it's just not my thing, Charlie."

"Then, you'll never discover your true potential…I carry all I've learned wherever I go. Being in touch with my true self…will help me tonight. Tonight…we will show the world, we are a force to be reckoned with."

"Who are you taking with you?" Eva asked.

"Actually…there's been a change of plans. I want you to come with us, Eva. God must have brought you here for a reason."

"Charlie…I can't…let me do something else, please." Eva thought about the pregnant woman in her dream; even she couldn't participate in something so heinous.

"You would go against what God has planned for you?" Charlie didn't like to argue about anything.

"I can't do it, Charlie…I'll do anything else for you but…not this…"

Tex knocked on the door, and then barged right in without waiting for a response.

"What is it?" Charlie growled.

"Is *she* coming?" Tex asked, nodding at Eva. She looked at Charlie with imploring eyes.

"Um…I don't think so," he said.

"Some chicks just don't have a taste for murder, Charlie," Tex said glaring at Eva. They clearly didn't like each other.

Charlie finished dressing without saying anything else; Eva studied him, trying to understand how she had ever found him attractive. It was time to go and she decided tonight was her chance; Charlie wouldn't be here to stop her. If things went as planned, there would be a multiple murder tonight, in Beverly Hills. Because of Charlie's prison record, Eva believed police would inevitably come sniffing around; she didn't want to be here when they did. She was also angry Charlie had lied to her about his nocturnal visits to the cave. It was time to get out of this mess, before it became more complicated.

Finally dressed, Charlie turned to Eva. "No one is keeping you here, Eva. None who live here are bound to stay…and can leave anytime they want." At times, Charlie seemed able to read her mind.

"Who said I wanted to leave?" Eva said a little too quickly.

"What we do tonight will be historic…I think you'll be sorry you weren't part of it," Charlie said, then turned and left the room.

"Be careful, Charlie," Eva called after him, but he was already gone.

An hour after they left for a night of sadistic murder, Eva said goodnight and locked herself in Charlie's room so she could escape out the bedroom window. Once outside, Eva moved to the rear paddock and chose a sandy-colored mare, mounting her without a saddle. She wasn't ready to head back east yet; and certainly not ready to face Dracula. Right now, her main goal was to get as far away from the ranch as possible. If Charlie went through with his plans, everyone at Spahn Ranch could be taken into custody; Eva had no intention of being one of them.

The porch light switched on; old George had seen her. He was cursing up a storm as he waved his shotgun at her. Eva's only alternative was to ride further up the mountain. The main road was no longer an option; George would expect her to go that way, and could easily overtake her with his truck. Suddenly, Eva remembered about the cave; she had only been there once, but she still remembered the way, and so did the mare. Sure enough, after about twenty minutes, she recognized the secluded entrance. Eva would stay here tonight; she needed time to figure out what to do next.

As Eva approached the cave entrance, she sensed an ominous presence. She heard a low, mean growl resonate from inside the cave. Eva stood her ground and waited for the animal to come outside. When it finally did, she was struck by the majestic beauty of the largest white wolf she had ever seen. Eva held out her hand to reassure the beast she meant no harm; they locked eyes, as if declaring a battle of wills. She dropped on one knee, and the wolf came right to her. The white wolf paused, and then started shaking violently; as Eva looked on, the furry beast morphed into a young man who was so striking, she was temporarily at a loss for words.

"Please...let me introduce myself...I am Sylvio. You know my secret, now." Sylvio held out a hand to help her to her feet.

"My name is Eva...I'm not one of your kind, but...I'm not human either."

"I know...you have no scent," Sylvio replied, as he sniffed the air around her head.

"I'm an earthbound spirit...I just wanted to see California," Eva explained, unwilling to reveal too much.

"Nice to meet you, Eva."

"Sylvio...that *can't* be your real name," Eva challenged.

"My human name was Imhotep...I got my ass kicked for it most of my life...that is until I became a vampire."

"I have to agree, Imhotep is not a very good name for a vampire, especially one as handsome as you," Eva replied.

Sylvio appeared to be a gentleman, but had a tough guy look Eva found very attractive. He wore his jet black hair slicked back to accentuate a pronounced widow's peak, and he had yellow-green eyes with flecks of silver. He wore faded jeans and dingy cowboy boots; any assumption he was a rancher, would quickly be dispelled by his fitted leather jacket. To Eva, he was the epitome of what it meant to be cool.

"Did you do that...or did it happen when you were turned?" she asked, pointing to the shock of white hair growing about his temples.

"Born this way...on my life." Eva realized he didn't want to tell her the truth.

"I guess I didn't expect to find your kind outside the city limits." Eva had no idea vampires had already migrated across the country.

"What...you think vampires only live in New York City?"

"I guess I never thought about it," Eva replied, wondering why he assumed she was from New York.

"California is the perfect place for us...the weather is great most of the year. Good weather brings people out to enjoy the nightlife... giving creatures of the night, plenty of opportunity to feed. But, that's not how we live up here."

"You don't kill humans?" Eva was intrigued.

"No...it is not our way. There are others like me...many of our kind live up here on the mountain. We deny our natural craving for human flesh, and settle for killing wild animals instead. We also eat the raw meat of what we kill...this provides sustenance that lasts much longer than drinking blood alone."

"I came from the ranch down there," Eva said, pointing to the foot of the mountain.

"Yes, I know that place...we all stay well away from Spahn Ranch... we believe Manson is crazy...and dangerous."

"I'm actually running away from them... I left because, I *know* they're crazy!"

"Sounds like a wise decision, but where will you go now? They all know about this cave, so you can't stay here...we live much higher up the mountain."

"I know this place isn't safe, but I didn't know where else to go."

"We'll...I'm glad you left...you have no place with them. Manson's war is one for humans to fight...not you." Sylvio said gently, taking her hand.

"Who is your father?" Eva had to ask.

"I wish I knew...I know it's hard to believe...I mean, who doesn't know the one who made them? All I can tell you is...I was out at a nightclub in L.A. I had way too much to drink...I think I took some mescaline, too. I woke up in a wine cellar beneath the nightclub with blood on my face and hands...but that's all I remember."

"You really have no idea?" Eva thought it was sad for a vampire not to know who made him.

"No, I'm afraid not. What's your story?"

"I found a new world inside a mirror when I died...in the year 1614." Eva expected more questions, but he said nothing.

"I lived in New York City before I came here, but...there is nothing for me there now," Eva said with a touch of regret.

"Such a corrupt and dirty city," Sylvio replied distastefully.

"It has its own kind of charm...especially when the city is lit up at night."

"Artificial lighting is nothing more than a manmade illusion," he replied, clearly unimpressed.

"You don't like big cities much, do you?" Eva asked playfully.

"Eva...ours is a simple life...there are five of us; we've been living up here for about five years, I think...but, I'm not really sure."

"What's it like to live in such a vast wilderness?"

"The only thing more beautiful than sunrise on the mountain...is when the evening sun sets the vast canyon wall on fire, with breathtaking shades of orange and yellow-gold."

"Sunrise?" Eva was puzzled.

"Yes...we all watch the sunrise up here...from the safety of our cave. Then we sleep until the night arrives with the sound of hawks and crickets. You see...the sun cannot kill us unless we walk out into it."

"I never realized." Eva was fascinated by the genteel vampire; he seemed born and bred in an ancient time.

"Why don't you stay with us...until you decide where you want to go?" As he spoke, something inside her began to change; Eva felt under a spell. She gazed into his silvery eyes, and saw the graceful white wolf living inside; surely, this had to be a good omen.

Eva agreed to stay with Sylvio, and his companions for the night; there was plenty of time to worry about what came next, tomorrow. Eva moved to untie the mare, giving her a slap on the rump to send her back down the mountain. With a trusting smile, Eva took Sylvio's hand as he prepared to bring her much further up the mountain, to a place few humans had ever been.

CHAPTER 117 - JACK - GREENWICH VILLAGE - (MARCH 1975)

The loss of his arm did nothing to deter Jack's love of men's fashion. Although long capes were sometimes difficult to find, they were quite flattering to his new physique. Jack still enjoyed wearing hats, but had surrendered his top hat for a stylish black Stetson; when the mood suited him, he wore his red tinted spectacles. Since losing his arm, Jack had managed to become quite expert at using his left hand; he still struggled to do many things, and that included killing. Out of necessity, Jack eased his way into a routine of bottled blood and eventually got used to it. Surprisingly, it was Rupert who made arrangements for Jack to have a ready supply; it was a gesture of good faith, and it sealed their partnership. The bottled stuff didn't taste the same as fresh blood, but it kept the cravings at bay and it kept him alive. The truth was Jack had stopped killing because he was no longer sure of his ability to overpower his prey; he'd been tempted a few times, but always ended up settling for bottled sustenance. As he walked up Bleecker Street, Jack thought about the fiasco at the zoo. Dracula had been right about one thing; they had reached an impasse that night; theirs was a battle neither could win. It didn't matter anymore; Jack accepted his handicap, believing it would never allow him a fair battle with Dracula.

Over the past eight years, Jack had found new purpose as an official member of the Van Helsings. It was a suitable arrangement for all parties; for Jack, it meant a place to belong and a guarantee he would no longer be hunted. Jack was mostly charged with keeping an eye on new vampire activity, and reporting anything problematic. As it turned out, he and Rupert made a great pair; for Jack, it was like old times. Rupert was the only one he could trust now; everyone else had turned on him, including Eva. After the crushing defeat in Central Park, the Van Helsings agreed to lay low for a while. Ever since the ghastly murders, security had gotten much tighter throughout the city. After dark, police officers were posted at every entrance to Central Park, from Columbus Circle to 85th Street.

Having no real place to live, Jack accepted Rupert's invitation to stay at his loft on McDougal Street; he lived there with Rory and an aspiring artist named Drew. The young black man happily paid most of the rent; he lived comfortably off his deceased parent's trust fund. Jack observed that unlike most artists, Drew didn't mind people watching him paint; surprisingly, Drew was a vampire too. As protection against sunlight, the windows were painted over with thick lead paint. Drew accommodated the lack of natural light, by flooding his studio with multiple sources of artificial illumination. Rory was greatly changed from what Jack remembered; she eventually warmed up to Jack, mostly because he had stopped killing. The two sometimes went scouting for trouble together; Jack was surprised at Rory's dogged determination to keep rogue vampires in line. Drew was an odd bird, but Jack liked him because he was different. Together, they compared the many varieties of bottled blood available through Rupert's channels, much like two friends comparing fine wines. Drew liked to stay in most of the time, painting was his passion. Jack was used to open spaces and had to be out in the night. The days were getting longer; Jack could already feel his strength increasing, along with his hunger. It was time to get outside, and take in the familiar ambiance of his favorite neighborhood.

He walked in silence, the click of his boot heel echoing in the night. The streets were sparsely populated, likely due to a biting cold; Jack decided to shoot over to 8th Street and do some shopping. Hustling past a florist shop and a pizza parlor called *Mama Mia's*, Jack reached the shopping district. Up ahead, two black men were playing Three-card Monte with an unsuspecting tourist; Jack stopped to watch them for a moment, trying to ignore his growing hunger. He reached the corner, and spotted a brick storefront called *Blacksmith*; the name itself, made Jack nostalgic for the cobblestone streets of London. The entrance was below street level; it took a moment to adjust his eyes to the store's dim lighting. Once inside, Jack was accosted by the overpowering scent of burning incense and new leather. Wrinkling his nose in distaste, Jack removed his hat and scanned the crowded store, confident he would find just what he was looking for.

The salesgirl saw him as soon as he entered; she worked on commission, and it had been slow all evening. The tall man had a hard looking face, with pronounced cheekbones; despite his odd dress, she found him interesting in a mysterious kind of way. She watched him move to the back of the store and her mood brightened; he was perusing a display of designer boots. The salesgirl casually worked her way toward him. The man abruptly turned around and handed her a Frye boot, asking for a size ten. Within minutes, the lovely young girl returned with a brown box. She bent down to help Jack try on the boots; because of his missing arm, the salesgirl assumed he was a veteran.

"When did you get back?" the salesgirl asked politely.

"Oh, no…nothing like that…it was an automobile accident," Jack replied. He had gotten used to people assuming he was a Vietnam vet.

"Terribly sorry…I shouldn't have assumed," the girl said apologetically with a casual flip of her wavy blonde hair; Jack became intoxicated by her delicious scent.

The salesgirl smiled at him with gleaming teeth, and lips the color of cinnamon. Jack studied her face and decided her eyes were her best feature. For the first time in a long while, he felt an attraction that had nothing to do with killing. Jack realized the girl was talking to him, but he hadn't heard a word.

"…should know that these boots are better than any of our imports… that's just between you and me."

"Irene…yes, thank you so much…"

"You know my name," the girl replied clearly puzzled.

"Your name badge." Jack pointed and the salesgirl laughed at her mistake.

"You know, I do that all the time." She smiled with a dimple Jack found irresistible.

"Irene of Thessalonica…you are named after the girl who refused to eat sacrificial food, all in the name of *Christianity*," Jack said, pronouncing the last word in a sarcastic tone.

"Yes, my mother has mentioned it a few times," she replied nervously, as she fingered a gold chain. Something in her expression changed, and Jack could feel her guard go up.

Two new customers entered the store, and the salesgirl took the opportunity to escape. Jack paid for his boots and lingered about a little longer, but didn't see her again. He found a coffee shop across the street;

he would wait there for her shift to end. Exactly thirty minutes later, Jack caught her slipping out a side door; she was going to cut through Washington Square Park. He felt a small thrill inside; it had been so long since he enjoyed a nice game of cat and mouse. Jack followed the perky blonde at a reasonable distance, until he realized she had begun walking as briskly as she dared, without appearing to run from him.

The salesgirl named Irene knew he was following her; she was trying very hard to pretend she didn't notice. She was a confident and striking girl with blonde hair and blue eyes; it was not uncommon for men to follow her. She recognized the weirdo from the store right away; something about this one really spooked her. Her mother had told her a hundred times not to walk home alone so late; Irene was a free spirit and loved walking through the park on clear nights. Her heart raced, as she made a sharp left turn; he changed direction too, slowly closing the gap between them. She had a brief vision of him as a killer, and imagined someone had cut off his arm; she had no idea how close to the truth she was. Like a gift from above, Irene spotted a group of middle-aged tourists; this was her only chance. The blonde moved toward the group, pretending she knew them; it was the only way to get away from the one-armed man.

Jack stopped in his tracks; the girl had begun conversing with a group of tourists. He couldn't believe his bad luck. The perky blonde linked arms with a silver-haired woman; the entire group walked past a bubbling fountain and out of the park. Jack cursed under his breath; maybe he'd lost his killing instinct altogether. With a deep sigh of resignation, Jack reached into a breast pocket to retrieve a metal flask; without an ounce of enjoyment, he downed its contents and headed home to his comfortable loft to watch television. He didn't kill anymore, so what else was there to do?

CHAPTER 118 - THE DARK ONE

The wolf stood proudly on a jagged rock, sniffing the air for the scent of humans. He didn't expect it, but he was ready if they came looking for the girl. He assumed his wolf-like form when he hunted, but always slumbered in his human form. Of course, Sylvio had lied to Eva about how and when he was turned, but it was necessary. The truth was Sylvio had been a creature of the night since before the reign of Nefertiti; he was likely one of Egypt's oldest vampires. Imhotep a.k.a. Sylvio, had been turned during an orgy with the pharaoh's daughter; although he did remember being bitten, Sylvio couldn't remember anything else. That first night, he passed out from exhaustion, hoping the whole thing was just a dream. When he had to hide from the sun the next morning, Sylvio knew what he had become. The soothing voice came to guide him shortly after; since then, the white wolf lived to please his master.

"You've done well…but you must keep her here for a while longer…" The Dark One spoke softly, so the others wouldn't hear.

The white wolf stretched out his front paws; a lean and muscular human back broke through the thick coat of fur. The Dark One watched in fascination, as the beast gracefully morphed into a perfectly proportioned man of thirty.

"Sh-h-h…she's just inside," Sylvio whispered, moving further away from the cave.

"Whatever you do…make sure she doesn't figure out who you really are."

"Do not worry, master…she is under my spell. Eva believes she has been with me only a few days…an ancient spell that distorts one's sense of time."

"She hasn't tried to seduce you?"

"No, why would she?"

"The countess finds you attractive…I can see it," the Dark One replied.

"Tell me, master… how will you recruit Manson without the girl's help?" Sylvio asked, changing the subject.

"Manson is my business...Sylvio. Your job is to keep her engaged here...I want time and distance between the countess and Dracula... long enough for them to forget their passion for one another."

"Perhaps, she needs a distraction...but what?" Sylvio was slow to come around sometimes.

"The former countess is a nymphomaniac!" the Dark One declared angrily.

"But, master...I don't really like women!" Sylvio whined.

"Close your eyes, then. The former countess needs a compelling reason to stay...unless you have forgotten how," the Dark One taunted; vampires didn't like their virility challenged.

"I still know how to please a woman, master."

"Good...time for some practice, then."

"But, for how much longer?" Sylvio was tired of living on a desert mountain.

"Until you hear from me," the Dark One hissed.

"Of course...but, I sense something else troubles you. What is it, master?" Sylvio felt certain there was something more on its devious mind.

"Sylvio, you are a loyal servant...so I will share my thoughts with you. As you know, Dracula has successfully amassed the legions I commanded...the vampire community is fanning out across a country, with enough open land to sustain both vampire and humankind for centuries to come...and yet..."

Sylvio broke protocol and interrupted, "It sounds like the Romanian prince fulfilled his destiny. Isn't that what we wanted, master?"

"Yes, but there's something different about this one...I fear the count is cursed with too much heart, despite what history books say about him. Even when he was first turned, Vlad Dracula resisted his natural craving...and still clung to the human world. Under my tutelage... the count finally learned to embrace his calling. Urban vampires have successfully imbedded themselves into the very fabric of society. Hiding in plain sight...who would have thought that would work?"

"Master...you still do not tell me what troubles you." Sylvio was tired of hearing about Dracula's accomplishments.

"I wanted Dracula to be more like Jack...that's why I brought them together in the first place! Instead, they made a family of ghosts and homeless children, putting them before anything else. They're both seasoned vampires...but act more like humans every day. Neither one is living up to their full potential...not by a long shot!"

"You are dissatisfied with what Dracula has accomplished, master?" Sylvio resisted the urge to gloat.

"No...and yet, it's all become so *civilized*."

"Isn't there enough killing in New York City already, without unleashing a new breed of vampires who shun bottled blood?" Sylvio loved to play devil's advocate.

"Violence pits humans against each other...and draws attention away from the nefarious activities of your kind. Everyone benefits... except the humans, of course."

"What part will the girl play in your plans, master?" Sylvio couldn't wait to be relieved of babysitting the former countess.

"I see no reason to reveal such plans to you!"

"I implore you, master, when can I leave this place? I miss my lovely penthouse." Sylvio loved big cities, especially Manhattan; he had lied to Eva about that, too.

"Keep the countess satisfied. That's your task!"

Sylvio knew better than to challenge the Dark One's wishes; he had done his homework, and knew all about Countess Bathory. Now, he was being tasked with seducing her. Sylvio preferred men, but was a skilled lover and knew how to tantalize a woman; with little effort she would soon crave his touch. Sylvio would disguise their passion inside the haze of Eva's dreams; the Egyptian vampire was a master at sorcery.

Inside the cave, Eva was lost in a dream about Sylvio; he was kissing her and dragging his wet tongue along the curve of her bare hip. With powerful hands, the Egyptian vampire positioned her body to receive him, as she moaned with anticipation. Eva sought Dracula's familiar face; yet, somehow knew her lover was someone else. His weight was on her now, as he became more forceful; Eva surrendered to her desire, deciding she was having a lovely dream from which she didn't want to wake. The sound of a screech owl pierced the night; Eva woke with a start to the soothing sound of crickets, her hands shoved deep inside the soft wetness of her womanhood.

CHAPTER 119 - A NEW KIND OF FAMILY - TUNNELTOWN - (MAY 1975)

"We simply have to find a way to get running water down here. There's a sink...there had to be running water at one time. Isn't there a way to reconnect it?" Virginia pleaded with Vincent; he was working on another portrait of Semele, and only paying half attention.

Prince stopped his work and turned to Virginia. "Let me take a look."

Having no access to fresh water was proving difficult, especially with several children living there now. Semele came first, and then the others followed; they fed Alice and came to live in Tunneltown, because their company made her happy. Virginia had never been this content; it didn't matter where they lived, having children to fuss over meant everything. Vincent put down his paintbrush, and stood back to admire his latest portrait of Semele. From the moment she first came to this place; the artist had been obsessed with the albino girl's wraithlike beauty. A face like this was every artist's dream; he marveled at Semele's flawless complexion and her rabbit-like eyes.

Semele had been immediately welcomed to Tunneltown without a lot of questions; something she hadn't expected. Alice brought her through the secret entrance, and introduced a street-wise kid to a whole new world. Alice lived with others like her, along with a group of misplaced ghosts. Vincent and Virginia were very protective of the children, including her; it was almost like having parents again. Semele no longer had to sleep outside and she never went hungry; for the first time ever, she had a place to call home. It didn't matter that it was cold in winter or that she slept on the floor; what mattered, was that Semele felt loved.

A breeze kicked up as Dracula emerged from a coal chute in his bat-like form; he flew in circles around the room with flapping wings, as he assumed his human form. Dracula gave the delicate white-haired girl a nod, and then went to examine Vincent's work.

"Dracula, over here...look at this." Prince called from across the room; he had his head stuck underneath the sink. Oliver stood nearby, holding an extra wrench.

"What is it?" Dracula asked.

"A means to a more sanitary way of life." Prince stood up, brushing his dirty hands on his trousers. "This sink was connected to a waterline at some point..."

"What are you getting at?" Dracula asked, as he admired Semele's portait.

"Look at us...we have six children here now, with very human needs. We need access to clean water!"

The black swans were all girls, between the ages of seven and ten years old; Alice seemed to need other children around for entertainment. Dracula watched the black swans playing cards at a discarded dining room table, with mismatched chairs; it was a rather small table for so many.

"Are you even listening to me?"

"I see...you need running water. Well...if we can't give you heat down here...we should be able to do something about water. Someone should be able to reconnect the sink, but it may require a new waterline. I'll get Nikos on it. I think we have someone over at the DEC we can *negotiate* with."

"Thanks," Prince replied; Virginia flashed Dracula a smile from across the room.

Dracula turned away, and then thought of something else. "One more thing...we'll get one of those extra-large library tables down here. Nikos can easily arrange it during the overnight hours...I will tell him to get some sturdier chairs, too."

Alice heard her father's voice, and ran to jump into his arms. Dracula lifted her into the air as she planted a kiss on his cold lips. "Good evening, Uncle Vlad!" Alice used her best adult voice; she grew more like Eva every day. Soon she will be trying on high heels and wearing makeup, just like Eva. How he missed her.

Dracula returned his attention to the vast collection of colorful canvases; Vincent's work truly brought their underground home to life. In the flickering candlelight, Dracula was suddenly struck by the dramatic change in Vincent's recent works. As he scanned the room,

Dracula noticed one that stood out from the others. He immediately recognized the Twin Towers, which were rendered beautifully. What Dracula found disturbing, was what Vincent added to the foreground; two commercial airplanes hovering dangerously close to the North Tower.

"Vincent...what inspired you to paint this one?" Dracula asked from across the room.

Vincent put down his paintbrush, and moved to where Dracula was standing. "Oh that one...I don't know really. Prince brought me a photo when they were first built...I just improvised the rest."

"What made you add the airplanes?"

"It just came to me...sometimes my paintbrush has a mind of its own. Virginia doesn't like this one either."

"Show him the other one," Virginia said, looking up from her journal. They both followed her gaze to a painting propped up in a corner, away from the others.

"I won't let him hang it," Virginia said. They all moved to get a better look.

The only words to describe the work were *eerie* and *terrifying*. It was a rather large canvas; the subject matter itself, was quite disconcerting. In the lower right hand corner was the face of a terrified man, whose hair was on fire. His bloodshot eyes bulged with fear; his mouth was open so wide, you could almost feel the trembling of his uvula, as it danced above his throat. Behind the screaming man, were two commercial airliners headed straight for the Twin Towers. No one spoke for a moment; even Vincent seemed rattled by his own creation.

"It just comes to me," Vincent said with a shrug.

Dracula finally turned away, and moved to kiss Alice on the cheek. "I will see you again soon." Alice smiled sweetly, anxious for him to leave because she had her own plans for tonight.

Alice was planning to take Semele for a ride on the Staten Island Ferry. It was a beautiful autumn night and she wanted to enjoy a few hours of unsupervised freedom. Semele was dressed the moment Dracula was gone; despite protests from Virginia about them going out alone. Once the girls made it to the subway tunnels, they would be home free; both looked forward to a night on the town *without* adult supervision.

As Alice and Semele came up the subway steps, a tall thin man watched them from the shadows; his eyes followed them until they disappeared into the crowd. He didn't recognize the albino girl, but he remembered little Alice well; the girl he carried safely across the street, as German bombs exploded all around them. Alice made it, but not poor Audrey. Jack had a family once, and he wanted them back. He missed showing Prince and Oliver new card tricks, and discussing politics with Vincent; he even missed the damn bird. He wanted to feel part of something bigger than himself; above all, Jack sought Dracula's favor and his forgiveness. He was finally ready to make amends; he would humble himself, if that's what it took to have his family back again.

Chapter 120 - Halloween Night - Times Square - (October 31, 1975)

The night started out well enough, despite a somber and murky sky. Alice and Semele helped the younger black swans with costumes for the annual Halloween parade; it had become an annual tradition for all of them. Dracula dressed as he always did, in outdated clothes the night forgave. Alice still looked like a child, but had the moody disposition of a budding adolescent; a voice inside her was always screaming, "I am a woman!" Semele walked beside them, holding Alice's hand. A lively Bruce Springsteen song called "Born to Run" was playing in the background; in the modern world, music was everywhere.

When they reached the next intersection, Semele recognized the Holy Apostles Soup Kitchen; she had eaten there many times. The windows were fogged over, but the warm glow inside looked inviting. Cooler nights meant winter was coming; at least she had a roof over her head. Semele let go of Alice's hand when her eye caught sight of a *Russell Stover.* Pressing her nose against the window, Semele marveled at a virtual mountain of candy corn and a glass shelf filled with cellophane-wrapped popcorn balls. Semele's mouth watered, as she watched a customer inside sample a piece of fudge. Realizing she had fallen behind, Semele ran to catch up with the others, but was distracted by a vendor selling warm pretzels. Their enticing aroma made her ravenous. A grotesquely overweight man turned to glare at her; Semele decided to risk snatching a pretzel. Unfortunately, she wasn't fast enough. The man grabbed her wrist and dragged her into his concession stand, blocking any chance of escape.

The vendor held Semele, until a police officer finally arrived, taking her into what he called *protective custody.* Once inside the police cruiser, the officer turned to face Semele. "I get that you were hungry…but you can't just steal food." Semele said nothing. What were they going to do to her?

"What's your name?" The officer looked into her eyes; they were like nothing he had ever seen.

"Semele."

"Do you have a last name?"

"No."

"Kind of old not to know that..."

Semele interrupted him, "My parents live underneath the library...I was at the parade with them and we got separated."

"The New York Public Library?"

"Yes."

"Maybe you mean somewhere behind it...an apartment building, maybe?"

Semele decided to stop talking for the rest of the drive. When they arrived at the precinct, the officer explained Semele had to stay at the precinct, until they found her parents. How long would she have to stay here, she wondered.

Semele longed for the stability of a real home, with working heat and a bed to sleep in. Maybe she *should* tell the officer she was homeless. At least she might have a chance to live in a real house with running water and heat; foster parents were better than none at all. If Semele didn't like it, she could always run away. She had become weary of being tethered Alice; feeding her made Semele feel like a slave to wickedness. Semele still embraced her humanity, and wanted to keep it that way.

"Mister..." Semele began, unsure of the policeman's name.

"I'm Sergeant Murphy...is there something else you want to tell me?"

"About my parents...I made that up. I am homeless...for about three years now." Semele couldn't tell the truth about how long she'd really been on her own.

"Uh huh...well, that means we need to call a social worker and this time of night..."

"Am I in trouble now?" Semele asked fearfully.

"No...but Semele...we can't get a social worker here until tomorrow morning...I'm afraid we're going to have to keep you overnight. We have a nice cot you can use, and we'll get you something to eat, anything you want."

Semele was shivering from the cold. "May I have a hot chocolate, please?"

As she sat across from Sergeant Murphy sipping hot chocolate, two officers brought in a man who was deadly pale. Semele recognized the cashew vendor, and quickly looked away. Officer Malone, the arresting officer, sat down across from the man and prepared to take his suspect's statement.

"Is that him?" asked a burly looking man with thick eyebrows and protruding jowls.

"Yes, captain…the one who tried to rob a blood bank over on 33rd Street."

The police captain scratched his head and muttered, "Don't that beat all."

Across town, Dracula and the others combed the streets searching for their white-haired princess; Vincent and Virginia were the most frantic of all. The parade had ended and the crowd was already thinning out, but still no Semele. None of them even considered police involvement, so Semele spent the night at a precinct, only blocks from her underground home. Curled up peacefully beneath a soft down comforter, Semele slept better than she had in years.

The next morning, Semele awoke with a start; someone was yelling right outside her door. She got up and tiptoed to the door, opening it so she could see who was screaming. It was the cashew vendor; he was handcuffed, but that didn't stop him from trying to get free.

"Don't bring me out into the sun…PLEASE!" the man pleaded, as Officer Malone brought the cashew vendor toward the door. Officer Denby came to assist, pulling the handcuffed man toward the glass doors. Their prisoner became so agitated; Officer Denby fastened a second set of handcuffs to the suspect's arm and his own.

Semele moved away from the screaming man, as he became even more vocal. "You can't bring me outside…THE SUN!!"

"Come on now, buddy…we're taking you over to Bellevue. They're going to take real good care of you." Both officers remained calm, even as the man resisted more violently.

Semele stood paralyzed by fear, they were dragging the cashew vendor toward the front steps; the man began shrieking like a wild animal. The officers ignored his desperate pleas, and brought him out into the sunny day. They're going to burn him up; Semele was terrified and no longer sure she was in good hands. Maybe it was a mistake to trust humans, even ones who wore badges.

Now in full sunlight, the cashew vendor's skin began to blister and burn; the officers watched in disbelief, unsure what to do. Officer Malone moved away from the man, as he began tearing at his clothes. Officer Denby was sweating profusely, and realized the suspect's clothes were smoking; he was going to ignite! He fumbled for the handcuff key, but instinct told Officer Denby, he was already a dead man.

Traffic had slowed to a crawl, as the horrific scene unfolded; eye witnesses would later attest they saw two men simultaneously burst into flames, on the steps of the 14th Precinct. Two good Samaritans tried to assist, but quickly realized both men were beyond saving. Horns blared as impatient commuters fought gridlock, caused by the bizarre scene; this tragedy would surely make front page news.

Police Captain Brady finally came outside to give a brief statement to the press. Behind him, a team of first responders gathered what remained of the two deceased men, and prepared to transport them to the coroner's office. The crowd wanted answers; but, the police captain couldn't provide anything that made sense. A prisoner and one of his officers had simply ignited on the steps of his precinct, and he had no idea how or why.

A reporter stepped forward, "Captain Brady...can you tell us anything about what happened here?"

"We are investigating the incident further. What I can confirm is this: a prisoner and one of my officers were apparently victims of a tragic accident."

"Come on...can't you give us any more than that?" another reporter persisted.

"We all witnessed the same thing. Officers Denby and Malone brought a prisoner out into the sunlight; within seconds, they both ignited. Unfortunately, because Officer Denby was handcuffed to the prisoner, they both perished."

"What could possibly have caused such a deadly fire?" asked another reporter.

"As of right now, we are considering all angles...including the possible use of an accelerant."

At the bottom of the steps, Rupert listened, and decided it was time to stir the pot a little. He snatched an unattended mike, and went in for the kill. "Captain Brady…are you aware that vampires are living underneath Bryant Park?" The crowd gasped, but then grew silent; they wanted to hear the police captain's response.

"I can't think of anything more ridiculous! I won't even dignify this question with a response…any other relevant questions?"

"I have a question, Captain Brady," a young black man asked.

"Final question…go ahead."

"Will the coroner be able to confirm that your prisoner was, in fact, human?"

Chapter 121 - Police Chief Rodriguez - NYPD Midtown - (November 2, 1975)

Police Chief Manuel Rodriguez sipped black coffee, wrinkling his nose as the bitter brew reached the back of his tongue. The *New York Post* was opened in front of him; there was a sensationalized article about the incident at the 14th Precinct. There were still no clues as to how a suspect ended up in flames, taking a police officer down with him. The newspaper article revealed the deceased suspect had been arrested for robbing a blood bank; this evolved into rumors vampires were invading Manhattan. *The Post* was known for distorting the truth, but this was not the first time these accusations had been made. The police chief felt certain something was going on that warranted further investigation. He pushed the intercom button and waited for a response.

"Detective Daly, here."

"Daly...do you remember that old file about Jack the Ripper and a Count Draco? You know...the one we got from that Scotland Yard detective several years back..."

"Inspector Poole...yes, I remember."

"I know we made a copy for our files...can you go downstairs and grab it. It should be in the archive room...tall gray cabinet.

"Have there been some new developments, chief?"

"I'm not sure, but I'd like to look at it again."

Rodriguez put the newspaper aside, and reviewed the official report completed by Sergeant Malone. In the file was a list of everyone inside the building at the time; that included NYPD staff and civilians. Police Chief Rodriguez combed through the names, pulling out several mug shots to review; he was hoping something would click. He pulled out a photo of the deceased man, referred to as NY-1624-1; he carried no ID and refused to give a name when he was arrested. What Rodriguez found most interesting, was the nature of the suspect's crime; attempting to rob a blood bank, but not for money. The man wanted blood; he even asked for a specific type. Was he planning to drink it?

The police chief picked up the last photo; it was a young girl with arresting pink eyes. According to the file, her first name was Semele, but no last name was listed. The incident report stated the girl had been picked up for stealing from a street vendor; according to Sergeant Murphy's report, the girl said she lived underneath the New York Public Library. This statement raised a red flag Rodriguez couldn't ignore. His thoughts were interrupted by a knock on the door; Detective Daly had returned with the file.

"Come in, Daly," Rodriguez said, reaching for the file. A cigarette burned in the ashtray; his sixth one already today.

"Anything else, chief?"

"Yeah...do you mind if I pick your brain about Poole?" Detective Daly sat down, squeezing his ample form into the chair.

"You personally met with the Scotland Yard detective...what did you think of him and his incredible story?"

"What can I say? He seemed to have all his marbles. But, chief...he claimed Jack the Ripper was consorting with vampires...and that they were living all over Manhattan. How could anyone take him seriously?"

"Daly...in your meeting with the inspector...did *anything* he had to say seem plausible?"

"It *was* several years ago...I was still a rookie then, but I do remember he was thoroughly convinced Jack the Ripper was still alive...I'm sure he meant, a copycat killer.

"What about this Count Draco...what did he say about him?"

"Honest to God...the inspector believed that Count Draco was a fictitious name; the man claimed he was actually Count Vlad Dracula a.k.a. Vlad the Impaler."

"The same Dracula, Bram Stoker wrote about?"

"The very one...that's why I remember it. I mean, who hasn't seen at least one Dracula flick?"

"So, according to Inspector Poole...what is Count Draco a.k.a. Count Dracula, doing in New York City?"

"Read it for yourself, chief. According to the inspector, this Count Draco has already fathered hundreds of vampires. If that's true...I wonder where they're living," Daly responded, only half serious.

"Good question..."

"What's going on, chief...why is this relevant now?"

359

"Daly…I'm going to be frank here. My interest in Inspector Poole's story is because of something a reporter asked the other day; it was right after that horrific accident at the 14th. He asked Captain Brady if he was aware vampires were living underneath Bryant Park. The night before that, police picked up a little homeless girl for petty theft; the girl claimed she lived underneath the New York Public Library."

"That is a rather strange coincidence but, *vampires*, chief?" Daly replied, with as much respect as he could muster.

"Of course, I don't believe New York City is infested with vampires. But I am concerned nefarious activities are going on that can't be explained…and, what about that man robbing a blood bank…why would anyone do that?"

"There should be mention of blood banks in the file, too…I remember the inspector saying they needed more of them…to feed the growing vampire community."

"Did the inspector actually call it a *vampire community*?"

"Yes…I'm sure of that. Inspector Poole also mentioned a night gowned woman who frequented Bryant Park; he even had a few witness statements, confirming she was seen roaming about with homeless children."

"You know what, Daly…I do recall receiving a few reports about strange nocturnal activity in Bryant Park."

"Did any of these reports mention anything about child abduction; *that*, we can act on, chief." Daly was relieved to be talking about real crimes again.

"Daly…you're a genius!"

"Me…what do you mean?"

"Missing children…we can obtain records on that. Get on the horn with your contact down at missing persons; request a list of juvenile abductions and missing children. Let's get records going back ten years, and see what they come up with. The main focus should be on children gone missing near Bryant Park and around Midtown Manhattan."

"It will take a few days, chief."

"That's okay…let me dig into this file…I'll let you know if I have any more questions."

The file Inspector Poole provided was amazingly detailed; after a few minutes, the police chief found himself engrossed in a tale no rational person could possibly believe. Included in the file were newspaper clippings from the late '60s; these piqued the police chief's curiosity even more. There was an informative article about the brutal killings at the Central Park Zoo, back in '68. Rodriguez remembered reading about it; to this day, he believed the public had been misled as to what really happened. He even remembered reading that they found a bloody stake at the scene; wasn't that considered the ultimate vampire weapon?

He picked up a second newspaper clipping about a horse carriage incident at Columbus Circle. He vaguely recalled something about two young girls spooking a horse, causing a major traffic accident. There were two photos contained within the article; it was the second one that caught his attention. The photo was of the intersection where the accident occurred. The police chief blinked twice when he saw her; the white-haired girl faced the camera with a defiant glare. The photo was a bit grainy, but there was no mistaking it; she was the same girl that had been at the 14th Precinct two days ago. How was that possible? The incident at the zoo happened nearly eight years ago. She hadn't aged at all!

Rodriguez grabbed the phone and dialed the 14th Precinct; Sergeant Murphy answered on the first ring.

"Police Chief Rodriguez speaking, do you have a minute, sergeant?"

"Yes, sir!"

"Terrible business the other day...I'm awfully sorry about Officer Denby."

"Thank you sir...how may I help you?"

"I'm actually calling about something else...can you talk now?"

"Sure."

"The day of the incident...there was a little albino girl at the station..."

"Yes...Semele...the girl who claimed she lived under the library."

"Yes...I read that in your report."

"We followed protocol and called social services right away, Chief Rodriguez." Murphy worried he might be blamed for the girl's disappearance.

"I'm sure you did...Sergeant Murphy...I would very much like to talk to this girl." Murphy's heart sank; the chief didn't know she had taken gone missing.

"Sorry, sir...she took off when we were dealing with crowd control... we don't really know where she went."

"I want an APB put out on that girl...NOW!" He hung up without saying goodbye; it had been that kind of day.

Disappointed to have reached a dead end, Rodriguez rolled up his sleeves and picked up the albino girl's photograph. He used a magnifying glass to have a better look; her eyes were hard-looking and her mouth was a bit lopsided. The white-haired girl had a disturbingly ethereal quality about her; her ivory skin was almost blinding. Who the hell was she?

Chapter 122 - A Murderous Rage - Bronx, New York - (December 24, 1975)

It was clear and cold as he walked purposefully through the night; his right hand was deep inside his jean pocket, fingering a bowie knife. Ducking down a trash-laden alley, he moved with robotic precision, following a persistent voice that told him it was time to kill. Tonight, he knew exactly where he needed to go. Because it was very late on Christmas Eve, there were few people on the street; this suited his purpose just fine. He was looking for a parked car with flashers on; that's what *Harvey* told him to look for. The man moved into the shadows and approached the car from behind; he pulled out his knife, as adrenalin pounded in his ears. The car was running and he could see two girls inside; the window was cracked to let a cloud of cigarette smoke escape.

The man took one last look around, before yanking the car door open; he surprised them with a sadistic smile, before plunging his knife deep into the driver's ample bosom. Her passenger screamed, and opened the car door to escape; the man gave chase catching hold of her hair. The girl stumbled to the ground and he stabbed her repeatedly, until she finally stopped moving. The female driver was still conscious, and struggling to exit the vehicle. The man was determined to finish his work, so he returned to the car and stabbed the driver five more times.

When he saw two men running toward him, the man threw his bloody knife to the ground. He had to get out of here, now! His heart was pumping so hard, he thought it would explode; the sensation was exhilarating. He made his escape through a narrow passageway between two fences; most didn't know it was even there. It didn't matter though; the men stopped chasing him when they discovered his bloody victims. He wasn't sure the women were actually dead; he only assumed so, based on the amount of blood. The man could feel the stickiness of it on his hands; he had to find another method. His clothes were ruined and so were his shoes. The man could hear police sirens coming his way; he abruptly changed direction and darted down a narrow street. There was so much blood; he never thought there would be so much of it. The man discarded his beige jacket in a trash can, because it was saturated; his black pants and shirt were covered too, but in the dark, it was virtually unnoticeable.

The man picked up his pace, anxious to get home, so he could scrub his whole body with disinfectant. The police sirens sounded much further away now; his breathing gradually return to normal. The man finally reached his Ford Galaxie, safely parked where he'd left it earlier that evening. As David Berkowitz warmed up his car, he was already making plans to acquire a handgun; knives were just too messy.

Chapter 123 - A Leap of Faith - Saint Patrick's Cathedral - (December 24, 1975)

Dracula despised the city during the holidays; there were just too many damn tourists. The sun had just set behind the familiar landscape of Central Park; the amber glow that followed served as a welcome mat to the glorious night. As he skillfully navigated crowded sidewalks, Dracula could feel the excitement of young children anxiously awaiting the arrival of Santa Clause. At Christmastime, a cold-hearted city opened up its heart and offered good will to all; Dracula had learned by now, the sentiment was momentary. How he detested the facade of exaggerated benevolence, associated with the season! Dracula passed a shifty-looking Santa ringing a brass bell; he saluted pedestrians with a white-gloved hand, as they dropped coins into a red bucket. The frigid air was tinged with the scent of pine needles; but nothing overpowered the delicious scent of humans. Two black men passed him, carrying huge radios on their shoulders; the music played so loud, a few scowled in disapproval.

High-end retail stores were starting to close; last-minute shoppers brushed past him with murmured apologies. Dracula crossed the street and headed up Fifth Avenue, toward Saint Patrick's Cathedral. It began snowing, but not too hard, just enough to get people into the spirit of things. Dracula had fed on bottled blood earlier; inbred religious guilt prevented him from ever killing on a holy day. Christmas Eve could be a difficult night for a vampire; especially, for one who was once a devout Christian. Tonight, Dracula didn't want to be alone; instead, he sought the comforting warmth of human beings.

Once inside the church, Dracula could feel his strength weaken; it would pass the moment he stepped outside again. It was already getting crowded, but he found an isle seat near the altar. Angelic-looking choir boys lit dozens of candles, as if attempting to ward off evil spirits lingering outside. Dracula caught the eye of an old black woman coming toward him; she was wheelchair bound, and used her powerful arms to propel herself with a determination he admired. When she reached his pew, the old woman leaned in and whispered, "There is still time." Dracula looked away, and she continued on to the front of the church.

Dracula tried to focus on his surroundings; statues of saints whose names he had forgotten glared at him from behind the anonymity of marble eyes. A life-sized nativity scene carved out of white marble, drew his attention; he got up from his seat to get a better look. As Dracula approached the most enduring symbol of his old religion, he longed to claim his humanity once more, even if just for a little while. To walk in the sunshine on a summer day, to have a faithful lover and friend; these were human pleasures Dracula sorely missed. He bowed his head and only pretended to pray, because he didn't feel worthy. The moment he closed his eyes, Dracula was accosted by a vision of Eva hiking on a desert road. He opened his eyes to find the old black woman beside him again. She put a hand on his muscular arm, and asked, "Are you lost, dear?" Dracula shook her off, only to realize she hadn't been there at all.

A choir of children began singing like angels; the song was "Joy to the World." Everywhere his eyes wandered, Dracula saw hope, faith and a sense of community. It tore him apart, because these things were unattainable for someone like him. Perhaps it was a mistake coming here. Dracula no longer felt comfortable, and became anxious to leave. He moved casually toward the far side of the church; suddenly sickened by the pungent odor of burning incense. All around him, long-dead saints eyed him disapprovingly, hissing the word *blasphemer*. He moved past a life-sized statue of Mary; bloody tears cascaded down her face and were pooling on the floor. Dracula turned around and realized no one else could see it; he had to get out of here! No longer concerned with discretion, Dracula made a beeline for the door, as a few last-minute parishioners came rushing in.

Night was a vampire's refuge and his salvation; it quickly restored Dracula's strength and determination. With a sudden surge of energy, he dashed down the church steps, his need to bond with humans evaporating almost instantly. The snow had stopped, and the stars had come out of hiding. Winter was a vampire's natural season, with its longer nights; it was a time of year when vampires reigned supreme.

Dracula glanced at his pocket watch, deciding the night was still young. He headed west of Times Square, to a lesser known area near Eighth Avenue. Tonight, he was looking for the kind of woman who would openly flaunt what she was selling. It didn't take long for Dracula to find a suitable plaything; he caught a fleeting glimpse of her, as she darted down a side street. She was a buxom brunette wearing a bright red mini-skirt, low-cut sweater and knee-high leather boots. Her long hair was piled high atop her head, and her hips swayed with a primal sexuality few men could avoid noticing. Just my type, he thought, abruptly changing direction. Dracula followed her for two blocks, trying to keep a reasonable distance. She finally turned around, and smiled at him. "It's been slow tonight…are you looking for a good time, honey?"

"I could ask you the same," Dracula replied seductively.

"That's a new approach." The brunette giggled, and he could see her blushing.

Dracula could almost taste the woman, as she moved closer to him. Although he was sexually aroused, there was a stronger need coming to the surface; Dracula craved the pulpy flesh of her lovely neck. Suddenly, he didn't give a crap about holy days; he needed to feed like the vampire he was.

"So, what do you say…do you want to have some fun?" The hooker was holding out her hand for payment.

"What if I told you…that I could please you more thoroughly, than any man has ever done?"

The brunette gazed up at him, and responded honestly, "Then I'd have to say…I've heard that before."

The vampire laughed with glowing eyes. Fear sparked in the woman's dark eyes and her lips began to tremble. "Don't be afraid…," Dracula said, as he folded a fifty dollar bill into her hand.

"Okay…where do you want to go?" The woman relaxed a little.

"I know a place." He took her hand, and together they walked toward the black waters of the Hudson River. The docks were quiet this time of year, especially on Christmas Eve.

The Hudson River was a sheet of black marble; harbor lights reflected a manmade world above. After centuries of time, the ancient vampire still found nighttime waters mesmerizing. In the distance, he could hear the low horn blast of a passing ferry.

"I love how the stars sparkle on the water." The woman turned toward him, attempting to unzip his pants.

"No…not that…"

Dracula moved to embrace the woman, burying his head in the crook of her neck; the sound of her heartbeat thundered in his ears. He wasn't planning to kill her; he just needed to feed on fresh, warm blood.

"It's okay, honey…we all need someone to hold on to now and then…" the woman said kindly, caressing him with more compassion than he deserved.

"You see…I'm just so hungry," he whispered, then plunged his teeth into her neck.

Although surprised, the woman did not pull away; this was not her first experience with what her kind called "kinky sex." Dracula restrained himself, pulling away after a few minutes. "Are you okay?" he asked, trying not to scare her off.

The hooker took one look at his bloodied teeth, and found her voice. A bloodcurdling scream pierced the night; Dracula clamped his hand over her mouth. The woman continued to struggle, until he was left with no choice but to snap her neck. As her lifeless body slipped to the ground, Dracula cursed himself for losing control. He hadn't wanted to kill her, but once she started screaming, what was he supposed to do? As he stood alone on the pier with a corpse at his feet, Dracula decided he was done with trying to regain his humanity; he was tired of the constant battle. Vampires didn't belong in churches! They belonged to the night. He would no longer deny his natural craving. It was time to satisfy his bloodlust with more than just bottled blood.

Out of the corner of his eye, Dracula noticed a solitary figure standing by the water; his guard went up, until he saw a flash of lush red hair. It was Mary. He called out her name, but she wouldn't answer.

"Mary…" he called again, but she merely flashed him an angry look, before diving into the Hudson. Dracula considered going after her, but his dislike of water prevailed. Besides, she was already dead.

A group of drunken men singing "Jingle Bells" came into view. Five of them clung together, as if holding one another up. One of the revelers shouted out a "Merry Christmas!" Dracula waited for them to pass, then assumed his bat-like form and flew into a night that neither judged nor condemned.

CHAPTER 124 - DREAMS DIE LAST - (DECEMBER 30, 1975)

She heard them whispering before she realized who was talking. Eva had gotten used to living with wolves, and was accustomed to solitude during daylight hours. Her head felt foggy and she wondered how long she had been stuck on this mountain. She couldn't even remember what day it was. Eva had only planned to stay for a few days, just long enough to make sure Charlie wasn't looking for her. The memories of her old life seemed distant and surreal, like watching someone else's life on a movie screen. She remembered she was not human, but Eva couldn't remember where she had come from anymore. She could feel herself slowly slipping away. What was happening to her in this place? A little piece of her was getting lost every day. But, how many days?

Eva looked around the dimly lit cave. Sylvio was gone and so were the others, despite daylight arriving an hour ago. Eva made her way toward the cave entrance. She could hear the rain, but there was another sound; it was the sound of human voices. Were Sylvio and his wolves roaming about during daylight hours because there was no sun? It was possible, but not their normal custom. The voices were clearly discernable, now. Sylvio was talking to someone.

"I am sure she has no idea how long it has been, master." Sylvio's voice was muffled against the sound of steady rain.

"After all this time...we have surely succeeded in our plan to erase him from her mind," a familiar voice spoke; Eva's throat clutched in fear.

"The end of another year arrives in a few days...time perhaps, to leave this place?" Sylvio asked hopefully.

"Not yet...we need to wait until the spring...it will be time for her to play another part by then."

"I never expected to be here this long," Sylvio whined.

"Six years of human time is *nothing* to a vampire!" the Dark One hissed.

"Babysitting gets very tiresome, master."

The conversation ended, and Eva hurried back to her blankets to feign sleep; she kept her eyes closed as Sylvio slipped back into the cave. Her thoughts were rambling as she tried to imagine how much had changed in six years. Was it really possible she had been here that long?

CHAPTER 125 - THE PRODIGAL SON - EMPIRE STATE BUILDING - (DECEMBER 31, 1975)

He had gotten used to living in the village. He enjoyed weaving his way through the narrow streets, sometimes stopping traffic as cabbies honked and shook their fists at him. Jack realized he had nothing to lose by living recklessly, and so he did. He began avoiding his loft when they started coming around, the dark-skinned men who wore towels for hats. Rupert insisted they were Van Helsing recruits, but something about their black eyes and furtive glances made Jack question their real agenda. By mid-December, Jack moved out of the loft and relocated to a basement apartment in lower Manhattan. It was a sublet, and he could pay in cash; this arrangement would make it harder for Rupert or anyone else to find him. When he wasn't in the city, Jack could be found hunting in the Catskill Mountains; it was the one place a vampire could hunt in peace.

As another year came to a close, Jack decided it was time to make his way back to Tunneltown. Jack had chosen New Year's Eve to show himself at everyone's favorite meeting place. His ultimate goal was to reconcile the past once and for all. He would humble himself, and could only hope Dracula would be receptive to his peace offering. Jack had also forgiven Eva; over time, he came to realize he owed her his life. Jack glanced at his watch anxiously; he wanted more than anything, to ring in the New Year with old friends.

Assuming his bat-like form, Jack became airborne and made his way toward Midtown Manhattan. He zeroed in on the Empire State Building, convinced this was where his family would be. The time was 11:15PM. Jack returned to his human form, and headed for the observation deck. He picked up the hum of voices as he came around a corner; sure enough, a New Year's Eve party was in full swing. Jack loved hobnobbing with wealthy people, and rather enjoyed crashing parties that were by invitation only. Feeling optimistic, Jack scanned the room, but didn't see anyone familiar. He weaved through the crowd and slowly began to realize, none of them were here.

Jack shrugged his shoulders in defeat, wondering where to look next. He knew one thing for sure, no self-respecting vampire stayed underground on the last night of the year. A flashy blonde called out for Jack to stay, but he waved her away dashing toward the fire escape. He should have known they weren't still coming here, but where else could they be?

Utterly disappointed, Jack returned to his neighborhood to seek comfort in the tiny graveyard behind St. Paul's Chapel. He liked being in a place where the dead found eternal rest, something that would forever elude him. Jack tried to think of where else Dracula could possibly be, on a night most vampires considered sacred. Jack contemplated looking for them in Tunneltown, but had a sixth sense they would be celebrating under a starry sky. But, where?

From the cemetery, Jack had a picturesque view of the World Trade Center; he was continually awed by modern architecture. The Twin Towers were now the tallest buildings in the world; the Empire State Building had been unceremoniously demoted. A crescent moon was caught between the two monolithic silhouettes; the towers were temporarily haloed by a shimmer of liquid silver. As Jack studied the flickering lights of the North Tower; he suddenly realized his mistake. The Empire State Building was no longer the tallest building in New York City, now was it? He couldn't believe he had been so stupid; now Jack knew exactly where to find them.

CHAPTER 126 - THE JOURNEY
BACK - (DECEMBER 31, 1975)

Eva pulled away from Sylvio; she had just woken from a dream they were lovers. Lately, her dreams left her mind feeling heavy, as if she was drugged. Something unnatural was keeping Eva here; she had fleeting glimpses of her old life, but the visions were fuzzy and seemed out of reach. It was time to get off this mountain, before she lost herself completely. Eva thought about Dracula, how she longed to see him again; he was the only man she had ever loved. It was time to leave this place of suspended time. The white wolf was keeping her here for a reason; Eva had to go now, before it was too late.

Eva confirmed Sylvio was asleep, then crept away to retrieve the backpack she had hidden outside the cave. She remembered the way back down the mountain; Eva had to move fast, before she fell under the white wolf's spell again. Was it really possible she had been living on this mountain for six years? What had she missed while she was gone? Had Dracula found a new love? Eva couldn't bear the thought.

Sylvio woke, opening one eye as he watched her leave. The Dark One hissed into the darkness, "Let her go…this is exactly what we want."

"She'll go back to him…I thought we didn't want that, master."

"I have changed my mind about that, Sylvio. As luck would have it, Jack has decided to reunite with Dracula…and that always brings out his darker side. Eva will only be a minor distraction. Besides, if his carnal needs are satisfied…Dracula can focus on acting like a true creature of the night."

"Let me be part of your plans, master…let me live and breathe among humans again," Sylvio pleaded.

"The countess does have a dubious sense of loyalty and must be watched closely…especially as she reunites with the others," the Dark One replied, willing to consider Sylvio's request.

"Please let me return to New York…there, I can keep an eye on the countess without her even knowing."

"Very well, Sylvio…I grant you this…on one condition…"

"Anything, master."

"There's no sun today…go follow the countess to make sure she makes it to the diner, and don't be seen!"

"Master, how can the girl return to New York City from a diner?"

"Just do it!" the Dark One replied dismissively.

Sylvio knew his place and always did what he was told; it was the main reason he had lived so long. He knew the girl overheard things she wasn't meant to, but it didn't matter now. He took a deep sigh, as his body morphed into wolf form. Shaking himself out once the transformation was complete; Sylvio left the cave with a snarl because he hated the stench of wet fur.

An hour later, Sylvio returned; he was soaking wet and in a surly mood. Inside the cave, four teenage boys slept like wolf cubs; they were playfully wrapped around one another. They had been with him since he came to this mountain, but now, they were nothing but a liability. Sylvio approached the sleeping boys and studied them for a moment; he tried to feel pity, but found it wasn't there. He carefully sprinkled kerosene over the sleeping boys; they didn't wake until Sylvio had already set them on fire. Their pitiful screams echoed through the canyons; the sound was deafening. Sylvio had spent nearly ten years with his progeny, but his cold, dead heart felt nothing. Outside the cave, a gust of wind cut through the lingering screams, as the smell of burning flesh assaulted his nostrils.

"The intoxicating aroma of death…" Sylvio cried, without a trace of remorse. The sky grew black, and released a downpour of heavy rain; as though offering up the tears, their father refused to shed.

CHAPTER 127 - COMING HOME - NEW YORK CITY - (DECEMBER 31, 1975)

On the last day of December, Countess Bathory returned to the city she loved like no other. A veil of light snow dusted her hair and clothing, as she walked briskly toward Central Park; her one purpose now, to find the one who held her heart. The luxury apartment building was a welcome sight and thankfully, it hadn't changed at all. As Eva got closer, she considered exactly what she would say, after such a long absence. She had left Dracula six years ago to find a psychotic killer; Eva wondered why she had ever believed Manson would make her happy. Now, he was serving a life sentence, and Eva was home where she belonged. Had she been gone too long to expect she still held Dracula's heart? Eva felt her stomach flutter at the possibility. Had he even tried to find her? As she stood in front of the glass double doors, Eva looked up to the top floor and tried to imagine Dracula waiting, as though he was expecting her.

Eva considered the possibility Dracula was still at home, primping for the New Year's Eve celebration. Suddenly, she couldn't wait to see him. Her clothes were wrinkled and dirty, but Eva didn't think any of that would matter, once he took her in his arms. There were too many people roaming about to even consider using the balcony, so Eva went the conventional route. With a polite nod to the door man, she took the elevator up to the penthouse. When she reached the door, Eva pulled out her key; no matter how much she jiggled it, the door wouldn't open. Frustrated, she rang the bell, hoping Dracula would answer.

The door was opened by an egg-headed butler with mild osteoporosis and a timid smile. "May I help you, miss?"

"I am looking for someone." Eva glanced around at the unfamiliar furnishings. The man took in her attire and his hooded eyes became reptilian. Perhaps she had made a mistake; it certainly looked that way.

"This is the Alderman residence and I am the only one here," the butler said curtly, as he closed the door a little.

Eva put her hand up to stop him, "Please…can you at least tell me, how long Mr. Alderman has been living here?"

"I most certainly will not…good evening," the butler replied as he pushed the door closed, before she could protest further.

Once outside again, Eva considered the Empire State Building as a possibility, and almost made the same mistake Jack did; but then she remembered the Twin Towers were taller. Of course, this is where, Eva would find him. Excited to celebrate New Year's Eve inside these magnificent buildings, she picked up her pace and headed for Bloomingdales. Every woman needed a new dress for such an occasion; Eva had no money, but that had never stopped her before.

Chapter 128 - A Family Reunion - North Tower - (December 31, 1975)

Dracula was always first to arrive; it was his custom to survey a situation where his enemies might try to expose him. Dracula planned to enjoy tonight, celebrating the passing of another year in human time had become a family tradition. Nikos and Prince were bringing Oliver and Alice; Vincent and Virginia remained underground to stay with the black swans. Virginia had secured some special treats for the children, including paper hats and horns to help them ring in the New Year.

A group of revelers came his way, and Dracula offered his most congenial smile as they passed him with cheerful greetings. It was easier to crash a New Year's Eve party than any other kind, likely due to excess alcohol consumption. Celebrations were getting started, as evidenced by the sound of an orchestra playing a popular Glenn Miller tune. Tonight, was the grand opening of the North Tower's famous restaurant, *Windows on the World*. Dracula learned the restaurant had a revolving floor; during the course of the evening, guests would be entertained by a three-hundred-and-sixty-degree view of the Manhattan skyline.

As if on cue, Nikos arrived in a stylish tux; on his arm were Alice and Oliver. They were all dressed so elegantly, they easily passed for invited guests. Semele was notably absent, but no one mentioned her, especially in front of Alice. Dracula surveyed the crowd, smiling when his old friend approached the dance floor.

"There you are!" Nikos called out to Dracula.

"Greetings!"

"Uncle!" Alice let go of Nikos, and ran to Dracula.

"I swear you are the most beautiful girl here!" Dracula said. He watched her spin around in an emerald green taffeta suitable for a much older girl, but this was no time to chastise.

"Thank you, Uncle Vlad...and you look smashing, too!" Alice loved using modern phrases.

Dracula took his daughter's hand, and brought her to the dance floor; Virginia had recently taught her how to waltz. Her dark hair had been washed and curled, she was also wearing lipstick. On impulse, he pulled her close and whispered, "Please don't grow up too fast."

"I promise."

The song ended and Nikos stepped in to dance with Alice, as Oliver hung back with Prince. Neither liked to dance, preferring to watch human socialization from a distance. The boys each held a cup of punch pretending to take sips; they were experts at blending in.

Dracula scanned the dance floor, searching for someone to catch his eye. Would he find a stunning blonde to dance with tonight, or perhaps, a sultry brunette? Dracula straightened his tie and sauntered across the room, just as she was making her grand entrance. Through a sea of colorful evening gowns, she saw only him.

The room darkened and everything else went out of focus, as he looked upon the lovely face of Elizabeth Bathory. Her white skin shimmered like a sea of pearls, and her red lips held the promise of total ecstasy. A curtain of luscious dark curls framed her lovely face. Her eyes were warm and full of love; in them, he saw Eva, the one who had softened the cold-hearted countess. She wore a burgundy gown that clung to each delicious curve; Dracula felt an urgent need to touch her, before she disappeared.

Eva couldn't move, but she held his gaze. She reached out her hand and that was all it took; Dracula rushed into her open arms. They kissed each other fiercely, oblivious to everyone around them. Dracula had found joy again, and never wanted to let her go.

"I can't believe you're real," Dracula said, as he gently stroked her cheek.

"I won't leave you again, Vlad...I promise."

"As it was meant to be...I see it now...," Dracula replied. He was lost inside her dark eyes.

"I remember you!" Prince exclaimed, pointing at an adult Eva.

"You look different," Alice said, as she scrutinized Eva's face.

"Come now...Eva's been gone for a long time and now she's all grown up." Eager to change the subject, Dracula whisked her away to the freshly polished dance floor.

"She gonna be his girlfriend now?" Oliver asked Prince, trying to decide how he felt about it. Prince was still in shock; Eva, the child had vanished. He remembered meeting Countess Bathory once, but how could this be her?

Dracula and Eva danced tirelessly; they couldn't get enough of each other. At one point, Eva believed the room was spinning; Dracula later explained about the revolving floor. Desperate to be alone, they excused themselves and went out to the terrace. There were a few people milling about; Dracula pulled her toward a secluded corner.

"I won't ask you anything you don't want to tell me..." Dracula said.

"It doesn't matter, now...the past is forgotten. I face you as a woman now, Vlad."

"Yes...so I've observed," Dracula said, as he spun her around to look at her.

"Vlad...," she paused, as a familiar figure approached.

"Jack!" Eva exclaimed with a broad smile; Dracula turned around to face him, too.

"Please...I come in good faith," Jack said, raising his arm to show he had no weapons.

"Really...why now?" Dracula replied suspiciously.

"Because, it's time to make amends. I have lost much and now...I just want to be part of *my* family again."

"Oh, so now we're *your* family...even after you betrayed my trust," Dracula said through his teeth.

"*You* left me to die in Berlin...but I hold no grudge...otherwise, why would I come?"

"Vlad...he is your own flesh and blood." Eva didn't realize until this moment, how much she had missed Jack.

"So what's the catch, Jack...you must want something. Did Rupert send you?" Dracula wasn't willing to trust Jack so easily.

"No catch...Rupert and I parted ways a while back."

"And why should I believe you?" Dracula persisted.

"Because...you're the one who made me...you are my father. Doesn't that count for something?" There was no mistaking Jack's sincerity, as he begged to be forgiven. Dracula's eyes softened, but he wanted Jack to grovel a bit more.

"I want to come home...to be part of something again. Is that so hard to understand?"

Dracula thought about his life and realized he *did* miss Jack, and the companionship of a seasoned vampire. What better choice than his own son? Before he could respond, Eva wrapped her arms around Jack, and Dracula knew a decision had already been made. Dracula took a step forward, and that was all it took for Jack to embrace the one who made him. Although the ancient vampire was wary, he returned Jack's embrace hoping he was not making a mistake.

Back inside, the New Year's Eve party was in full swing. Dracula decided it was time to reclaim his family, and that included Jack. Oliver saw him first, then Prince, as he entered the room; they could clearly see all had been forgiven. The two boys ran to Jack, and Alice followed; she had a soft spot for him and always would.

"Look at you boys!" Jack hugged them both, as Alice pulled on his sleeve to be lifted up.

"Uncle Jack...why were you gone so long?" Alice asked. She knew well enough not to ask about his arm.

"Where is your little friend...the white-haired girl?" Jack asked, looking for Semele.

"She's gone, Jack...since last October," Alice replied, losing her cheerful smile.

The music paused as an announcement was made; it was 11:45PM and time to refill champagne glasses for the big countdown. Dracula quickly located Eva, determined she would be in his arms at the stroke of midnight.

"Hey...why don't we go back out on the terrace?" Jack suggested. All agreed and within moments, they were all gathered together under the night sky.

"To the year ahead!" Dracula toasted a crescent moon.

"Happy New Year, everybody!" Alice and Oliver exclaimed, holding up empty glasses to the night. Nikos raised his glass in agreement, feeling no need for words.

"To a family reunited!" Eva declared, as she kissed Dracula's cheek.

Prince stepped forward and made his toast, "To Uncle Jack's return!"

Jack had no glass, so he made a mock toast. "Tonight, I'm thankful for family...and most especially, for a father's love."

When the ball dropped in Times Square, a family of vampires

and earthbound specters shouted their good wishes to each other, and to the stars above. It was a night they would remember always. The party started winding down, so the others went back to Tunneltown; but, Dracula and Eva stayed behind. They didn't want the night to end; both of them were stalling for time. They knew what was to come; they felt apprehension, accompanied by a crushing desire. They finally hailed a cab and snuggled together in the back seat; Dracula nibbled playfully at her neck, giving the nosy cabdriver quite a show.

Dracula's hotel room at the Doral was dark as pitch. Giggling like children, they opened the heavy brocade draperies to let in the night. It was just after 2:00AM, so the sunrise was far enough away. On this magical night, it seemed important to feel the night air blowing through the room. By the time Eva finished adjusting the drapes, Dracula had undressed and stood before her like a well-carved statue. He moved to unzip her gown and she let it drop to the floor, stepping out of it with the grace of a ballet dancer. They faced each other as man and woman for the first time, since the sixteenth century; Dracula vowed he would never let anything come between them again. Eva moved to kiss her count, but he offered his cheek instead; for a vampire, the mouth was for feeding. Eva persisted and began biting at him until he finally gave in, and put his tongue inside her mouth; the ancient vampire was surprised to find pleasure there. It seemed like ages since they had been lovers; tonight, felt like the first time all over again. He ran his tongue along her slender neck; he wanted to taste her skin, and savor the delicious scent that was uniquely hers. His lips moved to her glorious breasts; her nipples were like dimpled strawberries. They fell together onto an unmade bed, his desire became unbearable and Eva's passion all-consuming. She called his name as he planted gentle kisses along the length of her nymph-like body, one he remembered so well it was like coming home. Here with his long lost love, Dracula forgot about his loneliness and the anguish of being a creature of the night. All he wanted tonight was to give Eva everything a man could and more. Unable to delay their pleasure any longer, Dracula entered her; gently probing the very core of her femininity. Overcome with desire, Eva pulled him all the way inside, until he filled the aching in her soul. Dracula's eyes flew open when he realized that after all these years, he *could* reach orgasm. In his moment of ecstasy, the vampire found his humanity; if only for a fleeting moment in time.

Chapter 129 - Sylvio - Dakota Building - (January 1976)

The Dakota Building was an historical marvel, and perhaps one of the most fascinating landmarks in New York City. Built in 1884, the Dakota at one time was surrounded by a rural community, including several farms. Before the city was modernized, the Dakota was isolated from the rest of the city which only added to its intrigue. At one time, residents could see the Museum of Natural History; today apartment buildings and skyscrapers obscured it from view. The Dakota Building was situated on Central Park West, at the corner of 72nd Street, and was home to many prestigious and wealthy people, some movie stars and musicians. Ex-Beatle, John Lennon and his wife, Yoko, made their home here, which greatly increased the allure of the prestigious residence. Sylvio's wealthy family had secured the apartment in the 1950s; it now belonged to him. It was here Sylvio found anonymity, in a big city like New York; it was easy to get lost. He couldn't wait to bathe in his Venetian marble bathtub, to wash away all remnants of a desert mountain.

Sylvio stepped off the elevator with breathless anticipation. He immediately took off his shoes and socks, digging his toes into the most luxurious carpet money could buy. After years of walking on hard, rocky ground as both a human and a wolf, it was wonderful to return to a more civilized way of life. He reached the ornate bronze door he'd had imported from Italy and rung the bell; Sylvio wasn't expected. The door was opened by an exceedingly tall man with a shaved head. His eyes were wide with surprise, but he would never dare to speak before spoken to.

"Eadric," Sylvio said with a smile, handing the man his shoes and socks as though he'd only been gone for a few days.

"Master Sylvio...so good to see you again." Eadric had been his body slave at the time he was turned; Sylvio saw no reason not to continue that relationship, so he made him a vampire, too.

"It feels good to be home…Eadric. Run me a bath and open a bottle of my reserve, tonight…I'm feeling adventurous."

"Very good, sir," Eadric replied, as he turned to attend to his master's socks and shoes.

Eadric was a true and faithful servant; he also knew every one of Sylvio's darkest secrets. Eadric rarely left the penthouse; bottled blood was delivered in the guise of imported wine and he needed nothing else. He wasn't a slave any longer; Eadric was paid handsomely for his services. Funny thing was Sylvio couldn't remember ever seeing him buy anything. Then again, what did he need?

He surveyed his living room, taking in the splendor of a carefully appointed space he had decorated himself. Sylvio moved to a leather chaise lounge, stretching out his well-toned body in a distinctly feline manner. As he waited for his bath to be drawn, he contemplated what club he wanted to frequent tonight; he had a taste for testosterone-laden sustenance. He'd read somewhere, a group called the Ramones were playing at CBGB. A nightclub would be fun after so many years in isolation. He closed his eyes, but could feel someone watching; the Dark One was nearby.

"You look extremely comfortable," the Dark One said. It had something pressing to discuss.

"Compared to a bed of straw, how could it be anything else, master?" Sylvio replied sullenly. He was too comfortable to move.

"We have a problem…the albino girl."

"The black swan who fed little Alice, master?"

"Correct…the girl has been dodging police since November. She and the juvenile vampire used to ride the Staten Island Ferry…they also played around that atrocious statue in the harbor."

"The Statue of Liberty?"

"Yes…she will be there…wearing a wool hat to cover her white hair…and sunglasses because of her eyes. She is a clever one, I'll have to admit…but, her resolve is weakening as the weather gets colder. You need to find her before the police do."

"I guess I'll have to stalk the Staten Island Ferry, then," Sylvio said distastefully; like most vampires, he hated the water.

Eadric entered the room oblivious to their conversation. "Your bath is ready, Master Sylvio."

Sylvio nodded, unsure what to do. "By all means, *Master Sylvio*... go and have your bath first."

Chapter 130 - Police Chief Rodriguez - NYPD - Midtown - (January 1976)

Police Chief Rodriguez hated snowy days like this. Half his staff found excuses to stay home, leaving his precinct even more short-handed than usual. Puffing on a Camel, Rodriguez studied his notes as a curl of smoke snaked out of his mouth. Whenever he had a spare second, he always came back to this troubling case.

The girl named Semele had simply vanished; it pissed him off that none of his officers had ever found a single trace of her. The police chief felt certain she would turn up as the weather grew colder; instead, the frigid temperatures sent her deeper into hiding. Rodriguez looked down at his notes on recent developments based on Detective Daly's report.

* Coroner's Report on remains of incinerated prisoner - Nothing left of prisoner but ash (Inconsistent with remains of Officer Denby)

* Confirmed blood bank openings have increased by 300% over past decade - How can Red Cross be constantly complaining about a shortage? Notable increase in vandalism at blood banks (Satanic ritual motive doesn't seem to fit)

* Blood shipments redirected to "so-called" medical clinics - addresses turned out to be vacant lots or abandoned buildings - (Investigation ongoing)

* Missing Children Update: Significant increase in child abductions from Midtown to Rockefeller Plaza - Spike began in 1968

* Unsolved Disappearances near New York Public Library (First two were employees)
- Don Baker
- David Mitchell
- Mary & Maude Harding - (Twins -Age 9)
- Jill Porter (Age 7)

* DES report showed an unauthorized installation of a waterline under library?? Appears to be unrelated to any specific crimes - WHAT FOR?

Rodriguez sat back in his seat and lit another cigarette, as he reviewed Inspector Poole's report. It was hard to ignore blood-drained bodies, or prisoners who spontaneously burst into flames. Naturally, Rodriguez didn't believe in vampires, but what if there was a cult who *believed* they were vampires and actually consumed human blood? Granted, it was a bizarre twist, but it could explain the blood thefts and drained corpses; it might even explain the disappearance of two library employees. If his theory was correct, they were not only looking for thieves, they were searching for a cold-hearted killer. Maybe, even more than one.

Detective Daly knocked on the police chief's open door. "Hey, chief...we got a double homicide over at the Chrysler Building...two black men killed execution style in their car."

"Do we need crowd control?" Rodriguez asked stubbing out his cigarette, as he holstered his weapon.

"You bet...an angry crowd has already gathered claiming it was racially motivated."

"Sounds more like a gang war assassination to me."

"I'll drive, chief...already double-parked anyway. We called for a SWAT team, too."

"Good work, Daly...let's go."

As they rode to the crime scene, Rodriguez ruminated over the mention of a water line installation underneath the library. What need could there possibly be for running water inside a storage vault used for rare books? He didn't know a whole lot about the preservation of antiquities, but was he fairly certain moisture could do irreparable damage to aging books. He could always check in with the DES; but then the police chief decided against it, determined to focus on crimes he could actually solve. By the time they pulled up to the chaotic crime scene, all thoughts of vampires and blood banks had been put aside.

CHAPTER 131 - SEMELE - STATEN ISLAND FERRY - (JANUARY 1976)

The month of January had been exceptionally cold. Most nights, Semele found the Staten Island Ferry sparsely populated once rush hour was over. A steady breeze blew off water as she hovered in a corner, convinced it was the warmest place to be. Semele wore every piece of clothing she owned, including three pairs of socks under her rubber boots. She wore a black wool cap to conceal her white hair; she would draw unwanted attention otherwise. Sunglasses completed her disguise, although she got many strange looks from fellow passengers. Semele usually sat in the same seat, near the ferry captain. He appeared to take no notice of her, but his presence made her feel safer. The ferry captain had watched the girl travel back and forth each night since last November; she seemed compelled to remain in perpetual motion. When the boat reached Staten Island, Semele stepped off and moved to a favorite spot; she loved watching tugboats plough through the nighttime waters. Sometimes Semele thought about Alice and Tunneltown; they were part of her old life now. Semele felt betrayed by all of them; they had abandoned her at the parade and now she lived on the run. Semele was used to it; she should have known better than to try and make a home anywhere. The girl wiped an errant tear from her eye; she didn't need anyone!

Sylvio approached the pier and waited for the ferry to dock. It was after 9:00PM, so only one other man was waiting; he was engrossed in a thick paperback entitled *Jaws*. The black water made the vampire shiver, as he stepped onto the ferry boat. Sylvio moved about cautiously; if the girl was hiding, he didn't want to spook her. He reached into his pocket to retrieve a candy bar; he thought food might draw her out. After about twenty minutes, Sylvio realized she wasn't on the boat. The ferry was approaching St. George Terminal, now. There was nothing to do but return to the harbor and look somewhere else.

Sylvio watched as the ferry docked; a young couple boarded with huge smiles reserved for those who were in love. Love. Sylvio scoffed at the word; he had never known love in his human life, or in this one. He was about to give up his search, when he saw a third person boarding. It was clearly a child. Like all vampires, Sylvio had excellent night vision; he immediately spotted her wool cap and dime store sunglasses. He smiled maliciously, rubbing his hands together in triumph. Tonight, he was going to take her from this lonely life, and offer her a better one. He moved to the far end of the ferry, away from the amorous couple. Sylvio's plan was to attract the albino girl's attention in a manner she would least expect; he was a talented actor when the need arose.

Semele stepped onto the ferry, offering a weak smile to the captain. As she searched for a seat, she saw the young couple and decided to give them some privacy. Off to her right, was a well-dressed man in a wool overcoat; he appeared to be crying, but Semele couldn't be sure. The man was probably about thirty or so; she moved closer, and he looked up at her with bloodshot eyes. Without hesitation, Semele offered him her handkerchief.

"I think you need this more than I do."

"Thank you...I'm sorry...it's just that..." Sylvio played his part to perfection.

"Why are you crying?"

"Forgive me, child...it's just that my daughter and I used to ride the ferry every Saturday...before..." Sylvio covered his face and his smile, as he pretended to be overcome with grief.

"Your daughter is sick?"

"She was...but her body wasn't strong enough...and..."

"It'll get better...the pain goes away after a while..." Semele said, putting a hand on the man's arm.

"What is your name, child?"

"Semele," she said, there was no point in lying.

"You are very sweet, Semele. Where are your parents?" Sylvio asked, and he saw her guard go up.

"I know how to get by...I've been doing it for a long time."

"Semele...may I call you that?" The girl nodded and he continued, "You certainly seem capable of taking care of yourself...but, is this what you really want?"

Semele hung her head and spoke softly, "It is lonely sometimes…
and cold."

"I know," Sylvio said, putting a hand on hers; the girl didn't pull
away.

"*Who* are you really?" Semele asked. She removed her sunglasses and
looked deeply into his vampire eyes. In them she saw images of ancient
Egypt and the pyramids against a cerulean sky; but there was something
else, something dark and yet, so exciting.

"You ask me who I am, so I will tell you. I am the answer to your
prayers, dear child. Now come, we must leave this place," Sylvio said,
as he motioned for her to put her sunglasses back on.

Sylvio picked the girl up in his arms, and her scent made him dizzy.
He could smell Alice, but her scent would fade over time. He would
take her to a place where no one would ever hurt her again; together,
they would chase away the abysmal loneliness of eternal life.

"Hey, you there!" the ferry captain called after them.

"Tell him I'm your uncle," he whispered in her ear.

Semele turned and flashed the ferry captain a smile. "It's my Uncle
Dickie…come for me at last!" The ferry captain hesitated for a moment,
and then figured it was none of his business.

When they reached the pier, Sylvio set Semele down, and they
walked hand in hand toward the subway; it seemed the least conspicuous
way to travel. As they headed down the subway steps, Sylvio turned to
Semele with a smile and said, "Uncle *Dickie?*"

Semele looked up at him through dark glasses, as he tucked a tuft
of white hair into her woolen cap. "It was the only name that came to
mind!"

"Little miss…you will call me *Uncle Sylvio.*"

Semele was starving by the time they got to the Dakota; she
marveled at such a dwelling, which was well beyond anything she
had ever seen. Once inside Sylvio's apartment, Semele thought she'd
died and went to heaven. Everywhere she looked there were colorful
paintings, and fabulous sculptures she just had to touch. A bald-headed
butler answered the door; he smiled blandly at Semele, taking in her
dirty clothes and the unpleasant odor she exuded.

"Master, should I draw the child a bath?" Eadric asked hopefully.

"Yes…of course, but first you must make our guest something to drink," Sylvio replied with a nod. Eadric poured her a burgundy-colored beverage.

Semele didn't realize she was thirsty, until Sylvio held the glass out to her. "This will make you feel better…don't mind the taste, just drink it up."

She put the glass to her lips and wrinkled her nose; Sylvio's eyes glowed in a hypnotic way that made Semele want to drink. She finished the drink in several gulps; Eadric caught the wine glass, as she doubled over in her chair. Searing pain gripped Semele, as she began retching violently; the change was coming fast now.

Sylvio rushed to catch Semele, before she collapsed onto the floor. He held her tightly, cooing in her ear, "Let your body go now…you've no need for it any longer. I'm here little one…and I always will be."

Semele's breathing began to slow, as she lay cradled in Sylvio's arms; he held her until the transformation was complete. When Semele finally opened her vampire eyes, she saw the world in a whole new light. Her eyes were no longer pink; they had turned fluorescent silver.

"You feel better now?" Sylvio asked, caressing her delicate face.

"I'm still hungry," Semele replied, reaching for the empty glass.

"My sweet girl, you will feed from me, now…only then, shall I be your father." Sylvio pulled a tiny finger blade from his vest; he sliced his forearm and offered it to his new fledgling.

Semele took his arm and drank hungrily from her father; Sylvio closed his eyes as the exotic creature fed on his life blood. Her feeding was far more intoxicating than sex could ever be. He let her drink until he felt himself weaken; only then, did Sylvio gently pull her away. Once Semele understood what she had become; the world no longer seemed so scary.

Chapter 132 - Rory - Granary
Cemetery - Boston, MA - (April 1976)

Granary Cemetery was quiet this time of night; it was an historic landmark, so she never came here during the day. Rory liked to visit from time to time; her father's grave was a place where she could reflect on her life as daughter to an American hero. The name Paul Revere was getting more difficult to read, as were the dates; it was a very old marker. Next to her father's grave were the five victims of the Boston Massacre; Rory liked to believe they kept her father company. She could still see his face, sitting by a late night fire, as he tried to explain politics. Rory would never forget their special midnight ride together; on that wonderfully historic evening, she had felt truly alive!

Rory had a new life now, with a cause she believed in. Only problem was, she and Rupert were slowly growing apart. His recent association with the dark-skinned men unnerved her; there was something about them she didn't trust. After nearly taking out Dracula at the zoo, Rory became a bit of a celebrity among the Van Helsings. After the epic battle, Rory felt a new empowerment; she quickly discovered how exhilarating killing could be. Would her father be proud of her for fighting vampires? She didn't know but reasoned, her father had his enemies and she had hers. Rory liked to think of what she did as population control; for the most part, the Van Helsings only took vampire lives when it was absolutely necessary. Over the years, Rory had become proficient at taking out rogue vampires; some deserved it, others she killed for the fun of it. Some pleaded for their lives just before she staked them; others accepted their fate without a fight. Rupert trained her well and before long, Rory became one of the Van Helsing's fiercest killers. What she lacked in size, Rory made up in speed; Paul Revere's daughter had blossomed into a skilled assassin.

Rory's thoughts were interrupted by a security guard, who approached with a flashlight; she vaporized before his eyes. The guard convinced himself it was a trick of the light, using his flashlight to confirm the historical gravesite was undisturbed. Six feet underground, all that remained of Paul Revere was bone dust; he felt Rory's presence and silently wept for his inability to rescue his earthbound daughter.

CHAPTER 133 - THE VAN HELSINGS - WEST VILLAGE - (MAY 1976)

Rupert demanded loyalty above all things, and was bitterly disappointed Jack had defected; there was no denying he had gone back to the company of his own kind. At first Rupert blew it off; he could get others to do what Jack did, but deep inside he felt a burning need to hurt them all. Cruelty came naturally to Rupert. He had become a master at targeting weaknesses in those he chose to destroy; unfortunately, his battle against the vampire community had been lost long ago. Dracula and his legions had successfully infiltrated nearly every borough of New York. He had recently been advised a budding vampire community had also sprouted up on the West Coast, near Los Angeles; before long, vampires would have a nationwide presence.

A few years back, Rupert befriended two men named Abbud and Kamil; they had recently emigrated from Afghanistan. At first, they seemed interested in joining the Van Helsings; but after a few months, they seemed more interested in learning everything there was to know about national landmarks. The two Middle Eastern men rented an abandoned machine shop on Hudson Street; they claimed to be designing the ultimate vampire weapon: homemade bombs. Rupert warmed to the idea of flushing vampires out by incinerating them, sorry he hadn't thought of it himself. His first thought was to target Bryant Park; what a way to exact his revenge on Jack and the European count. Abbud and Kamil discarded his suggestion, explaining they had other targets in mind; it pissed Rupert off that they always spoke in Arabic, whenever he was around. A knock on the door interrupted Rupert's thoughts; he opened it, and came face to face with Nikos Fabri.

"Hello, Rupert," Nikos said. He grabbed him by the neck, kicking the door shut with his boot.

"Wh-h-hat do you want?" Rupert croaked; he was no match for the well muscled-man.

"I just want to talk..." Nikos released him, and Rupert collapsed on the floor.

"I've committed no crimes against your precious vampire!" Rupert said, rubbing his sore neck.

"And the girl, Semele…is she here?" Nikos asked, his keen eyes scanning the loft.

"No, why would she be?"

"I'll just have a look around then…why don't you come with me?" Without waiting for a response, he took Rupert by the arm. Nikos called out Semele's name, as he looked for any sign the girl was living here.

"Like I told you…the girl's not here!"

"Rupert…tell me about the dark-skinned men. What are they to you and why are they here?" Nikos kept a tight grip on Rupert's arm.

"Van Helsing recruits…what else?" Rupert replied innocently.

"Uh-huh…recruits you say…"

"That's right."

"Tell me then…why would vampire killers have the need for explosives?"

"I don't know what you're talking about."

"Very well…but know this…if I discover you or your associates are involved in anything that disturbs the sanctuary of our legions, my lord and I will come after you!"

"I'm not afraid of you!" Rupert declared, grabbing a rusted saber from the wall.

Nikos laughed and snatched it from him. Rupert watched in horror, as he thrust the saber through his own stomach, and then pulled it out from the other side.

Still not afraid?" Nikos asked with a malicious grin. For the first time ever, Rupert was speechless.

CHAPTER 134 - THE DARK ONE

"Wake up now...I have let you sulk long enough." The Dark One hissed. Jack awoke at once, even though it was still daylight outside. He tried to block out the familiar voice, but his will wasn't strong enough.

"Why do you torture me? I just want live in peace."

"Oh, come now...whoever told you a vampire was allowed to live in peace?"

"What is it then...what nefarious scheme do you have planned now?"

"Come on, Jack...I have an assignment I think you'll rather enjoy."

"The last time I did your bidding, it was...less than successful," Jack said, referring to his failed encounter with Adolf Hitler.

"Only because Dracula stepped in and ruined everything!" the Dark One countered.

"I guess me getting left for dead, was a minor event for you!" Jack snapped back.

"Not at all...you were very brave and did your best...I know that." The Dark One was setting him up for sure.

"What is it you want then?"

"There is a young man...a very troubled young man who lives in Yonkers. He has a killer's instinct, but lacks agility and skill...things that come naturally to you. He already tried to kill with a knife...it was a botched job...and David decided he had no stomach for it."

"Has this *David* actually killed anyone yet?"

"Not yet...he purchased a gun, and has been vacillating on his next move. He wants to kill...but there's no one to push him, Jack. Each day he tries to work up the nerve to do what he was born to do...that's where you come in."

"Knives and scalpels are my weapons of choice...I'm no marksman."

"Don't worry...he plans to shoot his victims at point-blank range."

"So, what comes next?"

"This man...David, is afraid of dogs. He actually believes they talk to him. His next door neighbor has a black dog named Harvey. You have

an amazing ability to shape shift; the wolf and dog are both canine...
after all."

"So, you want me to pose as a dog, and convince this guy to start shooting people?"

"We need a diversion, Jack! NYPD are digging deeper into rumors of a *vampire community*. We need something to distract both the police and the public."

Jack didn't want to get sucked into this. "Can't you get someone else...I have other plans..."

"I know all about your plans...they're laughable at best."

"What do you mean?"

"Your plan to create one big happy family...in the Catskill Mountains. Naturally, I know all about it. You want to take Dracula and his love-struck countess there...hoping to reconnect and shut out the rest of the world."

"Maybe...I'm just tired of living in a concrete jungle..."

"Snap out of it, Jack! Your soul is mine and so is your life. You'll do whatever I ask...or I will take away everything you hold dear!" Jack closed his eyes; he saw Oliver and Alice running toward him with happy smiles. He couldn't risk losing them again.

Jack let out a sigh of resignation. "Tell me again...what you want me to do."

"You must guide David along the path he has already chosen. I'll get you a photo and his home address...the dog will be impossible to miss."

"That's it then...no other hidden agenda?"

"Correct...feel free to spend your time living in bucolic bliss, but remember...three's a crowd...especially when love is involved."

"I assume this man targets women?" Jack replied ignoring the Dark One's taunt.

"Oh, yes...lovely young girls, Jack. Surely this part will interest you." Jack could feel a tinge of excitement; it had been so long since he had made a woman squeal.

"Tell me more about him."

"David Berkowitz is filled with a deep-seated anger...he has much contempt for pretty young girls. Most women won't even give him the time of day. He's average-looking and on the surface, he leads an ordinary life. David Berkowitz often feels invisible...I'm counting on you to change that, Jack."

"Great...I'm tasked with turning a loser into a serial killer."

"Just think of young Berkowitz as an extension of yourself. After all, no one has more disdain for women than you," the Dark One taunted.

"Whores...its whores I detest!"

"All women are whores, Jack...you know that better than anyone."

"Fair enough."

"What I ask of you is quite reasonable, don't you agree, Jack?"

"It doesn't sound like I have a choice."

"Not unless you want something to happen to little Alice."

Chapter 135 - Olana Estate - Hudson Valley, NY - (June 1976)

Once Dracula and Jack agreed to bury their mutual grudges, the two found tremendous comfort in one another's company. Tonight, they had chosen to hunt in the Hudson Valley, conveniently located in upstate New York. Once they left city limits, they were free to fly in human form, a rare and special treat for Dracula. Jack had become partial to the Catskill Mountains, lots of open space that provided an escape from a crowded city. Dracula let Jack lead the way; together they flew over lush green hills and valleys that made Dracula homesick for the English countryside. The two spent a few hours hunting white-tailed deer, for once agreeing there was no need to kill humans every night. After they successfully took down two bucks each, they made a small fire, then proceeded to gorge themselves on raw venison. It was the kind of night meant for sharing stories; under a starry sky, the two reminisced about London and their various adventures.

"Don't you ever miss the old days...you know, horse carriages and gas lights...when it was easy to get lost in the dark corners of a city..." Jack's voice trailed off, as he studied the burning embers of their dwindling fire.

"Still romanticizing Whitechapel?" Dracula asked with a knowing smile.

"Not a specific place...I miss the authenticity of Victorian England. Frankly, I'm utterly unimpressed with the modern world...surely you know what I'm talking about."

"I do know what you mean, Jack...I have a soft spot for Whitechapel myself...the clip-clop of horses on cobblestone streets, and the lovely flowing fabrics women used to wear...I'd give anything to ride in a hansom cab again."

"What else...don't you miss anything else?" Jack persisted.

"Well, of course, I miss Makefield Manor...and having a real home."

"Makefield Manor...a grand place of many comforts. What if I told you, I'd found a better place. It's unoccupied ...a grand estate overlooking the Hudson River," Jack said, waving his arm against the horizon.

"What place?" Dracula asked, knowing there had to be a catch.

"It's called Olana. Come…I'll show you. Best to let you fall in love with the place first…then I'll explain a few things." Jack was already up, kicking up the dirt to extinguish their fire.

The two seasoned vampires became airborne in one graceful motion, flying like eagles along the Hudson River. On the horizon, Dracula saw something unexpected and amazing. Jack was right: the glorious estate was far more beautiful than Makefield Manor could ever be. He flashed Jack a smile and they headed straight for it. They made a soft landing, and Dracula found himself standing in front of a well-preserved nineteenth-century estate. Olana was artfully illuminated with well-placed exterior lighting; the house welcomed, but in a reserved kind of way. The magnificent piece of eclectic architecture combined an old-world charm with a distinct European style that made Olana, one of a kind. An artfully designed wraparound porch was positioned in such a way, as to provide a nearly panoramic view of the Catskill Mountain range. Even though the night was waning fast, Dracula found himself compelled to explore this architectural wonder further.

"Tell me more about this place, Jack." Dracula asked; he was clearly under Olana's spell.

"It was built by a well known landscape artist named Frederic Church in the late 1800s. Right now, it's an historical landmark…they run tours on weekends, but after dusk, the place is deserted. I discovered it one night, when I was hunting in a little hamlet nearby called Sleepy Hollow."

"Amazing…have you been inside?"

"It has become a second home to me…come on, I'll show you the way in."

Dracula was intrigued, but kept his guard up in case Jack was wrong about the place being empty. Jack moved with amazing speed and agility as he approached a basement window that looked secure, but was easily opened. Once inside, Dracula's eyes settled on a comfortable wine cellar furnished with overstuffed chairs; it made him think about the London home they had been forced to abandon.

"So, these tours are only on weekends?"

"Yes…and only for eight months of the year. Maintenance and ground keeping staff only come during the day. I checked it all out…I'm telling you, no one ever comes here after dark. Maybe, people think the place is haunted," Jack said with a snicker.

"It could work," Dracula said, wondering how Eva would like it.

"Come on…don't you want her to have a real home again?" Jack said, as if reading his mind.

Dracula realized Jack was right; Eva would love this place. More importantly, they'd have privacy and endless open land to hunt on. Dracula knew the Doral Hotel had become risky; he had stayed there far too long.

"You haven't seen the best part yet…come on." Jack led Dracula out, securing the door behind them.

Outside once more, they became instantly airborne. Like two schoolboys, they soared up to a Victorian-style balcony overlooking the Hudson Valley. The Taconic Bridge stood proudly in the distance; a shining beacon in the night. Dracula suddenly realized how much he missed open land and hunting on the moors. Jack observed the wonder in Dracula's eyes; for the first time in years, Jack felt genuine affection for the one who made him. As they flew back toward Midtown Manhattan, the emptiness that had been holding Jack captive for so long slowly began to evaporate.

Chapter 136 - David Berkowitz a.k.a Son of Sam - Yonkers, NY - (July 29, 1976)

He picked up the gun and held it in his hand, as if weighing how he would use it. The apartment was dark even during daylight hours; he had hung comforters over the windows to keep the black dog from watching him. The neighbor's dog spoke to him, even as he hid in the darkness; David tried unsuccessfully to block it out. For the past week, he had observed a ritual of loading and unloading his gun, as if afraid to act; the man was still fixated on his first failed attempt. There had been too much blood using a knife; a handgun was far more efficient. The trouble was getting up the nerve, and finding women who deserved it. Tonight, his restlessness had become unbearable; he couldn't stay inside any longer. Already dressed, David went into the kitchen to get a brown lunch bag for his Bulldog revolver.

When David stepped outside, he felt compelled to see if Harvey was still on his lead. He approached the hurricane fence, careful to avoid the beam of light coming from a streetlight above. The dog named Harvey let out a low growl as David moved closer, his courage bolstered by the .44 in his pocket. Two yellow eyes watched as the man came closer; it was time for Jack to make his move.

"David…what are you waiting for?" a very human voice asked. He pulled his weapon from the paper bag and took aim at the talking demon.

"I'm not afraid to pull the trigger, Harvey…just give me a reason," David said in his best cop show voice.

"It's not me you want to kill now…is it David?"

"What kind of demon are you?"

"One who can help you get the balls to finally act. How long are you going to keep playing with that gun…don't you actually want to use it?"

"How can you know anything about my plans?" David kept the gun aimed at the dog; in the dark, all he could see was its eyes.

"As far as I can tell…you have no real plan at all, but I can help you." Harvey's eyes changed to red as David listened; his finger was no longer on the trigger.

"I hear you out here barking every night…why do you torture me?"

"I'm trying to get your attention…I can help you finally get even with all of them."

"Get even with who?"

"Oh, come now…you know very well who I mean…those pretty girls you pass on the street…the ones who don't even know you exist." Jack realized he was quite good at being a demon dog.

"I'm invisible to most women," David mumbled, nodding in agreement.

"Why not have satisfaction tonight?" Jack needed him to stay angry.

"Who would I kill? I've made no preparations for tonight," Berkowitz replied, finally lowering his weapon.

"All you need is that gun you're holding. I know a place where lots of young people go…lovely young girls in parked cars, with windows carelessly left open…"

David Berkowitz was intrigued and moved closer to the fence, as the black dog told him exactly where to find his next victim.

CHAPTER 137 - SYLVIO - DAKOTA BUILDING - (AUGUST 1976)

Semele woke from her twilight sleep with a start; she heard the sound of someone crying. Her room was always dark because her bedroom windows were painted black; a very necessary precaution for vampires. She sat up and listened for the sound again, and then she heard it; a woman was crying right outside her room. Semele threw off her covers and tiptoed to the door. She opened the door a crack, still not sure what time it was, and then she saw her. She was clearly a ghost, but nothing like Prince or Nikos. This woman appeared to be comprised of mist or vapors, Semele could see right through her. The specter's movements were slippery and slow, like someone moving underwater. The crying woman turned to face Semele; her blue eyes pleading for release. She took a step toward the specter; it rippled like water before fading away. Semele ran back to her bed and got under the covers, trying to shut out the vision; before long, she returned to her dreamless sleep.

An hour later, the sun finally gave up the day; Semele immediately snapped awake. She rose from her rumpled bed and went to the kitchen; Eadric was performing household tasks in a robotic manner. She rubbed the sleep from her eyes and gave him a smile.

"Good evening, miss," Eadric said, opening the refrigerator to retrieve a bottle of Sylvio's special reserve.

"Good evening, Eadric...this house is haunted," Semele stated matter-of-factly, as she plucked an empty glass from an overhead cupboard.

Eadric wasn't used to houseguests, but he enjoyed having Semele here, it gave him someone to fuss over. On most nights, Sylvio left her at home and the two would watch horror movies together until well after midnight. Semele's favorite movies were the ones about vampires and werewolves; she found them utterly fascinating. Eadric confessed to loving the Johnny Carson show; sometimes they watched it together as they snacked on bite-sized meatballs made of raw hamburger. Apparently, vampires consumed more than just human blood; Semele was pleasantly surprised at how much she enjoyed uncooked meat.

"No horror movies tonight, miss," Eadric said, looking up from the *TV Guide.*

Semele was about to respond, when Sylvio entered the kitchen, wearing only silk pajama bottoms. He was proud of his physique and enjoyed showing it off, with or without an audience.

"Good morning, little one," Sylvio said, planting a kiss on the top of Semele's head.

"Uncle Sylvio…are we still stargazing tonight before you go hunting?

"Well…I…"

"Come on, you promised!" Semele implored with silvery eyes; Sylvio knew it would be impossible to refuse her.

"I suppose, for a little while. Let me shower and dress…I'll meet you up on the roof in half an hour."

Semele loved being on the rooftop so high above the rest of the world; it made her feel like a queen watching over her kingdom. The night was unseasonably cool for late August; there was a hint of fall in the air. They sat atop two gargoyles, situated just below the Dakota's peaked roof. The seasoned vampire enjoyed Semele's company; he found himself caring about the girl, more than he had expected. He lavished her with clothes and anything else she asked for, which were mostly books. Sylvio occasionally took Semele to a wonderful bookstore called Brentanos; it was located in the Greenwich Village, and stayed open late on Friday nights. The owner was very kind and let her read books for free. Semele wasn't sure if he knew they were vampires; he was a little pale, but she didn't think he was one of her kind. She was surprised at how many vampires there were roaming about the city, mingling in with humans in a most discreet way; Semele had never noticed this, until she was turned. As the weeks passed, Sylvio opened up to his fledgling, telling her about his life and how, even now, he missed the mystique of ancient Egypt. Semele told Sylvio about life on the street, and about meeting Alice; she left out any reference to her home life or the reason she ran away.

It was the kind of summer evening one savored from childhood, a night for catching fireflies and playing tag. Carefree summer nights were something even Sylvio recalled from his boyhood days. Semele had never been carefree, but now in this comfortable place with someone who took care of her, she felt safe for the first time. Sylvio was someone she could trust, and little by little, Semele revealed her secrets. Tonight, the fledgling vampire wanted to ask about the crying ghost, but wasn't sure how to bring it up.

"What's on your mind, little one?" Sylvio asked, studying her profile.

"I think we have a ghost living in our apartment."

"Ah-h-h…you've met our *Crying Lady.*"

"Who is she, uncle?"

"It's a rather common story…about a woman who lived in a different time…when this building was still very new. Did you know at one time the Dakota stood on its own, one solitary structure on the west side of Central Park?"

"How could I? Please tell me about it…" Semele loved hearing about the past; Sylvio was an excellent orator of all things historical.

"It was a world still unfettered with modern conveniences. During the winter months, a favorite pastime was taking open sleigh rides through the park…Central Park, that is."

"Like in the song, "Jingle Bells?"

"It was more than just a song…child; it was a way of life. There were no televisions or radios…people made their own entertainment and didn't let cold weather chase them inside…like it does today."

"But, what about the *Crying Lady?*"

"She is part of my story…her name was Emily Parrish."

"Who was she…how did she die?"

"Patience is a virtue…hasn't anyone ever told you that?" Sylvio teased with a smile.

"Sorry, uncle…I wish I could have lived in old-fashioned times…a nighttime sleigh ride sounds like so much fun!"

"It certainly does…you could find out for yourself…if you really wanted to," Sylvio suggested, as an idea began to form.

"A sleigh ride…in the middle of summer?"

"Semele…haven't you ever daydreamed about sailing on a turquoise sea to some far away land…or wished you could build a snowman in the middle of a heat wave?"

"I never daydreamed much...I would think daydreaming for someone like you quite unnecessary...you've probably seen just about everything."

"You're right...I have traveled the world for centuries...yet, believe it or not, many things I experienced without ever stepping outside my door."

"It must be lonely to live for so long," she said thoughtfully.

"Sometimes...but not so much now...having you here, has made me happy."

"I never made my parents happy...all I remember is them fighting all the time."

"Tell me what happened, Semele...why did you leave home?" Semele decided it was time to tell Sylvio her awful secret.

"My father was a drunk...he beat us...me and my mother. He hated my pink eyes and accused her of sleeping around..."

"Go ahead...you can tell me anything."

"It got worse in the months before it happened...he was drunk all the time, and my mother took the brunt of it."

"Where are they now?"

"My father's dead...I don't know where my mother is. She ran away the night he died...and so did I. It was hard at first, but eventually I learned to survive on my own." Sylvio sensed she was still not telling him everything.

"Semele...how did your father die?" Her young face was filled with anguish.

"Speak the words and it will set you free. Tell me...*how* did your father die?"

"I...I killed him...he was beating on my mother! I couldn't take it anymore...so I stabbed him with a kitchen knife..." Semele cried, covering her face in shame.

"And that's why you ran away." Sylvio knew firsthand how cruel humans could be. He wanted to comfort her but held back; Semele would find a way to forgive herself in time.

"Semele...I am always going to take care of you. I will never hurt you in any way. I only want to help you realize what an amazing creature you really are."

407

Semele brightened at his words, and then changed the subject. "Can you show me how it's done, uncle...how I could take a sleigh ride through the snow...right now, in the middle of August?"

"You're a creature of the night...if you want something badly enough...it's yours for the taking."

"But *how*, uncle...can you show me how to be part of another time? I want to see the snow and Central Park as it used to be...it all sounds so lovely."

"You *already* know how, Semele...simply chase the summer away and your dreams of a winter wonderland will be waiting."

"I don't understand what you mean...it's not as if I can just close my eyes, and make it wintertime in another century."

"Who says you cannot? You are a vampire and have powers of the mind beyond imagining. I will show you how it's done...now close your eyes," Sylvio instructed, stretching out his arm to touch her fingertips; he could feel her power. Semele's breathing slowed and she squeezed her eyes shut, wanting so much to believe.

Sylvio spoke in a voice like silk, as Semele prepared for an adventure of the mind.

"Now...picture wintertime in Central Park...not the way it is today... visualize an open space where people gather to celebrate a winter's night. There are no automobiles...no yellow cabs or flashing billboards...picture a time of horse-drawn carriages gliding across a bed of crusted snow. A few children are building a snowman...further inside the park, several men are tending to a bonfire..." Semele took in a deep breath as she tried to picture a different time, but could feel her mind struggling to disengage from the modern world.

"The bonfire is roaring hot now...and there is laughter in the air. Open up your mind...feel the heat as you hold your hands out to the flames..."

"I smell smoke!" Semele said in disbelief, but she kept her eyes closed.

"Now...tell me what you *see*."

"I see people in the snow, uncle...it's blurry though...I can't see them clearly..."

"Concentrate...I know you can do it!"

"It's getting clearer now...I see them...horse-drawn carriages with lanterns to light the way..."

"Now *listen* child...listen for the sound of their voices..."

"I hear bells, uncle...I hear the sound of sleigh bells!" Semele exclaimed; her eyes snapped open to find a winter's night in 1894. She gasped when she saw a full view of Central Park; all the modern buildings she knew so well had simply vanished. In the distance was the Museum of Natural History; it was clearly visible from the rooftop, which seemed impossible.

"Where are the buildings?" she asked but already knew the answer; they hadn't been built yet.

"These are shadows of what once was...Emily Parrish is here tonight with her mother. She is keeping a terrible secret."

"Where is she? They're all too far away to see their faces."

"I will take you into the park so we can see them up close...we will be invisible to those around us."

Once inside the park, Semele was amazed to see the Dakota standing on its own; she had never realized the history behind Sylvio's residence.

"That's Emily over there." Sylvio pointed to a striking blonde. Semele's mouth hung open; it was her crying ghost.

"Uncle...tell me how she died?"

"There was a very wealthy gentleman who once lived in our building...during Emily's time. The girl was hired as a tutor to his son, but a romance developed and..."

"I'm not *that* naïve, you know...he got her pregnant, right?"

"Possibly, but no one really knows for sure. She fell down a spiral staircase and was killed. I'm not sure why, but... Emily has haunted my apartment for as long as I can remember."

"It looks like she's waiting for someone..." Semele said thoughtfully.

"He's not coming."

"Look...over there. An empty sleigh!" Sylvio saw his opportunity, so they jumped into the red leather seat. With a crack of the whip, they flew up the hill away from the crowd. It was a magical night for sure; Semele sighed as she took in the sights and sounds of a bygone era.

They were being chased now; likely someone trying to rescue the runaway sleigh. Sylvio pulled back on the reigns to stop the sleigh, and they both jumped out. Two strapping teenage boys arrived, breathless from exertion and took control of the abandoned sleigh. The young men's faces had the smoothness of untainted youth, and their eyes sparkled with the pure joy of a brisk winter night; the kind of night that provided comfortable memories when old age took away everything else.

"Semele...I need to explain something before we go."

"It sounds serious," Semele said lightly.

"It is...tonight, I wanted you to have a great adventure, but I brought you here for another reason too."

"What other reason could there be?" She was confused.

"I need you to understand...you have the ability to leave the modern world...I'm talking about a place of safety, if something should happen to me."

"Are you saying I could actually hide in another time?"

"Exactly...but there's something else. When I have travel to another time like this, I am usually invisible...but not always."

"You mean sometimes people see you?" Semele was intrigued by this idea.

"Mostly children...they are more receptive to it, I guess."

"Perhaps they thought *you* were a ghost," Semele replied, taking his hand.

"I hope you'll never need to hide from anyone, but unexpected things can happen. When you travel back in time, you are untouchable by anyone...except another vampire."

"I don't ever want to go anywhere unless you go too."

"I hope you never have to."

"Uncle...can we go back to 1976 now? I'm hungry." Sylvio nodded in agreement. Since they were mere shadows here, they could fly back to their gargoyles in human form; hand-carved statues welcomed them back with Halloween smiles. The wind carried them back to the Dakota's rooftop, but the moment they landed, the spell was broken; the sound of uptown traffic confirmed they had returned to the modern world.

Emily Parrish looked around. She couldn't believe no one else had seen them, the albino girl and the strangely dressed man. The man believed they were invisible, but not to her. Who were they? They looked familiar, but she couldn't be sure. Emily Parrish knew one thing for certain, neither one of them was human.

CHAPTER 138 - A HOME ON THE HUDSON - OLANA - (SEPTEMBER 1976)

Eva watched as the sun disappeared behind Rip Van Winkle's fabled mountain. The Catskill Mountains had already become a familiar landscape; in this wonderful place, Eva felt optimistic about the future. When Dracula first told her about Olana, Eva was skeptical; all that changed when she finally saw it. Dracula brought her here one summer night, and Eva found herself immediately bewitched by its majesty. It would be lovely to live in luxury again; Eva was tired of being chased from one place to another. Compared to this, the Doral was a fleabag! According to Jack, Olana was abandoned from dusk to dawn; what a perfect refuge for creatures of the night! All they had to do was leave before dawn, after clearing away any trace of their presence.

During daylight hours, Dracula and Jack took their rest in Sleepy Hollow Cemetery. They used the Archbold Mausoleum; Eva learned it was closed to tourists, and therefore, a safe choice. The seasoned vampires spent their daylight hours inside a borrowed tomb; it was deadly quiet, except during tourist season. After Halloween, most people lost interest in graveyards; even in a town whose only claim to fame was their legendary headless horseman.

Eva stood in the bell tower; a gentle wind caressed her face as she watched the sky. The soothing sound of crickets told her Dracula would arrive soon. Eva could already feel his presence, as a veil of darkness slowly consumed the last remnants of the day. In the past few months, she had become disenchanted by the city she once loved fiercely; maybe it was just the oppressive atmosphere of Tunneltown. The moon was a shimmering orb as it rose above the mountain; it claimed the sky with a gentle grace. Eva was glad to feel the weather turning cooler; autumn meant early sunsets and longer nights to be savored, like fine wine.

Dracula came up behind her; Eva could feel him before he touched her. She turned to face him, as a coyote cried out to the new moon. Dracula sniffed at the air, as several more cries rang out. His furrowed brow told Eva he sensed possible danger.

"What is it, Vlad?"

"I thought I caught a scent of something…"

"Wolves used to frighten me…not anymore."

"They're coyotes…not wolves, although there's little difference, except their size. The sounds of the wild are soothing to me, the noise of midtown traffic, not so much." Dracula moved to kiss her neck, under a moon much brighter than usual.

In the distance, a white wolf waited for the coyote pack to move away from the house. He wanted to get a little closer to Dracula's new residence. He knew of Olana; it had been abandoned for years before being declared an historical landmark in the 1960s. Sylvio couldn't help but be impressed at the clever hiding place they discovered. The countess had come out onto the balcony earlier, no doubt to watch the last bit of color drain from the sky. Eva seemed content; she was obviously with these two vampires by choice. He had done his duty. Countess Bathory was safe and accounted for. It was time to go, before Dracula caught his scent.

Jack was always last to wake from his daytime slumber. His dreams were full of blood, and the decayed faces of his unfortunate victims; these images made Jack's fingers twitch as he slept. He had been thinking more and more about resurrecting the Ripper; he missed the sadistic pleasure of tearing human flesh. Little by little, the beast living inside was clawing its way back out. Jack's demons had begun to catch up with him; he needed to start killing again. He craved the scent of humans up close, and the joy of drinking from an open neck. Jack could no longer fight his true nature. It was becoming stronger every day, perhaps exacerbated by his mentoring of a would-be serial killer. There was another thing fueling his burning rage; Dracula was slowly pulling away from him, and seemed almost brainwashed by his new love. Jack never realized how annoying it was, to be around a vampire in love; Eva was no better, with her sickening display of unrelenting adoration. Dracula was losing his edge and all desire for carnage; all he wanted to do lately was play house. Jack was beginning to feel like a third wheel here, just as the Dark One predicted. The ironic thing was Olana had been his home; now *he* felt like an outsider. He had no real beef with either of them; the problem was their love only magnified his abject loneliness.

Jack approached them as they embraced on the balcony, coughing politely to announce his presence. They smiled at him with love in their eyes; it took every ounce of his inner strength to suppress a snarl. Some nights it bothered him so much, he went off on his own; it was the perfect opportunity to spend some time grooming a serial killer. It was his secret and he guarded it closely. Jack didn't feel obligated to account to them for everything he did. He was a vampire, after all; vampires *killed people!*

CHAPTER 139 - MAKING OF A SERIAL KILLER - (OCTOBER 23, 1976)

David held the gun, consumed by an uncontrollable urge to kill. Harvey was doing it; that dog wanted him to strike again. He used to hate that dog; but lately, David had started to believe it was his only friend. After years of being ridiculed and ignored by women, he would finally have a chance to punish them. Harvey was going to help him.

Jack couldn't stand the stench of living inside the dog; it was worse than drinking blood from intoxicated victims. At last, his protégé was ready to come into his own; it was all because of him. Jack schooled him in developing his own modus operandi, which he explained to David, was critical if he expected to succeed. He gave him pointers on how to come at victims from behind, and helped bolster his absolute hatred of women. Jack also suggested David write letters to police after each kill; taunting police was half the fun of being a serial killer. The more time Jack spent mentoring the young man, the stronger his urge to start killing again became. The seasoned vampire couldn't help but wonder, if that had been the Dark One's plan all along.

Right on schedule, Berkowitz came outside, zipping up his windbreaker as he approached the metal fence. His Bulldog revolver was tucked into a deep pants pocket; he liked the comfort of its weight against his leg. Harvey was in the yard, waiting for him with red eyes David no longer feared. He tossed a dog biscuit over the fence; Jack played along and ate the tasteless thing. David leaned over the fence, as the black dog told him about a place called Browne Park; it was there he would find his next victim.

As it turned out, David Berkowitz failed miserably that night. He wounded two women, but that was all. Luckily for his protégé, neither woman could remember anything about their attacker. Jack cursed when he read about the botched attack in the newspaper. He was going to have to show him how to do it.

CHAPTER 140 - THE DARK ONE

Of course, Jack was correct in his assumptions. There was never a real plan to use young Berkowitz as a decoy for police; the Dark One's strategy had been to push Jack into killing again. Once that happened, it didn't matter whether Berkowitz continued his crime spree or not. For what it had in mind, only a vampire would do.

The Dark One was quite satisfied with how things were turning out. Jack was steps away from resuming his role as the *Ripper*, and Sylvio was leaving his own trail of corpses strewn about the city. Naturally, all of this meant the NYPD was being kept sufficiently busy; too busy to follow up on erroneous reports of vampire activity near Bryant Park. The Dark One would have preferred Sylvio be more discreet with his corpses; but it was no worse than a killer from Yonkers, who thus far, proved a very poor marksman.

Sylvio was the kind of vampire who needed to kill humans; he particularly enjoyed targeting handsome gay men. The Dark One found it amusing Sylvio's escapades had already earned him a nickname. The evil entity also knew about Sylvio's growing affection for Semele; it was the very thing it hoped for, when it brought them together. What a surprise it was to discover the Egyptian vampire had a heart, after all. The Dark One had found Sylvio's Achilles heel; its power over the handsome vampire was complete. Sometimes things just had a way of falling into place.

Sylvio was dressed to fit the era in which he found himself temporarily confined. Despite his dislike of modern fashion, he always stood out in a crowd. The sidewalks in Times Square were packed with an ever-growing number of tourists; Sylvio was annoyed to see many stores already decorated for Christmas. He focused on the young man walking a few paces in front of him; the vampire gracefully wove through the crowd, keeping his target in sight. The man was surely gay, he could tell by the way he carried himself; Sylvio was rarely wrong about such things.

The young man changed direction, and Sylvio realized he was hailing a cab; this fit into his plans perfectly. The vampire watched the man's hand go up; Sylvio slipped behind him to do the same. A black and yellow taxi screeched to a stop. As the man ducked into the empty cab, Sylvio pushed his way inside, coming face to face with his unsuspecting prey.

"I'm terribly sorry," Sylvio said in his most genteel tone. "It looks like we both hailed the same cab...where are you going?"

"To Bloomingdales," the man answered. He relaxed when he noted Sylvio's easy smile.

"Well, then...to Bloomingdales it is."

The man appeared shy and didn't offer his name. After a few minutes, the vampire moved a bit closer to the stranger; the man didn't move away. The cabdriver watched them in his rearview mirror and rolled his eyes; I hope they don't start making out, he thought. By the time they made it to Fifth Avenue, the two were locked in an embrace.

Sylvio was intoxicated by the stranger's scent; it was musky and full of promise. When the man reached for his groin, the vampire felt his hunger become unbearable. He nudged the man's cheek moving closer to his neck; Sylvio was desperate to calm a burning need that had nothing to do with sex. The man moaned with pleasure as Sylvio licked playfully at his neck, before piercing it with his razor sharp teeth. The man squealed for a moment, before his body went limp. The cabby glanced in his rearview mirror, but could no longer see them; he couldn't wait to get rid of these two lovebirds. When they reached the main entrance to Bloomingdales, the cabdriver turned around to find Sylvio inches from his face. His red eyes were terrifying; behind them, the cabby saw the very gates of hell. The vampire slipped a twenty into the cabdriver's palm; the man switched on the *Off Duty* sign, without even realizing he was doing so.

"Now…you will remember nothing about what you saw tonight. There was never a second passenger…just my poor friend here, who is apparently indisposed…" Sylvio flashed the cabdriver a ghoulish smile full of bloodied teeth.

"But what do I tell…" Sylvio grabbed the man's throat.

"Now, let's try this again. You will remember nothing about what you saw tonight…not my face or even that I rode in your cab…now, say it!" Sylvio hissed, as he loosened his hold.

"Nothing…I will remember nothing…," the cabby croaked, as his eyes glazed over.

Carefully wiping his mouth with a monogrammed handkerchief, Sylvio stepped out onto the sidewalk and decided to walk back to Tunneltown. Thanks to Semele, he knew exactly how to get in; it was well past time to meet the legendary vampire. Sylvio had only seen Dracula from a distance and found himself more than a little intrigued; it would be a pleasure to meet someone he could easily consider a peer. He was older than Dracula but, alas, there were still classes even among creatures of the night; it was hard to beat a Romanian prince. He would show the ancient vampire proper respect; it was much better to have the count as a friend, than as a foe.

As luck would have it, Dracula had not yet left to go hunting. He and Nikos were currently engaged in a heated conversation about a recent outbreak of vampire-style killings; Sylvio's crime spree was creating a stir already. The Egyptian vampire felt no guilt about taking human lives rationalizing, it was necessary for his survival. Sylvio made a habit of killing his prey, to avoid leaving eyewitnesses behind; a vampire, who expected to live for centuries, could hardly afford to show compassion.

"Vlad…the *Post* and the *Daily News* are calling him the *Curbside*

Killer. Bodies drained of blood and carelessly left out in the open...such brazen actions are dangerous!"

"Have any witnesses come forward?"

"None...all the killings happened inside cabs," Nikos replied.

"And the cabdrivers...what do they have to say?"

"That's the strange part...none of the cabdrivers can remember anything. One driver claimed he was hypnotized...you and I both know vampires are proficient at hypnosis."

"True...it could be a rogue fledgling though...why not let the Van Helsings take care of it," Dracula suggested.

"What if the culprit is closer to home, Vlad?"

"You think it's Jack?" Dracula asked.

"Who else could it be?"

"Jack hasn't killed a human since he lost his arm. If he *were* killing again, he would dispose of corpses with more efficiency."

Sylvio hated his bat-like form because it made him feel vulnerable; unfortunately, it was necessary in order to make his grand entrance into Tunneltown. Semele told him exactly where to enter so he would arrive in their living quarters, after swearing Sylvio to secrecy. Semele explained about the artist, the night-gowned woman and the street children who all enjoyed Dracula's protection. She also told him about the Van Helsings and their truce, most of which Sylvio already knew. What he wanted most was to uncover Dracula's lair and his secrets. He felt compelled to see how another vampire of wealth and status chose to live. Sylvio reached the library rooftop and with one last look around, descended down an unused coal chute to meet the infamous Count Vlad Dracula.

They all heard Sylvio coming, and watched as a cream-colored bat swirled above their heads. In a puff of smoke, the bat gracefully morphed into a chiseled vampire. He had a pronounced widow's peak, and his chocolate-brown eyes were rimmed in silver. Dracula turned away from Nikos and drew a loaded pistol from his belt. Sylvio held up his hands to show he was unarmed.

"Pardon my method of introduction...Count Dracula," Sylvio said, before bowing to Dracula respectfully.

"How did you know where to find us?" Nikos demanded, still holding his weapon.

Dracula remained silent, but moved closer to their guest and began circling him; he sniffed at the air to confirm that this was indeed, a very powerful vampire. Sylvio stood his ground, after years in the wilderness, his canine instincts were very strong and he was not easily intimidated.

"I certainly hope you're not going to piss on my Italian loafers," Sylvio said finally; his words sent Dracula into a fit of uncontrollable laughter.

"I think I like you!" Dracula exclaimed, as he clasped Sylvio by the shoulders in welcome.

"May we sit down…please? I would like to explain why I came."

"Very well," Dracula replied as they moved to a well-used table. He held up an open bottle of his special blend, but Sylvio waved it away.

"As you've already surmised…like you, I am a creature of the night… turned as a young man in ancient Egypt," Sylvio explained. He would be very selective about what he revealed; of course, they could never know about Semele.

"It is a privilege to meet a vampire older than myself…I imagine you could teach me much," Dracula said, appearing awestruck. Nikos glared at their uninvited guest with obvious contempt.

"Let me speak plainly…I was largely responsible for assisting Eva… the countess, with her escape from the Manson family. It was a sorted business. Out of respect for your position in the vampire community, I wanted to ensure she got home safely." Sylvio was a master at embellishing a story to make himself look like a hero.

"We appreciate that very much…Mister…?"

"Excuse my rudeness…my given name comes from an ancient alphabet…I never use it. Everyone just calls me Sylvio."

"Well, Sylvio…I appreciate what you did. You are an honorable representation of our kind," Dracula replied, extending his hand.

"And your reason for showing up here…uninvited?" Prince asked, moving to join them at the table. Like, Nikos, he didn't trust too easily.

"I was determined to make sure the countess was safe, but then I found out she wasn't living here…." Nikos cut Sylvio off.

"Where the countess resides is none of your business!"

"I needed to see for myself where she had gone…it took me awhile, but I eventually figured out where she went," Sylvio countered.

"And how was that possible…did you stalk her?" Prince asked.

"Let's just say…I'm resourceful. I knew she was living outside the city; from there, it was a process of elimination. I must say, your mountain retreat is quite lovely…such a clever hiding place…"

"So, you know about Olana!" Dracula felt violated, but not really angry.

"You've been spying on us!" Prince accused with narrowed eyes.

"Not at all. I only went to Olana to confirm the countess was living there…she never even saw me. I had to confirm she was safe, and in good company."

"Sounds like a fishy story, to me," Nikos said, stepping closer to their guest.

Can I be candid with you, then?" Sylvio replied; it was time for a little "ass-kissing."

"All of us would appreciate that very much," Nikos said his arms folded across his chest.

"Honestly, I'm here tonight because I wanted to meet you in person, Count Dracula. What happened with the countess, just gave me an excuse to pay you a visit; although it's true I rescued her from Manson. You can ask her yourself. …I can be devious at times, but I just had to meet you. To our kind, you are a god…the one who started it all. I come to you this night…as an ally and a friend." Sylvio bowed once more, as if to confirm his sincerity.

"I'm unsure how I feel about you knowing so much about us; we know so little about you. In regard to the countess, I do thank you for your valiant efforts."

"We *are* blood brothers, after all." Sylvio replied.

"Fair enough…we will consider you an ally then." Prince moved to shake Sylvio's hand.

"Now, if you'll excuse me, I have a rather pressing need," Dracula said, as he prepared to meet a crescent moon.

"Perhaps someday, I could meet your friend Jack…I am an expert hunter of game," Sylvio replied.

"As is Jack," Prince replied, he was warming up the Egyptian vampire.

"Ah-h-h…of course, he is a natural-born killer," Sylvio replied, and then showed off by vaporizing before their eyes.

"Wow…can you do that?" Alice asked Dracula. She had been eavesdropping on their conversation and witnessed Sylvio's unorthodox departure.

"I'll have to give it a try real soon," Dracula answered with a wink. He only vaporized when there was no other option for escape; it was a talent most vampires used with discretion.

Sylvio decided his meeting with Dracula had gone exceedingly well. He presented himself as a benevolent and cultured vampire; he knew right away they would hit it off. No doubt about it, the count was practically an Adonis. Few rivaled Sylvio as this one did, but this fact would only serve to keep him on his toes. His main objective tonight had been to befriend the inhabitants of Tunneltown; he might someday need an ally or even a hiding place.

Sylvio was luckier than most vampires; he enjoyed a comfortable lifestyle, through careful investment strategies and an occasional burglary. Sylvio had a thing for stealing fine jewelry, and would have continued, but one night, he almost got caught. After that, he decided it was time to find another way to supplement his income. A few weeks later, Sylvio was approached by a two men, who claimed they needed a translator. The pay they offered was too good to turn down; Sylvio had a gambling habit to feed. They all shook hands, and then the taller man thrust an envelope at him; they had a deal. At first, all Sylvio did was translate correspondence, and act as a messenger boy; after a few months, he was given more assignments. After a year, Sylvio was charged with managing several operatives in the field; unfortunately, he never took the time to learn a whole lot about his employer's ideology. Sylvio had inadvertently joined a war against Western civilization.

Sylvio glanced at his pocket watch, one he'd carried off and on since the late nineteenth century. It was refreshing to be reacquainted with his belongings, after such a long time in the wild. On the next corner he recognized the bodega, and found the place with little trouble. Sylvio pulled out his extra set of keys, and made sure he had his wallet. There were two locks and a deadbolt, so by the time the door was opened, his associates were in defense mode.

"*Marhaba…Abdal*," said Kamil, lowering his weapon; Abdal was the name Sylvio used for his special assignments, it was one of many.

"*Marhabtain*…please, let's speak English," Sylvio said, taking a seat facing the two men.

"It has become unsafe for you to remain here…in the city."

"Abdal?" Kamil absolutely hated the idea of relocating.

"Listen to what I say…we need to move everything to the outer boroughs. Our associates have arranged two new places we can use… one in Queens and the other is located in Yonkers. I will get you more details in a few days."

"Yonkers!" Kamil replied distastefully.

Sylvio stood up and glared at both of them, as he pulled out a large wad of cash. He counted it again and split it between them; they snatched the money up and were suddenly more amenable.

"It will be better this way…the places we found are in more remote areas. There is no immediate call for any action at this time…your only task is to build and safeguard the growing arsenal."

"Whatever you wish, Abdal," Kamil replied.

"When you get to the new location, you will continue to acquire weapons and ammunition but slowly…no quantities or items that would draw too much attention…a gun here or there…ammunition at sporting goods stores or gun shows only. Basically, just keep buying discreetly… but stay under the radar. This is your country for the next twenty years, so follow the Quran. Marry and multiply. Our best weapon will be in our numbers over the years to come." Sylvio gave instructions based on a document he had been asked to memorize.

"So, there are no immediate plans for an attack, Abdal?" asked Abbud, who was disappointed; he wanted to fight, not start a family!

"This is a war we will only win by increasing our numbers; arterially alone won't be enough. It is your responsibility to continue the legacy; you must start families and raise strong sons to fight alongside you. One day it will be American women and children who bleed and beg for mercy in the streets." Sylvio improvised his speech, based on directives he received from those who employed his services. Abbud and Kamil nodded with mock enthusiasm, anxious for him to leave so they could commiserate about having to live in Yonkers.

CHAPTER 142 - RUPERT - MIDTOWN MANHATTAN - (NOVEMBER 23, 1976)

He followed the man as he walked down 39ᵗʰ Street, leaving ample distance between them. Thanksgiving was tomorrow, and Sidewalk Santa's had already started to make their appearance. He despised everything about Christmas, but these most of all. Rupert pushed his way through the crowd, making sure he didn't lose sight of him; the tall, dark man had just left the library. This was no ordinary vampire; he carried himself well, exuding both confidence and sexuality. Rupert stayed on his tail, curious to see where he was going. The man stopped and Rupert flattened himself against a brick wall, not even daring to breathe. The tall man started walking again, but Rupert remained still until the gap between them widened. He continued tracking the vampire, careful to stay close to the buildings so he wouldn't be spotted. An old woman with a shopping cart hustled by, muttering under her breath. The tall man turned to look behind him, and Rupert froze.

The vampire glared at Rupert with the red eyes, hissing through sharp white teeth, "I could smell you a mile away...*black swan!* Be gone, or I will finish the job and make you one of our kind!"

Rupert stood transfixed by the eyes of evil; strangely he was not afraid.

"Well, black swan...what do you have to say for yourself?" Sylvio demanded. He took a few steps closer to Rupert, who appeared mesmerized.

Rupert finally snapped out of it. "You are very much like him...are you one of Dracula's unfortunate progeny?"

"Not even a remote possibility...why do you follow me?"

"I've never seen you before...you're not one of them," Rupert said, as Sylvio stepped out of the shadows. The vampire was even more handsome than Count Dracula; he had cold, silvery eyes that were void of compassion.

"If by *one of them*, you mean the residents of Tunneltown...you are correct. I suspect you're following me to see if I might be that killer...

you know, the *Curbside Killer*," Sylvio answered, taking in the delicious scent of Rupert's blood.

"Funny…the thought had crossed my mind…" Rupert was cut off, as Sylvio pounced on him, knocking his prey to the ground. The vampire subdued Rupert and dragged him behind a dumpster; he would rid Tunneltown of this nuisance, once and for all. The vampire hunter begged for mercy, as Sylvio plunged his teeth into Rupert's exposed neck. He would make this black swan a creature of the night; it was time he learned what it felt like to become the hunted. Rupert tried to twist away from Sylvio, but was no match for the seasoned vampire. Rupert's heartbeat slowed, but was still pumping when he lost consciousness. Sylvio stopped drinking and slapped his victim's face; he wanted Rupert to fully comprehend his fate.

"Wake up now…that's right. Now listen to me! I am going to feed you now…so you may know the curse of bloodlust." Sylvio used a pointed fingernail to slice his arm.

Rupert tried to scream, but found he couldn't; he gasped for air, only to get a mouthful of Sylvio's blood instead. There was no going back now; he would never walk in sunshine again. This was his last human thought, before his body surrendered itself to the night. Sylvio stood up and watched, as Rupert's clawed at the air, his scrawny limbs twisting in a most unnatural way. When the transformation was complete, Rupert crawled toward Sylvio with his bloodied mouth; at last justice had been served! Sylvio had taken all that was human from the leader of the Van Helsings, and made him the very thing he hunted. He would let Rupert discover the pain of a hunger that burned much stronger than anything he had ever known. This fledgling didn't deserve any guidance from him. The real punishment would be in finding he no longer had allies; Rupert was now an enemy to both humans and vampires. Taking one last look around to make sure no one was watching, Sylvio assumed his bat-like form and headed back uptown to his comfortable penthouse.

The scent of garbage was strong, making it hard to breathe. Rupert felt a stabbing pain in the pit of his stomach; this was a very different kind of hunger. He was a vampire now, but would have to hide it; otherwise, the Van Helsings would surely turn on him. They had only accepted Jack because he led them to Dracula; Rupert had nothing to bargain with. Sylvio had left him to fend for himself, but Rupert wasn't worried; he knew just about everything there was to know about vampires. Unfortunately, nothing prepared him for the physical pain of wanting blood; he would need to feed soon, or risk losing everything.

Chapter 143 - Son of Sam - (February 1977)

Jack was done with that idiot, David Berkowitz. Instead of leaving a trail of corpses, this "Son of Sam" was leaving his victims alive; eventually this would do him in. Jack had really tried to help him at first; it was he who suggested using a nickname, like Jack had during his illustrious career in Whitechapel. Berkowitz had written some letters to a newspaper columnist named Jimmy Breslin; even this had been Jack's idea. Either way, the public was both fascinated and frightened by a vicious killer who targeted young women. So far, the police had no leads. Surprisingly, his protégé had become a recent sensation, likely due to the deranged content of his written correspondence, as published by the *Daily News*. Jack was more than satisfied that young Berkowitz was on his way to notoriety, and no longer needed his help. The seasoned vampire had better things to do, such as learning how to hone his skills as a one-armed killer. Jack liked the sound of it; maybe he needed a new nickname.

An hour later he was out of breath, exhilarated to have finally killed again. Jack's unwitting victim was a young man by modern standards; he hadn't even planned on killing tonight, but when an intoxicated human tried to mug a vampire, what else could he expect? Tonight, he came to the amazing realization that his missing arm misled others about his physical strength; Jack's handicap allowed him to catch his victims off guard. After a fresh kill, Jack felt renewed; his bloodlust had been buried for a long while, and it was time to reawaken the raging beast. The dead man's blood had been sweet, likely because the poor fellow hadn't scraped up enough money for his nightly bottle of Thunderbird. His rheumy eyes stared up at Jack with something like surprise, the moment before he opened his throat. The vampire stood over the bloody corpse; adrenalin pumped wildly through his veins. With a shaking hand, Jack lit a cigarette to calm his nerves. This time he would leave the corpse for the police to discover; if the *Curbside Killer* could do it, then so could he. Adjusting his clothes, Jack turned and headed toward Tunneltown for a visit with his family, before heading to Olana, for a night of hunting. There would be three of them tonight; Dracula had invited the Egyptian vampire to live with them at Olana.

Sylvio didn't hesitate to accept the invitation; Dracula made the offer without consulting the others, pointing out they had plenty of room. Eva finally agreed, because she knew Dracula enjoyed his company. Jack had warmed up to Sylvio, but found himself feeling inadequate at times; they were both so worldly, compared to him. Eva found Sylvio charming, but whenever they were alone, he always managed to stand a little too close. Did Dracula know they shared a bed, when they lived together on the mountain? She always thought their relationship remained chaste; but Eva's dreams, were anything but. Sometimes, when no one else was looking, Sylvio shot her a knowing glance, making her wonder what had really happened in that cave. The countess had no idea Sylvio fantasized about her, but not in the way she thought. In his fantasy, Eva would be begging like a dog at his feet; he would buy her a diamond-studded neck collar, nothing was too good for a countess. But, of course, Sylvio couldn't go anywhere near her; he would have to seek such pleasures elsewhere.

After hunting together the first night Sylvio arrived, Jack took him to Sleepy Hollow Cemetery, offering him an empty crypt for his daytime slumber. Sylvio only stayed occasionally, but over time, his enjoyment of being with like company took over, and he left Semele with Eadric more and more. Sylvio was a very selfish vampire. Despite having deep affection for his fledgling, he had always been one to indulge his impulses; Sylvio needed constant stimulation and couldn't be tied down to any kind of routine. He justified his absences by ensuring Eadric had access to whatever it took to keep Semele happy. And just like that, Sylvio pushed away his old life, including his fledgling, so he could spend time doing what made him happy.

Olana was a wonderful reminder of the nineteenth century; the lavishly furnished estate made Sylvio feel like royalty. The grounds were surrounded by lush green forest; the estate itself was artfully placed high above the Hudson River. Miles and miles of dense forest all around, allowed the vampires to indulge their most savage inclinations. Sylvio was comfortable spending evenings in such a glorious place; it had been a long time since he consorted with others like him. The Egyptian vampire also enjoyed the camaraderie they shared after hunting; the three of them would tell stories, one more outlandish than the other. Sometimes Eva stayed to listen, but most nights she let them have their time together; she would share her lover's bed at some point before dawn. For Sylvio, life outside the city in this wide open place was like a dream and frankly, he just wasn't ready to wake up yet.

CHAPTER 144 - A TIME OF TRANQUILITY - (1977 - 1993)

After nearly ten years, Tunneltown remained a comfortable and safe home for New York City's growing vampire community. Most of those who lived under the library were sired by Dracula or were his descendants; the rest were Jack's progeny. Because of Dracula's meticulous plans to make vampires of powerful men in all areas of law enforcement, there was little need for concern their hiding place would ever be discovered. Jack had been an integral part of their plan; he turned street thugs into loyal and often vicious vampires who served Dracula, and his unconventional family. In addition to those who were turned, the inhabitants of Tunneltown also enjoyed protection from humans, who had been persuaded to serve the vampire community; some were motivated by financial compensation, while others were blackmailed into submission.

Tunneltown was now Jack's home again; when he showed up for frequent visits, everyone was happy to see him. Prince was always first to greet him; since their reunion on New Year's Eve, the two had rekindled their friendship. Oliver and Alice were older now, not in their bodies but in their minds. Oliver's face had matured, yet his skin was still smooth and wrinkle free. Alice was still a fresh-faced girl, but she wore makeup now; not so long ago, she was jumping into Jack's arms. The black swans were a bit reserved, but seemed to adore Virginia; they lived in a sheltered world and remained childlike, despite their advancing age. For this, Virginia was thankful; nurturing the children was what she lived for.

A harsh winter gave way to a brutally hot summer so severe; the city suffered a total blackout in mid-July. The following month, the NYPD finally caught the .44 caliber killer, known as *Son of Sam aka David Berkowitz*. The city breathed a collective sigh of relief, despite knowing another killer would soon take his place; New Yorkers were used to sleeping with one eye open. As the years passed, the vampire community continued to flourish, and this included expansion of the West Coast community. Not surprisingly, Sylvio had a hand in that, too.

The 1980s brought new ideas, new fashions and increasing technology; as America approached the 1990s, a new threat emerged, igniting a conflict in the Persian Gulf. The U.S. suffered some casualties, but at least, the fighting was overseas. Through it all, Tunneltown remained a secret and the vampire community continued to thrive.

The Dark One remained in the background, as human time passed with painful slowness. The evil entity had plenty of souls to corrupt and command; it was constantly engaged in driving human beings to commit acts of violence against one another. There was no rest for the devil, or any who served him.

Chapter 145 - A Different Kind of Enemy - (February 26, 1993)

A vampire's twilight slumber is bottomless, floating on wings of black velvet; sometimes their dreams were so vivid, creatures of the night often awoke ready for battle. There weren't many things that could wake a vampire when the sun was out, except danger or extreme hunger. At exactly12:17PM, Dracula woke with a start inside his crypt, sensing something terrible had happened. Although he felt no personal danger, the seasoned vampire had a premonition his world was about to be turned upside down. Dracula sensed the sun was still high in the sky, so he closed his eyes once again, slipping into a dreamless sleep that was, unfortunately, short-lived.

"Vlad," a voice whispered in the darkness. Dracula sprang from his tomb, clawing wildly at the air until he saw Nikos; his loyal friend was trying to tell him something.

"What is it?" Dracula asked in a hushed tone; Jack slept soundly in a crypt next to his own.

"Something has happened...about two hours ago. I came to tell you as soon as I could." Nikos tried to temper his voice, and to keep his lifelong friend calm.

"I knew I felt something...tell me!" Dracula demanded, now fully awake and squinting at a ray of sunlight that streamed across the room between them.

"It's the World Trade Center...they set off a bomb...and," Nikos couldn't speak fast enough for Dracula.

"Which building?" Dracula asked impatiently.

"The North Tower...the damage seems minimal...a few lives lost... lots of injuries, though." Nikos didn't know any more than what he had seen on the news. The whole city was in a state of shock.

"Are my children safe?"

"Yes...Prince is handling things in Tunneltown during my absence...authorities know very little. It appears to be the work of a terrorist organization, operating out of the Middle East somewhere."

"A radical religious group, then?"

"It appears so…they used a moving van to set off a bomb in the North Tower's basement…I guess they thought the bomb would decimate both buildings." Nikos was suddenly short of breath.

"But why, Nikos?"

"Who knows with these religious fanatics…from what I've read…" Nikos was cut off. Jack woke and threw the cover off his crypt.

"What's the matter?" Jack asked, observing their serious expressions.

"A bombing in Manhattan…the World Trade Center," Nikos replied matter-of-factly.

"Those bastards!"

"As I was explaining to Vlad…the damage is minimal…a failed attempt with some collateral damage…it could have been much worse."

"And Tunneltown?" Jack asked.

"All fine…I came to tell you what happened, but also to advise it might be best to stay up here for the next few days. NYPD and SWAT teams are swarming neighborhoods, looking for accomplices."

"And where is Sylvio?" Jack asked Dracula, when he observed his open crypt.

"Said he couldn't stay last night…had something to do," Dracula replied defensively. In his eyes, Sylvio could do no wrong.

"Seems a little too convenient…how well do you trust him, Vlad?" Nikos asked.

"Well enough to believe he would never be part of such a thing… just a coincidence that he didn't sleep here last night," Dracula insisted, but there was a shadow of doubt he couldn't ignore.

"Well, then…let's hope you're right," Nikos replied.

Police Chief Daly wasn't ready to retire yet, but rules were rules. He would be fifty-five next month; that meant a gold watch and a pension for life. He had gone into law enforcement right out of high school, and worked his way up the ladder; he was promoted to police chief seven years ago. The recent bombing attempt at the World Trade Center affected him deeply; as it did most New Yorkers. Granted, the poorly executed bomb plot had been deemed a failure, but there were still human casualties. Ramzi Yousef, who claimed to be the mastermind, had been arrested yesterday, after confessing to the whole thing; he claimed it was retaliation for U.S. interference in the Middle East. By all accounts, the police did an outstanding job in apprehending the suspect; however the F.B.I. concluded this attempt was too well coordinated to be the act of a single perpetrator. The F.B.I. faced a tremendous challenge in the days ahead; the arrest of one man hardly made New York neighborhoods any safer. The heinous attack on the World Trade Center had been a meticulously planned; it likely involved a network of individuals, who were hell-bent on destroying the American dream of democracy and religious freedom. A devout Catholic, Daly found it difficult to comprehend the ideals of those who were driven to commit mass murder, especially those willing to sacrifice their lives in the name of Islam. From what Daly had read, it almost seemed Islam was a religion at war with the world, and at times, even with itself. The extremists were dangerous people who firmly believed religious indifference was a violation of their faith; this made them a formidable enemy. Terrorism was certainly not a new threat, and for America, it was fast becoming a painful reality; it involved combat with an invisible foe. Daly was old-school, preferring to face criminals head on; these days, the city's greatest threat appeared to operate from anonymous locations, frequently catching law enforcement off guard and woefully unprepared.

Daly sat back in his swivel chair to take a sip of bitter coffee; he didn't drink it for the taste. The F.B.I. had pretty much taken over the investigation; however, each precinct within the city limits was tasked with what was referred to as a "neighborhood cleanup." Police Chief Daly knew what this meant, scouring the streets and homeless shelters looking for anyone who didn't fit in. Daly would start compiling a few search teams this afternoon; it was always a good idea to cooperate with the F.B.I.

It was nearly lunchtime; the police chief was extremely regimented about his meals. Daly was a big man; he'd married a gourmet cook and didn't mind being referred to as portly. He had a little time to spare before lunch, so Daly decided to tackle the file cabinet he had been meaning to finish cleaning out all week. His assistant, Cindy, emptied all but one drawer; she explained there were some old files he needed to sort through, before she just tossed them out. Bending down to open the drawer, Daly could really feel his age. He ignored his sore back, as he picked up the red accordion folder and brought it back to his desk. He knew the file well; it had belonged to his friend and mentor, Police Chief Manuel Rodriguez; he had passed away from lung cancer a few years back. Daly had no valid reason to keep the file, but he could never bring himself to toss it out. He pushed the file aside to peruse after lunch. As he slid the folder across his desk, an old floor plan for the New York Public Library slipped out, Daly automatically snatched it up. He smiled remembering the vampire craze back in the 1970s, and his former boss's conviction there was something illicit going on beneath the public library. Daly looked at some of the notes and flipped through a few newspaper clippings; there was an interesting article about wolf killings at the Central Park Zoo. He almost turned away, until he spotted a work order for a waterline installation. When he inspected the document more closely, Daly confirmed the installation was for a waterline underneath the New York Public Library. Referring to the library's floor plan, the police chief realized the line connected to one of the empty storage vaults. Why would a waterline be needed there? Daly looked at the plans again; anything could be stored there. His inquisitive mind started to work the puzzle in his head. There would be no need for running water, unless someone was either working or living down there. Homeless people were a possibility, but something in the back of his mind made Daly believe something more sinister was going on.

An unused storage area underneath a public library was a perfect place to hide; or perhaps to make arrangements for acts of aggression against the United States. It was dark, it was tucked away, and it was perfect place to store weapons and explosives. Perhaps they might even uncover an actual terrorist cell. Forgetting about lunch altogether, Daly grabbed the phone and dialed the police commissioner's private line.

"Police Commissioner Daniels here," a crisp, authoritative voice answered.

"Commissioner Daniels…Daly here…I think I have an idea where we might find us a terrorist cell…how fast can we get a SWAT team together?"

"Name the target, Daly, and I'll have one assembled within the hour."

Chapter 147 - Massacre of the Undead - Tunneltown - (March 5, 1993 - 2:17PM)

Alice and Oliver were playing a game of backgammon, as Virginia wrote furiously in her private journal. Oliver was winning, as usual; he had become an expert at playing games of strategy. Vincent had started painting more abstractly; Virginia wasn't sure if she liked his new style, but found it an improvement over some of his darker works. The black swans were out with Prince, getting their midday meal from a local food shelter; it was so quiet when the children weren't around.

One floor below them, a legion of undead hung from the rafters; they were lost in the solace of twilight sleep, as they waited for the sun to set. Their eyes rolled back and forth as they dreamed of glorious human blood. Miles away, in the picturesque Catskill Mountains, the ones who made them slept inside a mausoleum, with only dust and bones for company.

Two SWAT teams were stationed in front of the New York Public Library; they were greeted by Patience and Fortitude, the great lions looked ready to pounce at the slightest provocation. Fifth Avenue had been temporarily blocked off to pedestrian traffic, as authorities prepared to act on an improbable hunch. Police Chief Daly's car was safely positioned behind the barricade; some were skeptical of the location, but knew well enough not to challenge Daly's authority. The plan was to target both vacant storage areas simultaneously, allowing for the element of surprise. As Daly raised his arm to signal the team into action, he prayed his intuition was correct; the last thing he wanted was to retire from the NYPD in disgrace.

It was a cloudless, sunny day when the lair of Dracula's progeny was discovered by men, whose orders were to neutralize or destroy. When the first rifleman entered the vault, he could smell them and broke into a cold sweat. The others followed behind him, waving their flashlights wildly as they searched for any movement, or signs of life. A chirping sound above their heads put everyone on alert, as they stepped further into the cavernous room. In one swift movement, two officers flooded the ceiling with light; above them were hundreds of grotesque-looking bats. They began swarming the room with teeth bared; several men had to pull bats off their faces. Team members began firing at the ceiling with carbines, sending the bats into frenzy; then it got suddenly quiet as the bats disappeared into what appeared to be, abandoned coal chutes.

When a vampire is in its bat-like form, the fight or flight response takes over. The terrified bats lost their sense of time, completely forgetting about the sun, as they fled the thunderous sound of rapid gunfire. Hundreds of frightened bats flew into a clear blue sky; each was incinerated by a searing sun the moment they became airborne. Outside the library, people watched in horror as bats shot out from the building's rooftop, shrieking in pain as they ignited. Police officers used bull horns and advised pedestrians to clear the area, so they could deal with a severe bat infestation. The crowd knew they were being fed a white-washed story; who calls in a SWAT team to exterminate a colony of bats?

While Dracula and Jack's children were being incinerated, a second SWAT team moved to storm the heart of Tunneltown. When Virginia heard the gunshots below, she knew there was little time to waste; Oliver and Alice could not be exposed to daylight! Acting fast, Vincent and Virginia hustled them to the back staircase, so they could hide in the subway tunnels until sunset. The door burst open moments later; Virginia and Vincent held their hands up, the artist still grasping his paintbrush. The team leader was taken by surprise when he saw the couple; they hardly looked like terrorists. What was Chief Daly thinking?

"Don't move...who are you?" the team leader demanded, his gun pointed at Vincent. He noted their strange dress, Virginia's worn nightgown and her bare feet.

"We live here...I know we're probably not supposed to," Vincent said meekly, but the officer cut him off.

"Do either of you have any I.D.?"

"I.D.? No...I'm sorry," Vincent replied, not sure what else to say.

"We are homeless...officers...our only crime was using this empty space to live in," Virginia said calmly, as the man lowered his weapon. Two other team members were conducting a perimeter search and discovered no weapons of any kind, but there hundreds of paintings and a clear indication others were living here.

"Who else lives here with you?" asked the team leader.

"Just the children," Virginia answered with soulful eyes.

"And where are they now, Miss...?"

"Miss Woolf, Virginia Woolf."

"Is this your idea of a joke?"

"Certainly not!" Virginia declared.

"I supposed you're going to tell us you're Pablo Picasso," said another officer to Vincent with a sneer, and they all laughed.

Vincent took a step forward. "Actually no...I am Vincent van Gogh."

"Okay, pops...whatever you say. You'll both have to come with us now...you're trespassing at the very least...and who knows what else. Hal, grab those journals on the table, too," the team leader commanded, as he handcuffed both of them. Two rookies were tasked with taking the eccentric couple to the 5th Precinct, where Police Chief Daly planned to interrogate them personally.

"Hey...let the woman put on shoes and a coat, officer...it's cold out there!"

As they descended the library steps, Virginia thought about their options and realized there was only one. Vincent was shaking in fear, as he looked helplessly at Virginia. "Ginny...what do we do now?"

"What ghosts do, dear...disappear..." Before her words reached the air, Virginia vanished.

The stunned police officer held up the dangling handcuffs in disbelief, then turned to see Vincent vaporize into thin air as well. The two rookies glanced around to confirm no one had seen. Police Chief was busy giving reporters an exclusive interview at the bottom of the library steps. The rookies were speechless, both thinking the same thing; how were they ever going to explain how they allowed two handcuffed prisoners to escape?

It was a cold afternoon in midtown; Prince walked with the children to their favorite soup kitchen on the corner of 41st Street. Mary and Maude were the oldest and the first black swans Alice made after Semele disappeared. Susie was ten and Sara eight, when Alice brought them to Tunneltown. Jill was the youngest, at seven years old. She followed Alice home one night and they couldn't refuse her a place to stay; because she was so frail and small, they all spoiled her.

They had all just stepped inside the Holy Apostle's Soup Kitchen, when the horrific sound of screaming children pierced the frigid air; Prince instinctively knew Dracula had lost a brace of kinsmen. There was no mistaking the sound of vampires being burned alive. But what had chased them into the sunlight? Thankfully, the children had already gone inside, so they hadn't seen. Suddenly, Prince remembered about Alice and Oliver. Had they been exterminated with the others? Prince closed his eyes, trying to block out the vision of them being burned alive. The authorities had finally discovered their hiding place; there was no going back to Tunneltown. What were they supposed to do with the children now?

Tunneltown was no longer safe and might be lost to them forever. How could he subject children to life on the street during the coldest time of year? He had to leave them here. What choice did he have? Mattie ran the place, and was a kindhearted soul; surely she would take pity and help them find a foster home. Prince closed his eyes, remembering the joy of doing magic tricks for the girls by candlelight when they first came to live in Tunneltown. He didn't want to leave them, but what else could he do? Prince turned around to find he was no longer alone.

"You're going to leave us here aren't you?" Mary asked gazing up at Prince. Jill peered out from behind Mary's denim skirt.

Prince bent down taking Mary's hands in his, she was his favorite and he would miss her most of all, "Mary, I need you to be strong…yes I need to leave you here. Something has happened to Tunneltown and you can't go back…any of you."

"Why can't we come with you, then?"

"That's just it…I don't know where we're going…I don't want any of you living outside. Mattie will help you…she knows people who can help."

"They'll just put us in foster care, you know," Mary said bitterly.

"Think about it…you'll have a warm place to live and home cooked meals," Prince said weakly.

"Is that what you *really* believe?" Mary asked, her mouth quivering with anger.

Jill moved from behind Mary, her curly blonde hair framing a petite face. Her eyes filled with tears, as she looked up at Prince with a look that broke him in two, "You said you'd never leave...you told us we would always be together...," and then she began to sob.

Mary tried to comfort Jill, her face red with rage, "Go on then... we don't need you anyway!" Mary snapped, and then spun away with an arm around the little girl. Prince hesitated for a moment, and then moved toward the door; if he turned around, he would surely change his mind.

Chapter 148 - Sleepy Hollow Cemetery - (March 5, 1993)

The afternoon sun was brilliant in a cloudless sky; the ghosts of Sleepy Hollow Cemetery had been chased away with the sunrise, and now waited for the night to return. A gentle wind moved through the graveyard; bare trees created an ominous shadow on the headstones below, some so old the writing had almost disappeared.

Dracula woke the moment his progeny began to perish; he jumped wildly from his crypt, and then fell to his knees in agony. Jack opened his own crypt to find his maker writhing in pain. Something was wrong; Jack could feel it, too.

"What is it?" Jack croaked.

"My children...something terrible has happened..."

Jack's knees buckled, forcing him to the floor; he was too weak to move. They managed to crawl back to the protection of their crypts; but lay wide awake as they waited for dusk. Neither knew what to expect, but both were certain of one thing; their underground home had been exposed.

Akos flew like the wind with his important message; the bird was determined to deliver Virginia's note into Dracula's hands. When the bird reached the Archbold Mausoleum, the sun was still high in the sky; the faithful falcon perched on the peaked roof and waited for the moon.

Chapter 149 - Police Chief Daly - 5th Precinct - (March 7, 1993)

He had three major newspapers spread out on his desk; Chief Daly was trying to make sense of the recent bombing, and the subsequent raid on the New York Public Library. Like his mentor, Manuel Rodriguez, Daly liked to make lists, as he worked through the facts in criminal cases; the only difference, was that he used a desktop computer. Although Daly wasn't directly involved in the World Trade Center investigation, he couldn't shake the feeling that the bombing, and the discovery of inhabitants under the library, were somehow connected.

In front of him was an oil painting the SWAT team confiscated during the search of the library book vault; it was quite disturbing in its content. It was a large canvas, depicting a well-rendered silhouette of the Twin Towers against a bright blue sky; in the distance, two commercial airliners hovered nearby in a menacing way. What disturbed Daly most about the painting, was the wild-eyed man in the forefront; his hair was on fire and he appeared to be screaming in agony. What would possess someone to paint something like this, and what did it mean? Was it meant as some kind of future threat, or merely the creation of an artist with sadistic inclinations? Daly cursed out loud in frustration; he would never have the chance to interview the pale-faced artist or the woman. His two rookies had let their prisoners escape, and were now on desk duty for the foreseeable future; Daly was convinced they mishandled the handcuffs.

Daly turned to the journals; they were apparently written by the woman calling herself Virginia Woolf. In one journal, there was a whole section about vampires blending into society by seeking nightshift work. According to the journal, lots of bars and nightclubs hired vampires without ever knowing it. Supposedly, vampires slept as bats by day, underneath the library. Daly sat back after reading this part; exactly what kind of bats did we incinerate? The police chief pushed the journals aside. Vampires weren't real and everyone knew it. Such tales were best suited for writers like Stephen King. Supernatural or not, the police chief was convinced a dark and terrible secret lived within the bowels of his city.

Daly picked up the *New York Post* and read the headline: "WHERE IS EVERYBODY?" According to the paper, more than sixty people who either worked or lived within the midtown area had gone missing the day after the raid. Daly's precinct phone lines were flooded with calls about people that hadn't shown up for work or school. The general protocol for investigating missing persons was forty-eight hours; due to the huge number of mysterious disappearances, Daly decided to put a taskforce together. He scanned down the names of the missing, trying to zero in on something that made sense. There seemed to be no connection at all between those missing, and yet, he did take note that quite a few were employed in nocturnal occupations. Could these disappearances be somehow related to the mass extermination of bats? Daly didn't believe in vampires, of course, but there was no viable explanation for such a large number of people to go missing all at once. He took a slug of Pepsi, and prepared to address more pressing matters.

After a polite knock, his assistant, Cindy barged into his office. "Chief...just got a call from one of the F.B.I. investigators. Police officer found a wallet stashed somewhere behind the North Tower...initial crew must have missed it."

"And...?"

"The wallet contained four separate sets of identification, so there's a question about the owner's true identity."

"Okay...but, why did they call us?"

"Out of respect, I think they want you involved...and maybe because one of the names he used was Abdal Kadir...and with the recent bombing..." Cindy didn't need to finish.

"So, now they want our help with a diplomatic approach. Do we have any idea where to find him?"

"I think that's why they called you directly...two of his identities show an address at the Dakota Building...*the penthouse*, no less."

"Got it...building has a lot of wealthy and prestigious residents...I imagine he thinks it'll go better if I show up personally to question our suspect." Cindy beamed at him; she was going to miss him when he retired.

Chapter 150 - A Search for Abdal Kadir - New York City - (March 7, 1993)

Rory eventually decided not to kill him. The vampire hunter already had many chances to do so, but never followed through. She reasoned it was right to spare his life as payback for turning Rupert, which sent him into hiding and far away from her. Truthfully, Rory let Sylvio live because she found the Egyptian vampire handsome and enigmatic, like someone from the old world. She was fascinated by his essence and simply couldn't bring herself to take his life. Sometimes she followed Sylvio out of boredom; it was a way to live vicariously through someone else. Her other pastime was petty theft; she picked pockets with the precision of a seasoned criminal. The Egyptian vampire's patterns were very predictable. He usually went to nightclubs, but rarely the same place twice. It appeared he lived a hedonistic lifestyle, so typical of vampires with means. A few weeks before the bombing, the Egyptian vampire abruptly abandoned his normal pattern and began trolling the financial district. Rory followed Sylvio to the World Trade Center seven times over a period of several weeks; he brought a camera with him a few times, but only took pictures of the service entrances and security gates. Sometimes Sylvio met with another man, but other times he was alone; his focus was on the North Tower.

On the night before the bombing, Rory followed Sylvio once more; he met with the same man out on the sidewalk. After a brief embrace, they parted company; Rory thought she saw money exchange hands. What were they planning and was the North Tower their target, she wondered. Sylvio started walking in her direction; Rory crossed the street to a bus stop, and sat down on an empty bench. If she went to the authorities with her suspicions, they might think her involved and take her into custody; she had no legal means of identification. Maybe it was nothing at all; maybe Sylvio was just working one of his sly schemes. Rory eventually decided against doing anything; she convinced herself she was just being paranoid.

Two weeks after the bombing, Rory sat on the same bench; naturally,

Sylvio had vanished without a trace. This only served to confirm he was involved with Ramzi Yousef, the suspect police had in custody. Rory was hot for revenge; Sylvio had bested her, and she wanted to even the score. She dug into her coat pocket to retrieve Sylvio's wallet; she'd snatched it from him the day before the bombing. It had been so easy and only meant as a prank, that is, until Rory opened it. Inside she found four separate identities for her vampire, including a passport for someone named Abdal Kadir. With a name like that, Rory was certain he *had* to be involved in the attack, especially after seeing him at the North Tower so many times. For the first time ever, she had been duped by a vampire and it made her seethe. Sylvio was in cahoots with religious fanatics; these radicals were an enemy to vampires and humans alike. Rory cursed out loud at her stupidity; it was time for Sylvio to pay for his deception.

Across the street, the sidewalk surrounding the North Tower was still cordoned off where the worst damage had occurred. A police presence had also continued since the attack. Rory was holding the one thing that would incriminate the arrogant vampire; it would lead police right to his front door. Getting closer to the police barricade, Rory got into character, adjusting her demeanor from vampire hunter, to benevolent teenager.

The police officer watched as the girl approached him; she looked no more than thirteen or fourteen, with a hard-looking face. As she got closer, the officer saw her hold something out to him. "Officer…I found this wallet in the bushes over by the service elevator…thought I should turn in." The girl spoke with an innocence that belied her appearance.

"What's that?" The officer took the wallet from her as he sized her up.

"I found it…by the service elevator…so I wanted to turn it in."

The officer opened the wallet and his eyes grew wide. "I'm going to need more information miss…"

Rory didn't hear him, because she had already skittered away. He shrugged it off, knowing her identity wouldn't matter once his commanding officer got a look at the piece of evidence he was holding. He moved quickly to his squad car and radioed his precinct. Within minutes, his C.O. was on the line, as the officer told him all about a wallet *he* had just found at the crime scene.

Exactly one hour later, Rory stood across the street from the Dakota looking up at Sylvio's penthouse apartment. Three police cruisers pulled up in front of the building; they had flashers on, but kept their sirens off. Rory stayed in the shadows, she wanted to see Sylvio brought out in handcuffs. Although she had a mild feeling of regret, Rory was determined to witness his incineration. She looked up at the bright blue sky; there wasn't a cloud in sight. Goodbye Egyptian vampire!

The sun was still high in the sky, when they set up another round of cards. Semele played with precision and for the thrill of winning; she loved poker and beat Eadric most of the time. They didn't play for money; they played for shots of AB negative. A rare blood type, AB negative was difficult to obtain, but Eadric insisted on the occasional indulgence. He was a snob about his sustenance and besides, he had an extremely affluent master.

"Type O is okay for everyday consumption, Eadric, but it lacks body," Semele said, as she held a goblet to her lips.

"The young lady has excellent taste," Eadric replied with a bloody smile.

The doorbell rang and Eadric temporarily abandoned their game of poker to answer it. Certain it was a delivery of bottled blood he was expecting; Eadric opened the door and was thrown down on the floor as an officer handcuffed him.

Semele squealed and ran to her bedroom, locking the door. She grabbed an oversized scarf to cover her face, and then climbed out a dormer window. She quickly reached the rooftop, grateful for the shade of so many trees. She could hear them coming after her; Semele's only option was to assume her bat-like form and hide in one of the chimneys. The moment she ducked out of sight, four uniformed men came crashing through the metal door; despite a thorough search, the police couldn't find her.

Inside Sylvio's apartment, Police Chief Daly called his men together to discuss where the girl might have gone. He was extremely irritated that his team let her get away. He was equally disappointed to find their suspect was not in residence, but was determined to make his butler talk. All he needed was twenty minutes alone with the man, and the bastard would tell Daly everything he wanted to know. The police chief knew the F.B.I. would be all over his ass for interfering with their investigation, but he didn't care. What could they do, fire him?

Eadric bowed his head, refusing to speak. He had made a vow to Sylvio that he would sacrifice his life, in order to protect his master's secrets. He never expected to live forever and was resigned to his fate; Eadric stood mutely as an officer read the vampire his Miranda rights. It was a matter of honor; Sylvio had granted Eadric eternal life and he was going to repay him in kind. The vampire let the officers lead him out with amazing poise, despite a certainty that his death would be excruciatingly painful. Eadric's only regret in his final moments was for Semele; he had come to love her like a daughter. He could only hope she was clever enough to avoid his fate, by finding a safe place to hide.

Fortunately for the two officers, neither was handcuffed to their prisoner which most certainly saved their lives. Daly walked behind them and noticed the prisoner becoming agitated, as they reached the main entrance to the Dakota. The sun dominated a nearly cloudless sky; the prisoner's body slumped as they led him through the double doors. When they stepped into the glaring sunlight, there was a flash of light; Daly felt a heat so intense, he thought it was a silent explosion. The two officers quickly let go of their prisoner; despite handcuffs, he managed to contort his body into positions the police chief hadn't thought possible. His clothes started to singe as he was being roasted alive; Daly was overcome by the nauseating smell of burning flesh. Eadric let out one last gasp of air, before his body fell to the ground and became mercifully still.

"Jesus Christ…what's happening here?" Daly exclaimed.

Pedestrians gathered and stood mesmerized by the smoldering mess, unsure of what had happened. There were several calls to 911, but anyone could see the poor man was beyond help. Police Chief Daly ducked back inside the building to call his public relations manager. He needed to locate the rear entrance in order to evade the press; they would be there in droves before very long. As Daly dialed his precinct, he was assaulted by a vivid recollection of another burning prisoner; he was the one they apprehended for robbing a blood bank. With every passing minute, the police chief was starting to believe something supernatural might be going on after all.

For a while, Semele could hear the officers moving across the rooftop, but eventually they gave up. When the moon rose, Semele felt the cool night air and left the safety of her smokestack. Flying to her favorite gargoyle, Semele shook and resumed her human form. Her eyes filled with tears, when she thought about Eadric; he had been a dear friend for such a long time. Semele thought about Sylvio, sometimes; he haunted her dreams, but she didn't think he was coming back. She remembered the night Sylvio taught her the magic of time travel. Semele didn't know if she could do it again, but was willing to try; there was nothing left for her in the modern world now.

Semele held out her arms and closed her eyes tight; from memory she conjured up a vision of Central Park in another time. She heard the sounds of traffic below and tried to block them out; as her young heart cried out for a bygone era. It took a minute for the modern world to slip away; when it did, Semele caught the scent of evergreen. She was back. There were no electric lights, or cars; the park was one big winter wonderland just waiting to be explored. From the rooftop, Semele could see the bonfire; it was just as she remembered it the night Sylvio first brought her here. Using the fire escape, Semele found her way down to the ground level and raced toward Central Park. When she reached the street, there were no cars or traffic lights and no tall buildings at all; a few horse carriages passed her by, as a light snow fell all around them. Central Park had been turned into something magical. Everything was covered in fresh snow, making it look like a Currier and Ives Christmas card. Breathless, Semele entered the park searching for the beautiful young girl with blonde curls. As she searched the crowd it was clear that, as before, no one could see her.

She scanned the crowd and didn't see Emily Parrish anywhere; had she come on a different night? Semele now had second thoughts about coming here. What if no one could see her? Would she be stuck here, invisible to everyone, even her crying ghost?

As it turned out, it was Emily Parrish who found Semele, as she cautiously approached the bonfire. The pretty blonde came up behind her; Semele could feel the warmth of her presence right away. Semele turned around and their eyes met. "It's you," she whispered.

"Yes…and I've been waiting for you," Emily replied, taking her hand.

CHAPTER 151 - THE OTHERWORLD

This forgotten place was a welcome refuge during turbulent times; Virginia clung to Vincent, as they passed through the colored lights to a place they hadn't seen since leaving London. When the lights dimmed, both were shocked to find it no longer felt familiar; the magic of the Otherworld had notably waned. To Vincent, their old home now appeared almost two dimensional. The cavernous dwelling no longer offered a feeling of ease and comfort. Instead, it had merely become the home of discarded books, and a portal for seamless time travel. Without regular inhabitants, the Otherworld was no longer tasked with desires or wishes to fulfill, and had become a stagnant shell of its former self. Gone were the two princes, who made things, come alive with their desire and imagination; there were no more games of hide and seek, or mock battles to be fought. The enchanted bird had vanished too, along with the sound of children's laughter.

Vincent called out for the others, but received only the echo of his own words. Virginia took his arm, because she found the place unsettling; the only familiar thing was the massive library of books. The walls were slick with slime, and a damp odor permeated the air. Virginia worried about the children, but knew they couldn't go back to look for them now.

"Akos will get my note to them…I'm sure of it."

"What did you have time to write?" Vincent asked, surprised at her ingenuity.

"What else…H E L P!"

Colored lights flashed again, as the two siblings entered a place filled with a lifetime of memories. Oliver came through first, with Alice behind; as if by magic, they were back in a place where time didn't matter and there was no need to feed. Once they confirmed Tunneltown was deserted, there was no place else to go. They looked around, and like Vincent and Virginia; observed things were clearly not the same. Remnants of the tainted vine hung listlessly from the arched entrance; Alice reached out to touch it, but changed her mind.

What had happened to the place they used to find enchanting? The Otherworld now looked like a tainted fairytale, and nothing like Alice remembered.

They moved through the darkness battling cobwebs, until they reached the familiar living space they abandoned so long ago. As they took in their surroundings, they noticed an odd-looking mirror they didn't remember seeing before. Alice approached the mirror, but Oliver pulled her back; the mirror had started fogging up. Oliver knew well enough not to mess around with something like that.

"Let's go to the library!" Oliver declared.

They ran to the library, looking for their favorite books; some looked ready to crumble if touched. They sought the comfortable corner where they used to read, only to discover Nikos sitting on the floor. One glance told them he had been crying. All around him were history books Oliver recognized, ones they had discussed together at length; the precious books sat in ruins. Why would Nikos do this?

"Nikos…" Oliver knelt down, and tried unsuccessfully to pull him to his feet.

"Oliver…you knew to come here. Good. Vincent and Virginia are here too. I don't know about the others." Nikos appeared hypnotized.

"Nikos…what is it…what's wrong?" Oliver asked.

"Look around you, boy…books are mankind's only legacy! They contain countless stories that demonstrate the human need for conflict. It is the way of the world and has always been so…and now, it all seems pointless."

"What does that have to do with what happened to Tunneltown?" Oliver asked confused.

"Don't you see…no matter what we want to believe…vampires will never succeed in dominating the human race. I'm not sure it was ever meant to be."

"And how have you come to this conclusion?" Oliver asked.

"All right, Oliver…I'm going to speak to you man to man, and that means…brutal honesty."

"Go on…," Oliver urged; Alice stood behind him, taking in every word.

"I have been around long enough to make my own observations.

Believe me, not much has changed since my generation's time. Humans are still killing each other over religious differences; in my opinion, vampires are no better. I have lived in the shadow of Count Dracula for centuries, protecting a lifestyle I was brainwashed to believe in. Like most of his progeny…I was not given a choice when he fed on me…as I lay dying on a battlefield fighting his war."

"If he drank from you…then why aren't you one of us?" Oliver asked puzzled.

"I was his first kill…but I never drank from him. Instead, I became trapped in a state of limbo…halfway between the living and the dead. *I* should have been his first vampire, *not* that psychotic killer from Whitechapel!"

"I always thought you were a spirit…like Prince or Eva," Oliver replied.

"The only thing I have in common with them…is that I'm earthbound. I chose my path when I begged Dracula for release. I had nowhere to go, so I became his soldier and have served him faithfully, ever since. Funny, how until recently, I never questioned the lifestyle vampires lead…not even when Vlad made monsters of innocent children."

"He had to do it…you know he did!"

"But for his own selfish reasons. Remember…Dracula serves no one but himself!" Nikos spat angrily.

"Dracula told me vampires fight a noble cause!" Oliver declared defensively.

"Oliver…a vampire's only noble cause is their selfish need to feed. All vampires are heartless…and born with a natural craving for human carnage. There's nothing noble about killing for sustenance…when bottled blood will do. The one who made you kills for the thrill of it, and usually without an ounce of guilt." Nikos spoke with uncharacteristic bitterness.

"You don't know that for certain…and besides, a vampire's need to feed is not his responsibility. It should be borne by the one who made him," Oliver argued.

"None of that matters. Our plan to dominate humans has failed miserably. Vampires are losing the battle to survive in a world with increasing technology. In modern times…one can't go anywhere without being on film. Dracula has no idea how difficult it has all been to manage such responsibility...while he and Jack play house in the Catskill Mountains with the countess!"

"He is my father...I will not hear you speak against him!" Oliver yelled.

"Don't you see, Oliver...it's all part of a much bigger plan. Tunneltown was vulnerable from the start...because of its nefarious purpose."

"What are you trying to say?" Oliver asked.

"I'm saying the invasion of Tunneltown was inevitable. Frankly, it makes me wonder if the vampire community has finally gotten what they deserve. I have been loyal to Lord Dracula for centuries...and now, I realize my loyalty was misplaced."

"But it is your responsibility to serve him!" Oliver insisted.

"And what if I'm tired of being his Renfield?" Nikos replied bitterly.

Oliver put a hand on his shoulder and spoke softly, "There is no such person...this is real life and Dracula needs you now."

"And does that mean turning a blind eye, every time he feels inclined to take an innocent human life?"

"He only kills when he has to!"

"Is that what you really believe, Oliver? Look me in the eye and tell me so." Oliver remained silent.

Nikos continued with his tirade. "I'm going to admit something else to you...and it may be painful to hear. Instead of being horrified when the fledglings were burned up...I actually felt a sense of justice. It was a great victory for mankind."

"How can you say such a thing?"

His green eyes became angry slits, as Nikos looked Oliver in the eye. "Because I believe each one of Dracula's precious progeny was taken to compensate for a human life my old friend took, without a second thought...including my own."

"I'm going to find Virginia," Alice said nervously, taking Oliver's hand to pull him away.

CHAPTER 152 - A FINAL FAREWELL - OLANA ESTATE - (MARCH 9, 1993)

It would be their last night in this historic place. Thanks to the World Trade Center attack, all national and historical monuments were being fitted with surveillance cameras that ran twenty-four hours a day. That meant Olana would now be off limits. The dust had settled in the city after the library was re-opened, but the surviving vampire community understood they could never return to Tunneltown. Now that so many of his children had perished, they were outnumbered and it would take time to build his legions anew. Dracula silently cursed Nikos for disappearing when they needed him most. For the time being, there was only one place they could find sanctuary. Eva and Jack knew it too; the safest hiding place would be one where time didn't matter. As they sat together sipping from crystal goblets, they dined on raw filet mignon, one of Jack's favorites; Eva always set a place for herself, despite not consuming human food. Eva dreaded returning to the Otherworld; she couldn't think of any place more boring. Frankly, she was a lot more interested in seeing the new millennium; perhaps, even ahead of schedule. Eva's thoughts were interrupted as Dracula made a toast.

"To our last night in the year 1993!" Dracula said, raising a glass to salute the moon above. The clink of wine glasses lingered in the air for a moment.

Jack proceeded to change the subject. "Why not take the chance... get it over with?"

"What are you talking about, Jack?" Eva asked, spinning the stem of her wine glass with delicate fingers.

"Travel ahead in time, of course, past 2000...if the planet hasn't destroyed itself by then, we find a new home somewhere else. Maybe, Paris or..."

Dracula cut him off. "And if the world has gone dark and all life departed...then what?" He was very superstitious about the future, especially the possibility of facing his own personal judgment day.

"Do you *really* want to live forever?" Jack asked with a mischievous grin.

"Are *you* volunteering to go?" Eva taunted.

"Maybe we could draw straws," Jack replied, hating to be put on the spot.

"No one is taking that chance...now let's just enjoy our dinner," Dracula replied, eyeing Sylvio's empty chair.

Sylvio had been missing in action, since the World Trade Center bombing. This fact only served to convince Jack and Eva, he might somehow be involved. Dracula was blind when it came to Sylvio, because he admired the Egyptian vampire and considered him a peer. Dracula had his doubts, but remained unwilling to admit Sylvio played a part in the attack on his favorite landmark.

Tonight, the vampires dined on the veranda facing the Hudson River, as a mirror reflection of the night sky glimmered on the water.

"I can't believe we have to go back to that lifeless place," Jack complained.

"It's the only place we can go right now. Tomorrow, they install surveillance cameras...so we can't stay here anymore." Dracula sipped his beverage with relish.

"Stop whining, Jack...it's not like we have a choice," Eva said, tired of hearing him complain.

Jack threw down his fork. "How long will we be stuck there this time? The millennium is just seven years away, you never want to take any chances...do you even have a plan?"

"Settle down," Dracula said calmly, putting a hand on Jack's arm. "You know how this works. We have to make careful preparations... before we re-enter the human world again."

"I still don't understand why we can't send someone ahead, so we know...it doesn't have to be one of us," Jack replied.

Eva jumped into the debate. "You know the risks, Jack. Everything we've read about the millennium and possible complications. If things went wrong, we could end up stuck in limbo with no way back...I can't see how we could ask anyone to take that risk." Eva was anxious to discourage Jack from even considering this idea; if anyone of them was going to see the millennium first, it was going to be her.

"Eva is right, you know. They expect all kinds of technology issues…I even read something about computers crashing at the stroke of midnight," Dracula said, pouring Jack another glass of his special reserve.

"Yeah…I read all about it, too. Something called *Y2K*…it was on the news." Jack concurred, taking a slug of his beverage. "I know I say it all the time, but I hate the modern world…I'll take the streets of Whitechapel any day."

"I know what you mean, Jack. I miss the old world too…the formality of dress and the way people lived in the moment, not like it is today," Eva said, agreeing with Jack. She wanted their last night here to be without conflict.

"The world is different now…even hunting seems less like sport than it used to," Dracula replied, with a distant look in his eyes.

"Remember when you first took me hunting, Vlad?" Jack asked, suddenly anxious to reminisce about the old days.

Eva jumped at Jack's words and prompted him to tell his story, which was then followed by a tale from Dracula. Before long, they were all laughing and talking about adventures no sane person would believe to be true. Jack even spoke about the night of his attempted suicide all those years ago, and how Dracula's blood gave him a second chance. It was strange to hear Jack felt this way, when Dracula's intention had been to punish him with the curse of eternal life. After a few more stories, Jack knew it was time to leave them alone to enjoy one another, before the sacred night was over. He excused himself by claiming he wanted to feed one more time, before the sun forced them into hiding.

Once Jack was gone, Eva could feel the tone of the evening change. Dracula seemed greatly affected by Jack's declaration of gratitude for being turned. "You never spoke of it…I mean, exactly how Jack was turned." Eva prompted him to talk more about what happened.

"I told you already…he was on the run from Scotland Yard…I kept him from drowning…" Eva cut him off.

"Not exactly…he jumped in with the intention of killing himself, and you saved him by making him like you."

"I couldn't let him get away with it…he killed my beautiful Mary. You should have seen her corpse…she was unrecognizable." Eva suddenly regretted making him talk about this tonight but now, it was too late.

"Vlad...what's done is done. The two of you have a truce, and there is no need to think about it anymore. Look about, the night is fading fast."

Dracula took Eva in his arms and together, they took flight from the bell tower; they headed toward the Adirondack Mountains, to a place no human had ever seen. Their cave was well covered by a host of rhododendron plants, obscuring the entrance from view. Once inside, they stripped off their clothing and Eva moved to bury her head in his chest; her pelvis was thrust forward to invite his touch. Their lovemaking was bittersweet and filled with the longing of another time. When they were finished, Eva told her chiseled vampire she wanted to sleep under the stars, so they abandoned their cave and ran outside to claim a night sky full of twinkling diamonds.

Jack liked hunting game well enough, but it didn't satisfy his hunger for human prey. There was much more excitement in pursuing an intelligent adversary, than a panicked white-tailed deer. He was a born killer and often killed when he didn't need to feed. He had watched many die by his own hand; he was especially fond of watching his victims experience a wide range of emotions, during the last moments of their pathetic lives. Jack craved a human kill tonight; raw meat soothed the gnawing in his gut, but often left him unsatisfied. The seasoned vampire surveyed the valley below, knowing he would have no trouble finding a cozy little dwelling on the edge of the forest. With any luck, he would find a door left carelessly unlocked.

Dracula and Eva lay naked together; their limbs still wrapped around each other, as their campfire dwindled. Eva was wide awake, watching her vampire sleep in the soft glow of a dying fire. It was difficult to leave this wonderful place, where she and Dracula found such happiness. They had spent their last precious night underneath a sky full of stars; and now, it was almost over.

Eva moved to nuzzle Dracula awake; it was already growing lighter on the horizon. "Come love...wake up. We have to go now."

Dracula snapped awake and was instantly on his feet, pulling Eva up with him. Holding hands, they took flight, savoring the lush landscape of upstate New York as they flew back to Olana. The horizon brightened, as a sleepy sun climbed higher on the mountain. Eva pushed Dracula into the safety of a dark house; she smiled at him as they took one last look around. They moved away from the window and rushed to the main parlor, where a Louis XIV mirror promptly transported them to the Otherworld.

CHAPTER 153 - SUBMISSION OF A
VAMPIRE HUNTER - (APRIL 1, 1993)

The seasoned vampire hunter strutted down the street, with a confidence he wanted to squash. For the death of his lifelong friend, she would pay with her dignity, and her pride; he would bring her down lower than she ever thought possible. He had dyed his hair blond and donned red sunglasses to disguise his appearance; the Egyptian vampire walked up Bleecker Street and headed toward a seedier part of town. Naturally, Sylvio was too clever to go anywhere near the Dakota, once he realized his wallet had been stolen. When he heard about the raid of his apartment, he figured out who was responsible. Sylvio had caught a glimpse of her a few times, over the past few months; his vanity allowed him to believe her crush on him, was the only reason Rory stalked him. Now, he was a wanted man, and Sylvio was out for vengeance.

A little girl and her mother passed him on the street; it made Sylvio think about Semele for a moment. A vision of his fledgling flashed through his mind; the child's silvery eyes implored him to take her stargazing one more time. Sylvio squeezed his eyes shut, when a teardrop tried to escape. He didn't need her in his life to be happy. Sylvio didn't need anyone.

He pulled up his collar, as a muttering homeless man passed by; he exuded an odor that hung in the air. Sylvio followed the vampire hunter to a rather desolate section of Barrow Street; he wondered what her plans were for the evening. He took great satisfaction in knowing he was going to change them. Casually extracting a hand-rolled cigarette from his breast pocket, Sylvio tucked it behind his ear. He continued walking, careful to keep a safe distance as he stalked his unsuspecting prey. She could have been pretty, if she had lived to become a woman; instead, her human life had been cut short by a disease no one died from anymore. She was petite and compact, but Sylvio knew it could be deadly to underestimate her strength. Rory walked with amazing grace, and a certainty she was invincible. It only made the pursuit more interesting; having a worthy opponent always made the conquest so much sweeter. When she turned the corner, he gracefully lunged into the air. By the time the vampire hunter detected the flapping of his arms, it was already too late. There was no time to vaporize; Sylvio wrapped himself around her, and then everything went black.

She had no idea where she was; there was an almost deafening silence in the air, as though time were standing still. No sounds of traffic or human voices. The room was dark but she could see it was furnished lavishly; yet, the location was foreign to Rory. She was in a comfortable bed and her sheets felt like silk against her skin. She was surrounded by idols that appeared to be made of solid gold; the décor was clearly Egyptian. *Where* was she? Rory searched her memory, but could not remember anything about the night before. The door clicked open. Rory pulled the sheets up to cover her undeveloped breasts, as Sylvio entered the room; His presence took her completely by surprise.

"I see you've slept well...now let's have a look at you," Sylvio said with a leer. Rory knew it was useless to resist, so she slowly stood up, but kept the rumpled sheet against her unclothed body.

"Drop the sheet or I will take it from you."

She was in a no-win situation and assumed he meant to keep her as some sort of sex slave. Rory finally dropped the sheet; she put her hands across her chest, as if it would actually save her further embarrassment.

"None of that matters, my dear girl...I detest fleshy women so, you'll do."

"What do you want from me?"

"Not what you think."

Rory stood naked in front of him, no longer caring what happened. She had the ability to vaporize, but where would she go? There was nothing worse than being anonymous and alone.

"Do you know where you are, daughter of Paul Revere?"

"Not in New York City...that's for sure," Rory tried to conceal her fear.

"No, not a modern city...and certainly not a modern time."

"You brought us *back* in time...but when?"

"Back to my time...before I became what I am."

"You speak in riddles," Rory replied impatiently.

"How about brutal honesty, vampire killer! Because of you, I had to leave my favorite city…just to keep myself out of jail. You're lucky to be alive…but, no matter…I have found a suitable way for you to pay for ruining my cover and killing my loyal servant."

"I could have killed *you* several times, vampire! You're the one who's lucky to be alive!" she spat at him, but Sylvio only sneered.

"You should have killed me when you had the chance, dear girl. Now you are trapped in my time."

Tired of talking, Sylvio clapped his hands and the door opened. A bald man entered and after glancing at her for a moment, bowed to his master.

"Eadric…please prepare a bath for our guest," Sylvio commanded.

"Very good, sir."

When they were alone together again, Sylvio lost his smile. "You will get down on your knees now…please," Sylvio said; he pulled a leather studded neck collar out from behind his back.

Rory showed no fear, as he placed the collar around her slender neck. Sylvio caressed her cheek indulgently, as one might pet a dog. Rory looked up at his face; she still found him handsome, despite his treachery. Even now, when she was at her most vulnerable, Rory continued to deny the villain he was.

Sylvio removed only his shirt and sandals, as he stood before her. He cupped her chin and spoke more gently. "Now, what I want from you is to make sure my feet are always clean. You may start by licking them now, while I tell you about all the things I might step in. Sometimes…I can get into some pretty dirty things." He stroked her hair, with a tenderness that belied his true nature.

When she became a Van Helsing, Rory abandoned her femininity to become a fierce warrior and learned to kill without remorse. Her lifestyle eventually hardened her against emotions. She had watched vampires plead for their lives, as she held a knife to their necks; it only served to enhance her enjoyment as she slit their throats. Now, it was her turn to become the prey, and she wasn't sure how she felt about it. Rory thought for a moment about her human life; it seemed so remote, as though it belonged to someone else. Rory had lost her fight and realized there were worse things than living in bondage. In all honestly, she was grateful for a chance to be near the most charismatic man she had ever known.

Finally lowering her head to Sylvio's feet, Rory submitted to him without shame or guilt; after a few minutes, Rory realized, she had never felt so loved in her whole life.

Chapter 154 - New Year's Eve - World Trade Center - (December 31, 1999)

Eva loved to dress up and mingle with the rich and famous. She always remained on the fringes of things; she lingered just long enough to exchange glances with handsome men, and the occasional jealous female. Eva had procured a gown that accentuated her womanly curves; she would turn a lot of heads tonight, which was exactly her intention. There was something liberating about attending a party where no one knew her name: Eva had the freedom to do or say anything she wanted, without consequence. When she stepped out of the cab in her four inch heels, Eva felt like royalty; she would have no problem passing for an invited guest tonight. A beautiful young woman had an amazing ability to glide through life; Eva took great comfort in knowing she would stay this way forever. Selling her soul to the devil seemed worth it to her, especially now that Dracula shared her bed again.

As Eva entered the famed restaurant, she had a momentary feeling of regret the others weren't here to celebrate with her. The dance floor was packed as the band played a lively tune; for a brief moment, Eva wished she had a steady dance partner. A waiter wearing a crisp white shirt passed by with a tray of champagne flutes; Eva snatched one up without him even noticing. She didn't drink, but found champagne glasses an effective prop; over centuries of time, the countess had become an expert stem twirler. There were a lot of famous people Eva recognized from television and the newspapers, but the names of most eluded her.

As she looked around the room, Eva was amazed at the diversity in modern fashion. The rich and famous were dressed in the latest Paris fashions, while others set their own trend, by wearing outfits she considered outrageous. In her opinion, a lot of young people seemed to dress like slobs; Eva later learned this was called the "grunge look." A group of revelers passed her carrying handheld silver eye glasses that spelled out 2-0-0-0; she found the idea extremely clever. As Eva observed the growing crowd, she was astounded by the number of people using portable phones, and wondered what the obsession was all about.

Eva was about to check out the buffet table, when she felt someone watching her from across the room. The tall man gave her a wink, and immediately headed in her direction. He had a ruddy complexion with a horrendous spray tan; His wheat-colored hair was styled in a conspicuous comb over. The man had his hand out by the time he reached her; Eva had no choice but to shake it.

"Thank you for your support," he said without introducing himself; the man assumed she knew who he was.

"Excuse me?" Eva said, as she wracked her brain trying to place him.

"Gee, I'm sorry…I thought everybody knew I was running for president."

"Ah-h-h, yes," Eva said with undisguised sarcasm, when she finally remembered who he was.

"You're that successful real estate mogul…suddenly turned politician."

"The country needs a drastic change. I believe I can make America great again!"

"Well then…I certainly hope you plan to handle the country's finances a lot better than your own. As I recall, you've already declared bankruptcy twice." Eva knew his type; the man thought he could have any woman he wanted.

His face reddened as he took a sip of his Diet Coke, then he changed the subject. "You know, I'm hosting a little after party at one of my hotels…perhaps you'd like to stop by later…"

She cut him off. "Save it…*Mr. President*…you never know who might be watching." Before the tall man could respond, Eva had already walked away.

Eva made her way outside to take in the view of her favorite city; at the stroke of twelve midnight, she would witness the beginning of the twenty-first century. Everywhere Eva looked, people seemed genuinely happy to be alive at this exciting time; there was no sign anyone was concerned about the world blowing up. If she made it to midnight and nothing happened, then Eva could go back and tell the others it had all been a hoax. Maybe they could do what Jack suggested, and settle somewhere in the new millennium. Eva knew Dracula would be angry she came alone, but she didn't care; she had to know one way or the other. Unlike Dracula, Eva wasn't particularly superstitious, and she was willing to take the risk.

She went back inside again; Eva suddenly wanted to be around people when the midnight hour arrived. What if this turned out to be her last night on earth? She couldn't imagine what other form of death there would be. Her human body had perished centuries ago; what would the end of the world mean for her? All around her, Eva saw nothing but smiling faces; the sound of popping corks created their own beat against the thumping of a live rock band. The performer was a young black man dressed in a ruffled shirt and leather pants; he was thin and beautiful enough to be a woman. The artist's soulful music permeated the room; Eva found herself tuning everything out, as she listened to the sound of his guitar. When the captivating song ended, Eva was amused to discover the singer's name was Prince.

Someone knocked her arm, spilling champagne on her gown; Eva turned to find a stunning young man she recognized, he was a very famous actor. "I'm terribly sorry…it's just so crowded in here," the man apologized. His bright blue eyes sparkled beneath the crystal chandelier; the man's face was sheer perfection, and he was impeccably dressed in a midnight black tuxedo.

"I know you…you starred in that vampire movie with Tom Cruise." Eva had seen it recently at a premier, but she couldn't remember his name.

"The very same…," he nodded with a shy smile.

"Your performance took my breath away," Eva gushed, unable to look away from his arresting blue eyes.

"Thank you…it was quite interesting to play a vampire with heart." A stunning braless woman in a silk dress crept up beside him; without saying a word to Eva, she took his arm and pulled him away.

Feeling a bit nervous with only minutes to go, Eva felt a sense of panic and wondered if it was too late to reconsider. A middle-aged man moved next to her; based on his breath, he was feeling no pain. He looked at her with bloodshot eyes, raising his glass with a wobbly hand. The music stopped as the countdown began; there was no turning back now.

When the clock struck midnight, Eva held her breath. The inebriated man leaned over and kissed her cheek; under normal circumstances she might have slapped him, but she didn't. The millennium had arrived without incident and she was jubilant; Eva couldn't wait to tell the others.

CHAPTER 155 - WASHINGTON SQUARE PARK - NEW YEAR'S EVE - (DECEMBER 31, 1999)

Once nightfall came, Washington Square Park was transformed into a refuge for those who called the streets their home. In the dead of night, all that is foul lurks in the darkest corners of a heartless city. Rupert had become a nocturnal pigeon keeper, making friends with the homeless who accepted him as he was; odiferous and covered in bird shit. He roamed about Bryant Park each night, after he had fed on what he needed to survive. His presence was barely acknowledged by anyone, except tourists. Over time, Rupert became known as the "Night Watchman." Once or twice, another vampire tried to approach him with malicious intent, only to discover he was already one of them. After years of living outside, he had become immune to feeling anything at all. Rupert simply existed. The Van Helsings had disbanded by '94; after the massacre of so many vampires the year before, there was no longer a need to rein in rogue fledglings. With Dracula and his crew gone, the city slipped back into its natural rhythm. The police still had plenty of criminal activity to keep them busy, but none involved suspects who suddenly vanished, or prisoners who burst into spontaneous flames. Tonight, the sky looked like a sparkling wasteland; Rupert wondered if everyone would be catapulted into space, at the stroke of midnight. The thought made him giggle out loud. He glanced at the clock and noted there were only minutes remaining of the twentieth century; Rupert would surrender his regret and accept what fate had in store for him.

A few people gathered around a barrel fire; they drank from bottles tucked into brown bags. Rupert found himself moving closer, as he prepared to spend what might be his last moments on earth. When he caught the scent of their blood, he got weak in the knees; he disguised his bloodlust with a fake smile, and was instantly invited to the party. They were all homeless and without any family, yet they found communion with one another. If the world was really going to end in the next five minutes, at least Rupert wouldn't die alone.

Chapter 156 - The Dark One - New Year's Eve - (December 31, 1999)

The Dark One had no memory of being born; it wasn't really certain it had been born at all. The evil entity just was. The end of times had been foretold for centuries. The Dark One truly believed the world would end at the stroke of midnight; convinced mankind would never see the dawning of the twenty-first century. The prophecy claimed the sun would die and a shroud of darkness would spread itself across the world; every living thing would perish, including mankind. The Dark One wondered if creatures of the night could survive an apocalypse; it wouldn't matter though, without human blood to feed on, vampires were doomed.

Believing this would be the last night for planet earth, the Dark One decided to take on a living form. The evil entity longed to feel the pulse of a city in motion; this required a vehicle of flesh and blood. The Dark One had a preference for rats; they could tunnel anywhere and remain completely anonymous while doing so. The Dark One enjoyed the sensation of having a body, with blood pulsing beneath its fur-covered flesh; its red eyes could penetrate even the blackest night. As it skittered awkwardly down a cobble stoned alley, the Dark One heard the sound of traffic, as a jubilant crowd gathered in Times Square. From the filthy sewers of an overcrowded city, the Dark One listened to humans celebrate the passing of another year; that's all this was to them. They drank and laughed, as though they hadn't a care in the world; the humans had no idea what was about to happen. They didn't understand a thing about the prophecy, but the Dark One did. In a very short time, everyone would understand.

The Dark One didn't see it coming, until it was too late; the tomcat got hold of the rat, violently swatting it back and forth. The rat gnashed its teeth, trying to fight the determined feline, but was no match for the vicious tomcat. Blood flowed profusely from the rodent's mouth, as the gray tabby sunk its teeth into the belly of its prey; for the first time ever, the evil entity experienced physical pain.

Chapter 157 - The Y2K Hoax America Almost Believed - (January 1, 2000)

Mankind had been forecasting the proverbial "end of times" since the world began; this included the superstition surrounding the arrival of the twenty-first century. Many fortunetellers and psychics warned the world was headed for Armageddon; anything from asteroids to tidal waves could potentially mark the end of modern civilization. A total blackout was another possibility, along with a return of the plague and other infectious diseases; as the millennium approached, the list of potential catastrophes grew. Computers would crash or worse yet, the grid would go down. From there, who knew what would happen. Naturally, the majority of people believed nothing would happen when the twenty-first century dawned, but vampires and earthbound spirits were a superstitious lot; they approached the new millennium with much apprehension. Either way, retailers enjoyed record sales of generators in the fall of 1999; humans were easily swayed by advertisements that advised preparedness. Those with shelters made sure they were thoroughly stocked; for the media, it was an absolute field day. When the date grew closer, the anticipation began to build as the world speculated on Y2K, and how it could change the American way of life.

When the new century dawned the next day without incident, the city of New York, along with the rest of the world, breathed a collective sigh of relief. And just like that, everyone promptly went about the business of living day to day. Computer systems continued humming along without a glitch; all fears of the grid going down were cast aside. The temporary National Crisis Center located in Times Square disbanded, and by 4:00AM, the National Guard was advised they were no longer needed for crowd control. During the last twenty-four hours of 1999, all major buildings and landmarks throughout New York City, including the World Trade Centers, the Empire State Building and the Statue of Liberty, had been guarded closely by a discreet task force; all of them were relieved of their duties well before dawn. The world had dodged a bullet, and welcomed the twenty-first century with open arms.

Eva enjoyed walking around the city in the wee hours of the morning. The sky was already getting light; streets were peppered by a few stragglers, who were being chased away by cleanup crews. As a sleepy sun rose on the first day of a new millennium, Midtown Manhattan was quiet and nearly deserted; confetti fluttered about in the morning sunlight, as though refusing to leave the party. Eva couldn't wait to go back and tell the others it was safe; there was no reason to be apprehensive any longer. Humanity had survived the millennium!

The year 2000 was no more or less eventful than the year before; once the novelty of living in the twenty-first century wore off, life went back to normal. Outwardly, Americans seemed to embrace the new century with optimism; technology was advancing at a rapid pace, and the future looked bright. Most had forgotten about the bombing in 1993; terrorism still seemed like a remote concept to many Americans. The year flew by and suddenly, it was December; colored lights lit up the streets as New Yorkers prepared to celebrate their first holiday season in the new millennium. Caught up in the magic of the season, New Yorkers were blissfully unaware of a sinister plot in the works, one that would tear apart the very fabric of America.

In the second week of December 2000, an Egyptian man named Mohamed Atta traveled to the United States with a few others; they claimed to want commercial flying lessons, so they could become pilots. They registered for the accelerated program in the state of Florida. Despite the men's country of origin; their request was accommodated with no further scrutiny. When Atta sat in the pilot's seat and took his first lesson, the man knew what he was born to do; he firmly believed glory waited for him in the next life. Atta was an apt pupil and passed the test with flying colors; the instructor made note he needed to work on a smoother landing. What his instructor didn't know was that Mohamed Atta had no intention of ever landing his plane; the radicalized Egyptian man had signed up for a one-way flight.

Chapter 158 - A Reflection of Life - The Otherworld

Dracula examined the mirror after Alice and Oliver told them about its sudden appearance. It was curious indeed, but Dracula didn't feel the need for concern; as a precaution, they decided to cover it. Oliver also filled Dracula in on his disturbing conversation with Nikos; the ancient vampire was hurt to learn of his friend's deep-seated resentment, but felt certain he would come around. This wasn't the first time, Nikos decided to grow a conscience; Dracula was accustomed to waiting him out.

Prince entered the Otherworld right behind Dracula. He told them about his decision to leave the black swans at the soup kitchen; Mattie ran the place and even knew the children by name, so at least they were safe. Prince felt certain it was the only decision he could make. Everyone understood the dilemma; the black swans were half-human and couldn't reside in this realm. Prince had made a necessary and difficult decision, but it was a painful loss for them all. Virginia was heartbroken at the loss, and refused to talk to anyone except Vincent. Jack was last to arrive, captivating Alice and Oliver with adventurous stories; Akos hovered nearby, anxious to be a part of things. This was a rare chance for all of them to be together; despite the uncertainty of the future, they were all excited. Eva was notably absent; she claimed to have a special errand so Dracula didn't pry. Nikos was still missing in action, but Dracula shrugged it off; if his long-time friend refused to be part of planning their future, Dracula would engage Prince as his new right hand.

They were all congregated in the library, discussing their re-entry into the human world. It seemed everyone looked forward to living in a brand new century. The ancient vampire could hear ripples of laughter, as everyone talked excitedly about the future. Dracula moved away, suddenly compelled to take a closer look at the mysterious mirror. He flung off the cover and caught the odious scent of death. The mirror was an old piece in need of re-silvering; it was slightly concave, giving it a rather mystic appearance. His reflection started to change, and then the mirror went black. Dracula heard the sound of rushing water, as the unmistakable image of his beloved castle came into view. A woman screamed and Dracula watched, as his beautiful queen tumbled to her death in the Arges River. He squeezed his eyes shut, but it didn't stop the visions. The mirror flashed again, and Dracula beheld his young son; Mikolai had a bloodied mouth, and the red eyes of evil. Then the others came to him, not the humans he had killed for food; the ones who haunted him now, were those he had killed for sport or to protect his secrets. The brunette in a red taffeta he danced with one New Year's Eve appeared; she smiled at him, but he drew back when her face morphed into a grotesque-looking wolf. Audrey was there, too, pointing at him accusingly, her face disfigured by German artillery. Dracula cried out, "It was not my fault...I tried to save you!"

The faces were coming faster now and with them, the sound of his victims' voices crying out for vengeance. The mirror image changed and he recognized the cashew vendor. He glared at Dracula, his singed clothing creating a wreath of smoke around him; the ancient vampire could actually smell his burning flesh. The scene changed, and Dracula found himself on the rooftop of the New York Public Library; the sky exploded with a swarm of frightened bats, flying directly into a searing sun. Dracula covered his ears to block out the screams of his children being burned alive. He could have stopped it; instead, he hid himself away in a lavish estate, ignoring his responsibilities as their father. He blinked again and saw the face of Inspector Poole, followed by a vision of his broken body; the man had been killed for no other reason than to protect his dirty secrets. It had all seemed so righteous at the time; Dracula seldom felt remorse for the lives he had taken. Maybe Nikos was right, after all; perhaps, the vampire community had gotten what they deserved.

Dracula thought about his legacy, and his misguided belief he could find happiness in the modern world. What had been so damned important about living in modern times, he wondered. I skipped centuries of time and now, all I long for are the things I have lost. Dracula wondered what made him feel compelled to dominate the human race when; in truth, he found them fascinating and at times, even beautiful. Dracula redirected his focus to the matter at hand; he couldn't afford sentimentality at a time like this. In order to leave the

Otherworld, they needed a place far outside the city, a place virtually unknown to authorities. They needed shelter from the sun, privacy and access to what they needed to survive, but *where*? As Dracula was covering the mirror, it finally came to him. They already had the perfect place at their disposal; a place where wild game was plentiful. They could stay in the cave he and Eva had discovered; it would only be temporary, just long enough to secure a new place to live.

The sound of her voice made him turn, as Eva came up behind him. Dracula had been so engrossed with the mirror, he had no idea how much time had passed. He reached out to her, as though needing to confirm she was real.

"Vlad…I did it. I witnessed the dawn of the new millennium!" Eva declared, as she rushed into his arms.

"What do you mean?"

"I couldn't wait when so much was at stake…so I went ahead and saw it through."

Dracula pulled her closer, jubilant with the news. "And all went well…nothing strange happened?"

"Of course not, or I wouldn't be here. The whole thing was nothing but a hoax…if you ask me. Look, I'm perfectly fine. I went to a New Year's Eve party at the North Tower…the next morning…I watched the sun rise on the twenty-first century!"

"You're always taking crazy chances!" Dracula hissed, but his pleasure at her news was evident.

"You worry too much, Vlad," Eva said kissing his cheek, and then she called out to the others.

Prince came first and could see by the glow in Eva's eyes, she had been to the future. Oliver and even Alice gathered around, anxious to hear all about the New Year's Eve party and who she met there. Vincent and Virginia sat away from the others feigning interest in some crumbling books, but they didn't fool anyone. Dracula knew they were afraid to leave the comfort of what they knew, and he understood exactly how they felt.

Dracula listened as Eva told them about the grand party and what they served; she also told them about the singer named Prince. Even Jack hung on every word, he who hated all things modern. They all

472

agreed on the month of April in 2001; it was as good a date as any. An unknown cave in the Adirondacks would be the perfect place to stay while living arrangements were finalized; everyone was adamant they didn't want to stay in a timeless place any longer. The Otherworld had lost all dimension; its amber lights no longer the welcome sight they once were.

Chapter 159 - A Bittersweet Departure - The Otherworld

Virginia and Vincent stayed in a small room once used by Eva. Neither one of them slept really, it was just a habit carried over from their human lives. When nightfall came it seemed only natural to rest, and so they did. They both tossed and turned as they thought about Dracula's plan to hibernate in a remote cave, somewhere in the mountains of New York State. Virginia was horrified by the idea; she had no desire to live out in the wild like animals. Finally alone, she decided it was time to speak up.

"Vincent...I don't want to go with them."

"What do you mean...you want to stay here?" Vincent sat up and took her bony hand in his; he had come to love her like no other.

"No."

"Then where would we go?"

"There's nothing for us in the future, Vincent. You know it as well as I." Vincent felt the same way. Another whirlwind of time travel was the last thing he really wanted; he already missed their underground home.

"I want to stay in the year 1993...and I want to go back and look for the children, Vincent. Will you come with me?"

"They'll see us if we use the portal!"

"We don't need a portal, dear," she replied; Vincent could already see right through her.

"Wait for me...Ginny," Vincent whispered, and soon he was nothing more than a swirling cloud of white smoke.

CHAPTER 160 - THE DARK ONE

The heat was unbearable, but it was blind to the source; a feeling of weightlessness made the evil entity feel dizzy.

"Where am I?" the Dark One asked a void the color of midnight.

"That is not important," replied a malevolent voice.

"I thought I was killed…"

"You're already dead! Now, you need to finish what you started." The Dark One understood it was speaking with Satan himself.

"Master, what is your will?"

"My will…as if that mattered. The vampires are coming again… they've shed their superstitions, and plan to settle in the new millennium."

"I do not understand. Why is this a bad thing?"

"Because of our plans for 2001. We can't let them get in the way… or try to stop it!"

"What's going to happen?"

"The details are none of your concern! What matters, is that nothing stands in the way."

"Of course, I can arrange for their elimination."

"No, you idiot! The vampires may be useful yet. I don't want them harmed!"

"Very well, master…I will engage them somehow…perhaps, with a distraction."

"It will take more than that; you must find a way into their minds… help them get lost inside a world of their pitiful aspirations. Each one of them has an Achilles heel…I'm sure you already know this…"

"Where do they hide, master?"

"In a remote cave…discreetly hidden in the Adirondack Mountains… but, it should be easy enough for you to find; the Romanian vampire has a powerful scent…as does the whore killer. Hold them all there…until I command otherwise!"

The voice was gone and with it, a malodorous blanket of evil. The Dark One considered hypnosis at first, but knew a vampire's will was very strong and often resistant. In order to completely realign a vampire's sense of time and space, it would be necessary to use something from the old world. It was a craft few human beings even knew about; as a right hand to Satan, it had mastered many of the dark arts. The secluded cave would be the perfect place to hold them captive, by creating an alternate reality. For this, the Dark One would access a special talent discovered in ancient times: *enchantment*.

CHAPTER 161 - A DEADLY MISSION - (MARCH 2001)

Naturally, Sylvio didn't intend to waste away in ancient Egypt; it was merely a place to revisit his past and store his property, Rory being among them. She belonged to him now, and he treated her no differently than anything else he owned. Strangely, the former vampire hunter seemed content in her new role as his body slave; Sylvio left her in Eadric's care, as he made a second trip to the twenty-first century. His latest association was with a group of men who worked for an organization called al-Qaeda; they were men of few words and little patience, but they paid in advance for his special errands. Despite their nationality, they always paid him in U.S. currency; this was of utmost importance to him. Thanks to Rory, Sylvio was a fugitive now. His only chance to live in the modern world was to stay off the grid. Unfortunately, that meant doing business with individuals who had questionable agendas.

Tonight, Sylvio had been summoned to meet with two contacts at a Starbucks, on the corner of 51st and Lexington. He planned to take this opportunity to try and obtain more details about what they were planning; he hated working in the dark. One of the men had availed himself of Sylvio's services in the past; he kept staring at his smooth, unwrinkled face, clearly puzzled by so little change in eight years. Sylvio felt the man's eyes on him and tried to redirect his focus.

"Gentlemen, I have a question." They nodded and Sylvio continued, "I don't know exactly what you're planning, but why now? I thought your contacts would've chosen the millennium for maximum impact... just curious."

"In theory you are right...but there would have been no element of surprise." The older man spoke up; he was obviously offended Sylvio dared question their timing.

"I don't follow you."

"To strike when it was expected, would have been a foolish move... better to wait until no one is paying attention. You ask a lot of questions for a messenger boy."

"I meant no offense," Sylvio replied.

"Our leaders direct our actions and they are guided by Allah."

"Of course...forgive me." Sylvio replied with mock humility.

"We wait until summer is over...in the fall, office buildings will be full again," the man replied. He was certain Sylvio was a nonbeliever, and no better than plant life.

"And what exactly are you planning?" Sylvio persisted.

"Too many questions killed the cat," the older man said with a chortle.

"I'm no cat...and I don't like working in the dark."

The man looked at him with beady eyes settled deep inside his hooded brow; he leaned forward and motioned for Sylvio to come closer. "Our plans were made by those high above this realm as punishment to America for many things. The location, my friend...is none of your fucking business! Your job is to deliver packages!" The man thrust an envelope into Sylvio's hands under the table, and he stood up to leave.

"Yes...you are handsome delivery boy. Now you go and do your job," the younger one said with yellow teeth, as the older man eyed Sylvio with mistrust.

Sylvio wanted to keep pushing for more information, but knew it was best to let it go. He shoved the envelope into his pants pocket, deciding human casualties were not his concern. By the time Sylvio reached the next block, he was already thinking about a new suit for spring and perhaps a nice pair of Gucci loafers.

Walking behind him unnoticed was a loyal servant to Dracula; despite his recent doubts, he was determined to find the Achilles heel of the Egyptian vampire. The night was cool and refreshing as Nikos ducked in and out of doorways, tracking one he had never trusted since the day they first met.

CHAPTER 162 - AN ENCHANTED WORLD

A firm belief in spells of enchantment was quite common in both Medieval and Renaissance times. Many told tales of their own experiences, and these stories were passed on to the next generation. Whether it was the lovely Sirens of Greek mythology luring sailors into shallow waters, or a simple spell cast to change the weather, superstition was once a very real part of daily life. For most, the deep forest was a place to fear and respect; it was a place of threatening danger, but could also prove a welcome refuge. Dracula's love nest was just such a place; out of necessity, it would be their temporary home. The Adirondacks were more remote than the Catskill Mountains; there was little chance of them being discovered here. Even when they abandoned their cave, everyone understood they needed to reside outside the city. A twenty-first century vampire no longer owned the night; modern cities had surveillance cameras just about everywhere. Jack had located an abandoned estate not far from Olana, it was in a state of disrepair but seemed their best option; the property was privately owned but had been unoccupied for two decades. The home was not well-maintained or comfortably furnished, but that didn't matter; Dracula was happy to have any kind of home at all.

When it was time to leave the Otherworld, they were all surprised by the disappearance of Vincent and Virginia. The couple didn't leave a note; no one had any idea they planned to go back to reclaim their lost family. No one dared mention the notable absence of Nikos, but he was on everyone's mind nonetheless. There was an obvious battle of wills going on between Dracula and his loyal friend, but no one dared speak of it. It was time to leave this timeless place and see the new century. The Otherworld portal delivered them close to the cave's location, but they still had a short distance to travel on foot. They all agreed this would give them an opportunity to adapt to the mountainous terrain and confirm the cave was unoccupied. There was a little snow on the ground, but none of them felt the cold; Dracula couldn't help thinking, this was a hardly a place he wanted to stay for very long.

When they reached the entrance to the cave, Prince drew his sword and Jack kept a hand on his bowie knife; the main concern was making sure the cave was empty. Eva detected a foul odor, but the others didn't seem to notice. The smell became stronger, once they were inside the cavernous space. Eva sensed right away something had changed. It was the same place, and yet, there was an aura she couldn't ignore, as if something was waiting patiently to strike. Going ahead of the others who were chattering excitedly, Eva found her way to the back of the cave.

Eva stood in total darkness, hugging herself with excitement as she daydreamed about walking down Broadway in a designer dress. More than anything, she couldn't wait to return to the civilized world. Eva didn't care where they lived, because she planned to spend much of her time crashing parties of the rich and famous. To Eva, nothing was more exciting than being a part of the twenty-first century. Her thoughts turned once more to what she would wear; a trip to Bloomingdales would certainly be her first stop. Eva heard a soft whisper and turned to find an odd-looking mirror glowing in the darkness. She blinked as the ghost of Prince Richard approached the mirror; he looked exactly as she remembered. His image began to ripple like water and then suddenly; Eva saw a much younger, more beautiful version of herself. In the glass, she saw Countess Bathory at age sixteen. The girl had skin like fine porcelain, her sultry eyes smoldered beneath perfectly shaped eyebrows. Eva became spellbound, and desperate to claim her younger self again. She reached out to touch the glass, and could feel her own perfect face. Prince Richard came back into view, and took the sixteen-year-old apparition's hand; but as they turned away, Eva called out to them. She longed for her old life, even if only for a short while. She wanted to live and breathe again inside a perfect human body, still young and blemish free. The boy turned his head with a sly smile, as Eva took a step into the glass; that was all it took for Countess Bathory, to become lost in a world of her own making.

When they got bored with the tedious discussion about their future plans, Alice coaxed her brother outside to explore the nighttime forest. As they left the cave and walked out into the darkness, Oliver's radar went on high alert; the landscape of the forest had been completely transformed. Alice stood wide-eyed as she watched a web of coarse bracken-like foliage frantically weaving itself into a virtual dome around the entrance to their cave. The foliage was impossibly thick and had not been there when they arrived less than two hours ago; there was definitely something sinister about its presence. Oliver heard Alice scream from behind him. When he turned around, the sturdy vine had already begun to suck his sister into the bosom of its very being. Alice reached for him with her mouth opened to scream, but no sound came out. Oliver tried to pull on her feet, but she was already too far gone; the boy was left holding an empty shoe. He dropped to his knees and covered his face in defeat, completely unaware that the wicked vine had already wrapped itself around both of his ankles; Oliver was about to be reunited with his sister.

Prince suddenly noticed their absence, and excused himself as Dracula reminisced with Jack about hunting on the moors. Prince moved toward the cave entrance and his sixth sense told him an ominous presence loomed nearby. Grabbing his sword, Prince flattened his body against the stone wall and gradually worked his way outside. The first thing he noticed, was that there was no longer a view of the Oswegatchie River; dense foliage had insinuated itself around the cave entrance and completely obliterated his view of the night sky. He called out to Oliver and Alice, but there was no response; Prince realized the grotesque mass of spoiled greenery had imprisoned them. He moved along the perimeter of the obscene growth, keeping a safe distance as he listened for their voices. It took a second before he heard a voice, but it didn't sound human. Prince saw a small opening and stepped forward trying to look inside. He heard maniacal laughter and swung his sword at the malignant vine; slicing through the entrance to hell, itself.

Inside the cave, Dracula and Jack wrapped up discussions about their game plan. They looked around and observed they were alone. It was well after midnight and they still needed to feed. Jack folded up their notes and building plans, believing everyone must have gone outside. Feeling for his weapon, Jack stepped into the night and immediately detected the earthy scent of evil. The vine was denser than anything he'd ever seen, coarser than bracken with razor sharp thorns that wound around one another; it looked like a demented rose bush. Dracula came up from behind Jack, on high alert as he caught the musky odor of a malevolent presence.

Jack approached the vine with his knife drawn, as Dracula drew his sword putting a finger to his lips. They heard the wind pick up as it blew through the vine, a primal sound that promised something hungry was living inside. Jack stepped closer and slashed at the vine with his knife, revealing a celestial light. Waiting inside was a beautiful boy named Jericho, the innocent child whose soul he corrupted for all eternity. The boy's eyes were the color of a summer sea, his rose petal lips curling into a smile. Jack instantly became lost in the intoxicating geography of tiny purple veins running up the side of his neck. Jack took another step closer and felt Jericho's arms around him, but then, the spell was broken and he was left holding a bundle of charred bones. Jack fell to his knees and wept for all that had been lost. The vine traveled up his leg, weaving a tangled web around the seasoned vampire. Jack didn't feel a thing though; his mind was busy conjuring up a vision of his fledgling's perfect face.

Dracula charged at the vine trying to break its hold on Jack; he slashed wildly with his sword, but could not free him. Suddenly, the vine swelled into a grotesque thing with pulsing veins that thumped like a human heart. Dracula watched helplessly as the vine sucked Jack into its belly, like a Venus fly trap. Filled with rage, the ancient vampire slashed at the vine repeatedly as blood sprayed everywhere, saturating the vampire's face and clothing. The scent of human carnage was overpowering, and eventually became impossible to resist. Finally giving in, Dracula opened his hungry mouth and drank without restraint, oblivious that he had been lured into the belly of the beast.

Chapter 163 - The Darkest Day - (September 11, 2001)

There are certain historic events that stay with you for life. If you lived them, they became a part of you for the rest of your days. Like the day John F. Kennedy was assassinated. If you were of school age, it was likely the most frightening event of your young life. For most, it signaled a loss of innocence that could never be regained. The strange thing about living through a catastrophic event is that you remember mundane things, like what color suit the first lady was wearing or the weather. On the day Kennedy was shot, it had rained in the morning however, by the time the president's motorcade passed along its fatal route, the sun was out again. Bright blue skies greeted a happy crowd who would be part of history, in a way they never imagined.

September eleventh fell on a Tuesday. The New York City skyline was majestic against a cobalt blue sky; further proof a sunny day is momentary, and comes with no guarantee of a happy ending. It was the kind of day that made people glad to be alive; crisp, clean and full of promise. For many, it was the first week their children returned to school. Trees already boasted a hint of color, as autumn settled itself into the landscape of a city nicknamed the "Big Apple." Falling leaves were already gathering in doorways, as shopkeepers reined them in with straw brooms. Cool air had replaced the stifling humidity of August as another day began with comfortable routine, in a city where anything can happen. And on that Tuesday in early September, the worst thing imaginable *did* happen, changing the world forever.

Mohammed Atta flew the first plane into the North Tower at 8:46AM, killing himself along with everyone else on board. The Boeing 767 crashed into the eightieth floor and no one located on that floor or above survived. After the initial shock, authorities scrambled to determine whether this was an accident due to pilot error, or something much more sinister. Sirens went off in tandem, as police worked diligently to get people away from danger. Mass evacuation of the North Tower turned the streets of lower Manhattan, into an unrecognizable scene of chaos and hysteria. The heat of the fire was so intense, people anywhere near the site felt sunburned; many staggered around with injuries they didn't even feel. Everything became surreal as people emerged from dust clouds, covered in ash and stunned by the horror of what happened. This kind of thing didn't happen in real life, people thought, as they watched black smoke billowing against a cloudless horizon. A man pointed to the sky as people gathered around him, and then they saw it; a second plane was heading straight for the South Tower. There was no time to stop it. Pedestrians and first responders alike watched in disbelief, as another Boeing 767 crashed into the South Tower. The time was 9:03AM. President George Bush had to excuse himself from a classroom of second graders, because there was no doubt the United States was under attack. A short time later the world learned about the Pentagon attack, along with confirmation a fourth plane intended for the White House, had crashed into an open field in rural Pennsylvania. The concept of using an aircraft as weaponry caught everyone, including authorities, by surprise. The heinous attack was immediately declared an act of war.

When the first plane hit, Virginia dropped the pot she was holding, spilling soup all over the tile floor. Vincent moved to help her clean up, as the others went outside to see what had happened. The two specters had been unsuccessful in finding the black swans, but Virginia convinced Vincent to stay in the human world; they had been volunteering at a homeless shelter ever since. When they heard a second explosion, they both ran outside. Virginia put a hand to her mouth and cried, "Vincent…it's just like your painting!"

Sylvio watched the second plane hit, and he cursed the sky; the dark-skinned men and their cronies were behind this. He stayed on the outskirts of things, careful not to get too close to the action. Startled by a blood-curdling scream, Sylvio watched a desperate man catapult out a window, in order to escape being burned alive. He lost him in the smoke and wondered if he would have done the same under such circumstances. Wiping the dust from his jacket with a linen handkerchief, Sylvio surveyed the damage and wondered how many had been killed. Everywhere he looked people walked around with vacant eyes. Some were covered with so much blood; he was surprised to see them walking at all. Others were unhurt but completely disoriented, stumbling over debris hidden by smoke so thick; Sylvio didn't have to worry about the sun. The piercing sound of human suffering permeated the air, and mercilessly echoed in his ears. With a greater sense of urgency, Sylvio moved further away from the site and almost bumped into an ash-covered child. She looked up at him and said, "They killed my mommy." Sylvio turned away and walked past a cluster of fire trucks, as men in black and yellow rushed to rescue those still trapped inside. Sylvio decided to move on before someone pressed him for identification. He had to get to Dracula before anyone else did. Sylvio glanced at his Rolex and could barely read it through the smoke. The air around him seemed as heavy as the hearts of America. The cold-hearted vampire allowed himself a moment of regret, before heading upstate to plead his case to a vampire he couldn't afford to alienate.

People swarmed around public television sets as news reporters shared graphic footage of a horrific event that would forever be a black mark in America's history. The subway system shut down at 10:20AM and by 10:30AM the North and South Towers had both collapsed, leaving the skeletal remains of an architectural wonder standing idly in the middle of a wasteland called *Ground Zero*. A veil of smoke and sorrow hung over the city of Manhattan, marring an otherwise perfect autumn day; but then again, some of history's darkest moments happened on sunny days. A sunny day comes with no guarantees.

CHAPTER 164 - THE AWAKENING - ADIRONDACK MOUNTAINS - (SEPTEMBER II, 2001)

Dense forest allowed Sylvio to move about during daylight hours, and the Adirondack Mountains provided just that. Once he got out of the city, Sylvio felt a tremendous sense of urgency to get to Dracula before anyone else did. He wanted a chance to explain he had been nothing more than a messenger boy, caught up in a much larger plot. Sylvio's only objective was to minimize his role and maintain Dracula's respect. Never before had any of his nefarious activities resulted in anything this catastrophic, and now Sylvio was in panic mode. The Egyptian vampire had to make Dracula believe he had not known their target, which *was* true. Following Dracula's scent, he found his way to their mountain retreat, and prepared himself for a possible confrontation; Jack could often be hot-headed. Stuck up here in the middle of nowhere, none of them would have any way of knowing what happened; he would have to be the one to break the news.

As Sylvio got closer to the cave, he bristled when he caught the scent of something foul; the woods suddenly grew dark as midnight. Up ahead, there was an iron gate blocking his path; Sylvio stepped closer, and the gate morphed into the giant jaws of rabid beast. Sylvio realized sorcery was being used to detain him; the gate was a classic attempt to keep others away, and to prevent the spell from being broken. He surmised the vampires were somehow trapped inside the cave, and Sylvio was determined to rescue them. He pulled out a revolver and fired at the imaginary beast; it vanished in a cloud of smoke. This vine was certainly not born from nature; this malignant growth reeked of the Dark One. For once, he would defy the evil entity and fight for his own kind. Sylvio reached for his knife and slashed through the vine, trying to find its core; before long, his clothes were saturated in clotted blood.

When Sylvio finally reached the void where evil lived, he saw them; they hung suspended like giant peapods from a vine with diseased bark the color of death. The living pods pulsed with life, and appeared to be feeding from the vine inside a cocoon of safety; their minds were imprisoned by a world of their own making. One by one, Sylvio cut them down until finally, the vine slithered away. When he asked them what happened, they all claimed their last recollection was of making plans to leave the cave. They had no memory of being imprisoned by a thorny vine, and believed they simply got lost in the forest. The vine had receded and the sun threatened to shine through the trees, so they hurried back to the cave hoping to find Eva there.

When they reached the entrance, Prince heard singing and was relieved to hear Eva's voice. Overjoyed he ran inside and found her twirling in circles, as though looking at a dress in a mirror. Prince reached out to touch her shoulder; Eva stopped spinning and looked at him with surprise, as though he should have been someone else.

"Prince…are we ready to go yet? I'm dying to see New York City in springtime. I'll need a new dress and maybe some shoes…," Eva said dreamily, as if half asleep.

"Come…the others are outside…Sylvio has come and saved us all," Prince said, taking her hand.

"Sylvio?"

"Yes…come." Prince took Eva's hand; he was unnerved by her vacant stare.

Sylvio knew he could procrastinate no longer. It was time to tell them the horrible news. As if reading his thoughts, Jack came at him and demanded to know why he had come. Dracula and Jack moved away from the others to talk. Eva followed, after taking one last longing look at the phantom mirror.

"How'd you find us, anyway?" Jack asked, balling his fist in anger.

Dracula stepped between them. "Maybe I should ask the questions, Jack."

Jack was unwilling to back down. "I want to hear him say he doesn't consort with terrorists!"

"I do not! I had nothing to do with what happened in '93…and I had nothing to do with what happened today!"

"What are you talking about?" Eva demanded, now recovered from her drowsiness.

"It was on the news…," Sylvio stammered.

"Does it look like we have a television set here?" Jack asked angrily.

"You don't understand…I know you came here in April of 2000, but time has passed and…" Sylvio paused waiting for it to sink in.

"What do you mean…how much time?" Dracula asked.

"When you were held captive…in those pods…human time passed. I understand you arrived here in April 2000…but today's date is September 11th…2001. Believe me…*this date* will go down in history."

Dracula exhaled deeply. "You expect us to believe we lost a year and a half of human time trapped inside an oversized Venus Fly Trap?"

"I know it sounds crazy but, yes…how else can you explain it?" Sylvio replied.

"Then what about Eva…she never left the cave?" Jack challenged.

"She must have been spellbound in another way," Sylvio replied, trying to convince them.

"I don't believe *anything* you say!" Eva snapped angrily. She looked into the Egyptian vampire's eye, and saw a vivid image of them locked in a sexual embrace. Sylvio held her gaze with a sadistic grin, until she finally looked away.

"Show us some proof then…something that confirms what you're telling us is true," Jack challenged.

Sylvio smiled and rolled up his sleeve, revealing a Rolex watch; the date was 9-11-2001. They were all stunned to discover how much time had passed.

"So, we lost some time…it does not *really* matter to us," Eva reasoned.

"Why are you showing up now, after all this time, Sylvio?" Dracula asked in a wounded voice.

"I apologize…my business associates turned out not to be trustworthy…they lied about their plans and now the city…" He couldn't continue.

"Go on…," Dracula prompted.

"I didn't know everything about their plan…or that it would hit so close to home," Sylvio said weakly, not looking at any of them.

"*Tell* us…Sylvio!" Jack demanded.

"They used airplanes as bombs…," Sylvio trailed off.

"*Where*, Sylvio?" Dracula asked, shaking him.

"World Trade Center…both towers…they collapsed an hour ago," he whispered. Eva shrieked, as a painful vision of the city on fire filled her mind.

"Just like Vincent's painting," Prince whispered.

"How many killed, Sylvio?" Dracula asked more gently.

The Egyptian vampire swallowed hard and replied, "They don't have numbers yet...possibly two thousand."

"Jesus Christ!" Dracula declared, surprised he had chosen these words.

"Vlad...I didn't know they would do something like this," Sylvio insisted.

"You trusted him!" Jack said, pointing an accusing finger at Dracula. "I did."

"We have all been friends for a long time. Frankly, I don't see why any of this matters. People die all the time in natural disasters." Sylvio attempted to minimize the situation.

"Mass murder is not a natural disaster!" Eva said hotly.

"Come now, gentlemen," Sylvio said ignoring Eva, "we are vampires and take human lives all the time."

"It shouldn't be like this, Sylvio. Killing to feed is one thing...but, this is mass murder! What will you do for an encore?" Dracula was torn between his love for Sylvio, and his anger that he would choose to be a part of terrorism.

"Killing people with exploding airplanes is a cowardly act!" Eva spat.

"I never claimed my associates were brave...just clever," Sylvio replied smugly.

"Clever enough to be responsible for the murder of innocent people," Eva snapped.

"Why should that matter to you? I thought killing innocent people was your specialty, countess," Sylvio said with knowing eyes.

"On occasion, it has been necessary for every one of us to dispense of humans who are troublesome," Eva replied defensively.

"You're changing the subject...why don't you come clean and tell Vlad your dirty little secret," Sylvio replied, seizing the opportunity to deflect attention from himself.

"I don't know what you're talking about!" Eva tried to call his bluff.

"Oh, come now, countess…tell your handsome vampire what you did to his lady fair," Sylvio taunted.

"Don't listen to him Vlad…he's trying to trick you…we all know Jack killed Mary!" Eva said feeling cornered with no way out.

"Eva, what's he talking about?" Dracula felt a sick feeling in the pit of his stomach, as he watched her squirm.

"Yes…go ahead…countess, tell him or I will," Sylvio taunted.

Eva's eyes brimmed with tears; she had no choice but to come clean. "It wasn't Jack…"

"Eva…what are you saying?" Dracula asked, but he already knew.

"It was *me* that night, Vlad. I didn't want to share you with her…," Eva cried as Dracula digested her painful words.

"The girl in the bonnet…it *was* you!" Dracula remembered now, the young girl he saw the night Mary was killed; Eva had betrayed him in a most unexpected way.

"You were going to leave…I couldn't let that happen…" Eva was crying uncontrollably now.

Dracula smiled sardonically and cupped Eva's cheek; for a brief moment she thought he might forgive her. "My beautiful black-hearted countess…the last one I ever expected to betray me…and all because I was blinded by a pretty face." Dracula pushed her away, and Eva collapsed at his feet.

"Please…Vlad…it was a long time ago. Can't you find it in your heart to forgive me?"

"There's nothing to forgive…I've always known exactly who you were…but I loved you in spite of it. It doesn't matter now…I have to go."

"But where will you go?" Eva asked.

"I have to help them…I need to atone somehow."

"Why? What did humanity ever do for you?" Jack asked.

"I have to at least try," Dracula replied, already turning to go.

Jack charged after him, but Dracula had already taken flight, making his way toward disaster. Jack had no interest in going anywhere near the city right now, but he was suddenly ravenous; it was time to feed his burning need. Sylvio watched them both go, and tried to feel something like pity for the former countess; she was still on her knees, tears spilling down her cheeks.

"Now look what you've done!" Eva screamed at Sylvio.

"You did it to yourself, countess…and by the way, I just love seeing a woman on her knees," Sylvio taunted, leering at her cleavage.

"You pig!"

Sylvio laughed and left her broken on the ground, as he fantasized about having her lick the dirt off his feet; he was already getting bored with his current body slave.

CHAPTER 165 - THE AFTERMATH -
(SEPTEMBER 11, 2001)

The fateful day was sunny and bright, a difficult time for vampires to move about without protection from the sun. Once Dracula left the cover of dense forest, he took on his rodent form and tunneled his way to lower Manhattan. As soon as he reached the outskirts of the city, he could smell smoke and another odor he knew all too well. Subway service had shut down but it wouldn't matter for him; in fact, it might help him get there faster. As Dracula made his way closer to the devastated financial district, he felt tremendous remorse he hadn't made it his business to become more informed about Sylvio's extracurricular activities. Although heartbroken by Eva's confession, Dracula felt like a fool for ever trusting her at all. The ancient vampire couldn't change who he had been for centuries, and neither could the countess. They were both damned in this life and the next; it was just a matter of time before their penance came due.

When Dracula reached what was now being called *Ground Zero*, the scent of death became stronger; a lingering fog hung in the air, as if boasting a great conquest. Ducking into a blind corner, Dracula assumed his human form and ran into a thick cloud of smoke, looking for something he couldn't define. He wanted to be of help to the injured; perhaps it might even earn him a chance of redemption. The entire perimeter surrounding the fallen towers was cordoned off by police barriers, to keep people at a safe distance. The ancient vampire pressed himself against a barrier, momentarily stunned by a gaping void that would forever change the landscape of lower Manhattan. The majestic buildings were gone, but through the haze, Dracula could see the steeple of St. Paul's Church; he was surprised to find it still standing. A pile of rubble was all that remained, of what was once considered an icon of modern architecture. The Twin Towers had been standing only hours ago, and now they were reduced to a smoldering heap of twisted steel; a sadistic monument to human suffering. Children wailed for their mothers, as separated families stumbled around searching for one another, in a vast wasteland of building debris. The continuous blare of police sirens was deafening; above it all, Dracula could hear the mournful cries of collective anguish, as the American dream literally went up in smoke. An evil act born of hatred and intolerance had issued a killing blow; New York City had sustained wounds that would take a lifetime to heal. From what he'd seen, the ancient vampire had every confidence New Yorker's would be up to the challenge. They had stamina, grit and an inner strength Dracula admired; he watched as everyday heroes helped one another with selflessness often found lacking in a creature of the night. After centuries of believing mankind was inferior to his own kind, Dracula finally accepted he had been wrong in his assessment. While it was true humans were far more vulnerable than vampires, they found tremendous satisfaction in helping each other, even when they had lost everything themselves. Today, as Dracula observed people assisting complete strangers simply because it was the right thing to do, the ancient vampire understood compassion and human frailty were the very things that made mankind so fascinating. Their weakness was their strength, in that it brought out the best in everyone, even on a day like this. Everywhere he looked, New Yorkers were coming together to make the best, of the worst day in their lives.

As Vlad Dracula stood at a crossroads of not only history, but his own existence; he at long last, embraced his love of mankind and openly wept for the loss of human life, in a city he had come to love. How could he continue living among humans when he needed to feed on them to survive? How could he claim to love humanity, only to kill them in dark corners to feed his wickedness? There were no easy answers, but he was certain of one thing; he could no longer kill humans without conscience. As Dracula reflected on the time ahead, he saw nothing but endless hours to fill in a sea of earthbound spirits, who had once scorned their humanity. Humans were the lucky ones; they embraced their mortality, instead of cursing it. They were a rare species in spite of their frailty; he understood now, why their blood was more addicting than heroin. The conflict of being what he was had become too great for Dracula to bear; the ancient vampire could no longer endure a life of duplicity. As he stood in the middle of a decimated neighborhood, Dracula wanted more than anything to atone for how he had lived. Ahead of him was a fire burning deep inside the wreckage of the North Tower; an easy out for him, and after that, only an inviting blackness. He stepped forward but someone grabbed his arm, and yanked him back behind the barriers. Dracula tried to resist, until he came face to face with Nikos.

"Don't do it...it's not worth it," Nikos warned, holding tight to Dracula's arm.

"This shouldn't have happened," Dracula replied. He tried to pull away and fulfill his destiny.

"I warned you to beware of the Egyptian vampire...now, it's too late."

"Maybe not...maybe we could go back in time and change it."

"Vlad...it's too late for that, and you know it...we need to leave this place." Nikos tugged harder on his arm.

"Let me go...there's got to be something I can do."

"What are you going to do, Vlad...surrender your body to the flames, in some grand gesture?" Nikos said, finally letting go of his arm.

"Maybe...my penance for all the innocent lives I have taken, remember?" Dracula said, repeating his friend's harsh words. Before Nikos could respond, Dracula ducked under the police barrier and charged past a pile of misshapen metal that used to be an elevator shaft.

Dracula was deep inside the wreckage, now mesmerized by the flames. Suddenly, he was terrified. What if this was *the fire*? The one that meant your very existence ceased and your soul was damned for eternity. Was he spellbound again or, in fact, facing the very gates of hell? The thought of his own personal judgment day had always terrified him, but not any longer. If Satan was calling him, then so be it. Dracula felt certain his destiny lie within the wreckage of something he once loved. No one tried to stop him as he moved closer to the blaze; they were too busy trying to rescue the injured. Dracula fumbled his way through the ruins in a dreamlike haze. In the distance he could hear a man shrieking in fear or pain; it didn't matter which, or perhaps it was both.

As Dracula climbed over a pile of bricks and shattered glass, he felt an intense heat. The fire was close now, glowing with colors so beautiful, Dracula was temporarily awestruck and unable to move. From above the blaze came a swarm of lights Dracula at first thought were Luna Moths; when one got closer, he could see her very human face. She hovered in the air with her gossamer wings beating frantically; her tiny mouth open in a scream and then she charged at him. The others followed suit, stabbing at him with elfin fingers as Dracula swatted them away. They had no real substance and were merely spirits of those who had just perished. Some glared at him accusingly, as if knowing he was a creature of the night; maybe they feared he was there to claim their souls. Some understood what had happened and gravitated toward a bright light above, while others were confused or hadn't yet given up their earthly bodies.

Dracula moved away from them and went deeper into the wreckage. He moved cautiously, unsure what he was looking for; until he stumbled over the body of a small child. Dracula bent down and realized the little girl was badly injured; she was unconscious, but still breathing. Dracula believed he could save her, and in that pivotal moment, the vampire felt his sense of purpose return. He gently picked her up, moving quickly to get her away from the flames; Dracula passed a soot-covered fireman who motioned him to keep moving. There were other people sobbing and begging for help, but all he could think about was saving this one child. Dracula heard people up ahead and followed the sound of their voices, the need to save the little girl growing stronger. As he moved through the dangerous landscape of a fallen building, everything started to move in slow motion. Audrey's sweet face flashed through his mind, her sweet mouth smeared with chocolate; then he saw her broken body lying in the street, as German bombs sounded in the distance. Dracula fought these painful images, trying to focus on the little girl he was trying to save.

Up ahead, Dracula saw daylight; two paramedics rushed toward him and took the girl from his arms. Dracula could see her lips had turned blue; the girl's eyes were open but there was no life in them any longer. Already Dracula could see the moth-like spirit of the child, as she rose above the remains of a humbled and broken-hearted city. The spirit hovered around him detecting the unique aura of a lost soul, and beckoned him to join her. Her translucent hand reached out to him; for a moment the ancient vampire became lost in eyes the color of liquid sapphire. There was nothing out there for him in this century or the next. More than anything, Dracula wanted somewhere to belong. He reached out for the spirit, but he was too late; she had already ascended to meet an afterlife he would never know. He heard the sound of voices coming after him, but Vlad Dracula didn't want to be rescued; he was already home. The fire was his salvation and Dracula knew it was where he belonged. With one last look at the human world, the ancient vampire took a tentative step forward and surrendered his body to the flames.

* * * * * * * * * * * * * * * * *

She watched as he turned and headed deeper into the smoldering ruins of the North Tower, and suddenly realized what he planned to do. Eva always knew Dracula's love of humanity would be his undoing. She was a wicked soul, but fiercely loyal to the vampire she loved. Eva carefully weighed the painful decision she had to make, amidst the chaos of an American tragedy. She could not let him do this; she had made a promise to her lord, and it was one she meant to keep. Before anyone could stop her, Countess Bathory charged into the wreckage as shell-shocked New Yorker's struggled to hang onto what was left of their hopes and dreams.

When the sun at last set on one of the blackest days in American history, the New York City skyline stood proudly, despite a glaring space where two important symbols of freedom and democracy once stood. The low wail of human suffering still hung in the air, as a sorry moon rose with notable sobriety; and with it, the cry of a newborn wolf.

CPSIA information can be obtained
at www.ICGtesting.com
Printed in the USA
BVHW080946140819
555872BV00002B/17/P

9 781489 723550

1